PRAISE [illegible]

“Michael Flynn's future [illegible] of near space is finally complete. This story is a direct sequel to and conclusion of the series that began with *Firestar* and continued with *Rogue Star* and *Lodestar*. These novels carefully and in full detail map out the steps humanity takes to restore our space programs. Danger and excitement mount as several asteroids head for Earth, and ships are sent out past Mars to stop them. All this action is set against a complex background of worldwide financial collapse, political and economic maneuvering and personal challenges for beloved and familiar characters whom we have come to know over the previous volumes”

—Chase Coughlin, Jimmy Poole, Roberta, Jacinta, and of course Mariesa Van Huyten.

“Filled with exciting extrapolative ideas and scientific and technological wonders, *Falling Stars* is a wonderfully powerful and dramatic conclusion to this multi-volume epic of SF.

As Robert A. Heinlein did and all too few have done since, Michael Flynn writes about the near future as if he'd been there and was bringing back reports of what he'd seen. It's a near future I'd like to have, and it's a near future we can have if we reach out and take it. And Flynn remembers—when so many forget—that people come first, and that the future, like the present, is inhabited by human beings in all their splendid complexity, and reports with a clear head and sympathetic heart on that too. A splendid piece of work.”

—Harry Turtledove

“The conclusion of Flynn's grand-scale near-future epic combines the rapid pacing of SF action adventure with the subtle maneuverings of political intrigue in a panoramic drama of human courage and sacrifice.” —*Library Journal*

“. . . an exciting plot, and the mixture of personalities and ideologies guarantees tension, attraction, and enmity that will please fans of David Brin and Kim Stanley Robinson as well as Flynn's cohort.” —*Booklist*

"The four book series which concludes with *Falling Stars* deserves to be ranked among the classic science fiction series and should make Michael Flynn's name more well known within science fiction circles." —*Sfsite.com*

"*Falling Stars*, the fourth book in this exciting series, brings all the characters back from the previous tales for a glorious finale. The story line is packed with non-stop action expected from a hard core science fiction novel, but surprisingly is character driven, as Michael Flynn emphasizes the staff as much as the quest. Though the conclusion of a strong quartet, this novel easily stands alone as a great genre entry."
—*The Midwest Book Review*

Lodestar

". . . striking characters and well-crafted hard SF keep this series compelling." —*Locus*

"*Lodestar* stands on its own. No knowledge of the earlier works, *Firestar* and *Rogue Star*, is required to enjoy this new entry in the series . . ." —*Bookpage*

Rogue Star

"Flynn has scored again with his exciting tale of one possible future, leaving one eagerly anticipating the series finale."
—*Charleston Post & Courier* (Charleston, SC)

"This rare book is a combination of political thriller, hard SF of the near future, and a Dickensian mix of nearly one hundred major characters. Flynn ably juggles all of these elements in the fully lifelike world he has created . . . [this] will hopefully be just the second of many volumes in this fascinating universe." —*VOYA*

"For a hard SF writer Flynn has a surprisingly light touch and it's not necessary to have read the previous novel, *Firestar*, to follow the story. For my money, Flynn is a much better writer than Heinlein . . . In this fascinating book, full of incidental speculative detail, Flynn even has room for the fashionable 'will a big rock hit the Earth?' question. Hard SF is often authentic but rarely this well-written and Flynn's future history looks on course for enlivening the genre with intelligence and subtlety."
—*Vector*

Firestar

"*Firestar* is an extraordinary achievement, beautifully and vividly written, full of real people, the story exciting, many-sided, sometimes funny, sometimes sad, ultimately triumphant, altogether believable—the history of a future that can be ours, in our own lifetimes, if only we have the vision and courage to create it. I can't wait to find out what happens next!"
—Poul Anderson

Also by Michael Flynn

In the Country of the Blind
The Nanotech Chronicles
Fallen Angels (with Larry Niven and Jerry Pournelle)
*Firestar**
*The Forest of Time and Other Stories**
*Lodestar**
*Rogue Star**
*Falling Stars**

** denotes a Tor book*

FALLING STARS

Michael Flynn

TOR®
A TOM DOHERTY ASSOCIATES BOOK
NEW YORK

FALLING STARS

Edited by David G. Hartwell

A Tor Book
Published by Tom Doherty Associates, LLC
175 Fifth Avenue
New York, NY 10010

www.tor.com

ISBN: 0-812-56184-8
Library of Congress Catalog Card Number: 00-048020

First edition: February 2001
First mass market edition: March 2002

Printed in the United States of America

0 9 8 7 6 5 4 3 2 1

John Dunning,

for one heck of a novel-writing class
too many years ago to mention in polite company

FALLING STARS

Characters

The van Huytens

Mariesa van Huyten, chairman-emeritus of Van Huyten Industries.
Barry Fast, Mariesa's ex-husband.
Armando Herrera, butler at Silverpond.
Trish Niederman, Mariesa's valet.
Christiaan van Huyten V, chairman of Van Huyten Industries and Mariesa's older cousin.
Adam Jaeger van Huyten, Chris's son, ex-president of Argonaut Labs.
Norbert Wainwright van Huyten, Mariesa's second cousin.

The Coughlins

Chase Coughlin, Plank pilot with Pegasus Aerospace Lines.
Karen Coughlin, his wife, a teeping accountant.
Chase Coughlin, Jr., their son.

The Silver Apples

Jacinta Rosario, cadet.
Mother Linda Fernandez-Jacoby, director of the Torrance Refuge.
Lilly Katilla, Ginger, Tina, Visitacion—sisters at Torrance.
Darlene, a duenna.

The Pooles

S. James ("Jimmy") Poole, computer security consultant.
Tanuja ("Tani") Pandya, his wife, a novelist.
Steven James Poole, Jr., "Little Stevie," their son.
Stassy, the cook.
Rada, the nurse.

The Carsons

Roberta ("Styx") Carson, a poet and progressive.
Carson Albright, the future's hope.

The Otters

Gar Rustov, copilot aboard LTV *Buzz Aldrin*.
Choo-choo Honnycott, copilot aboard SSTO *Hubert Latham*.
Richard Sung-yi, flight engineer aboard LTV *Buzz Aldrin* and SSTO *Hubert Latham*.
Lakhmid Singh, pilot.
Kenji Yoshimura, flight engineer aboard SSTO *Bobbi Trout*.

Movers and Shakers

Nathan Rothschild.
Louis Dreyfuss.
Estéban Ortega.
Heinrich Schlossmann.
Prince al-Walid.
Ed Wilson, an entrepreneur, president of Wilson Enterprises.

Van Huyten Industries

Hamilton Pye, president of Ossa & Pelion Heavy Construction.
Correy Wilcox, president of Gaea Biotech.
Wallace Coyle, president of Aurora Ballistic Transport.

Marcel Reynaud, troubleshooter, turnaround expert.
João Pessoa, president of Daedalus Aerospace, Brazil.

Other Players

Chino Martinez and Ed TiQuba, a couple of dogs.
Marie, Wendy, and Victoria, pilot coordinators at Pegasus.
Yungduk Morrisey, cadet.
Blaise Rutell, president of the U.S.
Terrance McRobb, congressman from Illinois, head of the American Party.
Forrest Calhoun, superintendent of Glenn Spaceflight Academy.
Solomon Dark, presidential advisor, North American Planetary Defense Committee.
Ellis Harwood, a muscular progressive, head of The People's Crusade.

13th Deep Space Wing, Experimental

Colonel Bob Eatinger, USAF-SO, commanding.
Leland ("Hobie") Hobart, superconductor chemist for Argonaut.
Ladawan Chulalongkon, a scientist at Argonaut Labs.
Morris ("Meat") Tucker, ZG rigger.
Billie Whistle, a cheesehead.
Dr. Robert Zubrin, program manager.

Operation Intercept

DSV Jackie Cochran
Captain Alexandra Feathershaft, mission commander.
Alonzo Sulbertson, engineer/copilot.
Bai Deng ("Peterson") Ku, doctor/biologist.
"Bird" Winfrey, NDT technician.

DSV Billie Mitchell
Captain Chase Coughlin, command pilot.

Jacinta Rosario, engineer/copilot.
Flaco Mercado, technician.

DSV Igor Sikorsky
Captain Yvgeny Zaranovsky, command pilot.
Total Meredith, engineer/copilot.
Alois Frechet, geologist/physicist.

The Fingers

Norris Bosworth ("SuperNerd").
Chen Wahsi (in Guangzhou, Guangdong Republic).
Pete Rodriguez ("Pedro the Jouster").

Acknowledgments

One of the problems with writing "near future" SF is that the future has a pesky habit of creeping up on you, unexpected-like. Induction caps for controlling computers with "brain waves," for example, made at least two appearances on TV news shows before *Lodestar* was even finished. Aerogel manufacture in ziggy was tried on STS-95 (while all the cameras were pointed at John Glenn). Digital cameras were coming onto the market while *Rogue Star* with its "digital optical input devices" was in first draft. And private companies were being contracted to manage public schools even as *Firestar* was in production. "Neo-encephalitis" was named "West Nile," instead.

As for privately built SSTOs . . . Gary Hudson (Rotary Rocket), Michael Kelly (Kelly Aerospace), Buzz Aldrin (Starcraft Boosters), and others are currently vying to be the first civilian company to reach orbit and The Artemis Project (a registered trademark of the Lunar Resources Company) plans a lunar mine. "Artemis Mines" is mentioned in the text with their approval.

The world may not be quite ready for nanotechnology, but microtechnology is rolling along very well, thank you. Dr. Stephen O'Neil, vice president of research at Micromotion, Inc., was kind enough to explain some of the near-future potentials for micro-electromechanical devices (MEMS), such as the surgical procedures and *in vivo* monitoring devices mentioned in this novel (and which, naturally, appeared on the evening news before I got the copyedited manuscript back!). Craig Purdy, of NASA's Goddard Space Flight Center/Wallops Island, provided information and background on material extraction and microgravity manufacturing, including on-site oxygen production from ilmenite. Dr. Robert Zubrin, of Mars Direct, described the construction and operation of magnetic sails. My apologies to him for not going directly to Mars.

Others helped out with various details. Stan Schmidt graciously determined the apparent size of Earth as seen from the Bean: Kathleen Wong, Abdou Noor, and others provided bits of translation. David Hartwell, editor of this series, gave helpful advice on earlier drafts of this manuscript. Most of all, to Marge Flynn, who didn't have to do anything to earn my eternal gratitude, but did anyway.

"It is by incremental steps that we enter into strangeness. We plant each stride on familiar ground little different from yesterday. Only years later, looking back, do we see what a long way we have come."

—Tanuja Pandya,
Taj Mahal

FALLING STARS
2017–2023

Prologue:

Black Winter, 2017–2018

Musconetcong Mountain had barely abandoned its cloak of rust and orange when harsh, icy, northeast winds ushered in a winter of unusual brutality. Sullen, black clouds rolled down again and again from the northlands and the wind howled sleet and ice. The sky grew a perpetual, sullen slate and gave everything a close, hemmed-in feel, as if a lid had been pressed over all the world. The Interstate vanished under a shroud of snow and ice. It was not a gentle snow—not the hummocky, fluffy sort that filled with sleighbells and roasting chestnuts and laughing children—but a gritty, ice-filled abrasive that stung exposed cheeks and blasted them raw. You could cut your hands building snowmen.

All summer long and into the fall, Mariesa van Huyten had watched the dominoes topple with fascinated horror. The economy dried and curled with the leaves; and fell with them, too, in the first, harsh knife winds. Investors dropped Orbital Management and Klon-Am Holdings following revelations that OMC had deceived telepresent operators and researchers with a virtual reality simulation and leased the same volume several times over on Leo Station. They began dumping Pegasus when word leaked of CEO Dolores Pitchlynn's collusion with Klon-Am in fraudulent stock transactions. Then, as if fearing contagion, they began selling Boeing and Matsushita, and other partners in the LEO Consortium. Bids on volume in Leo Station dropped, sucking prices down all across Low Earth Orbit. Goddard, Tsiolkovsky, and the other stations began cutting back. By October, Earthside toolmakers were hurting for directionally solidified metals and chip-makers for gallium bismide. Supplies of Permovium began to dry up, leading to an upsurge in neo-encephalitis.

The Dow fell below 12,000.

By the time the first bite of winter set in, unemployment topped ten percent, and men and women who might otherwise have been blowing smoke, pharming genes, or hacking cheese were now hustling lunch money. The Dip, they called it, hoping by name-magic to lessen its severity. Riots broke out in Cleveland, the Bronx, and elsewhere—in January, in the bitter cold and knee-deep snow. Crowds bundled in down jackets and moon boots set buildings afire—though perhaps only for the heat. The magtrain line that wound through the valley below Musconetcong Mountain cut back to two trains a day, then ran sporadically, then stopped entirely.

It was foolish to ponder individual blame. Adam Van Huyten often chastised himself for causing the Dip: but his revelation of the fraud on Leo was only one factor among many. The Social Security crisis. Roberta Carson's announcement on the web of the oncoming asteroid. The federal shutdown of the orbital trade—as if the answer to high blood pressure was to stop the heart. Even had Mariesa known of her cousin's plans and foreseen their consequences and forestalled his actions, the trigger would only have been something else.

In itself, the Dip of '17 was no great thing; not in the same league as 1893, let alone 1929 or 1873. It was the timing more than the magnitude that mattered. For during all that long, cold, lonely winter the asteroid called "the Bean" spiraled closer and closer to Earth.

Sleet curled across the flank of First Watchung Mountain outside the broad windows of the chairman's office at Van Huyten Industries. Mariesa van Huyten waited patiently and studied the eddies and whorls while her cousin, Chris, dealt with yet another interruption. She did not envy the man on the screen, who was, after all, only doing his job. Mariesa drank her tea. There was a woman reflected in the window:

an old woman with lines around her eyes, soberly dressed in dark winter worsted. She did not know who it was.

"Of course, I understand, Chris," the man on the pee-phone said. "We all face unexpected shortfalls; that's what a line of credit is for. To even out those little bumps. Though I guess what Dolores Pitchlynn gave you was more like a pot-hole . . ."

Chris van Huyten never showed anger. He was never known to raise his voice or to pound the table. When his frustration with fools and villains grew overwhelming, it showed only in a slightly stiffer bearing and a tendency to esoteric sarcasm. Generally, he relied on an iron sense of fairness and an even more iron sense of honesty. As those who worked most closely with him said, you might not like where you stood with him, but at least there was no mistaking where that was.

"Pitchlynn, I can handle," Chris said. "Strap on a parachute and shove her out the plane. On second thought, no parachute. And she pays her own SEC fine. Bring Marcel Reynaud over from Ruger AG to clean shop. Pegasus rides out a bumpy year, but she keeps flying. It's the bureaucrats that've blind-sided me, Ira."

Ira spread his hands. "They had to do something."

"Did they? Okay, I can see the safety inspection on the station—Bullock may have cut more corners than we know of—but, be honest, Ira: Who would do a more thorough job? The Orbital Safety Commission, or the tenants and consortium partners, whose livelihoods—whose *lives*—depend on proper maintenance?"

"It's like the kids say, Chris. 'No flubber on that one.' "

A moment of silence followed. Then Chris's voice went flat. "You're not going to fulfill your end of the contract."

Ira stopped smiling. "The bank's in a liquidity crisis. Rutell's Social Security bond issue is sucking the capital pool dry."

"Wonderful. On the one hand, they screw with the interest

rates, like they did in '29, and turn a market crash into a full-blown depression. Meanwhile, with the other hand, they grab up all the spare change in sight. It must be a rule: Secure all livery portals, subsequent to equine egress."

"Chris, no offense, but you and I don't have to worry about retirement. When the economy downshifted, Congress lost a year's lead time on the Social Security Reform Bill. Rutell had to act fast."

"That's what King Louis thought at Crécy. Congress should have had a bill years ago; but somehow Boomer retirement still managed to take them by surprise."

Afterward, Chris rejoined Mariesa by the window. "I guess you heard," he said. He sounded, if not cheerful, resigned. "There went our line of credit."

But VHI's operating budget was the last thing on Mariesa's mind. "Solomon Dark told me that Rutell sequestered the funding for the North American Planetary Defense Committee. He's grabbing money wherever he can find it and stuffing it into the Social Security mattress. 'Just for the next quarter, until revenues straighten out.' But Solomon and I both think that's optimistic."

"How does the saying go? 'When you're up to your ass in alligators, it's hard to stay focused on swamp drainage.' Six years is a lot smaller on the radar screen than the next election—or the quarterly P&Ls."

"Dear Lord!" Mariesa's hands balled into fists and she turned sharply to face him. "They would let the planet be destroyed rather than lose an election?"

Chris took her by both arms. "Calmly, coz. The Bean isn't a planet-killer; and most of them don't really believe it will hit us at all. They've been down that road before, and it's always been false alarms."

Mariesa broke loose from his grip. She ran a hand through her hair. "I have spoken to Solomon about it. He says that Roberta's Net-wide announcement about the asteroid probably turned the economic 'adjustment' into a panic . . ."

"Recession," said Chris. "We don't call them 'panics' anymore."

". . . but I don't believe that. The market dip started *before* Roberta made her speech. It must have been something else."

Her cousin spread his hands. "Water under the bridge in either case."

"Chris . . ." She spoke hesitantly and faced the window while she did. "The reason why I came—your pledge to SkyWatch—is it still good?"

"SkyWatch!" She heard the surprise in his voice. "But, you've found your 'rogue star.' "

She turned to him. "We found *one.*"

He stared at her a moment and his right hand rose slowly to tug at his lower lip. He began to nod. "I see. And if some of SkyWatch's money winds up funding Planetary Defense programs, why it's all one and the same, right?"

"We cannot afford to lose who-knows-how-many months of planning just because the economy went into an unexpected funk."

A faint smile played around Chris's lips. "Resurrect the old Prometheus team?" he said playfully.

She had not thought of that until this very moment and gave her cousin a sharp look, wondering how seriously he had meant it. "We could do worse, you know." There had been people on Prometheus who knew the value of planning. And who might, given the new urgency, donate their time.

"Ah, well," Chris said, "that pledge of mine was small change, anyway. It wouldn't help VHI's balance sheet to take it back, and it might do some good where it is."

"Thank you, Chris." It did not matter how much she squinted. The reflection in the window would never be that of the brash, neurotic, thirtyish girl who had once kick-started the future. It was someone else, now. After six years in the wilderness, she wasn't sure who it was who had emerged.

1.

Prometheus, Bound

As Lunar Transfer Vessel-02, *Buzz Aldrin,* passed above the dark expanse of the Sea of Fecundity, Command Pilot Chase Coughlin eyeballed his progress against the landscape below. He watched the Foaming Sea fall behind and the ship coast over the abrupt, bright highlands around Banachiewicz Crater. On the money, he decided. A moment later, Gar Rustov, his copilot, confirmed their orbit against the groundside navigation beacons.

Chase studied the twisted, colorless, alien surface, a country of lights and shadows: all blacks and whites and grays. As the ship crossed the ridge between the Marginal and Smythe Seas, the white and gray surrendered entirely and the terminator shrouded the Moon in an unrelenting night. A single gleam broke the darkness where Artemis Mines nestled on the edge of the Smythe Sea.

At apogee, Chase hit the kick motor and the *Buzzer* entered Low Lunar Orbit. Used to be, back in Apollo days, that the insertion took place out of contact with Mission Control and the world held its collective breath until the ship came out from behind the Moon. Miss an insertion burn and you'd keep on going and never, ever come back. Even back in '09, when he and Ned DuBois had "moonstormed" in the old *Glenn Curtiss*, they had been out of contact at the critical times. Now Space Traffic Control had relays all over Farside.

"We have entered LoLO," Gar confirmed.

"Acknowledged." Of course, what did "contact" mean? Only that now, if someone ever did miss a burn, the world would know about it sooner rather than later.

"Artemis reports bucket is down rails," said Rustov. Chase glanced at the clock. The catapult launch was late by a few seconds, but not enough to affect closing distance or relative velocity. Chase had snagged enough pods in his time to know when he had to tickle his orbit. Still, you *never* depended on gut instinct—especially in ziggy, where your guts sometimes twisted inside out. He queried the navcomp and the Artificial Stupid agreed that the rendezvous would indeed fall within the envelope.

Too bad. There were times when Chase wished for something a little more exciting than catching pop flies. Something that would pump the old adrenaline; something that would take him out to the edge and test his mojo.

"Docking collar D-as-in-dog-Three is prepped," announced the flight engineer. Rick Sung-yi sat at right angles and "above" the two pilots; but in ziggy, who cared? The teep helmet enclosing his head made him look like The Human Fly. Telepresent, he could prep docking collars using remote-control waldos. The *Buzzer* was an ungainly craft—fully loaded, it looked like a bunch of grapes held together with Tinkertoys—but it got the job done.

"How's the balance?" Chase asked, not because he thought Rick would neglect The *Buzzer*'s center of mass, but because Chase always checked everything. Tedious, but it wasn't like he had something else he had to do; and three times in the past anal-retentiveness had saved his butt. Not very dramatic, but he was alive; so there were no complaints coming.

"Pod orbit is . . . in groove," announced Rustov. He leaned back in his seat. "Close approach in twenty minutes." Chase set the countdown clock and the crew relaxed. Nothing to do now but wait.

"So." Rustov turned his seat to face inboard. "Are you having sold your Pegasus stock?"

Chase shook his head. "Nah. I figure to hold on until the smoke clears."

Rick Sung-yi flipped the goggles from his teep helmet. "Me, I'd sell."

"Nothing wrong with the Old Gray Mare." Chase patted the winged stallion logo on his scarlet coveralls. "Pitchlynn ran a tight ship. Too bad she was seduced by the Dark Side."

"That won't impress the turkey herd," Sung-yi answered. "They spook easy. How much has the stock dropped in the last week?"

"Don't matter none. It's still higher than when I bought it." Chase hadn't bought it, exactly: it had been part of his comp package. But, still . . .

Below, dawn was a knife edge west of Riccioli. Off to the south, a gleaming line thrust two hundred meters from the ringwall into Grimaldi Flats. "Is new catapult," Rustov told them. On the telescope viewscreen robots and waldos slid a coil module onto the quenchgun's inner tube. "Superconducting coils," Rustov explained. "Coil ahead of payload attracts, and one behind repels. Bing, bing down tube—" His two fists moved in tandem left to right. "Is how they move maglev trains."

"I know the guy who made that possible," Chase said. "Leland Hobart—Hobie, we always called him. Back in school, we thought he was dumb as bricks, but he was only thinking deep, you know."

"Never heard of him," said Rick.

Rustov turned and looked at Chase. "You mean 'Hobie, the Master of Cool'? You were in school with him?"

Chase Coughlin, Hot Pilot, did not impress Gar—who was, after all, something of a hot pilot himself. But Chase Coughlin, Classmate of Leland Hobart, was another story. Chase grinned. He'd have to tell Hobie, next time they crossed orbits.

"Is almost no metal in catapult," Rustov told Sung-yi, "because barrel coils induce wery high circumferential currents. And 'slinky' springs between barrel and outer tube not only take recoil but also make long heat path for dissipation."

Chase caught the F/E's eye. "Hey, Rick, I thought *you* were the engineer here."

Sung-yi shrugged. "Everyone has a hobby."

"Yeah? Mine's women."

"Right. How many in your collection?"

"Well . . . okay, one. So far. But—"

Sung-yi laughed. "But Karen's more than you can handle anyway."

Rustov turned from the viewport as the catapult site fell behind and The *Buzzer* soared out over the dark soil of the Ocean of Storms. "Someday," he said, "they move ships with quenchguns. Shooting iron pellets behind at great velocity, ship moves forward. Action, reaction."

"Until then, Gar," said Chase, "we'll set you in the after-lock with a peashooter." Sung-yi laughed.

"Lobbing those canisters up onto L-1 will make pickups easier," the flight engineer admitted. "We won't have to duck down here to LoLO to make the retrieval. Save two klicks delta-V, easy." It was well known that an F/E would sell his grandmother for half a klick.

"*If* the cans don't fall off the saddle," Chase pointed out. "L-1 is unstable."

"They will be using spin stabilization," Rustov said, "and apolune kick motors. Cans will be reusable, too."

"Reusable?" said Chase. "You mean we'll get to lug the empties back to the Moon? Man, this job is a thrill a minute."

"Be glad it isn't," said Rick soberly.

They raised the Earth coming around the western limb of the Moon just as the countdown clock kicked in and the Artificial Stupid announced the five-minute warning. Rick flipped his teep goggles back in place and Chase and his crew swung back to their workstations.

The *Buzzer* swung between the Earth and Moon and there, directly forward and framed between the two, was red Mars.

There was an asteroid coming. Roberta Carson said so on her big webcast. Impact in six years? Jesus, no wonder the market had crashed. Chase had asked around and it seemed ol' Styxy had the straight skinny. A Planetary Defense Committee had been quietly meeting since April trying to put a plan in place before breaking the news to the public. The asteroid was somewhere out around Mars for now, but there would be a close approach in July of '21 and a new FarTrip expedition would go out to meet it.

Yeah, thought Chase. Something new. Something different. Something out on the edge.

There was nothing Chase Coughlin loved so much as the punch of acceleration when a big bird lifted, unless it was the euphoria of utter freedom that followed as the Earth relaxed its obstinate grip and he floated free above the world. He was not given much to poetry—people sometimes said that he lacked depth—yet the mixture of power and skill and delicate balance involved in orbital flight moved him in a way he was utterly unable to describe. So perhaps it was only that he seldom spoke about such things that led others to hasty judgment.

Yet, Earth held charms of its own, if of a different sort, and Chase approached his mandatory groundside rotation with a surge of visceral anticipation. Karen and Little Chase met him at the pilot's lounge at Phoenix Sky Port, where Chase tossed his screeching son high in the air to simulate free fall. "Lift into orbit!" he cried.

"De-orbit burn!" the five-year-old hollered coming down to a soft landing.

The three of them walked out together laughing, but the chuckles died as they passed the gate area. Chase noted that Gates Five and Six seemed to be shut down entirely—at least there were no lift announcements posted. Two men sat in the waiting lounge at Gate Six with the air of having sat there a long time and, to judge by the belongings spread about, intent on staying for a good deal longer. Chase didn't think they were waiting for the next lift. He shook his head. He hadn't seen that sort of thing since he'd been a kid.

"Pegasus is cutting back again," Karen said as they left the secured area. "I scread it on my daily newsbot."

Chase answered the question she hadn't asked. "No change in my schedule." Not yet, at any rate. Seniority counted for something and Chase was glad of it, even though he felt bad for the poor sap who got left on the ground because he was low man on the pyramid. "I'm still down for an orbital cruise next month, after my R and R."

"A month is a long time," Karen said.

Chase looked at her eyes. "Worried, hon?"

"My firm lost two medium-big accounts . . ."

"They dropped your firm?"

"No, the client closed up shop. Went on the block."

He put his arm across her shoulders and hugged her to him. "This Dip won't last long," he said. "That's what the experts are saying. There are all kinds of policies and stuff to deal with it."

"And stuff," she said, giving him a little shove. "Who's the accountant here?"

Chase did a double take as they passed a newsprinter at the base of the escalator to the magrail. "Aw, hell . . ." He left her and walked to the stand, where he hit <stop> then <scroll back> and reread the teaser that had caught his eye. "They can't do that!"

Karen and Little Chase joined him. "Can't do what?" she asked.

"Says here they're closing down the Space Academy for the rest of the semester. It's funded by the lift taxes, and with traffic cut back so much . . ." He swiped his key card through the reader to print the rest of the article. Scuttlebutt you could get for free on the web, but copyright you had to pay. The scuttlebutt was accurate more often than not, but this newsgroupie, Aleta Jackson, had a reputation for the inside skinny.

One more omen, he thought as he read the article on the

maglev back to the Park 'n' Ride. He read it a second time, but the news hadn't changed at all.

Three weeks later, Pegasus called a staff meeting at their Phoenix Operations Center. Technically, Chase was on vacation, but the skinny said that to miss the meeting would be unwise, and Chase had never made an issue of watching the clock, anyway.

He zipped up the red coveralls with the flying stallion logo and checked the hang in the bedroom mirror with satisfaction. Still slim; still flat at thirty-four. He ran his hands down both sides of his head and felt the stubble growing out. Time for another trim. He wore his hair longish in the center, but shaved on either side. Rummaging in his jewelry box, he located a Jolly Roger ear stud, which he affixed in his right lobe; then he pulled the red baseball "gimme" cap over his head, tilted it at a cocky angle, and smiled at his reflection.

Someone had told him years ago that seeing a smile first thing in the morning helped you get through the day, so you might as well look happy when you checked your reflection because chances were you'd get damn-few smiles from anyone else.

That wasn't true for him, of course, as Karen proved when he came into the kitchen. Teeth flashed bright against a tan that a lifetime in Phoenix seemed to have made permanent, and a kiss too long to be the perfunctory, old-married kind almost convinced him to ditch the meeting and spend the day in bed. Karen, after all, telecommuted for an accounting firm and normally logged her time at home. How would the partners know what she was banging in between banging the keyboard?

"My assets will be wasting all day," he told her, releasing her at last.

"We'll calculate your ROA tonight," she promised.

Chase grinned. "My market share is rising already."

Playfully, she swatted his arm. "Don't get too jolly with it and invest it somewhere else."

"Direct deposit," he vowed, "I only do at home."

It was an old routine between them. Sometimes they used the language of space flight, more often that of accounting to talk of sex. So much so that Karen sometimes complained that she could no longer read a corporate report without becoming aroused. Whereupon Chase had acquired several annual reports and presented them to her in plain brown wrappers . . .

Little Chase was still asleep, so Chase left the house after no more than a lingering look into his son's bedroom. Outside, the sun was rising into a cloudless sky. His red Ford Panther started with the roar of a predator. Long and sleek, it had more power than some Third World dictators, but Chase kept his speed moderate as he negotiated the curving streets of his subdivision. You didn't find power in brute strength or speed, but in subtlety and control; and his 'chine was always perfectly under his command—responsive, quick, precise. Besides, Little Chase played on these streets and neighbors ought to show a sense of community.

By the time he reached the flight ops center of Pegasus Spacelines, his good mood had evaporated somewhat. He recognized way-too-many of the cars slotted in the pilots' lot. Big schedule shuffle coming up, he guessed. They were only flying three out of five lifts from the original schedule as it was; how many more flights could they cut? He waved to Lakhmid Singh and Reeney Cue as he cruised for a parking place. Definitely too many pilots on the ground. He was ninety percent sure that Reeney had been booked for today's Prague-to-Europa lift.

There were no open spaces in the pilots' lot, so he had to park among the commoners. As he walked toward the building, jiggling his keys in his hand, he noticed cars with New Mexico plates in the spaces reserved for the big hats. Bosses over from Albuquerque. Not a good sign.

In the meeting room, he hung out in the back with Singh and Choo-choo Honnycott, drinking bad coffee from a row of urns set up on a table there. Plates held the usual assortment of bagels and croissants, but few of the pilots touched them. "Desk jockey feed," they called it. Chase noticed that the chairs were set up auditorium-style. No tables, no notepads. Which meant whatever the big hats had to say, it would be short and simple. Chase scowled and drained his coffee.

He tried to remember who was booked to be up this week. What with cutbacks and cancellations, the lift schedule had been changed more often than a newborn's diaper, so it was hard to keep straight. Felicity Corazón, he thought. Maybe Gerhardt Brunnemacher. "Who has the lunar run this month?" he asked the others. He spotted Felicity's shaved head over near the windows, so either he had misremembered the schedule, or her lift had been canceled, too.

"I am thinking the schedule is to be revised again," Singh suggested with a fatalistic gust of breath.

Chase shook his head, but said nothing. Alexandra Feathershaft, Pegasus's chief pilot, had taken a seat in the front of the room and was bumping heads with a dark-haired man whom Chase failed to recognize. New CEO? he wondered. But you didn't need a general meeting to announce a new snout at the top trough; and Sandy was looking *very* unhappy. Chase handed his empty coffee cup to Choo-choo and walked up the center aisle of the room to where some of the office staff had already taken seats.

The three pilot coordinators were sitting together, as they usually did at these meetings. Heads close, chatting; but no smiles—which *was* unusual. If anyone knew who was up, it was this trio. Virginia saw him coming and nudged her companions and they fell silent at his approach. "Why, hel*lo*, Chase," sang Marie with broad enthusiasm. She was a certified Italian grandmother, gray of hair and short of frame. She seemed as frail as a bird, but was as tough and resilient as spring steel. Not only did she know who was flying which birds, but also which hotel or orbital station they were flopping at and—more important—who had birthdays and anniversaries coming up. Somehow she made sure that you were never on the far side of the Moon when you were supposed to be celebrating with your significant other. The pilots all called her "Mom."

"Big meeting," Chase said, letting his head indicate the crowded auditorium.

Marie's smile wavered just a bit. "The biggest ever, I guess." And was there just a touch of wistfulness in her voice?

"Is there anyone who's *not* here?"

The coordinator exchanged a glance with Wendy. If Marie was everyone's mother, Wendy was everyone's big sister. She swept back her brown, shoulder-length hair. "We're not supposed to release that information."

Chase digested that. Theoretically, the pilot schedule was public information, and while some confidentiality safeguards had been installed after the bomb scare back in '11, no one inside Pegasus had ever had any trouble locating friends and colleagues before.

"Oh, why not tell him?" asked Victoria. The third coordinator was tall, slim, and dark-chocolate. "Won't make any difference an hour from now. Will it?"

The three again exchanged mutual glances and somehow achieved consensus without words. Marie spoke for them. "Captain Brunnemacher, Antonov, and Scott are bringing *Gagarin* back from the Moon. *Artie Smith* and *Bobbi Trout* are docked at Goddard; *Chkalov II* at Tsiolkovsky; and *Henri Farman* and *Neta Snook* at Europa. But their crews are attending the meeting by telepresence. Wendy, do you have the crew lists for the orbitals?"

Chase said, "Don't go to any bother. I was just curious." They traded a few more pleasantries, then Chase worked his way to the back of the room. He repeated for Singh and Honnycott what the coordinators had told him. Lakhmid scowled.

"Only five vessels up?" he said. "That does not sound very good."

"Six, counting the LTV," Chase reminded him. "And all but the LTV in dock."

"Where are all the other ships?" Honnycott asked.

Chase twisted the spigot on a coffee urn and filled another cup. He gazed at the foul black brew, suddenly wishing it was something stronger. "Groundside," he said before gulping a swallow.

"It oughta be tea," said Honnycott. Chase looked at him.

"What?"

The other pilot gestured toward the cup. "Tea leaves," he said. "Read the future."

Chase downed the rest of the coffee. "I don't need no freaking tea leaves." On the slowest commercial day in the history of Pegasus Spacelines, there had never been a day with only six ships in the air. Five docked. Loading, unloading? Or just docked? *Gagarin* would have been docked, too, he suddenly realized, if it hadn't been on an irreversible lunar orbit.

"I don't get it," he said. "There's this asteroid coming, right? And they're shutting down the biggest orbital carrier in the world and putting its pilots on the beach."

"You don't know they're shutting down," Singh temporized. Chase could hear the anxiety and denial in the other's voice. "Maybe it's just another schedule change." Bad news is never real until someone official says it out loud. But the way Sandy Feathershaft looked, up there in the front of the room, the news must be pretty damn bad, and Chase wasn't any too sure he wanted to hear it. He tried to catch Sandy's eye, but she wasn't pitching any looks. Chase felt his stomach knot up.

"Asteroid's not for six years," Honnycott said. "Plenty of time to put the pieces back together." He nodded toward the front of the room. "Give the new CEO a chance."

Chase shook his head. "Ballistics," was all he said; but the other two knew what he meant. You couldn't wait until the last minute. There would be only a few launch windows where they could shoot missiles at the thing—what had Roberta called it in that press conference? The Jenuine Bean. Shoot missiles, or go there bonebag and blow the sumbitch up. Only a few windows, and who knew when those windows would open and shut?

There was no point in racing the bad news home. Karen followed the financial news closely and her spyder had probably downloaded the skinny as soon as the shutdown and layoffs were posted on the Net. So all he'd find when he got there would be sympathy and understanding, and Chase wasn't quite up for that.

Impulse pulled him off Interstate 10 and onto the surface streets—past traffic lights, car dealerships, restaurants, strip malls, and body shops. There were a few people about, though not many, and all of them in cars. Pedestrians in the Arizona desert were as rare as the dodo, and for much the same reason—too stupid to live. Daytime Phoenix was never actually *cool*. Even now, in the butt end of winter, the temperature hovered in the high seventies. The Sierra Estrellita gleamed in the distance. The sun was approaching noon and Chase decided he was hungry—but perversely, once he started looking, all the eateries seemed to have vanished.

He passed up a couple of bun-and-runs—he wanted a cool one as much as he wanted a burger—and was just about to say the hell with it when he spotted the roadhouse.

It was a ramshackle affair with a gravel lot and a wriggling MEMS sign above it that named it The Sidewinder. Some of the micro-electromechanical devices had failed, so the snake's motions seemed a little spastic. A battered pickup and an old SUV sat on the side of the building and three bikes, chopped, stood out front. But the haze from the black stack had the tang of barbecue in it, and Chase decided to check it out.

He pulled his Predator up beside the bikes and locked it. Three Harleys, he saw; battered, but kept in good shape. Repaired with dealer aftermarket parts; no homemade junk. Before entering the bar, he doffed his cap and held it over the sun while he looked at the sky. Yep. There was the Moon, all right: a fingernail paring just west of the sun. *Enjoy the trip, Gerhard,* he thought. He recoiled from the notion that it might be the last one. Somehow, the Moon seemed much farther away than usual, but maybe that was in his head.

Inside, the bar was warm and smoky, but not hot for all that. A floor fan at the far end stirred the air as it hunted back and forth. A long bar lined the back wall with a decently varied rack of bottles against the mirror. Above the mirror an improbably long rattlesnake was mounted on a wooden board. The bartender, a solid, dark-haired, happy-faced man, drank from a bottle of water while he chatted with the waitress. Chase tried to guess which was the pickup and which the SUV. The bikers occupied a booth near the door. They studied Chase as he slid onto a bar stool.

"Skull Mountain," said Chase, dropping his cap to the bar. The barman looked at the cap, at Chase's red Pegasus coveralls, then reached under the bar and pulled up two longneck Skulls and a glass. The glass looked clean. Chase took one of the bottles and popped the cap. He didn't use the glass. "Why two?" he said, pointing to the second bottle.

"First one's on the house," the barman said.

Chase thought about that. "Which am I drinking?"

"Second one."

Chase grinned. "I'm smelling some good 'cue. Can I get a plate of pulled pork?"

"Beans?"

"Why not? My wife's put up with worse."

The barman turned away. "Heard the news," he said. " 'Bout Pegasus shutting down. Damn shame. A lot of the welders and assemblers from the maintenance shops stop in here."

Chase grunted. He'd been so immersed in his own troubles

he'd forgotten there were others, with jobs a lot less glamorous than space pilot.

Sensing a presence beside him, Chase looked up into the broad, bearded face of one of the bikers. The man was heavyset, though not fat, and wore a black T-shirt under his leather vest. Intricate tattoos of eagles and hawks twined up both his arms. The T-shirt read: "No Fear? You Haven't Met *Me,* Yet!" When he bunched his muscles, the raptors stirred. "Your money's no good here," he said.

"I hope not," Chase said mildly. He lifted his bottle of Skull Mountain, "This here's my second bottle, so I got to pay for it."

"You hear me, Al?" the biker called after the barman, who was heaping pork on a plate. "I'm buying." The barman gave a sign and the biker slid onto the stool beside Chase. He stuck a hand out. "Bird Winfrey. You're Chase Coughlin, aren't you?"

"Gotta be," Chase told him. "No one else wants the job." He gripped hands.

Winfrey's laugh rumbled in his chest. "Thought I recognized you. I lifted with you a time or three back when we were building Leo Station."

Chase tilted his long-neck toward the other man. "Here's to you, otter."

"You want to join us over in the booth? Chino and Ed are two dogs—mechanics from Phoenix Yards. We were on our way to meet our wives up in the White Tanks."

Chase grabbed both his bottles and slid off the stool. "Your wives drive Harleys, too?"

"Yeah, I saw you checking the bikes out when you came in. Sure. When it comes to bikes, Yamaha makes a great piano."

Chase followed him to the booth and slid in beside a stocky Hispanic with oriental eyes. Winfrey introduced him as Chino Martinez and the other as Ed Tiquba. "That's 'TiQuba,' " the black man said, giving a click in place of the Q-sound Winfrey had used. It seemed to Chase's ear like the sound that a rider made with his cheek to giddyup his horse. He lifted his bottle. "Here's to the big hats . . ."

". . . And the swelled heads that wear 'em." Winfrey and his buddies were drinking Dos Equis. "I was making myself a nice piece of cash," Winfrey went on. "Up Goddard, you know? Testing DSM for Straight Arrow." He shook his head. "When you guys started cutting back on your lift schedules, we had a hard time lifting raws and dropping stuff groundside. So Straight Arrow had to close up shop."

"Wasn't my idea," Chase said. "Cutting back."

"Yeah, otter, I hear you." Winfrey fell silent. He exchanged looks with the dogs, but no one said anything more for a while. The waitress came and set a plate of tangy barbecue with a side of beans and dill pickles in front of Chase.

Her clothing affected a compromise between the maximum tolerable in the heat and the minimum required by decency. If the compromise conceded a little more to one side than the other, it was a compromise Chase approved.

Chase had never strayed from his marriage—it was part of his code—but putting a ring on his finger hadn't made him blind, and he frankly admired the female of the species. Drop-dead gorgeous was not the only factor, nor even a necessary one—he admired grit and quiet competency, too—but neither was it much of a drawback.

Winfrey looked up. "Put in on my tab, Honey."

"You don't have a tab," she said.

"So start one. Do I have to do all the thinking around here?"

"We're in deep trouble if you do," she said. "You can't pay with your good looks. First off, you don't have any and—"

Winfrey flushed under his bushy beard. "C'mon, cut a guy a break . . ."

Chase pulled his wallet out and laid a couple of presidents on the table. "Don't worry about it." Winfrey hesitated and looked embarrassed, but did not push the money back. The waitress counted the bills as she picked them up. She dropped a smile on Chase.

"Now, if *you* wanted to pay with your good looks . . ." She let the suggestion hang before turning away. Chase watched her go.

"There's a word in Shona," said Ed with a wistful grin, "for walking that way."

Chase grunted. "I just bet there is." He turned back to the table. Winfrey wouldn't meet his eye.

"Look, I'll pay you back, soon as—"

"You're starting to worry," Chase cautioned him.

Winfrey slumped in his chair. He looked at his two companions. "Life's a bitch," he said.

"And then you die," agreed Chino.

Winfrey's hands bunched on the tabletop, fingers interlaced. Then, bumping the table once, he sighed and picked up his drink. "How long you think this Dip'll go on?" he asked.

"Beats me," Chase said. "I'm no bean counter. Marcel Reynaud—he's the new CEO Pegasus brought in—he told us at the meeting today that there's no money to operate while the lawsuits are pending because the Social Security bonds have sucked up all the loose change. I guess *anyone* who needs cash is having trouble scrounging it up. So, they cut costs."

"Costs," said Ed. "That's you an' me."

"Something like that, anyway. Here's a freaking asteroid gonna whack us upside the head and the big hats are letting all the money go down the toilet." Chase took a slug of Skull. He supposed he might have felt different if he'd been on the receiving end of Social Security. Anything to keep those checks a-coming. But now a whole cartload of guys who would have been paying *into* the fund were out of work, so go figure.

Winfrey was watching the waitress chat with Al. He pursed his lips. "You think that Bean's for real?"

Chase cocked his head. "Don't you?"

Winfrey shrugged. "Don't much care, as long as it puts us back to work."

Chino checked his watch. "Hey, we better get humping, *'mano*, if we gonna meet the girls in time." The three bikers finished their beers, saluted Al, shook hands with Chase, and took their leave. "Anything comes up," Winfrey said to Chase before he left, "let me know, one otter to another." He blew a kiss to the waitress and the screen door slammed behind him.

Chase grinned and shook his head over his long-neck. Just goes to show. Three rough-looking bikers done up in leather and denim and steel, and they turn out to be a trio of family guys on an outing. A couple of dogs and an otter.

He was just finishing his pulled pork when the waitress slid into the booth opposite him with her own lunch in hand. A sandwich and a beer. She was dusky-complexioned with high cheekbones and dark eyes and hair. More than a little Indian blood in there. A fine line of heat perspiration beaded her forehead. When she leaned over the table, she displayed an impressive amount of cleavage. "Hi," she said. "I'm Honey."

"I bet you are." Chase stopped himself before he asked for a taste. He glanced over at Al, but got no clue from the bartender's expressionless face.

"Iron Al tells me you're a space pilot," Honey said, sucking sauce from her fingertips. "Mmm. Al makes one bad barbecue sandwich. What's it like? The Moon, I mean."

"Not much. Couple of mines. Farside Observatory. Mostly robots and waldos. A few miners and scientists. Nightlife really sucks."

"Do you go there a lot?"

"I've landed a few times," he allowed, "but mostly it's just fly-by pickups. The mines use catapults to launch pods into LoLO—that's Low Lunar Orbit—and we circle around and around and snatch them up. Silicon for the chip-makers in Goddard and Europa; oxygen for all the stations. Metals." He shrugged. "Nothing glamorous. They were building a bigger catapult, one that can park cargo in L-1, but I guess the Dip has stopped work on that, too, by now."

"How do you make a pickup? I mean, isn't that dangerous?"

"Oh, I move up real close and nudge my prong into the coupling basket."

Honey paused, then laid her sandwich in the basket. "That sounds . . . fun. Do you dock often?"

Chase began to imagine docking with Honey . . . He was treading dangerous ground, he knew. The thought was mother to the deed. But the talk was pleasant and he had nowhere he had to be, so any conversation was better than stewing in his own problems. He told her some of his shopworn yarns and received some gratifying gasps or laughs. Well, it had been a long time since he had a fresh audience. Some of the yarns were good enough that they needed very little in the way of embellishment.

When he described how he and Ned DuBois had flown into Skopje to rescue the UN peacekeepers, Honey placed her hand over his and said he must be very brave. "I ain't no hero," Chase told her with just the right touch of humility. "Just a guy with a job to do." He'd learned that from Ned DuBois. *Once you learn to fake sincerity,* The Man Who had told him, *the rest comes easy.*

"On my cadet flight," he said, "Forrest Calhoun and I lifted the rocket motors to raise the first external tank into orbit with Mir. Me and him and Ned DuBois and—" And who had been the Russian commander on Mir? Sugachev? No matter. "We hooked the motors onto the tank and lifted it into co-orbit with Mir; so you might say that we were the ones who proved it was possible to build Leo and the other stations that way." Okay, if it hadn't been him it would have been someone else, but it never hurt to exaggerate your own importance when you were talking with a pretty woman.

"Must be a bitch, getting laid off," she said. "Allen told me about that. Real bitch."

Chase tried to be blasé about it. "Oh, they can't keep the ships grounded forever. When they start lifting again, they know where to find me."

"Well, handsome, if you need a shoulder to cry on," the waitress said, "you know where to find me, too."

Chase hesitated. There was more to her offer than a shoulder. He could see that in the curl of her mouth. A friendly invitation. There was none of the weary hardness he'd seen on some women—just a healthy, good ol' gal who knew better ways than serving pork to get a guy's morale up and have a little fun herself in the bargain. "Wouldn't be your shoulders I'd cry on," he said with an answering grin.

Honey laughed and squeezed his hand. "Nah, you never would." She pushed out of the booth and piled her basket on his plate. "A gal knows when a guy's on the reservation; and, handsome, you are one Agency Indian." She cocked her head and studied him as he rose, too. "Too damn bad. I bet you would've been good."

"Not just good. Outstanding." He raised both hands. "Understand, I'm just repeating what I've been told."

"Yeah, modest, too. You better hit the road, 'otter,' before you change your mind."

Chase left the bar feeling far better than he had going in. Nothing improved a guy's outlook more than having a good-looking gal hit on him.

Of course, maybe Honey knew that, too, and that's why she'd done it. Cheer the poor bastard up. Still, Chase was as certain that her offer was sincere as she had been that he would turn it down. He tossed his car keys in the air and caught them on the way down. Yeah, too bad. They'd've been good together. But pledged virgins were not the only ones who took their vows seriously.

It wasn't something predictable; it wasn't something Chase himself could have predicted all those years ago at Witherspoon High, when he had been groping the girls and handing out black eyes. He'd been phat nasty back then. Bully, casual extortion, angry all the time, a couple of smash-and-grabs where he'd been lucky enough not to get caught . . . Wealing on Jimmy Poole. When he thought about it, it was like remembering a stranger.

Danny Coughlin, his father, had been a good enough man when sober, but prone to casual violence and thoughtless lust when the drink was on him, which was all too often. But there was enough to admire, even to love, that Chase had begun to follow his dad down the same path. If hot pilot Ned DuBois hadn't taken him under his wing, who knew which jail's cot he'd be warming today?

He hadn't seen it at the time. He hadn't thought he was teetering on a cusp, like a hot 'chine banking hard, just on the edge of losing lift and going into a spin. Yet, looking backward, it was as clear as the stars from orbit that his entire life had been decided that summer and everything since had been a working out of those choices. He had pulled on the yoke—No, he had *taken hold* of the yoke for the very first time in his life and flown on his own bearings.

Mentor Academies must have seen something in him; more than he had seen in himself. Something more than a nobody taking the bruises his father handed out wholesale and passing them along to others at retail. They had set him up with a job as a machinist's helper at Thor Tools, where he'd been miking a component for a tool build when Ned DuBois showed up.

Of course, he hadn't known who Ned was; not then. It was only later, with his heart pounding in his throat, that he followed the news of the first SSTO flight and the rescue of Gregor Levkin; and later still that he had taken Ned's dare and flown with him to the long-abandoned Moon and the whole world shook itself awake and said, *We can go back again* . . . Yet he had sensed something deeper in the older man than mere cockiness. Here was a man fully in command of himself.

Chase had latched on to Ned with the fervor of a drowning swimmer, and found a courage he had never known he lacked. After all, what sort of courage did it take to smack around the likes of Jimmy Poole? Not the sort you needed to thread the needle landing tail-down at the Fernando de Noronha test field; or snatch a shipping pod lobbed by the lunar catapults in what amounted to a "controlled collision."

Ned DuBois had been a womanizer—for a test pilot, it went with the territory—but when the chips were down and the hand was called, he had gone back to his Betsy. He had even given up command of the FarTrip mission to stay with her. That choice had impressed Chase more than all the swagger. Doing the right thing counted for a lot with Chase; though he wasn't always sure what the right thing was. There might be circumstances that would tempt him into arms like Honey's. He couldn't say. But those circumstances hadn't happened yet; and more to the point, he didn't go out looking.

The house was empty when he got back. A note posted on the microwave reminded him about Little Chase's one o'clock dental appointment. Officially a cleaning, but really just to get the tyke used to a dentist's office.

Chase doffed his coverall and hung it in the closet. He paused before shutting the door and wondered when he next might put on Pegasus red, if ever. He traced the silhouette of the winged stallion with his fingertip. He'd given the Old Gray Mare seven years of his life. Wham, bam, thank you, ma'am. Maybe they would get the economic mess cleaned up quick, but somehow he didn't think so. The market dive had caught more companies than Pegasus in its slipstream.

Aurora Ballistic and Orbital hired pilots. Earth-to-Earth ballistic runs were for weenies—bus drivers—but better than nothing; and Katya Volkovna, Aurora's chief of operations, was, like Ned DuBois and Forrest Calhoun, one of the original SSTO test pilots. But Aurora would have the same problem borrowing money as everyone else if they wanted to buy up Pegasus ships and routes and expand their service. As for Daedalus and Energia, the otter fraternity was worldwide and Chase didn't think the Social Security crisis affected Brazil and Russia, but that big sucking sound could vacuum up *reals* and *novy rubles* as easily as dollars. It was a global economy. That's what they all said.

The hell with it. Whatever happened, he couldn't change it by fretting. He pulled on a pair of ragged chinos and a T-shirt and headed for the basement, where he set up his lathe to turn some table legs. He liked using his hands and he liked working in wood and metal. He never used the voice commands built into the lathe's Artificial Stupid. Voice commands were for weenies, too. You had to *feel* the wood and the pressure and the bite of the tool.

The spindle wound up and Chase applied the tool. Feather light, at first, and wood peeled off in delicate spirals. He glanced at the template and adjusted the depth.

Honey. He shook his head. What a name. He hoped she hadn't had to grow up wearing it. Maybe he'd ask her the next time he dropped in for the barbecue. He pulled the tool away and the lathe whined down to a stop, a fair groove cut near what would become the base, once he squared it off.

Who was he kidding? Honey was a nice enough gal. Good-looking, sassy, autonomous. But there was something missing. Chase didn't know what it was, only that Honey didn't have it. And maybe that was good luck for the both of them—not to mention for Karen and Little Chase. He could drop by the Sidewinder and talk flirty and they'd both have a few laughs and no one would be hurt. He knew some guys who went pelt-hunting, convinced they were missing out on something. They were always a little disoriented, Chase thought. After all the furtive nooners and cheatin' evenings, they somehow never managed to fill the emptiness inside them. Could be there was someone perfect out there; at least, perfect for him. Someone who had whatever "it" was; but he could spend the rest of his life looking and never accomplish anything besides making miserable the lives of people that he loved.

He remembered what he had told Honey about his first flight. How he and Ned and Forrest had mounted engines on a derelict Shuttle ET that had been put accidentally-on-purpose into orbit. Could they do the same thing with that Bean? Mount rocket engines on it. A *lot* of rockets, maybe; but the basic techniques were known; and sure, the people who were paid to think of things like that had probably already thought of things like that, but he'd drop Ned a line, anyway, just to make sure. Ned knew people, or knew those who did, and people didn't always do what they were paid for.

He'd scope the mission first. It wasn't like he had a whole lot of work to do. Might as well lay a phat proposal on Ned's hard drive and not just a vague suggestion. He was a ship's captain. He knew to the gram how much a Plank freshly refueled in orbit could carry. He could call up Forrest at the Space Academy and pick his brain over his experiences on FarTrip I.

FarTrip II would be one phat stoopid mission. He'd told Hobie once that he was bored with commercial flights, with their space traffic controllers, port captains, bills of lading, and passenger manifests. A new FarTrip, out beyond the reach of ground control, depending on your own mojo, would be anything but run-of-the-mill. Maybe if he worked up a good enough proposal, they'd pick him to fly it.

Of course, as of now he didn't even have a damned commercial flight. He was laid off and earthbound, chained to a big honking rock.

2.

Virgin Berth

After the cab dropped her off at the curb, Jacinta Rosario lost herself for a few moments in the ritual of payment and tip before turning to face the building. Overhead, gulls shrieked under the razor sun. Something thundered out of LAX, a few miles north. An 803. She identified it easily by its engine signature.

Torrance was a community of small frame houses packed along winding streets. The lots weren't all that big—about the size of a swimming pool, which was what most of them had for backyards—but they were big enough to separate each house from its neighbors and save them from the label of "row homes." The silver apple refuge must have been a school at one time—and still was, since the sisterhood ran under charter one of the better public schools in the district—a boarding school for "girls at risk." Jacinta shaded her eyes against the sun and peered at the upper floors. They'd find a place for her. That was one of the rules. The First Precept read, "The apple is never far from the tree." Yet, it felt more like exile than homecoming; and that was wrong. She was a silver apple. She belonged here.

Another jetliner took off. Her mind transmuted the roar into the holy rumble of high-impulse rockets lifting from Phoenix Sky Port, hundreds of miles east.

But nothing would be lifting from Phoenix—or Allentown, or Prague, or anywhere else—until the financial crisis had passed. And even then, would anyone remember the cadet training schedules that had gotten shredded when it all hit the fan?

Just a short sabbatical, was how Mr. Calhoun put it when he announced that shortfalls in the lift tax on ballistic and orbital flights required drastic economies at the Glenn Spaceflight Academy. *They can't afford to keep the orbital fleets grounded for too long: and they sure as hell can't afford not to train the next generation of pilots.*

Brave words, but Jacinta wished she hadn't heard him trying to convince himself as much as the cadets. Sometimes, the ability to read voices and postures told you more than you wanted to know. Self-deception could be a comfort.

She stood for a while on the portico calling on her Inner Strength before she dared look into the DoorWarden and let it scan her appearance against the "master dataface." Tears, she told herself, could short the optics.

After a few days to settle in, Jacinta Rosario was invited to meet the director—an encounter she approached with hesitation. Ostensibly, it was to welcome Jacinta officially to the Torrance Refuge. *The hand is always open for those in need.* But there was an unspoken stigma attached to those who reached too quickly for that hand. Fledgling fluttering back to us? Was Outside more than you could handle, dear? Maybe you shouldn't *need* quite so easily. But, expecting the knives of kindness, Jacinta found no condescension in the refuge director's voice or posture. The concern and sympathy were genuine. Perhaps the circumstances—the recession, the temporary closing of the Academy—were so clearly elements beyond anyone's control that no stigma could attach to Jacinta seeking shelter. She was only one more storm-tossed pebble on the beach. And yet, Jacinta herself could not help but feel that in some indefinable fashion she had failed.

Failure, after all, had nothing to do with Fault.

Mother Linda Fernandez-Jacoby was a lean and narrow-faced woman who, despite her age, still wore the Maiden's Shawl over her shoulders. She would probably be buried in it. Most apples joined only for a term or two, to get their lives in order; but no organization could survive without its "lifers." Self-consciously, Jacinta adjusted the hang of her own shawl. The fabric tickled her neck and she tried not to scratch there. She had not worn it in over a year. Public displays were not required by the Precepts—the Shawl could attract unwanted approaches—but Jacinta had not worn it even in private, and she felt as if the mother, somehow, knew that.

"Have you settled in, sister?" Mother Linda asked. She had a pot of hot water on a sideboard and busied herself with the steeping of a cup of tea. Like all the apples, she dressed in bright, affirming colors. Her office was comfortable—feminine without being dainty—with soft chairs and low tables. The computer pixwall on standby portrayed an ocean beach.

"Yes, ma'am," Jacinta said. "Thank you again for taking me in. It'll only be until the Academy reorganizes and reopens."

Mother Linda turned and handed her a cup; kept one for herself. "Yes," she said, "though you don't want to depend on the future unfolding to your plans. All the economists say that this—'Dip,' I think is the approved term—will be short. Perhaps they are right; though I wish they didn't feel the need to repeat the assurance quite so much."

Jacinta shivered. "How bad is it?"

"Oh, our workshops are busy enough. More people are looking for low-cost goods. But our investments lost value along with everyone else's. And next quarter's tithes from our fledglings—like yourself—will fall terribly short. But the Council decided to sit on the portfolio. Our losses are only real if we start selling. When the market recovers, we'll be no worse off."

There was more to the world than the sisterhood's endowment, but Mother Linda might be forgiven for viewing the question through the lens of her immediate concerns. And Jacinta's scholarship was funded through the interest off the sisterhood's holdings. "I guess the good times are over."

Mother Linda waved a hand. "We've gotten so used to the

'good times,' that this episode may *seem* worse than it is. It's a crisis of *confidence*; nothing more. After all, Klon-Am resorted to fraud because the demand for their services exceeded their supply. But a great many foolish decisions were made. Panic selling. Hasty interventions. The desire to preen before the newsgroups. Short-term thinking. The sisterhood," she added in the Voice of Confidence, "takes a longer view; and we have urged other orders to do the same." The mother smiled. "There may even be opportunities to further our work. Every panicked seller needs a thoughtful buyer. And if the underlying investment is fundamentally sound . . . Well, the silver apples will come through. Remember, 'Patience resolves . . .' "

" ' . . . more problems than action,' " Jacinta finished. "But 'more' isn't 'all.' The trick is knowing which problems need patience and which need action."

The mother raised an eyebrow, took a sip of tea. "That's not part of the Precept," she said quietly. Jacinta flushed and looked at her feet.

"Sorry."

"May I see your copy of the *Precepts*?" The hand was extended, waiting.

Jacinta's blush deepened. "I . . . left it in my room."

"You should carry it with you at all times." The admonition, gently spoken, was an admonishment nonetheless. "Go fetch it and bring it here, *muchacha*."

The mother didn't understand, Jacinta thought as she hurried down the corridor to the elevator. How could you take a copy of the *Precepts* up a scaling tower or through an obstacle course? *No excuses*, she told herself firmly. *That's why they invented zippered pockets.* And yet . . . And yet . . . When she pulled the slim booklet from her duffel bag, she clutched it to her. How could she let the director see it? It was marked up with her own comments in the margins and the spaces between. She flipped rapidly through it. Every page was scribbled. Her throat tightened.

Maybe mother would not inspect the book. Maybe Jacinta could claim it as lost. She sat on the edge of the bed. Maybe . . .

No excuses. You are responsible for your own actions. That was the Fifth Precept.

But what about the recession and the shutdown . . . How am I *responsible?*

She thumbed through the dog-eared booklet until she came to the Fifth Precept and read her own gloss. "The world can do what it damn well pleases," she read aloud to the pleasantly colored walls. "But I am responsible for how I *respond* to the world. If someone knocks me down, it's *me* that decides whether to lie in the dirt and cry; to leap to my feet and strike back; or to turn my back and walk away." The words comforted her. Her own words.

Still, the corridor to mother's office stretched toward infinity. Chatter, both subdued and cheerful, surrounded her. The murmur of recitations in the classrooms downstairs. The smell of paint and leather and freshly cut lumber from the workshops. The rasp of a buzz saw. Friendly greetings from passing strangers who were also her sisters. The bright sun through the skylights bringing the day into the building. One of the panes was cracked. She ought to offer to replace it. She hadn't forgotten her glaziering, nor the other crafts she had learned at North Orange. *We educate your minds.* Sister Jennifer had once told a much younger Jacinta, *but also your hands and feet. There will always be* something *you can do.*

Bluff, for one. She patted her jumper pocket when she reentered the office. "Got it," she announced, just like that was the end to it.

But Mother Linda wasn't buying it. She held her hand out once more. "May I see it?"

Brazen it out, for another. Let what would happen, happen; and not exhaust herself on contingencies. Mother Linda paged through the booklet, pausing now and again to read what Jacinta had scrawled there. On one page, she paused a very long time.

"I can explain—" Jacinta said; but the house mother held up her palm and Jacinta sagged back in her chair.

An agonizing time later—no clock could measure its passage—Mother Linda closed the booklet and handed it back to her. "How do you explain this?"

"Well . . ." What was her explanation? She could not remember why she had started doing it; only that the world had begun making more sense once she had. A deep breath prepared her. "I guess, I ran into situations, almost died, watched friends fail . . ." She stopped. Who was that babbling so inarticulately? She looked for steel within herself, found it. "Some of the Precepts seemed too simple for what I ran into. I didn't reject any of them, but I thought they needed, well, amendments. I'm sorry if I—"

A cup of tea appeared before her. Jacinta searched Mother Linda's face and found . . .

Approval?

"Don't apologize," the director said. "Nearly all our fledglings annotate their *Precepts* sooner or later. We expect it. It marks the end of their fledging. To push against your boundaries is the most natural thing in the world—which is why the boundaries must be there in the first place. Without rules, why, there is nothing for the young to rebel against; nor any center to come back to. Our young girls need rules and boundaries; but an adult must guide herself through a more ambiguous world. There are always exceptions and special cases and times when the rules do not quite apply. Yet, the world is not *all* exceptions. It is not made up entirely of special cases. There really is a pole star, and as long as you fix on it, you can never lose your course for long."

That was all finely said, but losing your course implied that you had one. What exactly was hers? To spend her days waiting for the Academy to reopen? It would, of course; but no one said it would be soon enough for Jacinta Rosario to step back into harness or that the apples would be able to fund her scholarship when it did.

Or should she settle into the comfortable routine of the Refuge? "Study and recital and the care-absorbing task." She had known peace and respect growing up in the North Orange Retreat; more than she had ever known at home; but she had been fledged only a year, and already it seemed an alien world.

As for home . . . The Retreat had saved, if not her life, her sanity. Maria Rosario had been too young herself to comprehend that motherhood might actually require some of her time—away from the television, away from the phone, away from the message boards and chat rooms. She had left Jacinta to fend for herself—to dress herself in the morning, to find her own meals in an often-empty fridge—only to turn on her with shouts and sarcasm when Jacinta selected the wrong clothes or made a five-year-old's mess in the kitchen. Clueless to the end, she had watched in stunned amazement when her daughter walked out of the house at thirteen to join "that cult."

No, she couldn't go back there, either.

And where did that leave?

Jacinta lay on her bunk that night, trying to sort out her thoughts. The room was simple, not very different from her dorm room at Glenn Academy. A desk with a Net-browser, a reference shelf of "seedies," a closet where she had hung her few clothes—mostly coveralls with their Academy patches. She wondered if she'd ever wear them again.

Almost as far back as her memory could take her, Jacinta had yearned to leave the ground behind and soar through the skies into the blackness of space. And from nearly as early an age, she had learned to hide those yearnings. *Learn your limits, girl,* her mother had once said with cruel indifference, *before you smash into them.*

Well, she had smashed into them, right enough. Not, thankfully, because of her limits—she had yet to find those—but because the world had shrugged its shoulders and tossed an entire cohort of cadets from their perches.

But I wouldn't trade that year at the Academy for anything. She had hung a pixure over the desk. Grinning cadets, looking a little queasy and a little uncertain on their legs, posing in front of NASA's Vomit Comet after their training flight. That was her in the middle—the short, dusky one with cropped dark hair, high cheekbones, and a smile like helium, so that she still seemed to be floating, even back on the ground. She stood in front of Colonel Hancock, their free-fall instructor. Flanking the group were the two pinned cadets, Total Meredith and Lonzo Sulbertson, who had gone up with them as cadet-instructors shortly before their own graduation. And around her were the others: Kenn Rowley and Kiesha Ames and Karyl Krzyzanowkski (everyone called him "Kadet Konsonant") and . . . standing beside Jacinta (where he so often contrived to be) was Yungduk Morrisey—slim, serious, even a little exotic with the slight upturn in his eyelids. His eyes, she noted, were on her and not on the camera.

Friends, all of them. Close friends, some of them. Dreamers of the same dreams. Where were they now? In what refuge had they found themselves?

The Refuge's print shop had not been used in a while. The odors of old inks and papers and lead types in their California cases competed with the smell of dust and rust and stale oil. Jacinta spent a few days cleaning the shop. She sorted through the type cases for strays, cleaned the ink rollers and platens, scrubbed down the letterpress—it was a Heidelberg upright—and disposed of the warped and curled paper and dried-out ink buckets. She set in fresh stores, though not too great a variety because money was tight and she wasn't sure how many students would sign up when she started the craft class.

Lilly Katilla found her there. The child entered the shop so quietly that Jacinta did not know she was there until, with a slug of type in her hands, she turned toward the stone and almost collided with her. Lilly jumped back and Jacinta gasped and the types went flying.

"Oh, no!" the girl cried. "Oh, sister, I'm sorry!" And she scurried about the shop retrieving the scattered letters. Jacinta smiled to herself and knelt to pick up the ones that had fallen by her feet.

"No harm," she said.

"I thought you saw me come in."

"My mind was somewhere else."

"We were waiting for you on the roof and you didn't show up, so someone said she thought you were down here and I came to get you."

"What?" Jacinta looked at her watch. "I'm sorry, I wasn't watching the time. Are the Star Gazers still up there?"

Lilly nodded. The girl was ten, thin and awkward; and, while very conscious of no longer being a child, was still uncertain whether she was quite yet a woman. She looked around the shop, taking in the type cabinets, the stone, the press, the bindery, the shelves of paper and ink buckets. "What are you doing down here?" She didn't quite skip as she crossed the room with the types clutched in her hands.

Jacinta took them and set them on the make-ready table along with the tray and the remaining types. She would reset the lines later. She untied the apron, hung it on a hook by the stone, and washed her hands in the little sink there. "I learned specialty printing when I grew up at the North Orange Retreat," she told the girl. "I thought as long as I was here, I'd pass the skill along. You know the Sixth Precept."

" 'There will always be *something* you can do,' " the girl recited.

Jacinta nodded. "So this is another 'something.' When you're ready to fledge, you should be able to walk into any of a half-dozen places with at least an apprentice's level of skill."

"I'm going to college."

"Including college. That's why we teach you *how* to learn, by—"

"By 'observation, research, calculation, and experiment.' I know. But I thought you were a space pilot, not a printer."

Jacinta paused while she rinsed the protective lotion from her hands and forearms. For a moment, she saw the cockpit of Ned DuBois's jump jet the time she and Yungduk had snuck aboard, gotten shanghaied, and The Man Who had let them take a turn at the controls; and she felt again that same bottomless feeling she had experienced as the plane peaked and dived. Then she shook her hands and dried them on a towel. "I thought so, too."

Okay, if she couldn't *go* out there, she could at least look. The Star Gazers club she had organized focused on practical urban astronomy: how to tell time and direction from the stars, but it was really just an excuse for her to look at the sky, the way she used to do on the quad at Glenn Academy. They were waiting for her on the roof—six sisters ranging in age from seven to thirty sitting on the sundry lawn furniture that had been placed there. Jacinta gasped an apology for being late, but nobody seemed to mind. It was a lazy August evening and with sunset a cool breeze had come in from the ocean, seasoning the odor of asphalt roofing with salt. So what better place to hang than up on the roof?

A few of the brightest stars pierced the city-lit haze overhead. Remembering how boundless the sky had been near Mojave and how fiercely the stars had burned in the desert night, Jacinta thought this display pale and featureless in comparison. Yet, you played the hand you were dealt. "Does everyone remember why the stars move across the sky?" she asked. "Ginger?"

The youngest girl put a finger in her mouth and nodded solemnly. "It's because we're all moving *that* way"—she pointed east—"so the stars move *that* way"—pointing west—"but I don't *feel* like I'm moving."

The girl had said the same the previous night. That was why learning required repetition. "It's like riding in a car," Jacinta explained. "You feel it when the car bounces or turns or goes faster or slower—when something changes. But the Earth keeps turning with the same speed in the same direction. Did you remember to mark where the sun set on our 'Stonehenge Board'? Good. That will help us know when the seasons are about to change. Now everyone find the Pole Star for me . . ."

She told them how they could use the Little Dipper like the hour hand on a clock. By then, the orange glow had faded from the western sky and Jupiter blazed with ruthless clarity twenty-five degrees above the ocean. Sister Tina had brought a pair of high-powered binoculars she owned and they passed them around the group. Jacinta thought she could just make out the four big moons, but wasn't sure the others would be able to, so she didn't mention them. A telescope would have been nice to have, but there was no money these days for nice-to-have.

After the meeting was over and Sister Tina had taken Lilly and Ginger below for bedtime stories, Jacinta remained on the roof, lying on one of the chaise lounges. She imagined it was the pilot's acceleration couch and gravity was the launch force of an SSTO she was taking to LEO. But it was a pale pretense and she soon gave it up. Such imaginations were for a young girl looking forward, not for a disillusioned one looking back. The difference between anticipation and might-have-been.

"What was the Academy like?"

Jacinta started at the voice and, turning, saw Sister Visitacion in one of the lawn chairs. "Tassy" was fifteen; she could still have dreams. Jacinta looked back at the sky. "It was rough," she said. "They break your body and burn your brain. I almost washed out." I almost *died,* she remembered. Drowned in the Neutral Buoyancy Tank. Well, that was one way to wash out. "A lot of cadets didn't make the cut." Ludwig Schimmelpfennig, the one they all called "Lou Penny," had developed asthma. He had been a class-A pain-in-the-butt, but he had shared the same dream and you hated to see that happen. And Ursula Kittmann, who had lost an arm in a plane wreck even before First Muster and who had come back with a strange, new prosthesis to make the try anyway. A bitter, angry, cynical girl, yet Jacinta's comrade, regardless.

"That's not what I meant," Tassy said. "I meant . . . Well . . . There were boys there, right?"

Jacinta tried not to smile. At fifteen, not all dreams involved flying. "More boys than girls."

"Did any of them ever try to . . . You know. Touch you?" The inflection in her voice made it clear what sort of "touch" she meant.

The question had been seriously asked and so deserved a serious answer. "No," Jacinta said after a moment's reflection. "I'm sure some of them wanted to—I guess I wasn't the least attractive girl there—and there were some boys you had to be careful not to give them the wrong signals. Their wishful thinking could read friendliness as permission. But I let them know where I stood, and it's true: If you respect yourself, others will, too."

"Did you meet anyone special?"

"They were all special."

"You know what I mean . . ."

"Oh, all right. Yes."

Tassy's voice dropped a notch. "Did you kiss him?"

"Just once."

Jacinta heard the younger girl's intake of breath. Scandalized at the kiss? Or envious? "Out of gratitude. He saved my life in a training accident. And I did like him well enough. He used his head for something more than a hat rack."

"Did you *love* him? How can you tell the difference between gratitude and liking and love?"

Same questions Jacinta herself still struggled with. How did anyone tell the one from the other? There were no rules, no Precepts. "You'll know it when it happens."

"You all say that," the younger said with frustration. "Does everyone have to work it out for herself? How do you avoid mistakes?"

"Maybe the mistakes are how we work it out." Jacinta had made a mistake once, with Soren Thorvaldsson, one of the cadets she had met at the airport. She didn't reached out when she had the chance, and then Soren was dead. There had been no bond between them. Nothing had been broken, nothing had been lost; and that had been the greatest loss of all.

"How do you know it's love when you see it?" Tassy asked her.

"I don't know," Jacinta admitted. "I've never been close enough to see it clearly."

The younger girl shook her head. "There ought to be a way to tell. Some sign, you know?"

After Visitacion left, Jacinta resumed her contemplation of the mocking heavens. She tried to imagine learning to fly by "working it out for herself" and could imagine nothing but disaster. Was that why nearly one marriage in three ended in divorce? Of course, no one ever said you could learn only by your *own* mistakes. Others made mistakes in plenty, and you could learn from their accumulated errors, too. Still, at that age, no one ever did.

Jacinta eventually drifted into a confused dream, in which flying and floating and Yungduk Morrisey figured in a chaotic blend. When she started awake, Cancer was rising in the east, which meant sunrise was just behind. In the calm, pale light of the false dawn she tried to recapture the feelings of her dream, but they ran like water through her fingers.

Jacinta was installing a new electrical outlet in the Refuge's laundry room when she was beeped. "Answer," she told her wrist strap, activating its pea brain. "This is Sister Jacinta. May I do you a service?" Using a needle-nosed pliers, she twisted the hot leads together and then screwed a plastic cap onto the exposed ends.

"Could you come up to the reception area, dear?" It was Mother Linda.

"I'm in the middle of that new four-forty for the dryers." Jacinta did not make it a refusal, only a bit of information. Did Linda want to see Jacinta, or did she want to see Jacinta *now*?

"Sister Natalie is on her way down. She'll finish up."

In other words, now. Jacinta rocked back on her heels and scowled at the tracey on her wrist. "What is it?"

"You have a visitor."

Jacinta pushed herself to her feet and hitched her tool belt up. A visitor? Who on earth would be visiting her here? Her mother? But Mama had never approved of the "cult," and it was a long way to New Jersey, in any case. Total was with AFSO, posted to the Emergency Response Team at the Cape; and Lonzo was serving as midshipman on board *Chuck Yeager,* if the government's experimental nuke ships were still flying. Yungduk was back with his parents at Pope AFB in North Carolina. Ursula was down in Texas somewhere. And she didn't really know anyone else well enough to expect a casual visit.

Mr. Calhoun? The superintendent lived in Tehachapi, near the Academy, so a visit to Los Angeles would not be out of the question. Her heart hit an air pocket. Could the Academy be reopening? Oh, please, let it be! Before her hard-won skills grew rusty with disuse.

When Sister Natalie arrived, Jacinta turned the electrical job over to her and scampered up the stairs, her tools clattering against her hips. She did not quite run down the central hall to the reception area. Sister Darlene, manning the reception desk, looked up at Jacinta's precipitous arrival. Mother Linda, who was sitting in one of the visitor chairs, turned, too.

Jacinta staggered to a halt.

In the other visitor chair sat Yungduk Morrisey.

Jacinta pointed a finger at him. "But . . . you're in North Carolina." Then she heard how silly she sounded and added, "What are you doing here?" Which sounded just as silly.

"I came to see how you were doing," he said solemnly. He was dressed casually in white canvas trousers and a tan, buttoned shirt and soft shoes. She almost hadn't recognized him without his Academy coveralls. "I thought, maybe, I could take you out to dinner," he added, "maybe, go take in a morphie?"

Jacinta turned to Mother Linda, who said before Jacinta could even ask, "You're fledged, but you *are* staying in the Refuge and we must set an example for the younger ones."

Jacinta nodded. The implication was clear. "Sister Darlene, then." The sister at the reception desk raised an eyebrow, but made no comment. She spoke briefly on the phone, then gathered her things. Jacinta turned to face Yungduk. "I'm ready."

Yungduk smiled. "Are tool belts the hot new fashion, this year?"

Jacinta suddenly remembered how she was dressed. She gasped. "I've got to change." She turned away; turned back. "Wait for me." She had already dashed for the elevator when she realized how air she had sounded. Wait for her? Duh. He hadn't come all the way from North Carolina just to walk off because of a few minutes' delay . . .

The building's elevator was a decrepit affair; it took forever to reach the dorm floor. She caught a glimpse of a smile in the polished aluminum doors. Had she been grinning that way the whole time? In front of Mother Linda? Why should Yungduk's unexpected appearance affect her this way?

In her room, she chucked her tool belt and maintenance coveralls and washed her face and hands; pawed through her closet. Where was her number one blouse? In the laundry . . . ? She'd have to wear number two. Her good slacks needed pressing, but there was no help for that. There was no number two. She fell on her back on her bed as she tugged them up both legs at once. Her hair was growing out from her "otter cut" and had neither the grace of longer locks nor the edge of the close-crop. She ran a hasty brush through it, but it still looked awful.

How could Yungduk show up like this, with no warning! She should have told him to come back later. Tomorrow maybe.

But he was here now. He might only be in town for one day. (And he had nothing better to do than drop by and see her?) Her hair wouldn't look any better tomorrow, anyway. Jacinta draped her Maiden's Shawl around her shoulders and took the stairs down.

Before she reached the lobby she slowed her stride to a more dignified gait. By then she had gotten some of her equilibrium back, too. Why was she in such a flubber? She didn't live her life around Mister Yungduk Morrisey, thank you very much. If he didn't like her clothes or her haircut, that was too bad. There was a Carson poem that started, "Take me as you find me/Or don't take me at all . . ." Besides, who did he think he was, expecting her to drop everything and go out with him just like that? Maybe she had important work to do tonight.

Yeah. Like installing that four-forty line . . .

Jacinta logged out at the desk and linked her wrist strap to the Refuge's "angel board." Sister Tassy, who had taken over the desk from Darlene, told her the signal was clear and had her check the panic button, too. When everything was ready, Jacinta turned and faced her . . . date? "Let's go, then," she said.

When Sister Darlene followed them out the door. Yungduk said nothing, but Jacinta caught his crooked smile, so Mother Linda must have told him about chaperonage. "Just pretend Darlene isn't there," she told him sotto voce.

"She's kinda hard to miss," he whispered back.

His car, a tattered, brown '12 Hidalgo, was parked by the curb in front of the Refuge. Yungduk opened the passenger door and Jacinta slid in. Darlene squeezed into one of the backseats. "What was that all about?" she asked while Yungduk circled around to the driver's side.

"Nothing. The Duck's okay, for a boy."

He drove them to a mid-scale Korean restaurant on Sepulveda called José Yee's. When the waiter came to their table with three menus, Yungduk said carefully, *"Je il ma sit nun yum sik ju se yo,"* and the waiter beamed and warbled something back.

"I got us the special," he said when the waiter had gone.

"Must be good," Jacinta said. "I heard you say 'yum.' "

"I heard him say 'sick,' " Darlene said. "What is the special?"

Yungduk shrugged. "Not a clue. I don't speak Korean. Mom coached me on what to say. She said that's how you get the authentic cuisine."

Whatever it was, the special managed to be both sweet and spicy. Jacinta noticed that Darlene was the only one of them who tried the chopsticks. Jacinta and Yungduk both used forks.

"Dad's unit was transferred to Edwards," Yungduk told them. "Tasked to FarTrip II. We moved into a shotgun shack up by Rosamond just last week. What with the Academy closed and all, I was just hanging, so I thought I'd cruise by and see how you were." The way he said it, it sounded like a casual, spur-of-the-moment thing. No big deal.

Darlene made choking sounds and hunched over her kimchee. " 'Cruise by,' " Jacinta said. "Just like that." It was a drive of several hours from the high desert down to Torrance.

Yungduk shrugged. "It was either drop in on you or watch the cactus grow. I figured you'd be more interesting and I wouldn't get jabbed by so many needles."

Why couldn't he just say, *I came down to see you and take you out.* "Guess again," Jacinta said. "I can be pretty prickly."

"I know that. Don't I know that."

"I'm doing fine."

"What?" Yungduk shook his head.

"You cruised by to see how I was doing. I'm doing fine."

"Oh. Yeah. Me, too."

Darlene rose, dabbed at her lips. "Excuse me," she said, fleeing the table.

"What's with her?" Yungduk asked.

Jacinta watched Darlene duck into the rest rooms. If she didn't know any better, she would have said the older woman was laughing. "Kimchee's getting to her," she suggested.

"Why do you have to have a chaperone, anyway? Aren't you legally an adult?"

"It's not that. I'm fledged. I was on my own at the Academy for over a year. But we want to set an example for the younger girls, like Tassy. They're budding, and might weaken."

"Can't have that." He grinned.

Jacinta stiffened. "It won't be the smooth-talking boy who gets stuck with the baby," she told him. "Until girls like Tassy learn to use their heads along with their hearts, it's up to us who are farther along the road to look out for them."

Yungduk's smile died. "Sorry," he said. "I shouldn't have made a joke of it."

"Forget it. What's your father doing for FarTrip? I heard the project was back-burnered."

"Everyone's budget got raided," Yungduk answered gravely. "NASA. Air Force. The Academy. President needed the money to prop up Social Security. That doesn't mean the secretaries and directors have their priorities mixed up, too. The Joint Chiefs had some discretionary funds. NASA canceled a couple of pure science missions and shifted the money to FarTrip. The research scientists howled, but that was just reflex. What's more important than getting whacked by an asteroid?"

"Getting your Social Security check?" Jacinta suggested.

Yungduk made a face. "I guess we'd feel different if it was our rent not getting paid, but still . . ."

"Boomers," Jacinta said, as if that said it all.

"Probably a lot of them flat out don't believe there is an asteroid coming. Have you listened to that McRobb character? It's all a government hoax."

Jacinta ran her fork around her plate, stirring the food, but not eating. "Has your dad heard anything about an intercept mission?" The asteroid would make a close approach in the summer of '21. It was impossible to imagine that the world would let the opportunity slip by.

Yungduk nodded. "That's what his unit is supposed to do. They're reviewing the maintenance records for all the ships capable of the voyage. He's not supposed to say anything—top secret is sort of a reflex where the Air Force comes in—but from some things he's said, I figure there will be three ships . . ."

"Three!"

"Maybe four. And the go date is January of '21."

Jacinta slumped back in her chair. It was already August of '17 and she had two more years before she'd be pinned. They'd never send an unpinned cadet! She had to get zig time; she had to earn at least a copilot's berth! But if the Academy stayed closed, her skills would grow rusty. She might have to repeat months of practice—in the simulator and the buoyancy tank. She had kept her books, so her skull skills could stay fresh; but it wasn't just your head they lifted aloft. "Have you been over to the Academy?" she asked.

Yungduk grimaced. "Yeah. Dropped in on Mr. Calhoun. Just a few cadre there—and the third-year students who were too far along to furlough."

"Adrienne Coster?"

"Yeah, she was one of them. In fact, she's cadet colonel now. Say, wasn't she a sister, too?"

"A star of the sea. They're not connected with the silver apples. I think they started in a religious convent. The apples started as a safe house for battered women. Then Mother Smythe started taking in girls who weren't battered but were under a lot of pressure from boys to jolly with them. They wanted to say no, but they were afraid of being considered sidestreet instead of mainstreet."

"There ought to be a name for that," Yungduk said. "Un-cool-a-phobia."

"It's not a joke."

"I didn't mean for it to be. One of the things I like most about you is that you respect yourself."

Jacinta had just begun to parse that sentence when Sister Darlene rejoined them. "I miss anything?" she asked with a slight smile.

"Nothing important," Yungduk said.

Nothing important? Did Morrisey like her or not? Or was he afraid of making unwanted advances and getting rebuffed? What was the phobia for being shot down? It was important to keep a distance between them, lest she send his hormones the wrong signals; but there could be such a thing as too much reserve. She didn't want him to get too close until she knew him better; but how could she get to know him better unless he got closer? It was a paradox.

"We were talking about the FarTrip expedition," Jacinta said. To Yungduk: "Do you think they'll use the *Ares*?"

"Doubt it. Technology and layout is too new. No one's trained on it. Black Horses are too small, and LTVs are too specialized. No, they'll use Planks, just like Calhoun did back for FarTrip I. Too much riding on the mission to rely on anything but proven technology."

Of course, Calhoun's *Bullard* almost hadn't made it back; but neither of them laid that particular thought on the table.

Darlene turned to Yungduk. "So, how have you been keeping yourself busy?"

"Dad got me a job on the base. It doesn't pay anything. It's an internship, but I have clearance to use the simulator, so I—"

Jacinta gasped. "They let you use the flight simulator at Edwards?"

"Not the big one. Need a crew—and a project authorization—to operate *that* sucker. It's just a desktop software simulator."

Just a software simulator? Jacinta dropped her fork to her plate. The food had grown cold. "I'm not feeling well." She began to rise from the table and Darlene, startled, followed her lead.

Yungduk looked back and forth between Jacinta and Darlene, clearly bewildered. "Are you all right?"

"The food," she said. "It's a little too spicy."

Yungduk studied the food, then Jacinta's expression. "You want to skip the morphie? It's that new comedy with W. C. Fields and John Candy . . . ?"

"Just take me home."

"But . . ."

Darlene spoke. "You heard her."

Yungduk's face went still. "All right." He dropped his napkin on his plate and called the waiter. Jacinta fled to the street outside. It was early yet. Sepulveda buzzed with traffic, a continuous stream of people who had someplace to go. Jacinta clenched her fists as tight as she could, then crossed her arms over her chest and straightened her hands into spear points. The ritual was supposed to call up her inner strength, but the mind had to be in it, and just now her mind was not focusing. Darlene stepped up behind her and straightened Jacinta's shawl.

"What's wrong?" she asked.

Jacinta brushed at her cheeks. "Nothing."

"That's a lot of upset over nothing."

"I'm not going to make it."

Darlene frowned. "What do you mean, 'make it'?"

"Into space. It's something I've always wanted. But now the Academy's as good as closed and the recession just keeps getting deeper and they keep cutting back the number of flights and the Academy operates on the lift taxes that Space Traffic Control levies and . . ."

Darlene wrapped an arm around her shoulder. "And?"

Jacinta leaned against the older sister, feeling the warmth and comfort of her body. A pedestrian paused as he walked past and gave them a glance half disapproval, half leer; but Sister Darlene sent him scuttling off. "And Yungduk gets to use the simulator and he's just a short drive from the Academy and what do you want to bet he slips over now and then and mingles with the third-year cadets on his own dime? I'll bet 'Uncle John' even lets him into the Neutral Buoyancy Tank." She accepted the handkerchief Darlene handed her and dabbed at her eyes. *"He's staying in practice!"*

"Maybe he is," Darlene allowed, "but is his good fortune something bad for you?"

Jacinta clenched her fists again, but made no effort to cross them. "He didn't have to come all the way down here to rub it in."

Yungduk sensed something wrong when he emerged from the restaurant a moment later. Silently, he led them to the parking lot and drove them back to the Refuge. It was not a very long drive, but it seemed to take forever. Jacinta drifted inside herself, or else it was the world that drifted away.

So this is what it feels like when dreams die; when the road you are traveling is suddenly blocked by a mud slide and you have to change course for some new destination. If it had been her own fault, she might have borne it better. If she had failed to measure up, her heart would have learned to let go of the dream long before it faded from reach. Instead, it had been snatched from her with her arms still eagerly outstretched.

The car halted in front of the Refuge. For a moment, all three of them sat still. Then Jacinta turned and tugged the door handle. Yungduk laid a hand on her arm and Jacinta swatted it away. *"Don't you* ever *touch me without my permission!"*

Yungduk blanched, then his face darkened with anger. "Here," he said, reaching into his pocket. "I was going to give this to you later; but I guess there won't be a later." He held out a small package, gaily wrapped, with a white ribbon inexpertly tied around it. A bracelet, Jacinta thought from the size.

"I don't need your presents!" She knocked it aside and it dropped to the floor of the car. Yungduk bent over to retrieve it and in that moment Jacinta was out of the car. Darlene caught up to her at the top of the steps leading to the Refuge and steadied her with both arms.

"Jacinta!"

Yungduk's car peeled away from the curb and Jacinta watched it until it reached the corner and turned out of sight. Then, she broke down and cried onto Darlene's shoulder. "I'll never see him again."

"The way you were just acting, I wouldn't think that would bother you."

"I was depressed. I took it out on him. I shouldn't have done it."

"He'll be back, or he'll call you."

Jacinta lifted her head and sniffed. "How do you know. You only just met him."

"You told me yourself. The Academy's closed except for the third-year cadets, but he found a way to keep in practice. That means he doesn't give up easy."

Jacinta shook her head. "This is different. Flying in space is something he wants more than anything else in the world. I'm just . . . well, a pretty girl he met one year at school."

She opened the door to the Refuge and Darlene stepped inside. Before Jacinta followed, she looked up the long block, as if expecting an old, brown Hidalgo to come back around the corner, but it never did.

The package from Yungduk arrived two days later. A courier delivered it at ten o'clock but Jacinta let the express pouch sit on the dresser in her bedroom the rest of the day before she opened it. She was half afraid it would contain an apology that they both knew was not his to give and half afraid that it would not, because the only alternative to *I'm sorry* was *Hasta la vista, baby.*

In the end, not opening the pouch proved worse than the alternative and she ripped the drawstring with a sudden, savage tug. Expecting either abjection or defiance, she was not prepared for the contents: the same small present he had tried to give her in the car, its wrapping and ribbon all the worse for the extra days' wear and tear.

Jacinta sat slowly on the edge of her bed. She considered for a moment returning the gift unopened, but thought better of it. There was no point in being rude, and she was curious as to what sort of jewelry Yungduk thought she would wear.

She tore the wrappings off and found a flat, opaque plastic case about three by three. Taped to it was a handwritten note: *Let's go swimming sometime soon.* And an icon that took her a few moments to recognize as a stylized image of a duck.

She felt vaguely disappointed. Somehow she had expected more of Morrisey than the usual "I give you presents; you show me skin" trade-off. Of course, Jacinta's swimsuit revealed far less skin than he undoubtedly hoped to see.

She wondered what he would be like. He was lean and strong, she knew. He had taken her in his arms one time, when she had been drowning in the Neutral Buoyancy Tank, and carried her to the top, where Total Meredith had breathed life into her. But that embrace didn't count. She could not remember the feel of his arms around her. Later, as a reward, she had allowed him to kiss her; and that counted very little more, since she had stood there wooden as a board with her tongue firmly barricaded behind clenched teeth. She had kissed Total to greater effect.

She had gone to his room intending to offer him far more than a kiss.

It was a sudden, intrusive thought, one that she had thought safely forgotten. She had come so close to betraying all that her sisters had taught her. Brushing death often had that libidinous effect, she had learned afterward, but that was no excuse. She had offered herself shamelessly, but Yungduk had turned her down—when he could have satisfied his own longings so easily and pleaded permission after.

How do you know it's love when you see it? young Tassy had asked her.

I don't know. I've never been close enough to see it clearly.

How much closer did she need to get to see what was with her in Yungduk's room that night?

She looked up into the mirror above her dresser and was surprised at how hollow she appeared. Her eyes were dark-circled and seemed to have sunk deeper into her head, as if her insides had been all vacuumed out and her features were slowly sinking into the emptiness within. Well, she had been pithed, all right; first of family, then of dreams, last of all of love.

She opened the case at last. Perhaps she could regard the bracelet as a peace offering. After all, Yungduk had not intended to hurt her by rubbing her nose in his own good fortune, and it was small of her to hold that fortune against him.

It wasn't a bracelet.

It was a micro-CD. "Moo-seedy," people said. Jacinta frowned over it. An ordinary, commercial Write-Once/Read-Many disc that you could buy in any strip mall or cyberstore in the country. There was no label on the WORM, only a tag that read "Six Teras."

The Refuge had two salamander computers that rated six teraflops: one in the main office and the backup in the resource center. Jacinta took the seedy worm to the resource center and logged on. It was dinnertime and most of the sisters were in the refectory, but Jacinta had lost her appetite anyway. Darlene was reading a bound hardcopy novel in one of the tall, soft chairs in the alcove. Tassy sat at one of the tables with a workbook open and the screen showing some web page or other. "Big test coming up?" Jacinta asked, trying to sound cheerful.

"Project due," Tassy answered distractedly.

Jacinta sat before the salamander's wide-screen Gyricon and placed the seedy in the tray. The drive booted and the screen flashed a deep cerulean blue, then cleared to a gateway screen.

<OPERATIONAL SIMULATION OF SSTO VESSELS, MARK VII-C PLANKS>
<©2015, DAEDALUS AEROSPACE, S.A.>
<FORTALEZA DA NOVA BRAGANÇA, REP. FED. do BRASIL>

She stared at the announcement for perhaps a minute before the reality of it hit her.

<PLEASE SELECT INTERFACE:>
<TOUCH SCREEN ( ) MOCK-UP PANEL Model F2846/R2( )>

She toggled TOUCH SCREEN and hit RETURN and the screen dissolved to a replica of the pilot's control panel for an orbital Plank. A popper window listed scenario starting points. The default was <**Begin preflight checklist.**>

Jacinta whooped out loud, which earned her a startled look from the other girls in the resource center. *Let's go swimming?* Sure. Where else but in the Academy's Neutral Buoyancy Tank?

Sometimes you really did get a sign, clear and unambiguous.

"He loves me!" she told the library—indeed, the whole world, had the world been of a mind to listen. Let other swains bestow flowers or jewels. The perceptive suitor knows what his beloved treasures over all else. "He loves me," she said, this time more in a whisper, feeling the sound of the words in her heart.

3.

Fortunes

Spring came, cool and pleasant, and the mountainside burst into riotous colors as pinxter and violet and foamflower opened themselves to a new year. Two magtrains a day passed through the valley now. Flowers of another sort, perhaps; foretelling another sort of spring.

Ridgeview House snuggled atop Musconetcong Mountain at the far end of a dirt road that wound through thick stands of birch and maple and blossoming springtime flowers. From the crest, broad vistas rolled away to either side. Undulating dales, checkerboarded by soil newly turned, broken here and there by copses and windbreaks and by the flanks of other ridges. Northward, past Pohatcong Mountain and Ragged Ridge and Jenny Jump, the pale, blue, spruce-hazy line of Kittatinny Mountain marked the horizon.

Her guests had complimented her on the view, but Mariesa barely noticed scenery anymore. There were worlds to be saved. She felt filled with a vigor that she hadn't felt in years. A sense of purpose. And of guilt.

"We have a golden opportunity," she told the dinner guests gathered around her long, dark dining table. There was money seated at that table; perhaps more money than had ever dined so intimately together. They had come from courtesy and from curiosity or simply to enjoy the food; but they had come. You couldn't hook a fish that failed to nibble.

"An opportunity to go bankrupt," Louis Dreyfuss responded. He spoke with a languid French drawl. Nathan Rothschild, directly across from him, said nothing but indicated by his posture his agreement with his colleague. The others made no sign. Ed Wilson, at the foot of the table, smiled slightly and bent over his dinner. Silver clattered on china in the silence. Armando stood gravely impassive by the kitchen door, his white-gloved hands clasped before him, waiting for a request or an instruction.

"Opportunity means risk," Mariesa conceded, raising a water goblet to her lips. "With the deflation and bankruptcies," she said, "a great many assets are lying about at bargain prices."

"Because they are not worth buying, *hein?*" suggested Dreyfuss.

"C'mon, Louis," Wilson said. "Has the physical plant suddenly lost its capability? Have the workers forgotten their skills?"

"The most skilled of workers with the best of tools cannot sell a product that no one will buy," the Frenchman countered.

"Ed does have a point," Mariesa said. "The real value is still there—equipment and know-how; capital and labor—but the stuffing has been knocked out of them by people like us. When investment capital goes into hiding due to some mob panic . . ."

Estéban Ortega squinted, Heinrich Schlossmann puffed his cheeks, and Rothschild said, "Now, see here—" in precise British public-school tones. Mariesa hadn't meant to put it quite that way; but she could not now unsay the words. ". . . orders get canceled," she concluded, "production is cut back, skills grow rusty."

Nicholson looked up, all bland. "Is VHI in hard straits, then?" His tongue touched his lips—in anticipation, or just licking the gravy? Mariesa clenched her knife like a weapon and sliced her venison with a single stroke.

"Chris and Adam handle all that, now."

"And take no advice from you." That was Schlossmann, again; all smiles and with a hint of suggestion. Good Lord, were these men really so blind as all that? Did they think she had invited them here to underwrite a *coup* to regain control of VHI? And Nicholson, so much more practiced at dismantling enterprises than erecting them, angling for advantage while the world counted its days. Fools, and worse. The words pressed at her lips, eager to be spat out. Yet, she had invited these people to coax their money from them. They wanted stroking, not scolding.

"Well," she said airily, "sometimes we talk, Chris and I. We have a few purchases in mind."

"A bit risky, that," observed Rothschild. "Considering the times."

Mariesa shook her head. "Not really, Nathan. The best time to buy is at the bottom. We believe the economy has begun to turn."

"Had the gold standard been restored . . ." Schlossmann began with a wag of his finger.

It was Dreyfuss who raised a hand. "No, Heinrich. It is one thing to maintain a fixed rate of conversion against a common store of value; but can you imagine if people were turning in their currencies and securities for gold? *Mon Dieu!* It would be 1895 all over again."

"I think, Louis," said Rothschild, dabbing his lips with a napkin, "that that is what our hostess has in mind." He beckoned to Armando and the butler, ever attentive, refilled the man's wineglass.

Mariesa gave the Englishman a long look. Someone, it seemed, had done his homework. And the Rothschilds had been involved in the 1895 bailout, too. She wondered if she had found an ally. "We need to restore the faith," she said. "We need to be seen investing in the future, not hiding our money under the mattress. We could begin by backing the securities needed to fund the Planetary Defense Committee—"

Schlossmann sawed at his venison. "Ah, yes. The asteroid." Flesh, richly herbed with sage and rosemary, entered his mouth. Jaws worked and bulged. He said nothing more, but his eyes darted to Mariesa. "Almost six years hence," he said after swallowing. "If at all."

"You don't believe the astronomers?" Wilson asked with his head cocked.

"Pfaugh!" The German waved a fork, attacked the potatoes. "They have been wrong before. In a few months, we have, what, perhaps an announcement that, no, this thing too will miss by many thousands of kilometers."

Rothschild spoke dryly. "Even if it is true, Mariesa, there's not much the likes of us can do about it, is there? We can't *bribe* the bloody thing to turn aside." A wave of chuckles lapped the dining table. Mariesa locked gazes with the British banker, saw his sardonic smile, remembered the rumors. A war averted through bribery; a loan conditioned on ending a pogrom. The House of Rothschild went for the main chance, but was not immune to sporadic outbursts of altruism.

"This recession must end," she told them bluntly, "if we're to have any hope of mounting a serious defense in time. Ships and life support for rendezvous missions, deep space missiles for intercept, battle lasers, civil defense preparations—"

"None of which would be necessary," Nicholson said, "if we hadn't gone poking around out there." A wave of the hand encompassing the universe.

A polite silence followed. Nicholson had said "we," but Mariesa had clearly heard "you," and judging from their suddenly neutral attention to carrots and potatoes, the others had also heard the same veiled pronoun. Unless one believed in hellish coincidence, it had been the close approach of the Visitor Probe that had awakened slumbering alien mechanisms on the Bean and set it on a collision course for Earth—and the probes had been sent out in large measure on Mariesa's urging.

Yet, Nicholson's silent accusation was one she had flogged herself with daily since the new orbit had been confirmed; and like the flagellant, she had grown inured to the whip. Now and then, however, the sting could unexpectedly cut. *Mea culpa*, as the Catholics used to say. *Mea maxima culpa.* "Spilt milk," she said, a bit more harshly than she had intended. She was not about to divulge her remorse to confessors such as these. "We must deal with the world as it is, not as it might have been."

"She's right," Prince al-Walid said matter-of-factly, surprising Mariesa with his unexpected support. He had sat quietly through the entire meal, exchanging only light pleasantries with his dining companions. But the prince, they said, liked the long shot. The risk, for him, could well be an enticement.

Schlossmann asked, "And what income can we expect from such investments, *sayyed*?"

An elaborate Arab shrug. "Incalculable, perhaps."

"Ach. I run that 'incalculable' past my accountants . . ."

Ortega brushed at a mustache with his knuckle. "In classical Greece, great men would fund their cities' defense for no more return than the regard of their fellows . . ."

Dreyfuss laughed. "In which column on the balance sheet do you write that, Estéban?"

". . . not a very large asteroid; so the damage may be minimal . . ."

". . . and hope it doesn't fall on *your* head, eh?"

". . . a neglect of fiduciary duties to risk . . ."

". . . a greater neglect to . . ."

They were all talking now. Mariesa did not try to follow all the threads and turned her attention back to the meal. She beckoned Armando and told him to ready the desserts and aperitifs. Perhaps wisdom would condense out of the cloud of babel now that she had stirred the pot. *Just prime the pump, that's all I ask.* Get the economic engine back up to speed. She crossed her knife and fork over the plate, a signal to Armando to remove it.

Ed Wilson sat with her on the patio afterward and watched the sun set over Pennsylvania, a great, red swath across the heavens. Low cumulus clouds turned golden on their keels. Wilson sat on the edge of a patio chair, hunkered over his knees, and sipped the whiskey sour Mariesa had presented him. His own taste ran to more tropical concoctions, so his free hand moved oddly, at a loss without fruit and umbrellas to play with.

"You didn't really think they'd all rally 'round the defense of the planet, did you?" he said.

Mariesa sighed and closed her eyes. The wooded hillside harbored a chorus of crickets. A hint of sassafras scented the air. "I had hoped," she said. "I still have hopes. Nathan, in particular. They aren't fools."

"No," Ed allowed, "not fools. But, Mariesa, you're asking them to be the financial equivalent of the first wave to hit Omaha Beach. It's got to be done, and someone's got to do it; but I can understand it when they don't form a line to volunteer."

She regarded him coolly. "Which landing boat do you plan to be in, Ed?"

He grinned. "I'll do what I can. I've got money, but I'm also a techie. I *know* what the world is facing. Down *here*—" He struck himself in the gut. "And, yeah, I wouldn't like going bankrupt any better than they would—but I'd like it even less if the world got whacked and I could've done something to stop it. What about you, Mariesa? Are you willing to lay Van Huyten Industries and your trust fund on the chopping block?"

"Chris runs VHI these days. And the Trust is not mine to—"

Wilson rose from the patio chair and loomed over her. "Fish or cut bait, Mariesa. Are you going to *send* us into battle, or are you going to *lead* us there?"

Mariesa stood, too, facing him. They were close enough that she could feel the heat of his body, see her own reflection in the intensity of his eyes. At one time, the thought of an oncoming asteroid had filled her with paralyzing dread; but now it filled her with numbing guilt. "Lead," she said. No modifiers; no exclusions.

Wilson switched his drink glass to his left hand, wiped the right on his trousers, and held it out. "Whatever it takes?"

She met his grip with the same firmness he gave. Hard. Solid. A pledge. "Lives," she said, "and fortunes, and honor."

The rust-colored Ossa & Pelion Building occupied a small campus set back from Van Dyke Avenue north of Sterling Heights. Hamilton Pye, president of Ossa & Pelion Heavy Construction, met Mariesa in the lobby, asked how things were, and kept his questions to himself until they were alone in his office, where he cleared drawings and reports from the meeting table and sat Mariesa down with a cup of decent coffee. The walls were decorated with renderings of O&P projects. Leo Station and Goddard City; the Allentown–New York maglev line; the Triton-3 fish farm off the Louisiana coast; and others—buildings, dams, or highways—that were more mundane and anonymous.

Pye himself was a short, solidly built man with a bald, bullet-shaped head. Muscular, with hands that bore old scars; a square face that showed expression only to order, and then only fleetingly; grizzled black hair that curled on the backs of the hands and forearms. In all, he looked remarkably like something his company might have erected: built to specs and measured with plumb and square. Mariesa had never known him well, except as a man who, once given a job, would see it through.

"What are you up to these days, Ham?" she asked by way of opening.

Pye shrugged. "Not much. A couple office buildings here and there where the client figures he's sunk too much in to pull out now. The MidAmerica Maglev is still being built, but only the Chicago–St. Louis leg; and the PATH line conversion budget got zeroed out completely."

"Nothing on orbit." It was not a question.

Pye made a face. "Government's seen to that. They couldn't just clean up the mess Bullock made and keep going. No, they have to shut everything down. You know what the funny thing is?" He didn't wait for an answer. "The excuse they used was that maybe Bullock's people hadn't been doing the required maintenance. Well, the maintenance sure as shit isn't getting done now, you should pardon my French. Ahhhh . . ." A swatting of the hand and a grunt of dismissal. He swallowed some coffee. "You didn't come out here to hear me gripe." He set his cup down and sat with the angle of his head inviting the question.

Mariesa said, "How much of O&P's orbital capabilities are still available? I realize you cannot expect experienced craftsmen to hang around when there is no work for them; but unused skills grow rusty."

Ham's eyes narrowed. He rubbed his chin with his hand. "Who's asking, you or Chris?"

She hesitated only a moment. "Me."

"And you're just curious, right?"

Mariesa reached into her purse and pulled out a ring, which she handed to him. It was a heavy gold ring—a man's ring—solid, with its face embossed in an outstretched hand whose fingers curled around a small ruby. Pye grunted as he studied it. "Haven't seen one of these in donkey's years," he said. He held it to the light and the ruby gleamed. "Project Prometheus . . . I remember those days. Your little cabal. Secret plans . . . Black projects . . . Do you know how young I was? I actually had hair. Now look at me." He ran a hand across his bare scalp. His smile was rueful. "I was just a program manager back then. Drake, he was CEO, but you bypassed him and recruited me, instead. That pumped me. I ever tell you that? Didn't make me Drake's best friend when he found out, but I figured you'd take care of me. Now, every time I look up at night and I see Leo or Goddard, I tell myself"—his eyes drifted to the pixures on the wall and his voice dropped to a whisper—" 'Ham, boyo . . . You. Did. That. You made it happen.' Biggest construction job since Cheops piled rocks in the desert." He shook his head and studied the ring again. "You know, I always thought this logo was a hand giving fire to the humans. Now I see it's reaching out to catch an asteroid or a comet."

"You could read it either way," Mariesa said.

He looked at her and his eyes turned shrewd. "But the second reading, that was the way you always saw it. God's 'incoming.' It was a pet fear of yours."

"Now it's real."

"Yeah . . . now it's real." He stared at the way the ruby twinkled in the light.

"I'm calling a meeting of the new Prometheus team for next Thursday, in VHI's boardroom."

He nodded abstractly, his attention still fixed on the ring. "Chris in on this?"

"Are *you*?"

He looked at her and grunted. Then he shoved the ring onto his left hand, twisted it a little to test it, and flexed the fingers. The ruby caught the light through the window and flashed. "Seems to fit," he said.

"Ham . . ." Mariesa needed a moment before she could trust her voice. Then, more businesslike, "Ham, we built up a tremendous bank of assets training people, working out the SOPs for zero-gee work, designing the tooling and fixtures. How much is still available?"

"Available for . . . ?" He didn't let the question linger. "Never mind. I can add two and two. I'll tell you the same thing I told that Solomon Dark guy from the government. We haven't burned any prints or manuals. The people haven't died. And, yeah, maybe the edge is off their ziggy, but they haven't forgotten. Did you know that ever since that Carson gal made her wake-up speech last fall, we've been getting calls from the old hands, volunteering to help out. Not just the leads and supervisors, but your basic otter. They're not even asking full pay, some of them—and I suppose that forty hours on half pay is better than no hours on no pay—so, I would say—yeah—the most important asset of all is still there."

"And what's that?"

"The heart."

Norbert Wainwright van Huyten, treasurer for the Van Huyten Trust, lived alone in a Back Bay town house and spent evenings in his club or at receptions for the symphony or the museum. During the season, he allowed himself one night a week at Fenway when the Sox were in town, and followed them diligently when they were not. A dispassionate man, one of habits more than avocations, yet his home was not at all the musty, conservative environment that his demeanor implied. The paintings were bright and lively, though more to the modern than the post-modern taste; the carpeting: simple area rugs over hardwood; the furniture: vaguely Scandinavian, though Mariesa found the chairs more pleasing to look at than to sit in. She tried not to squirm while Norbert read the proposal her accountants had drawn up.

It was not easy to surprise him.

"You want to what?" Norbert very nearly dropped his bifocals.

"I want to cash out my share of the Trust."

He shook his head. "Why? It's safe enough where it is. We took some losses in the Dip, like everyone else; but they're paper losses. If you cash out now, you'll realize them. In a few months, I'm sure, we'll earn back what was lost and . . ."

"Months are precious," she told him. "They're worth more than the paper."

"If you have a cash flow problem . . ."

"No, Norbert, nothing like that. There are some investments that need to be made; but they're risky, and I can't ask you to commit the entire Trust. That's not my money."

"Mm." Norbert tented his hands and tapped the fingertips against his lips. "Strictly speaking, none of it is 'yours.' If you pull out a proportionate share of the principal, it affects the earnings of all the shares, so we all have a stake in what each other does. In fact, moving your assets into cash would pull the pins out on a lot of financial hand grenades. Share prices would drop like Lucifer. We've always gotten along quite well on the interest. Where did you plan to put the money? Not in a mattress, I hope."

"The Planetary Defense Committee."

He leaned back in his chair, folded his glasses, and placed them in a protective case. "I thought so. Well, orbital technologies were sound investments—and will be again. But now is not the right time to take a flier."

Norbert had his history garbled. When Mariesa and the original Prometheus team had put the original LEO Consortium together, orbital investments had been anything but risk-free. "Time is at a premium," she said. "I'm not looking for returns. I'm looking to defend the planet."

Norbert's smile was restrained. "Which you can't do by pouring your wealth down a rathole. In a few more months, as I've said, the markets will recover on their own, without a need to risk your principal."

"I do not intend to risk my principles, either. Norbert, you've got an analytical mind. Pauline and the others haven't a clue; but you must realize that orbital mechanics are like the tides. There are only certain times when launch windows for rendezvous open up and we can 'catch the tide.' Whatever we do—battle lasers in orbit, long-range deep-space missiles, rendezvous—infrastructure has got to be in place and ready before those dates. We can crash some schedules to make up for a late start, but time is not infinitely compressible."

Norbert nodded solemnly. "I won't belittle the seriousness of the situation. I've made inquiries." He fell silent and tugged at his lip. "What does Chris say?"

Sometimes, Mariesa grew tired of needing Chris's go-ahead. "He's committing VHI assets to the PDC."

"At cost plus five."

Mariesa gave a half smile to acknowledge the point. Norbert might live a circumscribed life, but that did not mean he was uninformed. "As you said, Norbert. If VHI goes under, we can't help defend the planet. And five percent is not exactly an exciting return. It's enough to cover maintenance, waste, and depreciation, and not much more."

"And maybe the money supply needs a jump to get it circulating faster. I know that you've been consulting with the House of Rothschild and the others; but these economic contractions are organic—you can't hurry out of them. Besides, 'the common defense' is not our business."

"We have allies in the government. Rutell wants to issue Planetary Defense Bonds, short-term paper at eight percent. But the recession dragged federal receipts down and forced them into a premature bailout of Social Security, so the government has no more credit to back the bonds. Rutell knows better than to issue unsecured paper—it'd be the greenback fiasco all over again—so he's looking for a consortium to underwrite the issue."

"Like Grover Cleveland did in 1895."

"He hopes to come out of it in better political shape than Cleveland did."

Norbert flipped a hand. "Rutell's in the political ashcan already. He's got nothing to lose, and he just might earn his reputation back. Mariesa, I can't authorize even a partial dissolution of the Trust; but if the right sort of people underwrite these bonds—if they seem secure enough—I'll pledge my shares along with yours and Chris's to help collateralize the issue."

Mariesa said nothing for a moment. She hadn't expected to pry her portion loose from Norbert's clutch; but neither had she expected any such commitment from him. "I'm . . ." She stopped, flustered. She could find no words.

Norbert cackled. That was the only way to describe it. He was so pleased at putting her at a loss; but for the sake of the world's survival, Mariesa tolerated his self-amusement. Norbert held a hand up, palm out. "Oh, you don't have to thank me, Riesey. You always were a crackerjack CEO. You had good instincts. And what if that damned Bean dropped on Fenway Park? Could ruin the Sox pennant hopes."

"Norbert, Impact is five and a half years away."

The ends of his lips curled up. "So are the Red Sox pennant hopes."

The men on the other side of the table tried their best to look stoic as the lawyers conveyed the papers from chair to chair. After all, they were parting with a treasured bit of corporate property. The two women directors did not try, and a certain glee marked their features in unguarded moments. Unloading a turkey, *their* faces said. Take it and welcome to it.

Mariesa ignored both factions, and scrawled her name at the bottom of the contract. Khan Gagrat, VHI's chief financial officer, witnessed and passed the portfolio over to Ira Wappenthiel and the other bankers who had helped leverage the deal. Khan shaved his head and wore hoop earrings and a ferocious mustache. When he smiled, he looked like an Afghan bandit chief contemplating an undefended village. Accounting was his scimitar; and options and derivatives, his jezail rifles. The look he shared with Mariesa said *I hope you and Chris know what you're doing,* but he was too much the freebooter himself not to show a little glee in a takeover. Any takeover.

It was the best sort of deal, Mariesa thought. One where both parties thought they had screwed the other.

One of them was necessarily wrong; but if North American Pressure Vessels had cooked their books, they had a damn-poor chef. Fraud generally tried to pretty things up, not the other way around. No, the owners were starved for cash; so, actually, both sides could win, because each side had different objectives. The sellers got the cash they needed and Mariesa obtained a fabricator of pressure vessels—with all the machine tools, skilled workforce, and design staff. Vessels for fuel pods; vessels for habitats. The only things lacking were orders—that was why the company was on the chopping block—and Solomon Dark was taking care of that end of things.

Provided the PDC bond issue floated.

A lot of balls in the air, and none of them allowed to hit the ground.

Leaving the meeting, she stopped in the small conference room down the hall from NAPV's boardroom, where Marcel Reynaud, VHI's turnaround specialist, was shirtsleeved with his staff in front of a row of temporary terminals. He looked up when Mariesa entered.

She handed him a portfolio with his copy of the papers. "It's done," she said.

Reynaud nodded, took a deep breath. "Very well, people," he told the staffers who had been analyzing the company and preparing the contingency plans. "You have the new organization and budget. We meet with the management tomorrow to review of the status and the vision. Paul, you will finish the physical inventory by Thursday, no? Bond the stockroom. At handoffs like this machine tools sometimes 'walk with Jesus.' And a meeting with the technical staff on . . ." He raised an eyebrow to Mariesa.

"A week from Friday. Solomon promised us a week from Friday."

"Let us hope that he comes through, *hein?*" Reynaud said with Gallic fatalism. "Otherwise, we must liquidate"—he riffled a sheaf of hardcopy with his thumb—"and you have just paid more than the physical plant is worth."

"If the orders don't come in," Mariesa told him, "the financial loss is the least of our worries."

Mariesa watched the markets climb, falter, dip again. Friday came and went. On the Monday after, she peeped Solomon Dark to ask him what had happened.

"It's McRobb," he said. Solomon's pee-phone image was

grainy and flickered from time to time. A fibrop was loose somewhere in the system and no one had traced the fault and fixed it yet. *Broken windows,* Mariesa thought. There was a psychological border where despair set in; where challenge evoked not response, but surrender. Often, it was the little things that triggered it: windows not repaired, paint not refreshed, potholes not filled, petty mischief not pursued. Life grew generally more and more shabby.

"What about McRobb?"

Solomon ran a hand through his hair. Mariesa had never seen him do that before. A dapper man, always perfectly groomed, never garbed in less than the cutting edge of fashion—indeed, often defining that edge himself. It was a crack in his facade; a broken window of another sort. Was that gray flecking his hair, or was that noise from the malfing fibrop? "He's got the bond issue tied up in the House. The Appropriations chair is nominally Democrat, but Lowe is a 'McRobb Democrat.' He just hasn't bothered changing parties. Truscott and his Whip are huffing and puffing, but they can't scare Lowe into releasing the bill if Lowe doesn't want anything from them that he can't get from McRobb."

"Can't Rutell do anything?"

Solomon shook his head. "Lowe won't even return the Man's calls. Mariesa, Blaise can't even get a decent table at a restaurant, these days. None of this mess is his fault; but that doesn't stop people from blaming him."

"No," said Mariesa. *Nor does it stop him from taking credit when the times are good,* she thought. "What is McRobb's problem?"

"To be blunt: you and your friends. He says the whole bond issue is just a cover for handing the Treasury over to Wall Street and the international bankers. The 'New World Order.' To be even blunter: Lord Rothschild and Prince al-Walid should have kept a lower profile."

"Maybe I should fly over in my black helicopter and check

the microchip in McRobb's buttock. It seems to be malfunctioning."

Solomon spread his hands. "What can I tell you, Mariesa. He's as low as they come, and shit flows downhill. But he's also a hell of a speech-maker, and he comes across as absolutely confident. People follow him because they don't like 'if, but, and maybe.' They want their leaders to sound like they know what they're doing."

"Even when they don't."

"Oh, especially when they don't. Keep an eye on the fall elections, Mariesa. The American Party may take the House."

And what a time, Mariesa thought, for the inmates to get jobs in asylum management. "Does he know he's gambling with the planet?"

Solomon paused and considered. "I honestly don't know. I used to know him, years ago, when he was with the Crusades; but now . . . ? He sees a government-industry conspiracy behind every potted plant, but he may only be playing on our sense of urgency in his quest for power."

"Meaning, he'll sell his vote if we dance to his tune."

"He doesn't see it that way."

"Can he be stopped?"

Solomon's tongue darted out and touched his lips. He did not look directly into the optical pickup. "Legally? No."

"Solomon," she said sharply, "whatever you do, don't prove McRobb right about government conspiracies."

The car dropped Mariesa off near Sixteenth and Pennsylvania, in a modest Washington neighborhood out of sight of the alabaster citadels of power. It was a row house: a block long but sliced like a bread loaf into individual units. The front yards were small, and mostly dirt in which patches of tired grass struggled for a foothold. A low wrought-iron fence, out of plumb, bordered the plot. Mariesa told the driver to come back in an hour, and tipped him generously enough to be sure he would.

The gate squeaked when Mariesa opened it. The wooden porch steps groaned. Roberta opened the door before Mariesa could ring the bell, and stood aside to let her enter.

Inside was a small foyer with coat racks and house shoes. Roberta said nothing, but Mariesa shed her own street shoes and selected a pair of guest slippers that did not look too used. Roberta led her past a flight of narrow stairs and through a living room of art posters, plank-and-cinder-block bookcases, and low-slung "ergonomic" furniture that bore a faintly old-fashioned look. Those were working bookshelves, Mariesa noted, full of tattered volumes, some lying atop the disorderly rows, many festooned with bookmarks.

The archway between living room and dining room was wide enough that they were distinct only by courtesy. The dining set, with its stained maple, ornately carved feet, and lyre-backed chairs, was more in tune with the current "coke" style than was the "modern" furniture in the living room. So old it was cutting edge. There was a painting on the wall that Mariesa recognized as an early Janácek original, a memento of the Prague years. Its value probably outweighed the entire remainder of the house, perhaps even the house itself. Mariesa was certain that Roberta knew the painting's value and equally certain that the memory of Karel Janácek meant more. *Ah, the comrades of our youth . . .*

Half the dining table was occupied by an old-model salamander computer, with its cardboard-thin Gyricon screen and a flash-rack of memory. A fibrop modem cable curled snakelike from a port on the farther wall through a litter of hardcopies and old-style floppies. The room was more office than dining room. Roberta, Mariesa guessed, did not throw many dinner parties.

A bassinet of white wicker decorated with red and blue ribbons stood nearby. Mariesa peered inside as she passed and saw the baby sleeping quietly. "He has his father's brow," she said, sitting in one of the chairs beside the computer.

"As long as he has his father's heart," Roberta answered

with a soft glance, utterly private, directed at the child. "I'd thought about naming him Alexander—did I tell you that before?—because his father was Philip and when he grows up he'll conquer the world. But there were some family resonances there I didn't care for. I didn't want him to be 'Junior,' either. He's not Phil; he'll never be Phil, and I didn't want him growing up thinking he had to be. As for 'Robert' . . ." She shuddered. "Robert and Roberta?"

" 'Carson' is a fine name for a young man," Mariesa assured her.

Roberta took a last look at the slumbering five-month-old, and Mariesa wondered (with a flash of sudden regret that she would never live to see it) what the man that lay within the boy might do when another thirty years had seasoned him.

Roberta sat before the computer. "You'll come for his birthday party, won't you? Won't be too busy saving the planet? You're sort of an honorary aunt, after all."

"I wouldn't miss it for the world."

Roberta blinked and cocked her head at her. "Was that pun deliberate?"

Mariesa tried not to smile. "You said you had something to show me."

"Yeah. I scread on the Net how you were coming to Washington to talk with Rutell and them, and I thought . . . You know markets and all. Maybe you can tell me if I'm seeing things." Roberta handed her a cliputer screen slaved to the salamander. "This is a graph of stock market activity," Roberta told her, "for the companies associated with the LEO Consortium. Phil set Isaac Kohl working on this before he—Anyway, here's the activity just before the Dip."

The cursor zeroed out, then jitterbugged across the screen, leaving a jagged trail behind it. Hourly activity, Mariesa guessed. A sedate, yellow line tracked behind it, winding up and down in slow curves. "That yellow line . . . it's the rolling average?" Mariesa asked.

Roberta shook her head. "Something like that. Isaac called

it an 'exponentially weighted moving average,' whatever that means. The little dotted V that projects forward like a pair of jaws . . . that's the one-day-forward predictor. You see how the hourly track stays inside the cusp of the V? Isaac says that means it's a stable process around the trendline." Roberta looked up. "Understand—when it comes to numeracy, I defer to Isaac. He's no people-person, but give him some numbers to run and he's 'Lightspeed' Bikolu in the hundred-meter dash. Watch careful, now. The cursor's approaching Dip Day. I'll slow it down. Tell me what you see."

As Mariesa watched, the hourly activity line jogged suddenly just above the V and stayed there for several hours; then "all hell broke loose for Texas" and sell offers rocketed off the top of the chart, leaving buys in the dust. Mariesa laid the flatscreen down and pondered the pattern. After a moment, Roberta gave an impatient cough. *Well?*

"Investors began selling Consortium stocks," Mariesa said carefully, "the same day Adam announced Bullock's fraud and posted the evidence on the web."

Roberta shook her head and her smile was vaguely triumphant. "Hunh-uh, Rich Lady. That first bump, a couple hours before the big spike? That came *before* your nephew's press conference."

Mariesa leaned back in her chair. "Someone bailed out early. Insider information?"

"Sure, that's why Isaac and me checked it out. *Any* major move in the market, Phil always said: 'Look for evidence that someone jumped the gun.' A lot of buys before a jump, or a lot of sells before a dip. That how we got Shotwell for insider trading two years ago. But Isaac says it took a *lot* of sells to make that hump. Either a lot of somebodies or one honking rich dude. So, I got curious. Isaac is a cholo number cruncher, but he's no virtchuoso; so I hired a troll. You know that cheesehead that testified for Adam? Billie Whistle? Well, she was at Dayton Middle when I was at Dear Old Witherspoon.

I read some terrible poetry in her class when I was a Teenage Wonder—"

"Why didn't you ask Jimmy Poole? Didn't he help you once before?"

"Call it a hunch. Billie trolled the public stock deebies for me and what she found was a cattle call of different deals, mostly on the New York board, but some in São Paolo, the Paris Bourse, and Hong Kong. All electronic sales, all small change, and no two from the same source, though a lot of them were brokered through a low profile Exchange member named D. G. Stockman."

"So, it was 'a lot of somebodies' . . ." Mariesa frowned and nibbled her lip. That didn't feel right. Roberta nodded.

"You see the problem. A whole lot of somebodies, all over the world, all decided to dump the Consortium within an hour of each other? Billie says there couldn't be that many insiders, anyway. Adam, his wife, his lawyer. Maybe his kids. Billie herself. Jimmy Poole. *Maybe* the other Baleens—though she doesn't think they knew Adam was up to anything, let alone a market-crashing announcement. An eavesdropping Net-walker named Captain Cat who started a pirate operation in Malaysia is a 'possible' . . . So is Hobie, who did some sniff-ing around for Adam when he was on LEO. But if *that* many people knew what was about to go down . . . Well, the press conference would have been anticlimactic, don't you think? The rumor mill would have been way ahead of him. So it must have been one person masquerading as many—someone who had a lot of wealth squirreled away anonymously in LEO stocks. Someone who didn't know or didn't care whether that much stock flying south that fast would spook the herd. *Now* do you know why I didn't go to Jimmy for help?"

Mariesa pondered the implications. "Are you trying to say," she managed, "that Jimmy Poole crashed the market? I know there are rumors about his wealth, but . . ."

"Believe them. Billie told me he was Baleen's number two sugar daddy after Adam, and he financed a whole second factory—in orbit!—out of pocket change. Even he doesn't know how much he has. It's all just a game to him. He probably doesn't even *know* what he did, and he's sitting out there in California patting himself on the crotch for being smart enough to duck out the back door before the riot started."

"When, in effect," Mariesa finished the thought, "it was his ducking out that started it."

The silence that followed was broken by an irritated wail. His I'm-hungry-*now* cry, Roberta explained, excusing herself while she rescued Carson from his prison. She greeted and cooed at the baby and received a crooked grin in return. "He can pull himself up, now," Roberta announced, as if such a feat had never been accomplished before. "He'll be walking soon, and I'll be lucky to keep up."

Mariesa followed Roberta into the kitchen, where the baby was enthroned in a high chair and the Bib of Power tied into place. Mariesa lowered herself into a kitchen chair. "It's what happens when your children insist on growing."

Roberta gave her a puzzled glance, as if wondering what Mariesa knew of children growing; but Mariesa said nothing to resolve the puzzle. It was just a fancy of hers, anyway, that Roberta and Jimmy and the others were somehow her children. She watched Roberta spoon out strained squash into a bowl. That was something she had never done. She had never looked into young, trusting eyes and given nourishment. Yet, had William not died before ever being born, Mariesa might have merely hired a nanny and shed the burden for the sake of her more important task of world-saving. Mariesa-then had been younger more impatient, more obsessed. Mariesa-then had still had more years in front than behind.

"May I feed him?" she asked suddenly. Roberta hesitated with the spoon poised, and raised her eyebrows. "Sure," she said after a moment. "If you want."

They traded places. "I don't know what to do about Jimmy Poole," Mariesa said as she offered the squash to the five-month-old. "Even if he did knock over the first domino, I don't think asking him to set it back up again would help much. Entropy only flows one direction."

"I wasn't thinking in terms of 'asking' him to do anything."

Mariesa looked at the grim-faced younger woman. "It wasn't his fault, really. There were other players"—Little Carson jerked his head away from the offered spoon. Mariesa tracked the stubborn mouth—"there were other players. It's *really* good, Carson."

"I don't care if it wasn't Jimmy's fault. All that wealth, just sitting around, just 'keeping score.' He ought to *do* something with it."

It was a time of crisis. Everyone thought everyone ought to *do something*. Yet, sometimes, the doing only made things worse. Mariesa was sure Rutell had had only good intentions. Yet, raising the interest rates had shoved a sock in the economy and broadened the market contraction into a recession. He should have taken a lesson from his own policies in 2011 and let the wound heal. But the pressure to *act*, to play the hero, was too great.

"There's a proposal from Leland Hobart that ought to be looked into," Mariesa said. "Carson!" The sharp voice made the baby jump, but his lips remained adamantly sealed. Was this how we learn to shake our head no, Mariesa wondered.

"Hobie?"

"Yes. Solomon Dark has doubts about it, but I think we should investigate all our options. Hobart was a schoolmate. Jimmy may want to invest."

Roberta laughed. "Out of friendship? That's not his button."

"Still, as you said, he ought to do something. I give up." Mariesa shoved the spoon into the squash and set the bowl down on the high chair's tray. "He wants his mommy to feed him, I suppose."

Roberta's laugh changed a note. "No," she said, pointing; and Mariesa looked back to see that the youngster had grabbed the spoon himself and was shoving the squash toward his mouth with modest success.

"You just want to do it yourself," Roberta cooed. "You just wanted to prove you could do it."

"Yes," said Mariesa, watching the child's triumph. "It's a human thing. We have a need to prove ourselves to ourselves. It may be our salvation."

4.

The Damocles Imperative

Of all the people that Jimmy Poole expected to show up on his doorstep in the mountains west of San Jose, Roberta Carson did not even make the first cut.

For years during and after high school, he had fantasized about this very event. Roberta would knock on his door, having realized that he was the one man she needed, and they would do the deed, right then and there. Sometimes he had imagined them on the floor of his living room in front of a snapping fire; other times in a silk-and-satined bedroom; still other times wantonly vertical in the kitchen, or straddled in his command chair in his Sanctum. Years and reality had whacked him upside the head. When he lost his virginity at long last, it had been Tani Pandya who took it—and who kept it still.

Jimmy supposed that his teenaged crush on Roberta had been born of their mutual status as outsiders in a tightly cliqued school. He, the despised nerd and genius; she, the pale-faced, black-garbed goth. "Styx," she had called herself then. "Morticia the Mushroom," the other kids said, evoking Jimmy's sympathy and exciting his desire to share miseries with the one person who might possibly understand. She had been a quiet girl, though often cutting and sarcastic when she spoke, and gave the impression of deep waters, of hard, secret desires.

Now, thinking back and knowing what it was like to lie nightly with Tani beside him, he thought that Styx would not have been good for him. She would have hurt him, somehow, and badly; not so much from intent as from her nature. Where Tani was cool, soothing water, Styx had been all searing fire.

Roberta dressed more brightly now, though her face had never quite lost that doleful look, and in moments when she was not consciously smiling, her countenance would settle into somber pensiveness. But if Roberta's unexpected arrival surprised Jimmy, that she had come with a committee in tow startled him even more.

It was quite a parade. Roberta, Leland Hobart—with a woman on his arm, and . . . Chase Coughlin: shaven sidewalls, punked hair, jewelry piercing places that it hurt Jimmy even to think about. Jimmy hesitated fractionally before letting the space pilot into his house. Hobie, he could take or leave alone. But Chase evoked memories of countless humiliations.

High school had been four years of hell. Not the roughing up, not the lunch money stolen or the stupid pranks. Those could be endured. The dim had always persecuted the bright, and Chase's attentions had, in a way, validated Jimmy's status as a human in the monkey house. No, what grated was the *humiliation*. The way the others had laughed at him or looked the other way. Chase had made Jimmy into a object of *ridicule*. In a *school*! A place where, had there been justice, Jimmy should have been a role model. For that Chase had yet to suffer.

Someday, Jimmy promised himself. Payback. Humiliation. Someday.

Jimmy hunted for some remark sufficiently cutting to put Chase in his place, yet sufficiently esoteric that the punk wouldn't get it; but Tani intervened before he could take a breath and she ushered them all inside.

As for Chase, sensitivity to the nuances of body language was never his strong suit. He crushed Jimmy's hand indifferently and his first question was whether Jimmy had any Skull Mountain handy. Jimmy spoke briefly into his wrist tracey and, shortly after, a messenger boy from a nearby supermarket knocked and delivered a case of the brew. If Chase was impressed, he didn't show it.

Meanwhile, they settled into Jimmy's library. It was a broad, open room flooded with sunlight from a floor-to-ceiling window of metallocene plastic at one end. The floor was a parquetry of light and dark woods inlaid in complex, fractal patterns. Racks of seedies and other media filled one wall. A Gyricon screen and reader in the severely functional style of the Naughty Oughts hung on a "diplodocus" that could be pulled to almost any point in the room. The hot, new style was "coke," heavily ornate and neo-Victorian, but Jimmy delighted in going against the trends.

Stocky, wide, and black, Hobie had morphed improbably from a famous high school jock to a famous world-class chemist. Almost single-handedly he had made superconductors commercially feasible. "The Master of Cool," the web sites named him. He introduced the slim, fine-featured, golden-skinned woman with him as Ladawan Chulalongkon, his wife and a coworker at Argonaut Labs.

Jimmy frowned. "I thought your wife was named Charlene . . . ?" He turned to Tani. "When the Hobarts were out here, the two of you went up to the City and—" Tani was making shushing motions at him.

"That was more than two years ago," she said.

"Oh." He looked again at Hobie and said, "Oh. Sorry."

The chemist waved a hand. "Don't be. I'm not." He looked at Ladawan. "Never been happier."

"When I went looking for Hobie," Roberta said, "all I had was his old address. Got the door slammed in my face."

Hobie frowned. "Charli had no cause to do that. Thinks every woman who comes by is someone I've jollied."

Watching Tani, Jimmy felt again how lucky he had been. He knew he wasn't the easiest person to live with. His passions and his appetites were often orthogonal to the mundane world's, and despite Tani's best efforts, his social skills often fell short. How many other women, he thought, would have walked out years ago?

So Roberta was a widow—which is sort of what you'd expect if you married an old fart like Phil Albright—and Hobie was divorced. He looked at Chase and guessed three wives with three adulterous breakups. Chase had run a string of bimbos back in high school and changed them as often as he changed his underwear.

"How about you, Chase?" he asked in a knowing voice.

"Dunno," the pilot answered. "Karen hasn't thrown me out yet. So I guess I'm still upchecked on her flight readiness list."

The answer surprised him. It didn't seem right, somehow. Jimmy wiggled his eyebrows. "I guess she hasn't caught you yet."

Chase's mouth settled into a flat line and his eyes hardened. It was just a flash and normally Jimmy never picked up on such things, but this he did. *Jesus,* he thought. *The guy's straight arrow.* Unaccountably, that irritated Jimmy. Space pilot. Moonwalker. The guy could have his pick. So why didn't he? It was out of character.

When the beer arrived, Tani solemnly passed the bottles around. Hobie and Chase sat on the floor and kicked with the Skulls while the others settled into soft chairs and sofas. Chase leaned close to Hobie. "Only need Meat here," he said, "and we got the Three Musketeers of Ziggy."

"All for one . . ." Hobie tipped the neck of his bottle.

Chase tapped it with his own. ". . . and every man for himself."

The chitchat drifted onto children and Jimmy tuned out.

Small talk bored him. Tani had told him once—after an especially disastrous dinner party—that he couldn't open his mouth without performing an information dump or showing off how clever he was. Uncertain what it was he was doing wrong, Jimmy took refuge mostly in silence, solitude, and the virtch.

Of one thing Jimmy was absolutely certain: This was *not* the class reunion committee. Roberta and the others wanted something from him. Well, it wouldn't be the first time. What they wanted remained to be seen, as did his response. He had always sort of liked Roberta, and Hobie was neither here nor there; but if Chase wanted something bad enough to come to Jimmy's door, Jimmy would have to think long and hard about his answer.

Something virtchuous, he decided. He was Poole sEcurity Consultants. The Wizard of Baud. He made everyone's short list of world-class virtchuosi. So if anyone came to him for favors, it was almost certain to be for the cheese, and more often than not something that required confidentiality and discretion.

Which was a polite way of saying gray work. If they had wanted a white bread hack, they could have simply submitted an R-4-P, Request-for-Proposal, over Poole sEcurity's web site. But if they wanted the Wizard to walk the wild side, what more secure channel than from their lips to Jimmy's ear?

And, what the h*ll. It wasn't as though he'd never cakewalked before. He'd given up cracking for Tani's sake. He no longer broke laws, but sometimes laws could be bent to get a client what he needed. You just had to check the tensile strength first. So whatever Roberta and her motley crew wanted, it was probably not a straight-on, honkie handshake. Some street jive would be called for.

And there was always the possibility that it would be something new and interesting. Jimmy had grown weary of the succession of banks and corporations and agencies who came to him with the same-old same-old month after month, always imagining that their electronic security concerns were somehow new and unprecedented; and pathetically grateful to Jimmy for hacking a solution. They never dreamed—or refused to dream—that their problems were the stale residue of their own ineptness and that Jimmy hacked the cheese so swiftly because he had seen the same problems innumerable times and (more often than not) from both sides of the firewall.

Of course, what better way to rub Chase's nose in Jimmy's virtchuosity than to extemporize whatever fluff they needed, right off the old keyboard.

"So tell me, Styxy," he said during a pause in the chatter, "to what do I owe the honor of this visit?"

Roberta smiled. "You and me, Jimmy—and Hobie and Chase—we're going to save the whole damn world."

It was a dog and pony show, but without bells and whistles. Jimmy had listened to enough of them in the past to appreciate the simplicity. No glossy GBC-bound booklets, no wall-size projections of multicolored bar charts and pies and trend lines. Just Hobie explaining things and drinking beer.

"We want to build a new kind of spaceship," Hobie said. "You know I've developed super-high temperature superconductors, don't you?"

"I've heard," Jimmy replied sardonically. "Something about a Nobel Prize?"

The chemist looked embarrassed and his eyes dropped. "There's talk of that."

"But it's bad luck to say it out loud," Chase interjected. "Right, Hobe?"

"Well, the prize would be for the theoretical work. The so-called Periodic Table of Superconducting Compounds. I was extending Anderson's work to anomalous spin liquids and found a relation between the parameters of superconducting compounds and the chemical properties of the constituent materials. You see, each compound is quenched—loses its superconduction—if the temperature gets too high. But it's also quenched if the magnetic field penetrates it. There's a critical current density, too, since a current through the wire generates its own magfield. So I correlated known compounds against those three qualities, and . . ."

Jimmy made old-time radio noises and tuned imaginary knobs. "Earth calling Hobart," he said in a high nasal voice. "Earth calling Hobart."

Chase laughed and Hobie grimaced. Ladawan said sternly, "Let him talk."

"Oh, that's okay," said Hobie. "Charli always did tell me I had a tendency to throw long. The point is, Jimmy, that once you kick a current into a loop of superconductor, it keeps going and going . . ."

"Like that damn rabbit on the tube," said Chase.

"I know what a superconductor is," Jimmy said impatiently. "Next point."

Hobie scowled. Even in his placid moods, Leland Hobart looked like a building that had just imploded and was about to fall on you. When irritation crossed his features he could be positively frightening. "Next point is the solar wind. Do you know what *that* is?"

Jimmy grinned. "Charged particles whipping off the sun."

Hobie grunted. "How fast?"

"Speed of light."

Chase Coughlin honked like an old-time auto horn. "Wrong! Sorry, contestant, would you care to try again?"

Jimmy looked at him. "I was talking with Dr. Hobart."

Chase straightened infinitesimally. Just enough for Jimmy to notice, and just enough for Hobie to lay a hand on the pilot's arm. "I'll handle it," he said; then, turning back to Jimmy, said, "Solar wind blows past Earth orbit at an average of 450 klicks a second. That's more than a million miles an hour. The flow's supersonic and you get turbulences, so . . ."

He looked again at his audience and chuckled. "Okay. I'm not even the physicist in our little group—"

"Who is? Ladawan?" asked Jimmy.

"No. She's a chemist, like me. Otul Ganesh, at Argonaut Labs, is our physicist. All right. You put a superloop out in the solar wind, what do you think happens?"

Jimmy leaned back in his chair and stuck his lower lip out. "You're good," he told Hobie. "You're getting me involved, not just spouting off like some people do." Chase made a strangled sound, but was the picture of innocence when Jimmy glanced his way. "If I remember my EM courses," Jimmy continued to Hobie, "and if it works the same way as computer hardware, I'd guess the charged particles bounce off the magnetic field."

Hobie nodded. "Sort of. They sleet around it, following the lines of magnetic force. But each time a particle hits the magnetic field, it imparts some of its momentum so—"

"So the field moves," said Jimmy, beginning to see where the other was taking this.

"Right. You get an acceleration to starward."

"Not a million miles a hour . . ." said Jimmy.

"There's tricks you can play with the current density, orientation, and a bunch of other factors to adjust the amount of force; but, let's say about a thousandth of a gee."

Jimmy rolled his eyes. "Well, I'm impressed . . ."

"A thousandth of a gee *nonstop*."

Jimmy blinked, studied the smug look on the chemist's face. "Okay. What?"

"Adds up. SSTOs are chemical, they burn at a high gee force because they can carry only a limited amount of fuel; so they go for high specific impulse—hard, short burns. They have to use fuel to move fuel. A magnetic sail pushes more gently, but *it keeps on pushing* so your velocity keeps building. You don't run out of fuel any more than a sailing ship on the ocean. Less, because there are no calms in the solar wind. At one milligee—figuring you accelerate to the halfway point, then decelerate to parking orbit at your destination—Mars orbit is maybe ten weeks away."

"And freaking *Pluto*," said Chase, butting in, "is only two years out. Isn't that phat stoopid? Old-time whaling ships went on voyages longer than that."

Jimmy nodded. The others watched him silently. He nodded some more, wondering how long he could drag out the silence. The others continued to watch him. "And my role is . . . ?" he said at last.

"Financing," said Roberta. "Rutell left a bunch of IOUs in the funding for the Planetary Defense Committee when he raided it to save Social Security. The PDC is pinching pennies for now and putting most of its efforts into proven technology; so Hobie's project has official sanction, but no official funding. Solomon Dark and Mariesa van Huyten and some of the Committee think magsails have potential down the road and authorized us to solicit private funding."

Jimmy blinked and looked at them hard. Money? Who the hell cared about *money*? Money was how you kept score; it wasn't the game. He bit hard and his lips tightened. "You want me to risk my savings on some herbie theory that's never been tested?" he said.

"Chase and I launched some scale models last year," Hobie said. "They were designed to use the solar wind to cancel out the sun's gravity. Hang in place, you see. Four of the ten survived the year and—"

"And the other six?"

"Don't know. Lost telemetry. And we weren't able to recover the hardware because of the federal stand-down and the Pegasus bankruptcy."

Chase grimaced. "Sorry about that."

"Not your fault, otter. Jimmy, the technology looks promising; so if we can build these ships and prove them out—"

" ' . . . If we can build these ships and prove them out . . .' " Jimmy repeated. "Meaning, you don't know if you can; or whether they'll work the way you think. I *do* know the difference between science and engineering."

Hobie shrugged. "That's the way the world works. No guarantees. We gotta go ziggy and draw wire."

"Ziggy's shut down," Jimmy pointed out. "There's a recession on, in case you haven't noticed."

Chase snorted. "Trust me. I've noticed."

Roberta opened her mouth, then appeared to change her mind about something. "A recession means the project can get stuff dirt cheap," she said instead. "Buy a lift, rent space on LEO, take up some rare earths and shit . . . Argonaut's equipment is still installed up there. *If* we can find the troy." She gave him a significant look.

Jimmy shook his head, as if to clear it. "And the reason I should fund all this is . . . ?"

"Save the planet?" Chase suggested with affected innocence. Roberta shot him an angry glance, and Hobie gave him the elbow. Jimmy snorted to himself. *Yeah. Don't piss off the money.*

"Screw the planet," he said. "What's the planet done for me lately? Save Jimmy Poole is more like it. All that needs is I get out of the way. It's not all that big a rock coming."

"If it hits the water—" Roberta said.

Jimmy wagged his hand. "Yeah, yeah. Tsunami. So if it hits nearby in the Pacific. I'll vacation in Dakota."

"And what if it hits fucking Dakota?" said Chase.

"Then I stay here." Jimmy spoke as if to a child.

"And if it hits the Gulf?" Hobie asked in a low, soft voice.

Jimmy spread his hands. "Not my problem."

"No," Hobie said through his teeth. "But Ladawan and me, we live in Houston."

"Then, *you* go to Dakota. It's not like they won't have the trajectory worked out way ahead."

Tani Pandya stood up. She had always had soft, doughy features; but now her face was set in hard planes and she seemed somehow darker than before. "I'll get more beer," she said through lips that barely moved, and left the room.

"Besides," Jimmy continued, "it's not like the planet depends on you guys. If it does, we're in worse trouble than I thought." His laugh echoed through his nose. "I'm sure the government's doing something. Those Planetary Defense Bonds . . ."

"Bottlenecked in the House," said Roberta.

"So why rag on me? Write your congress-critter. Or the van Huytens . . . I hear they have a little cash. Maybe they can spare some for your pet project."

"VHI is committed to other tasks—You're right, there *are* operations under way—but Mariesa has pledged part of her personal fortune to this venture. Hobie's idea may give us an extra edge. Hobie? Do you want to explain?"

"You don't need a launch window with a magsail," Hobie said. "Well, not much of one—you just 'hoist the mains'l' and head on out. *Because you're not dependent on free fall and gravity.* That gives us a lot more chances to reach the Bean and stop it."

"You see what that means," Roberta interrupted. "The way things stand now, we only get two shots. The close approach in 2021, three and a half years from now; and the final approach in 2023. With magships, we could get a few extra shots in."

Jimmy tugged at his lip. "And Chase here is going to be test pilot? I should risk my money to make him famous?"

"Christ, Jimmy, get a life," Chase said. "High school was twenty years ago. I'm not the same guy you knew. None of us are. I'm not a thug; and Hobie, here, he ain't a tongue-tied jock; and Roberta ain't a stuck-up poser. Even you, Jimmy. You're not a whiny, know-it-all asshole, anymore." His eyes said he didn't quite believe that last one, but Jimmy didn't care what Chase believed.

"More to it," Hobie put in quietly. "What I told VHI; reason why Styxy came to see me. Set up a superloop *on* the asteroid, with shrouds and lines and A/S motors and shit.

Enough lead time, we can *steer* the damn thing and park it wherever we want."

Tani returned with fresh bottles and passed them out. The one she set in front of Jimmy sounded like a knacker's hammer. He tracked her around the room with a puzzled frown. What had gotten into her?

"We've already lost most of a year," Roberta said, "because Wall Street bettors have been running headless chicken sims. Once Congress gets its enema and the appropriations begin to flow, we're supposed to get a spoonful of the federal gravy. When that happens, you'll get your money back."

Jimmy laughed. "If I lay my personal wallet on the line, *maybe* I'll get my troy back later from a grateful world; but the chances are that the Grateful World will vote me a Hearty Handshake and a Certificate Suitable for Framing, and not much more. Never saw in the Bible where the Samaritan got repaid."

"Will you at least think about it?" Roberta's voice had gone low. Her deep-set eyes, through some trick and angle of the lighting, seemed to have disappeared into shadows, catching only a stray gleam, almost as if he were seeing twin stars through two long tubes.

"Sure. I'll think about it." Thinking didn't cost anything.

A silence settled over the group that slowly grew embarrassing, until Tani spoke up and suggested they all have dinner together. Jimmy didn't think it would be a fun meal for the others, considering how their pocket-picking mission had gone. Hell had no fury like someone who knew how to spend your money and failed to get his hands on it. Hobie, in particular, looked less than thrilled. Scientists always thought they were entitled to other people's money. But no one could get a flight home until the red-eye, anyway—except Chase, Jimmy pointed out—so Tani brooked no excuses and left to make reservations.

Roberta asked to speak privately with Jimmy, so he told the others to make themselves at home and that Stassy, the household's cook, would get them anything they wanted. Then he led Roberta to his Sanctum, where he plopped in his command chair—a huge, comfortable, high-backed swivel with armrests built up to avoid carping and joysticks and scroll buttons mounted in them. Stacks of monitors and drives and zippers and trees and Y-racks surrounded him like the crenels and merlons of some electronic battlement. Jimmy had always felt safe in his castle—only once had it ever been breached, and he had dealt with the assailant, with a little help from some friends—although lately he had grown more aware that the heart of every castle was its donjon, and walls could confine as much as protect.

"What is it you wanted, Styxy?" he asked.

Roberta looked around for a second chair and found none, so she left him sitting there while she rolled one in from the file archive room next door. She looked around the Sanctum with frank interest. "So this is where it all happens . . ."

"Not all," said Jimmy, wagging his eyebrows and leering so she would understand the innuendo.

But Roberta was not put off. "You should see my equipment."

That depended on what she meant by her "equipment" . . . But Jimmy forbore from doubling the *entendre*. "I'm sure it's appropriate to your needs," he assured her. He could not imagine finding Roberta's computer setup interesting.

The poet laughed. "Different strokes for different folks, as my grandmother used to say. I'm sure your equipment does everything you want it to. Maybe more, sometimes."

Jimmy considered that. "Meaning?" He cocked his head to the side.

"What did you do the night you learned about Adam van Huyten's plans for OMC?"

Jimmy was silent for a moment, puzzled at the abrupt change in topic. "What do you know about that?"

"You and Adam were the money on Baleen Filters and Adam used the facility on Leo Station to ferret out OMC's fraud. So you had to know what was going down."

Now where had she learned that? From Adam by way of Mariesa? From Billie Whistle? Not that it mattered. Jimmy was clean. "I was just the money," he said. "I had no part in operations, and I didn't write the fly in their software."

"Yeah, I know. Billie Whistle did. You were just a stalwart, upstanding citizen. But that's not what I asked. I asked what you did the evening before Adam made his big announcement."

"Is it any of your business?"

"I think it is. You sold off big blocks of shares in the LEO Consortium."

Most of Jimmy's stocks had not been in his own name; but some had, and that was a public record. "So why ask me if you already know? Lots of people bailed out."

"Sure. *After* the announcement."

"It wasn't insider trading."

"I don't care if it was or not. You used an Artificial Stupid to run the trades, didn't you?"

"Do you think I have time to stay up all night making calls to the Shanghai Exchange or the Paris Bourse?"

"And you didn't just dump Orbital Management Corporation or Bullock's Klon-Am Holding Company. You dumped them all. Pegasus, Boeing, Matsushita, Ossa & Pelion, Energia, Hoechst, Roche . . . Went heavy into cash and gold."

"Wait a minute, there, Styx. I never gave orders to sell all those. Members of the Consortium, sure. I knew they'd get splattered with some of the mud Adam dug up on OMC, because, after all, they're the ones who gave Bullock the management contract in the first place. But not Roche and Motorola and the others."

Roberta leaned forward. "Do you want me to guess? You told your construct—I'll bet its name is D. G. Stockman—to sell your holdings 'in any company connected with Leo.' Well, genius, do you know how many companies are 'connected' with Leo? Suppliers, tenants. Companies with standalones in the sub-orbs who have to pass through Port Leo for Earthside drop-downs?"

Jimmy scowled. "That wasn't what I—"

"That wasn't what you meant to do. Sure. But that's how your construct construed it. There's a reason neural nets are still called Artificial *Stupids*. Jimmy, do you have any idea how much stock you dumped that night?"

He shook his head. "I have no idea how much I own or what it's worth, and I don't care. I'm not into the materialism thing. As long as Tani and I can live comfortably, anything else is just keeping score."

"Enough to catch the interest of the People's Crusades. We keep a 'stock watch' for evidence of insider trading. Jimmy, you tanked the market."

"Oh, come on—"

"I'm serious. Sure Adam's revelations had something to do with it. And my speech about the asteroid coming. I'll accept that share. And the original frauds, by Pitchlynn and Bullock when they slicked Adam's stock and by dell'Bosco with his musical chairs on Leo. And the government sucking the capital pool dry with their Social Security rescue . . . Each and every one of us thought we were doing the right thing, given the pressures of the moment and our own value systems. Whatever happens, there's never just one thing that causes it. So sure, you don't get *full* blame; but, Jimmy, that doesn't mean you don't get *any* blame."

"I didn't do anything illegal."

" 'Illegal' isn't the issue here. It's a question of doing what's right."

"I didn't do anything wrong."

Roberta shook her head. "There's a difference between 'not doing anything wrong' and 'doing right.' This plan of Hobie's . . . even if it doesn't pan out, we've got to try."

"The shares were my property," Jimmy insisted. "I have the right to sell them when I please." He thought the punning on "right" and "rights" was quite clever, but Roberta didn't buy in. She stood and straightened her skirt.

"I never said you didn't have the *right,"* she told him stiffly. "Lots of things, we have 'rights.' Doesn't mean we have to abandon common sense or a commitment to the community to exercise them."

"What's 'community' ever done for me?"

"You're a bright boy. You figure it out." Roberta stormed out and left him alone in his Sanctum.

Jimmy swiveled back and forth in his chair and scowled. Who was Roberta Carson to wag her finger in his face? A poet. And what good had poets ever done the world? Did poetry feed the hungry? Clothe the naked? Cure the sick? Jimmy had written programs that seined the Net and concatenated data into information that had allowed one team of researchers to develop Permovium—and how many sufferers from neo-encephalitis had lived productively because of that? Another A/S he had taught to work the "traveling salesman" problem for a shipping company—and how well stocked was your local supermarket today, Styxy?

He hadn't done any of that for altruism. Screw altruism. He'd been contracted to do a job and he'd done it the best he knew how—and he knew a lot of "how" when it came to logics and software—and because of that there was a little less hunger and a little less suffering in the world. If he deserved blame for the unintended consequences of his actions, then didn't he deserve credit, too?

At least, Styxy was true to type. Her sort was always generous—with other people's money. She was as much to blame for the Dip with her doomsday speech as he was for looking after his own interests, so where did she get off lecturing him? Why wasn't *she* doing penance?

Dinner was at a private restaurant called Timothy's. It was the sort of place that never advertised, seated seven tables, and did one service a night. It was also the sort of place where if you were as well hung as Jimmy Poole's wallet, you were guaranteed a table even if you called at the last minute.

Table talk focused on this and that. Children. Careers. Jokes heard. Jimmy noticed how distracted Roberta was—how she kept looking around from time to time—and guessed that this was the first evening she had spent away from her child since the boy had been born. He asked her how her poetry was going, not because he was charlie for poetry, but just to get her talking. That led the talk around to Tani's new book, *The Flesh Made Word*. Doing well, his wife said. She dismissed some of the negative media criticism. "They just wanted me to write *Taj Mahal* over and over—I'm an 'Indo-American writer,' so I should only write about the Indo-American experience—which proves they never really understood *Taj Mahal*."

That led to a host of remember-whens about Pandya's In-and-Out and about North Orange in general—what was Azim Thomas up to these days? Or Meat Tucker? Or Cheng-I Yeh? Name followed name. Ladawan asked Chase about the lunar run so Chase told them about Artemis and Selene and "catching flies" launched by the lunar catapult; and Hobie mentioned the scale model magships he and Chase had launched the year before the Dip.

"Solar storm flared up," Chase remembered.

"And Chase and me and the cadet—"

"Sulbertson."

"Yeah, Lonzo Sulbertson . . . We had to bunker up," Hobie added.

Ladawan said, "But why not put a superloop around the ship and shield it?"

Chase swatted Hobie on the arm. "That's what I told Genius, here, when he mentioned it afterward. Me, I want to die in bed—preferably with a hot babe in my arms. Getting microwaved is not my first choice."

"Lots of opportunities in superloops," Hobie agreed. "A

Deep Space Vessel can use it for shielding as well as propulsion."

"Different sort of piloting, though," Chase commented. "More like sailing than ballistics. Adjusting the loop angle, the field strength. Playing gravity against the solar wind. Not just the same old 'burn at anomaly' or 'two-gets-you-twenty.' "

Hobie shook his head. "Need some cholo flight programming, for sure. Clean sheet stuff; not just redlining the current SOPs." He didn't quite look straight at Jimmy.

Jimmy sat straighter and preened inwardly, though he did not let the smile reach his face. For something like this they needed a programming genius. Someone who could assemble a team of virtchuosi and cut new cheese. Already his mind was racing with possibilities. Get SuperNerd and the Jouster and the other Fingers. Write sims for the wind and the sail and play them against each other. Navigational programming for the sail . . . Something new, at any rate. Not the same-old same-old.

When Jimmy blinked and came to himself, Chase and the others were busy at their plates. But Tanuja Pandya, whose eyes could see inside the human heart, was staring at them all with frank interest. Flustered, Jimmy attacked his filet. When he looked up again, he saw a curiously satisfied smile on her face and knew with sudden intuition that his wife had just decided on her third novel.

Voices: Genesis

Tani Pandya speaking. I suppose it's only fair that if I ask the others to reveal their private thoughts and hopes and fears for my new book, I should do the same. After all, I'm the only one who will ever listen to these tapes . . . Jimmy says

I shouldn't call them "tapes." Micro-CDs? Whatever. Roberta and Chase and Hobie and the others I've given recorders know that I'll hear their innermost thoughts; so they might hold back. But no one else will ever hear mine. So, I can be more open than any of them.

Only, I find that I can't be.

I poured my soul into *Taj Mahal* and a bit of cynicism into *Flesh Made Word.* (Oh, God, if Jimmy only knew. Yet, I did grow to love him. I did, in spite of himself. Because I know, more than he does, that there is a better Jimmy in there.) But I could be open in my novels, because I could hold my characters in front of me, like shields. *They* were the ones exposing their underbellies, not I.

Not I.

But this is different. This is me, speaking straight out, and it's harder than I thought it would be. Yet a novel, even a novelization of true events, is hollow if the characters aren't stuffed full. And yes, I will change them around and shuffle them and tell the lies that make fiction more true than fact; but . . .

I'm delaying, aren't I?

I was wrong about no one else hearing this. *I* will listen to it—maybe a few months from now when I'm ready to start a rough draft—and I will not be the same person then as I am now.

So let's stick with the surface facts.

Name: Tanuja Pandya. Age . . . that old already? Thirty-five? I was in high school only moments ago. Now I'm middle-aged. A private joke of Jimmy's: if the average lifespan is eighty, then forty is the midpoint and twenty-to-sixty, the middle half. Trust Jimmy to quantify something like that. Jimmy will never be middle-aged, because he is the eternal child. He likes to . . . play. That's the only word for it. A different game now, but still play.

I'm a writer. I think I am. I tell myself that. I'm obviously not an extemporaneous speaker. <laughs.> Ever since I was a child, stocking shelves in Baba's store. I knew this was what I wanted to be. I love people, even the ones who don't want to be loved. Even the ones who make it hard to love them. I don't mean the gooshy sort of love, because sometimes love has to be hard and without illusions; but I want to know them all and I want to show them all to each other.

I guess I could have had an afternoon talk show . . .

The plan for my new book, if you can call something so inchoate a plan . . . let alone a book . . . The idea came to me the evening Jimmy and I took Roberta and the others to Timothy's and I realized that Hobie had slicked my Jimmy into joining their project. Hobie was always such a lump in school—though he began to blossom toward the end—that I never imagined him capable of subtlety. God, that sounds racist, almost; but it's not his color, it's his demeanor. I never expected such a combination of absentminded professor and tough football jock could play mind games. It was then, when I realized there were surprises buried inside familiar people, that I knew what I had to write about. Whether Hobie's magships ever fly or not doesn't matter, except maybe to the Earth; but I want to plumb the minds of the people who try to make it happen and find the surprises each one hides.

Anyway, that's the beginning, the genesis. Who knows how it will end?

Actually, Jimmy Poole thought she was wrong about no one else hearing the μCDs, since the encryption was trivial; but dead nuts on about people surprising you. Tani had given him some thoughts to ponder; but he was astonished later, when, in retrospect, he realized that they were not the thoughts he had expected them to be.

5.

Nothing More Perilous

The meeting would start in an hour and a half, but the drive to VHI headquarters was only forty-five minutes. Mariesa paused in the hallway at Ridgeview and adjusted her scarf. A useless gesture—she would certainly have to freshen up once she arrived—but one long-ingrained by habit and by Harriet's ancient scolds. One did not step outside except looking one's best.

Yes, Mummy.

She paused with one hand against her lapel. Every now and then she would remember with unbearable poignancy that her mother was dead. Most days, it was a simple fact, like the fact that the sky was blue; but occasionally, some trifling scene would flash through her memory as vividly as if she were reliving it. Young Mariesa, twelve years old, garbed in lace and flouncy dress, held back by Harriet's hand while her mother carefully straightened her bow. Odd, that she could not remember where they had been going or why, but her mother's voice and the touch of her hand were as real as the face before her in the mirror.

With a shiver, she recognized that face as Harriet's. She was older now than Harriet had been then; and though her mother had dyed her hair and worn it up and favored fashions a generation more antique, the reflection that regarded her now had the same round jaw, the same odd, slightly pointed ears. It was as if Harriet were still looking after her.

The limo's engine, idling on the driveway outside, came to her as a faint buzz. The phone rang and from the corner of the eye she saw Armando cross the front room to answer it.

Time to go. She gave the white-haired matron in the mirror one last glance and turned away.

"Who was that, Armando?" she asked the butler as he entered the hallway and opened the front door for her.

"On the phone, miss? No one. A wrong number."

She could see the lie in his eyes. Another crank had somehow gotten her access code. *The Bean's your fault, lady. You better watch your back.* She smiled at Armando and for his sake accepted the lie. Undoubtedly, he had checked the caller ID and just as undoubtedly the caller had been ID-protected. Another victory for "privacy rights," though only for those of the harassers. The one solace was that future calls from that number would be shunted to Charlie Schwar at Cerberus Security.

"I had best be going," she told Armando. "Hold down the fort."

The breeze outside was warm, and May flowers had burst out in abundance. The small garden surrounding the fountain in the circular driveway was a riot of white and yellow and violet. Wildflowers, though a different suite up here on the ridge crest than had colored the meadows and lawns around Silverpond. Bluebead lily and Dutchman's breeches had replaced foamflowers and mayapples. The sassafras was in bloom, infusing the air with its piquant "root-beer" odor. As summer grew high, there would be shinleaf and the wild sarsparilla. A northern oriole atop the fountain regarded her with cocked head, then took sudden wing.

The snow was gone—except in the cut for the Interstate, where the south face lay in perpetual shadow. Ice sometimes sheathed those rocks well into summer. Eastward, the waters of a broad lake sparkled in the morning sun; westward, thick forests flanked the gorge along the Musconetcong River. A canopy of oak and hickory hid most of the works of man, a bit of the landscaper's craft creating—at this one spot—the illusion of a house alone in a forested wilderness.

Until one remembered that the lake was a reservoir and

that Musconetcong Gorge was a preserve. Or until one raised one's eyes to the more distant views, where houses and farms, office parks and roadways, spoiled the illusion. She couldn't see the cluster of houses at Swinesburg—the angle was wrong—but she could pick out Pattenburg and The Hickory and Little York. And there was the maglev line that had once been the Lehigh Valley Railroad and, before that, the Bound Brook and Easton Rail Road.

The chauffeur helped her into the car and, when she was settled in, drove out. At the end of the driveway, where it opened onto Sweet Hollow Road, he signaled left toward Little York. An ancient '08 Wraith, whose faded green was mottled with putty and retouch, was parked against the traffic on the far side of the road, where it overlooked Hakihokake Creek. The Wraith pulled onto the paving in a spatter of dirt and gravel and swerved to within inches of the limo's right rear door. Mariesa gasped and snatched with one hand at the strap and with the other at the papers she had spread across the limo's folding table. The limo bounced on the shoulder; bushes and shrubs scratched at the paintwork. The Wraith roared down the western side of the ridge toward Bloomsbury, leaving a faint cloud of dust suspended in the spring air. The chauffeur loosed a few invectives after the vanished car, glanced over his shoulder at her to see if she was all right, then continued down the ridge toward Little York.

In 1628, the Dutch admiral Heyn captured the Spanish Treasure Fleet off Cuba. Among the captains sharing out the eleven and a half million gold florins was one Henryk van Huyten, who proposed in a letter to his brother "to use the sum more productively than would have the Spanish *tercios,* who meant to blow the same from the mouths of their cannon and muskets upon our homes and families." And so he did, developing close ties with the Seventeen Gentlemen and loaning sixty guilders to *Mynheer* Minuit to buy an island in the New World "whereon to build a new Amsterdam." His self-satisfied smile had been captured in oil by Rembrandt's teacher, Piet Lastmann, in a portrait whose long journeys had come to rest in the boardroom at Van Huyten Industries headquarters, nestled against the slope of First Watchung Mountain in rural Wessex County.

The painting, which hung above the boardroom's double doors, had recently been cleaned and restored, and some of Henryk's dour solemnity had lightened with the colors. He was still a pirate; but one with a sunnier countenance than heretofore. Mariesa was struck again, when Chris took his accustomed seat beneath it, how much of that face had survived the four centuries since brushstrokes had captured it. Chris was lighter, thinner, and taller than his ancestor, but nonetheless owned the same high cheekbones and the same cold, piercing, snakelike eyes. Dress him in ruff collar, beaver hat, and pantaloons and he wouldn't have raised an eyebrow along the old Heren Gracht.

Chris looked at his watch, then at Mariesa, but said nothing. Mariesa took the hint and rapped her knuckles on the boardroom table. "People?" she said. "Let's get started, shall we?"

There was a brief rustle as those physically present shifted their seats for comfort. Attentive looks from around the table and from the three active telepresence monitors. Adam van Huyten leaned close to his father and whispered something to which Chris responded with a raised palm.

Mariesa took a deep breath and said, "First item is FYI. The defense bonds are still bottled up in Congress because, to be frank, some people do not believe that there is an asteroid threat and think the whole thing is a power grab by the government. Solomon Dark does not see a light at the end of this particular tunnel."

"Small wonder," said Correy Wilcox, "when he's dealing with a troglodyte. It's a cave, not a tunnel." Correy, president of Gaea Biotech, was an original Promethean. Thickset and athletic, he wore a blond crew cut that had faded to a pale platinum even as it receded from his brow. One of the few alert to the possibility of an asteroid strike even back then, he believed firmly in the Goal; but he also believed firmly in Correy Wilcox. Mariesa had never fully warmed to him; though she had to admit that, in the end, his open ambitions had proven less harmful than had Dolores Pitchlynn's secret ones.

Hamilton Pye grunted. "Somebody better give that boy a nudge. We get our best shot July of '21, when the Bean makes a close approach. A FarTrip-style rendezvous is doable, but the ship has to go out in January."

"Thirty-three months," Wallace Coyle added, "isn't as much time as it sounds, even if we convert ships in the current fleet . . ." His eyes took on a distant look and his lips moved slightly. Mariesa had once compared him to a chocolate teddy bear, a verdict in which his wife Georgia had concurred. Now he looked like a very troubled chocolate teddy bear. "Aurora Ballistic and Orbital can supply the primary vehicle, of course; but without Pegasus to do the mods . . ."

"That is why I have invited João to rejoin us," Mariesa said. "Daedalus Aerospace has the same capabilities as Pegasus."

João Pessoa, telepresent from Recife, bowed his head in acknowledgment. João had grown more gaunt during the intervening years—he did not look well—and his hair, though still tied in a ponytail, had lost its sooty black color. He dressed more formally than the others, wearing a light-colored tropical suit. "It would be best if Wallace sent his ship to our yards at Fortaleza. That would be simpler than bringing my people north."

Mariesa made a note. "We'll come to that issue presently. There will certainly be more than one ship. Considering the stakes, such an expedition cannot put all of its eggs in one basket. The next item is the stockpiling of pressure vessels to serve as fuel tanks and habitats for the rendezvous mission. Marcel?"

The Frenchman rubbed his hand over his mustache. "The production reports, they are in your deebies. The link is . . . thus." A hyperbutton appeared on everyone's flatscreen. Inevitably, some attendees clicked over to study the spreadsheets. "We have been building to the NASA specs for the Shuttle hydrogen tank, for the efficiencies of scale. We have two completed and two more are begun fabrication. I understand that Ham will do the internal fittings to convert them into living quarters." He glanced at the O&P president, who nodded.

"My program manager's been running design options past Solomon Dark's planning team," the construction boss said. "We expect to subcontract the detail work with Lock-Mar, Boeing, and the other players. But . . ." He hesitated fractionally. "The skinny is that the steering committee prefers the Salyut Gamma to our modified hydrogen tank. The Salyuts would be more cramped, of course, which cuts down on crew size; but they're also a lot less massive, which cuts down on fuel needs—"

"Sure," said Correy, "but you can't pack as many supplies. You'd have to rely on pod rendezvous."

"Well," said Mariesa, "that is a chance we will have to take."

Adam raised his hand. It was more a traffic cop's gesture than one asking permission to speak. "I don't see that," he said. "If Dark's team picks the Salyut design—and I can't think why they wouldn't; it's a proven one *and* it gives the Russians a role—then we'll be left with four honking big en-route habitats and no way to unload them."

"Something will turn up, Adam. If not the Damocles expedition, then later, for LEO installations. The orbital trade will revive and someone will want pre-fab housing . . ."

"At fire sale prices. Marcel—" Adam turned to Reynaud. "What financial state is NAPV in?"

Reynaud looked uncomfortable and did not meet Mariesa's eyes. "Not good. Our suppliers, but naturally, want the cash on delivery for their parts and materials; while we, in turn, receive no payment for our product. We stockpile the vessels, the fuel pods, and the quarters of living. But there is no customer."

"There will be," Mariesa insisted.

"Bottom line, Marcel," Adam insisted. His glance ran around the table, demanding eye contact of each one. "Everyone knows the economic situation. No one holds you to blame if NAPV goes in the pot."

Reynaud sighed and leaned back in his seat. He tossed his flatscreen and stylus to the table. "Bottom line? In three weeks, we will not meet the payroll. We must close down."

"Marcel!" Mariesa leaned forward over the table, as if to reach him. "The world is in crisis. We must all sacrifice."

A shrug. "Certainly. But can I ask my workmen to labor without the pay? Will the greengrocers fill their shopping baskets for nothing because they work for nothing? Will our suppliers donate the parts and materials we must have to build the fuel pods?"

"When the Planetary Defense Bonds are issued—"

Hamilton Pye snorted. "Which'll happen over McRobb's dead body."

"Then someone should shoot the son of a bitch," Correy said, "so we can get on with it."

Adam looked at him. "That isn't funny, even as a joke. McRobb wouldn't even reach room temperature before half the whackos in the country took to the hills. And that, on top of everything else, we do not need."

Chris stood up. "Mariesa, may I see you for a moment, outside?"

It wasn't quite an order. "A fifteen-minute break," she told the others; and they gathered up their organizers and left the room, cell phones and traceys already beeping. All but Marcel Reynaud, who remained seated, staring morosely at the table, and Adam, who closed up his portfolio with a snap.

"I'm meeting with Dr. Desphande and Dr. Hobart in an

hour," he announced. "These magnetic ships of theirs may be blue sky, but at least they're funded."

Mariesa watched him go, then followed Chris outside to the sitting area. "It was a mistake to invite Adam onto Prometheus," she said. "He doesn't have the proper attitude."

"You don't run VHI anymore, Riesey," Chris reminded her, "and soon enough, I won't either. So who will the Trust pick next?"

"I'm happy the two of you have reconciled; but—"

"Marianne left me over it, did you know that?" He held up his hand. "Oh, officially, it was just a short vacation; but that wasn't why I contacted Adam, why we started meeting. It was your asteroid."

" 'My' asteroid . . . ?"

"Yes. It made our quarrel seem very small and mean. Further estrangement seemed pointless. He and I haven't cleared the air completely, but he is back in the family business. Prometheus is using VHI resources and Adam feels an obligation to the owners. That includes you and me."

"I'll forgo a dividend check or two, if it means saving the world."

"You can forgo the sarcasm, too, while you're at it."

"Chris—" A rebuke died on her lips and instead she sank onto one of the padded benches that lined the walls outside the boardroom. How many of Chris's decisions from now on would be predicated on preserving the fragile peace between him and Adam and Marianne? She looked up and saw the portrait of Albert Henryk, primped up in periwig and wide-collared powder-blue coat. His was an age when men still emulated peacocks. By all accounts "Bertie" had been an amiable man, still the curl on his lips seemed to Mariesa to be one of contempt. "It's not the same, is it?"

Chris frowned. "What? What isn't the same?"

"Prometheus. The . . . joy isn't there. The sense of purpose. It all seems so frustrating."

Chris sat down beside her. "You're trying to do too much.

You can't save the whole wide world by yourself."

She covered her face with her hands, rubbed her eyes and sinuses. "I can try. Chris, we kick-started the whole space enterprise. You and me and Prometheus."

"Yes, but kick-start is all we did. There were other players. Wilson and his rams, for one. Our friends inside the government, at NASA and the Air Force. The Artemis group. The world was pregnant. We induced labor."

She looked at him and laid her hand on his forearm. "I thought . . . it would be like it was."

"You can't go back. Things were different then. It's a bigger game we're playing now. Contingency planning and stockpiling are fine, up to a point—and maybe NAPV *should* go to the mat for the larger good—but you can't go off your own way anymore and hope to drag the world with you."

Mariesa gave her cousin a thin smile. "I so detest being a bystander."

"Don't be." Chris clapped her on the shoulder. "Look. What is the most urgent problem facing Project Damocles?"

"The funding. Voluntary contributions are coming in, thanks to Roberta and the People's Crusades; but there is no systematic—"

"And what is the major obstacle to the funding?"

"McRobb."

"So, where should you concentrate your efforts? Building vessels that the Damocles expedition may or may not use, or . . . ?"

She laughed, but without humor. "I doubt I could persuade a man like McRobb."

Chris shrugged. "You can give it a shot; but even if you can't, so what? Go to the public. Go to his support base and cut him off at his roots. Make speeches. You're the Moon Lady, for crying out loud! People will listen to you."

"I am not very good at speeches. I become nervous and grow excessively grammatical."

"Enlist your friend Carson, then. She's a wordsmith, isn't

she? Make her your speechwriter. Who else are people going to listen to? Phil Albright is dead, more's the pity. Rutell . . . they boo him. Unfairly, in my opinion, but a fact is a fact. Dark . . . they don't know him. Who else is there?"

"Ned DuBois. Forrest Calhoun. Mikhail Krasnarov."

"Now you're thinking. Get enough celebrities stirring up the masses and who knows? Inundate McRobb with E-mail and phone calls and even he might perk up and take notice."

She could feel the rush. "I don't even need to reach him," Mariesa said. "Some of his congressmen won their seats by razor-thin pluralities in four-way races. You wouldn't need near as many E-mails to spook a few of them. Why . . . !" She stood up. Straightened her skirt. "Why, we might even turn Congress without him."

Terrance McRobb had grown up dirt-poor in the streets of Chicago and, in consequence, projected a rough-hewn and aggressive confidence. The system had flagged him for a life in Joliet, but he'd escaped the streets by grit and determination. That others failed to do the same he ascribed to *would* not rather than *could* not. He had built a political career on combating the misdeeds of the government and often joked that while he had once dealt with the juvenile authorities, he now dealt with juvenile authority.

In build, he was stocky with a shock of unruly hair halfway between brown and sandy. He had large hands—he'd worked the docks before moving into politics—and his bright hazel eyes peeked from under deceptively sleepy lids. Having absorbed an abiding suspicion of "the bosses" at his father's kitchen table, he had championed "Joe and Jane Sixpack" from his first day in Congress. The American Party, he declared at its founding a few years later, would be *their* party—the party of workers, long-forsaken by money-hungry politicos and their string-pullers. *"More interested in sipping cocktails with the high and mighty than hoisting a cold one with the hoi polloi."* McRobb had cultivated the habit of dropping in at neighborhood bars around the country to ask people their opinions. He didn't always win their agreement—indeed, some raucous give-and-take often developed—but he did win their respect.

As a public speaker, he used the full range of voices from stage whisper to shout, and had mastered the grandiose gesture, the rhetorical question, and . . . the dramatic pause. Bryan would have recognized him immediately; or Jackson or Huey Long. He was cast in their mold: a "Man of the People"—or a "Rabble-Rouser," depending on the spin. To a generation raised on script-written, blown-dry, smiling-slick media clones, his crude drama was nothing short of electrifying.

What Mariesa did not expect, when she met him in his office in the Rayburn Building, was that he was charming, as well. His smile revealed uneven teeth, but it was genuinely friendly; and his handshake was neither brusque nor challenging. He made her comfortable in the small conference room attached to his office and sent his assistant to fetch coffee—No! Tea for Mizz van Huyten. A clever touch that, to have researched her caffeine of preference; and more clever still to let her know it. Yet, his self-correction seemed unscripted.

"I apologize for the close quarters," he said, lowering his wide, solid body into a seat opposite her. "The dinosaurs diss me every chance they get; so they gave me this broom closet, even though I'm a party leader."

"I think it's because the offices were laid out with the expectation of only two parties. Thank you," she added to the young man who set the tea service before her. McRobb leaned across the table and poured a cup for her.

"Yeah?" As if that were a sudden new aspect to consider. "Could be, I guess. But we're working on that, too. Get back to two parties. Except"—with a deep chuckle—"maybe not the same two."

There were those who claimed that McRobb's goal encompassed even fewer parties than that, though they could point to nothing overt in the man's public statements to support their suspicions. Hidden agendas, his foes warned darkly. Odd, how the same man could gain a reputation for both crudity and foxlike subtlety. On the wall behind him, and just above his head, hung a framed epigram:

> *There is nothing more difficult to take in hand, more perilous to conduct, or more uncertain in its success, than to take the lead in the introduction of a new order of things.*
>
> *—Niccolò Machiavelli*

But perilous for whom, she wondered. Mariesa noticed how McRobb sat with the left side of his face turned slightly forward, displaying the scar he had kept from a botched assassination attempt three years before. ("Kept," since minor plastic surgery would have rendered it invisible.) The rumor mill called the attack a setup, but that carried Machiavelli to new heights. What sort of man offers his face to the knife for mere gesture? The assailant wasn't talking, having been killed on the instant by McRobb's bodyguards. If he had been a hireling, he had been an especially stupid one to expect his payoff in any other coin.

McRobb's smile broadened a fraction. "Surprised I don't have fangs?"

Caught in her appraisal of him, Mariesa replied coolly, "Fangs, I never expected. Horns and a tail, though, were distinct possibilities."

McRobb laughed. "Yeah. Well, the System makes you 'n' me enemies, but there's no reason we can't act decent. Man-to-man," he added provocatively.

My God, he's got a twinkle in his eye! "I didn't come here to discuss philosophies," she said, removing her gloves and setting her portfolio on the table.

"Too bad. We wouldn't accomplish nothing, but it's so

much fun to kick BS. So, what can I do you for?"

"I had hoped we could discuss the Planetary Defense Bonds . . ."

"Ah." He nodded, as if expectations had been confirmed. "Or—as I like to think of it—the Rich Dude Raid on the Treasury."

"Those same 'rich dudes' are risking their fortunes by underwriting the bond issue."

"Right. See you in the soup kitchen."

"Mr. McRobb—"

"Please. Terry." The spread of his arms was all-embracing. Innocence inviting familiarity.

She declined the invitation. "The Planetary Defense Committee does not understand why you are obstructing the enabling legislation. We have barely more than five years to impact, and each day lost is another day less prepared. Asteroid 2004AS"—she pulled the photographs and orbital plots from her portfolio and laid them on the table—"is large enough to cause substantial damage when it hits—"

"If it hits."

She studied his perfect composure for a moment. "The odds on impact," she said carefully, "are nineteen-to-one."

"The odds don't mean nothing," he replied, "if the fix is in."

Forbearance struggled with impatience. "What does that mean?"

McRobb lifted the photograph of the asteroid, the famous one taken in December of '16, that showed the plume of plasma erupting from the massive nozzle. "It's wonderful what they can do with computers these days," he said offhandedly. Then he waved his hand, as if swatting a fly. "I mean you people will pick the pockets of some gullible but patriotic Joes; spend part of it on flashy construction projects; pocket the rest; then announce in a few years that 'the danger has been averted.' Hip, hooray, calloo, callay! But who's going to ask if there ever was a real danger in the first place?"

His smile displayed the self-satisfaction of a man who knew hidden truths. Wink, wink; nudge, nudge: the genuflections of the modern gnostic.

"How can you be so certain the game is rigged?" she asked in genuine puzzlement. "Has every astronomer on the planet joined some vast conspiracy?"

"Not *every* astronomer," he pointed out. "Only those who depend on grants from the Establishment. But it's not a 'conspiracy,' Mariesa." The voice of sweet reason, sung in condescending tones. "Astronomers have to eat, too; so they'll say what they think their pointy-haired bosses want them to say. No one has to give them instructions. Least of all . . ." And again, he flashed that inviting grin. "Least of all, a secret cabal."

Someone had famously said that every noble cause—from feminism to family values—attracted its share of woo-woos. The same could be said of ignoble causes, where the woo-woos made the merely whacky seem wise, old heads in comparison. Yet, it was the essence, not the extremes, that really mattered. McRobb did not believe in anything so outré as black helicopters or trilateral councils of capitalists; but he was convinced that when bad things happened, it was because bad people made them happen.

And Mariesa knew that no matter how pleasantly he might host her, McRobb considered her one of the bad people. One day, she would have to be put down "for the good of Joe and Jane." Her pride formed a lump in her belly. "Terry," she said, forcing the familiarity, "take this as seriously meant. There *is* an asteroid coming toward the Earth. That asteroid was deliberately guided to hit us; so where there is one, there may be others. Our options are limited and our time is short. The common defense needs money to build the ships, to scan the skies, and mount other defenses—and to pay Joe and Jane for building them. The bond issue is designed to mobilize that money."

McRobb shook his head in admiration. "And they say that

I'm into conspiracy theories . . ." He placed his coffee cup on its saucer. "You really think aliens are running around the solar system throwing rocks at us? Why?"

"We don't know why. It may not even be deliberate. But accident or design make little difference to those of us living on the bull's-eye." Mariesa rose from her seat. You did not pull a stump by hammering on it. The goal was to unblock passage of the bond issue, not drag McRobb out of his personal Twilight Zone. "Promise me that you will look into the matter. Talk to the experts. But we must do something quickly, or hundreds of thousands of your 'Joes and Janes' could die . . . And then, who will the survivors hang?"

She left the office under the watchful escort of two bodyguards. Big men, with muscles verging on fat, they walked with tough-guy swagger rather than military precision. Long hair, the one in a ponytail. An intricate, serpentine tattoo on the other man's arm. Multiply-pierced ears. Mariesa could imagine them in biker's leather, but not in a soldier's uniform. An SA; not yet an SS. They made no overt move, but the aura of threat was there.

The taller one held the outer door open for her. "Thy days are numbered," he said as she passed him, "and the number is one hundred and forty-four."

"Don't you mean two hundred and two?" she answered sweetly, leaving him puzzled by the door. Let him figure it out. Pseudo-religious numerology . . . Besides, it was silly to quibble over January 3 versus the first Tuesday in November when the Number of the Beast was actually one thousand nine hundred and fifty.

And counting.

Who will the survivors hang?

Among others, herself. If McRobb went up the tree for impeding the defense; Mariesa would surely dangle beside him for instigating the crisis in the first place. At least, so certain callers and correspondents assured her, and there were times when she was not inclined to argue. The thought niggled at her, haunted her as badly as the thought of impact itself. She had called in Charlie Schwar's people to screen her mail and stand watch by her driveway.

"You can't keep this up without any rest," Solomon Dark told her.

Hunched over the papers, Mariesa looked up and squinted at him. The table was a pool of light in an otherwise darkened room in the Pentagon basement. The flock of government and industry aides had departed. Mariesa checked her tracey. Ten o'clock. There was a time when by ten o'clock she was just hitting speed, shuffling deals in the Asian markets while her competitors slept; bulking up VHI so it could take that first giant step the planet needed. "Just a little while longer," she said. "These project schedules . . ."

"You have staff to work those out, identify the critical paths, assign dates . . . All you have to do is authorize the resources."

Her eyes dropped to the PERT for the LEO refurbishment. A tangle of lines that stubbornly refused to make sense. They blurred suddenly and she closed her eyes, rubbing the bridge of her nose. Keith McReynolds used to tell her the same thing, back in the early days of Prometheus, chastising her for her urge to micromanage. *The conductor,* he had said, *need not play each instrument in the orchestra.* A wise man, one whose counsel she sorely missed. "More like marshaling the resources," she told Solomon. She felt like a cowboy on a roundup—chasing maverick capital and driving it into the corral. Too often, there was no margin to risk. Who was that financier who had helped underwrite the American Revolution? Morris? He had gone bankrupt and died in poverty and schoolchildren had forgotten his name. As the kids liked to say today, *You stone for that?* And the answer from far too many potential backers was, *Not very.*

And yet . . .

The Consortium members had all contributed. So had Caldero. Bennett and Ochs, venture capitalists who had helped underwrite the IPO for Leo Station. Most of LEO's erstwhile tenants had squinted at their P&Ls, bit down hard, and found either cash or kind to donate. Boeing Outfitters had supplied space suits and supplies. Roche, medical equipment. Motorola, communications gear. Even Bullock had kicked into the pot; and that was most astonishing of all. A personal check for five figures with no note or explanation. The Bean would fall on the just and the unjust alike; impending death made comrades of us all.

Mariesa folded the chart over. "I suppose you're right." She pressed her left hand to her temple to still a sudden, sharp pain there.

"Are you all right?" Dark asked her.

"Just a headache."

Dark sighed and sank into a seat beside her. "You have it easy. Tomorrow, I meet with the Joint Chiefs. Then with FEMA. Your friend Krish still can't pin down the impact site, so General Sapper says the Corps of Engineers doesn't know whether to duck left or right."

"With luck, it won't matter." On the wall, an orbital schematic showed the positions, dates, and delta-Vs that could nudge the Bean aside. Dark followed her gaze.

"We can't afford optimism." Was his tie loosened? Mariesa looked closer. It was. Just a little bit, as if the man were slowly unraveling. "Oh," he added as an afterthought, "I heard from Air Force Space Operations that your Argonaut Labs project is now officially *13th Deep Space Wing, Experimental.* They've even got their own patch. AFSO's assigning a colonel to take charge."

"I'm not sure that's wise. I know those people. They don't favor uniforms."

Dark shrugged. "So, it's a logo, not a patch. Eatinger knows he's been handed a civilian research project. He's an administrator, not a martinet. And no one's asking where the money came from."

He left the question open, but Mariesa did not fill him in. She wasn't sure herself where the funding had come from. The thought that Jimmy Poole might have orchestrated the "anonymous and untraceable donations" was somehow disturbing.

Mariesa left the paperwork on the table. There'd be time enough in the morning. She flipped open her notebook and scrolled down the next day's appointments. "Dinner?" she suggested.

"Sure. In or out?"

She hesitated fractionally. "In."

Dark nodded and pressed a button on the table. A Marine guard entered from the anteroom and stood at ease. "Any preferences, Mariesa?" She had none and Dark told the man to send an orderly to the cafeteria to "rustle up whatever's handy."

Mariesa watched the Marine's eyes scan the room, take in the orbital charts and photographs, the timelines and PERTs hanging on the wall. A war room, but not his kind of war. There'd be no heroic storming of beachheads in this conflict. The map on the wall showed the enemy's position and projected movements, but the strategies and tactics were alien to the Marine's training. *As useful as a cavalryman in a tank attack.*

When they were alone once more, Dark stood by the table with his arms folded. "Do you still get threatening calls?"

Mariesa made room on the table for the anticipated tray. She had no idea what sort of food would be available at this time of night. Nothing very palatable, she supposed. "Why do you ask?"

"You didn't want to go out."

"All the good places are closed, anyway."

"Is that an answer?"

Mariesa sighed and stood up—a trifle unsteadily. She braced herself for a moment against the table until the dizziness passed; then she walked to the pixwall, where the orbital chart glowed in soft colors. With her finger, she traced the asteroid's path. Around and around the sun, forever. Until something got in its way.

"I cannot blame them, in a way," Mariesa said. "The callers, I mean. Sometimes, I think they may be right. Had we not sent the probes out, the Bean might not have changed course." The Bean. Somehow that bit of slang from Roberta's speech had become the common coinage. Because it was less threatening a name than "The Rock"?

"Launching the probes was hardly your decision," Dark pointed out.

"I was one of the instigators." She folded her arms and turned to face him. "Sleeping dogs," she said, "and we had to go poke at them with a stick."

"It could have been a malfunction. The probes found two other altered asteroids. Neither of those have been launched at us."

"Maybe *those* were the ones that malfunctioned—they were thousands of years on standby—or maybe they just didn't have a good launch window."

"You can't blame yourself."

"Why not? Others do." Her laugh sounded strained. "Oh, God! My whole life I lived in fear of this; and here I've gone and brought it on us. Ironic, don't you think?" By the look Dark gave her, he didn't think it was funny, either. Odd, that, though she hardly knew the man—and knew the private man not at all—she could confess her fears to him. Was it *because* he was so aloof and impersonal?

Dark pushed away from the table and came to her side. For a moment, Mariesa thought he would put his arm around her or clap a hand on her shoulder. But he only stood beside her awkwardly, as if he knew he should make some comforting gesture, but was not quite sure what it should be.

"It's not the threats," she continued. "Mostly the messages are just venting fear and anger. It's the vilification. It's being unloved."

Strange, how that came out sounding more universal than she had meant it.

"Most people are reasonable," Dark assured her. "They know the Bean would have headed our way sooner or later. Ninety-nine percent of them don't think you're to blame."

"Which still leaves three million people on my case."

He burst into sputtering laughter, and after a moment, Mariesa joined him. "Solomon, are you married?"

"Once or twice," he admitted.

"Any children?"

"Two. They're in their twenties now. Law school and finance."

Mariesa shook her head slowly. "What sort of world will we leave them?"

A sharp rap on the door forestalled whatever response he might have made. "Must be dinner," he said and went to open it.

It wasn't dinner. A second Marine handed Dark a sealed envelope, waited for the receipt, and left. Dark broke the seal and pulled a flimsy out. Mariesa saw his face grow pale. He crumpled the message in his fist and half sat on the table, as if his legs would no longer support him.

"What is it?" she asked.

"Bolivar Array's found another one."

For a moment, the message did not register. Then a strange sense of unreality overwhelmed her and she seemed to float far away. "Another one . . ." she said. "Which one."

"No previous sighting." Dark's voice was tinny and distant. "It's a new one, Mariesa." He uncrumpled the message and read it again. "It's maybe three-quarters the size of the Bean. Estimated impact, thirteen months after the first."

Surreality faded slowly. The sheet she took from his hands was a jumble of letters and numbers. She couldn't focus on it. The pain in her temple intensified. "Why?" she said.

It was a rhetorical plea, not a request for information, but

Solomon Dark answered anyway. "Maybe it's a contingency plan, in case the first one misses."

"Maybe," Mariesa said, "we won't leave them any sort of world, at all."

6.

Maiden Flight

Chase Coughlin arrived early at Phoenix Spaceport because he liked to check out his bird before lifting it. Not that he knew jack about aerospace engineering, but he acted like he did; and often that was enough to keep the dust bunnies on their toes. He would show up while the ship was still in the prep building off to the side of the lift pads and he would do the walk-around and he would do the crawl-through and he would kick the tires. An i-dotter, the ground crew called him; but Chase figured it was his butt on the sharp end if the damn thing malfed, and that gave him a whole different perspective than it gave some dog mechanic going home to his bed.

Besides, this particular bird hadn't flown for a while. RS-84 *Hubert Latham,* Port Bristol, had been mothballed for a year, and everyone knew that idle time reduced reliability. The "dust and rust effect." Equipment could go silently bad and you never knew until you depended on it. Equipment was a lot like people that way. Now *Latham* had a fresh ablative coating and the defunct Kensington Aerospace logo had been painted over with the Planetary Defense Council globe. Just like new, the dogs told him.

Latham was Chkalov-class. Having flown both *Artie Smith* and *Bobbi Trout,* Chase knew the layout, which was good; but RSX-32 *Valeri Chkalov I* had augered in on its second test flight and no one to this day knew why, which was not so good.

Damn superstition, Chase thought while he checked the gimbals in the steering jets. The Chkalovs had been flying for a couple years before the Dip and no lurking design malf had ever popped. Something had gone wrong in flight test, but Chase didn't think it was the hardware. Poor ol' Jonesy had had a bad streak, that was all. Okay, one bad flight. But in this business, bad streaks didn't get much longer.

Richard Sung-yi, the flight engineer, showed up with his cliputer and sniffer about halfway through Chase's inspection. Chase approved of flight engineers in general; and of Sung-yi, in particular. F/Es weren't pilots; but they put their hide on the line, too. Sung-yi had the official system checklist, so Chase turned the bird over and left while the engineer powered up the on-boards to run the diagnostics.

The sun was just cutting the horizon. Not bright enough yet to call it daylight, but sufficient to pull shapes and textures out of the dying night. Overhead, the sky had lightened from black to purple and the stars seemed to glimmer now more brightly against it. A band of burnt umber lined the eastern hills. The world was painted all the colors of anticipation. It was his favorite time of day for a lift.

There were no waiting ships to weave among, what with the recession and the federal stand-down, but the driver conscientiously guided the scoot-buggy along the proper serpentine path marked with double yellow lines, skirting the empty launch pads. "Too goddam early in the day," the driver complained. Chase said nothing. Complaining was for losers. He'd be skybreaking again; that was all that mattered. They could invent a whole new time of day for it, and he'd still show up.

Choo-choo Honnycott was inside the pilot's lounge checking the manifest and he slapped a casual five with Chase without rising from his seat. Chase went horizontal on the leather couch. He'd pulled rank and called in favors to get this gig, and that was something he had once sworn he'd never do. But it felt good to be lifting again, and he wasn't sorry he'd done it.

"Cargo's starting to show up," Honnycott commented.

"What, they don't have a life? Lift isn't for four hours yet."

"*We're* here," Choo-choo pointed out.

"That's different. You're verifying the manifest and shit; and Rick's out there playing with the on-boards."

"And what are you doing?"

"Catching sack." He stretched out on the sofa and laid his gimme cap over his face. "I'm command pilot," he said through the cap. "That makes me God. Wake me up for the Ascension." A moment later, he lifted the cap. "Hey. Any bunnies in the cargo?"

Choo-choo shook his head. "All otters. Mostly senior level, but working below grade. They pulled rank, just like you 'n' me and Rick."

"Yeah?" Chase repositioned the cap. "They're nuts, too."

"Oh, wait. Almost forgot. Forrest Calhoun called. He's sending down a cadet; one of those that missed their training flights last year when the economy tanked."

Chase crushed the hat against his face. "Oh, great. Not just a bunny . . ."

". . . but a bunny on the flight deck," Chooch finished.

"Chooch, I swear, if this kid ralphs on me, he's out the 'lock."

"Couldn't you just flunk him?"

"Don't be a herbert. Too much paperwork, you do that."

When Chase and Choo-choo came out to the waiting area, they found Wesley Bensalem in charge of the construction crew. Chase grinned. "Hey, Rector! Long time, no see." Bensalem was a square-faced, solid man with iron-gray hair combed forward in the "Roman emperor" look that had been fashionable a few years before. His mouth was a slit and his eyes were hard and humorless. The skinny said that he had smiled only one time in his life and it had hurt his face so bad that he never tried it again. He glanced at Chase's purple coveralls and the "bursting sunrise" shoulder patch.

"You're with Aurora B&O, now." It wasn't a question. The Rector asked damn-few questions; and those he did, he generally already knew the answers.

Chase shrugged. When Pegasus Aerospace went belly up in the Dip, Aurora Ballistic and Orbital had bought up most of its assets, including senior pilots. "Not many gigs at Pegasus these days," he said. "But purple instead of red still feels wrong."

Bensalem, who wore the blue-black of Ossa & Pelion Heavy Construction, shrugged. "As long as my people have a good lift, you can fly buck-naked, for all I care."

Chase shook his head. "I couldn't do that to Chooch." He looked over the passengers in the gate area, nodded to those he knew, like Flaco Mercado and Bird Winfrey. The crew looked heavy on inspectors and technicians, which made sense. The mission objective was to verify Leo Station's condition after nearly a year of neglect. Like *Hubert Latham,* the orbital stations had been virtually abandoned during the Dip.

Chooch nudged him in the ribs. "Here comes our supercargo."

Chase didn't ask where because cries of "Babe alert!" and "Chica, chica!" and "Yolki-palki!" told him all he needed to know. The otters parted for a slim, black-eyed girl in the light blue coveralls of Glenn Academy. Short-cropped hair and skin of pure honey, she walked with fluid grace, ignoring the comments that bubbled in her wake.

"Ouch!" said Chase, biting a knuckle. "First the Rector; now the Erector."

Choo-choo was unimpressed. "Not my bandwidth, brother."

Chase rolled his eyes. "Great. I gotta worry about *you* coming on to me?"

"In your dreams."

"No way, Chooch. My dreams are headed this way."

The cadet approached them, glanced quickly at their sleeves, and held her hand out to Chase. "You'd be Captain Coughlin. Cadet Jacinta Rosario reporting for duty."

One of the otters said, "Report here, *a cuisle!* I'm havin' duties for you!" Rosario's throat darkened deliciously and her eyes narrowed.

"Permission to bust some chops, sir?"

Chase had noticed the silver apple pin—a pledged virgin—and sighed for lost opportunity. "Permission denied. Chop-busting is why we have the Rector along." A thumb identified the chop-buster-in-chief. "And this here's Choo-choo Honnycott, who you don't gotta worry about on account of he's bent. Rick Sung-yi you'll meet when we board." He checked his watch. "You just have time to slip into your Liquid Cooling Garment. Need any help with the spandex?" he added hopefully.

Rosario's face went very still. "No, sir," she said in a voice twelve degrees colder. Then, after a moment's hesitation, "Permission to ask a question?"

"You're a cadet. Questions are all you got."

"Why do we put on our LCGs groundside? I mean, I know it's SOP, but . . ."

"It's in case we got to suit up in orbit," Chase told her. "You ever try to pull on spandex in ziggy? Even the cargo is wearing their underwear."

Later, on the shuttle bus to the *Latham*, Choo-choo nudged him and whispered, "Still gonna throw her out the lock if she spews?"

"Nah. But maybe I gotta frisk her in case, you know, she has anything in her pockets that could bruise during acceleration . . ."

"Hey," said Choo-choo, "aren't you married or something?"

Chase slapped himself upside the head. "Damn! Now why'd you hafta go remind me?"

* * *

Chase watched Rosario prepare for lift and nodded silent approval. Forrest was turning out a good product these days. He liked the way Rosario had handled the wolf calls back in the gate area, too. She hadn't been flustered and she hadn't gone ballistic, but had let her mission commander know that she was not pleased at the reception; and Bensalem had passed that useful datum on to his crew.

Still—and Chase stole a sidelong glance at the cadet while she buckled into the jump seat—you couldn't really blame the guys for noticing a tasty treat like that.

Chooch cross-loaded the weather advisory onto Chase's screen. Heightened risk of solar storms—with a probability running out to four decimal places, as if STC-Weather actually knew what they were talking about. Probabilities didn't mean jack. It if happened, it happened. The only thing certain was that sunspots were on the uptick and storms would grow larger and more frequent until '22. At least this lift was entirely below the Van Allens, so it was unlikely they'd have to depend on the new hobartium shields that had been fitted.

Chase signed off the advisory with his stylus. What anyone thought his acknowledgment meant was a mystery to him. He imagined that, deep in the bowels of STC, some hapless clerk would shortly acknowledge Chase's acknowledgment of the original missive and pass it on for a superior's initials. What happened to it after that was anyone's guess.

The boards were green and Rick declared everything ready for lift.

"Y'know," Chase said. "My own cadet flight, back in '09, it was Forrest Calhoun himself that flew me up. Just me an' him. Those were Mark IIs back then. *Bleriot* class. Now here I am, a big-deal mentor."

"I wouldn't call it a 'big deal,' " Chooch supplied helpfully. "There are only four lifts going up this week: Leo, Europa, T-grad, and Goddard City. The Academy couldn't be choosy about pilot-instructors. Don't worry, cadet"—he twisted around in his seat—"if Chase here gives you any disinformation, I'll set you straight."

Chase laughed. "Chooch, you're the last person to go to for 'straight.' "

After chest-crushing acceleration gave way to free fall, Chase granted Rosario permission to unclip and float around the flight deck. It was a bunny's right to cavort, her first time in ziggy.

Rick and Choo-choo went through their checklists and reported everything nominal. Landing gear retracted. Fuel usage within tolerance. Pressure leakage below detection threshold. Number two engine had been a fraction of a second slow on the cutoff and launch vibration had messed the calibration on the number three attitude indicator; but nothing outside the envelope. Chase told Rick to run the standard and recalibrate the gyro before the flight engineer did it on his own. That was the secret to being mission commander.

He spun his seat until he was facing Rosario. *Latham*'s flight deck was arranged in a circle around the central companionway, with the copilot, pilot, and flight engineer stations at ten, twelve, and two o'clock. The fourth seat, at six, was for supercargo. It had readouts slaved to the other boards, but no live controls. Some junketeers—there had been the vice president two years back—expressed surprise that the crew did not face the nose of the ship. But the ship was VTOL. Under acceleration, the deck was a floor and the ship's nose was "up," not "forward." And under ziggy, there was no "up" or "forward" to speak of. There was no reason for "airplane thinking" to influence the layout.

"You may be a cadet," Chase warned Rosario, "but for this lift, you are also crew—and signing the articles means you got certain legal obligations. If STC raises the storm flag—they watch the sun's luminosity, which gives 'em a few minutes warning on the storm front—we yaw the ship to put the water tanks and the fuel train between us and the particle stream, and the flight engineer goes aft to make sure the man-lock below the passenger module is dogged. That's D, the shielded deck, which it don't do no good if you leave an aperture open. That'll be *your* job. Now, when you go aft, you'll find the hatch already dogged, because there's no one but experienced otters in the Rector's work gang and they know the drill. But you still go back and check, *because it's what you do*. Understand?"

The cadet nodded meekly, "I dog the hatch, but only *after* I check the cargo hold and make sure none of the passengers is back there rooting in his luggage for a comic book."

Chase grinned broadly and nudged Chooch. "Give the lady a see-gar. I was wondering if you'd pick up on that, Rosario. Your mama raised a smart gal."

Her answering smile died a-borning, but Chase didn't notice right away, so after putting one foot in it, he carefully planted the other. "After all, your parents sacrificed a lot to put you through Glenn Academy."

"The sisterhood paid for my education, sir," she said stiffly.

"Oh." Chase thought about it. "Did you lose your parents, then? That's—"

"I'd rather not discuss that. Sir."

Rick Sung-yi glanced over from his workstation. Honnycott remained intent on the commlink to STC. Neither said anything. This won't hunt, Chase told himself. "Just conversation."

"I'm on board for familiarization. My private life isn't relevant."

Actually, Chase thought it rather might be. He did not have a reputation for character insight; yet a mission commander learned something about people or he didn't stay mission commander for long. There were two Rosarios: Professional Rosario, who was eager and open, and Personal Rosario, who remained mute and uncommunicative. That could be a problem, because it wasn't easy to keep the professional and personal separate. He decided to let it lie for now. A crew didn't have to be bosom buddies to work together.

Although, speaking of bosoms . . .

Chase unbuckled and kicked himself out of his seat, floating to the center of the deck until he hovered over the companionway. "Cadet Rosario, you have crossed the New Equator. You are now in ziggy. Stand and receive."

The cadet, obviously confused, maneuvered herself into the centerline of the ship. Above her the ladder led to the auxiliary tanks and the nose lock. Beneath her feet, the gangway ran open all the way to E-deck and the airlock to the unpressurized fuel train. Half the nooboos who made orbit became nervous about standing over such a deep "well," but Rosario did not even glance down. Chase gave her mental points for poise.

He gripped her by the shoulders and kissed her three times. Once on each cheek and once full on the lips. He felt her stiffen and her hands pushed against his chest. When he released her, they each sailed backward toward their respective seats. Chase tucked and bent and landed sitting in the pilot's couch. Rosario, less practiced, bounced off the arm of hers. The glare she directed at Chase, shaded into puzzlement, then wariness. "Hazing ritual?"

Chooch Honnycott answered, "Initiation, actually. Welcome to ziggy." He wagged a thumb at Chase. "It was this dude who gave me the Three Kisses on my first flight, too."

"Yeah," said Chase, "but you enjoyed it."

Rosario visibly calmed herself. She dropped her eyes and concentrated on refastening her seat belt. When she looked up, she said, "That won't happen again."

Chase swallowed his natural reply—which was *Your loss*—and respected her dignity. "No," he said. "Of course not." He paused a moment before adding, "Haven't kissed Choo-choo since then, either."

The copilot, listening with half his attention, shook his head; then he perked up and touched a hand to his earphones.

"Recife STC says go for planar passage," he announced. "Next orbit."

Chase welcomed the change of topic. "I hate changing orbital plane. Sucks too much fuel." But a Phoenix lift meant an orbital inclination of thirty-three degrees while Leo Station spun in equatorial orbit, so there was no help for it. "Mr. Honnycott, mark your cue over Zulu passage and burn at ascending node."

"Aye. Start countdown over Greenwich meridian."

Choo-choo knew his job. Like Chase, he had been a mission commander on the Luna trade, snapping up pods launched by the catapults at Artemis and Selene. Chase quizzed the cadet about planar changes and burn schedules until he satisfied himself that she knew her textbooks.

"Why do we execute a Hohmann transfer to the target altitude *before* we execute the planar change?" he demanded.

"Sir," the cadet answered. "It takes more energy to turn when you're moving faster. The target altitude is higher, and therefore slower, than our present altitude. A planar change from Phoenix orbit to equatorial orbit needs a delta-V of, uh . . . fifty-two percent. It might as well be fifty-two percent of a smaller number. That way we use less propellant."

"A textbook answer. You pass; but textbooks aren't everything," Chase said. "We got us an Artificial Stupid on board named Clarence. Say hello, Clarence."

An exaggerated country-yokel voice responded. "Gol-lee, h-yuk."

"That's the limit of his conversational prowess. What he's got is a deeby full of orbital maneuvers: burn schedules, vectors, delta-Vs, and crap. Just before lift, Rick entered the fuel load from the SGS certification and the I_{sp} from the most recent static test fire on the engines. Clarence puts it all together, figures how much fuel each maneuver would need, and sets up a screen display so we can choose the best combination of fuel usage and passage time. Why don't you run the calculations for the rendezvous with Leo Station."

Chase wasn't herbie enough to trust her with the actual burn calculations—that was Rick's job—but he did let her work the problem in parallel to see how well she matched the flight engineer's figures. "When shifting to a Hohmann transfer orbit," he said, feeling as mentor an obligation to instruct, "we do a posigrade burn which lifts—"

"Which lifts all points on the orbit except the burn point," Rosario finished. "The burn point becomes the perigee of the Hohmann ellipse. When we coast up to apogee, we do another posigrade burn and that raises all the points again, including the original perigee, and we're in a new, higher circular orbit."

Chooch clapped his hands in a slow cadence that was not quite mocking, and even Rick turned his seat to stare at the girl, who flushed moderately darker. Chase covered his smile with a stern look. He held up the sleeve of his coverall. "Hey, Chooch, how many stripes you see here?"

"Looks like four," the copilot said, "though it beats me where you got 'em from."

"How many stripes the cadet got?"

"None that I can see."

"That's what I thought." He could see Rosario flushing under the sarcasm and cut to the main point. "Okay. We have to double our altitude. What delta-V do we need to enter and exit the transfer ellipse?"

Rosario fell silent and a frown creased her brow. "Double the altitude? Uh, sixteen and thirteen percent of prior velocity, respectively."

"Wrong."

She looked stricken and suddenly uncertain. "Okay, fifteen and a half. I rounded."

Chase shook his head. "That's not where you went wrong. It's fine to keep a few standard orbit changes in your head; but for something like this, you *always* look it up in the deeby. As a matter of fact . . ." He glanced sidelong at Chooch, who gave a single nod. "As a matter of fact, those delta-Vs were correct. Okay, people, let's get located. Rosario," he called out. "You're the navigator. Find me three GPS beacons. What's so funny?"

"Nothing." The sad smile faded as Personal Rosario, briefly pondering some bittersweet memory, went back into hiding. "I've got three fixes," she said after a moment. "Popcorn at seventeen-seven klicks; Bathtub at nineteen-three; and Mimosa at twenty-nine-ought." Chase glanced again at Choo-choo, who confirmed.

"Good enough," the copilot said. "I used Unicorn instead of Mimosa; but those are three good sitings."

"You pass, Rosario. Now which way is Aries, so we can get oriented on the J2000 coordinates?"

"Wouldn't it be easier to verify our location through Space Traffic Control?"

"Sure," said Chase, "and Choo-choo is doing that, even as we speak. But normally there are too many ships up for STC to do all the calculations. The burns are precalculated in the flight plan, but we still do a complete check to verify time and location. Sometimes launch doesn't place you in quite the right position and you gotta adjust the burn schedule."

He checked the ship's chronometer. "Everything entered and verified?" Chooch and Rick acknowledged and Chase flipped the intercom open. "Transfer orbit commencing in two minutes," he announced for the benefit of the passenger cabin. "If you ain't strapped in, grab somebody fat and hope it's *you* that lands on *him*. Wheezer Hottlemeyer forgot to strap in during a burn one time and now he's a stain on the aft bulkhead." Sung-yi told him the board showed all harnesses buckled. But the cargo were all otters and knew the drill. He'd had the devil's own time with that vice president. The man hadn't grasped that his importance didn't matter bean dip to Clarence. "Okay," Chase added for the ship's log, "committing to Hohmann burn." He entered his personal code on the burn board.

"Confirmed," the computer answered.

"Once we enter our GPS location and altitude," he told Rosario. "Clarence figures out the exact timing of the burn. The Artificial Stupid does all the work. What I do is abort if it don't go right."

"For which," said Chooch, "the natural sort is sufficient."

They set their chairs to reclined position, and when the kick came, it gave Chase the illusion that the nose of the ship was *up*. He listened to the complaints and creaks of the load-bearing structures, waiting for the one wrong note in the symphony. His seat vibrated from the acceleration, and his body integrated that datum, too. Engines not quite in balance, he thought, but not off enough to matter more than a little shaking around.

"Coming up on main engine shutdown," Sung-yi announced. A few beats later, he said, "Uh-oh."

Chase looked at Choo-choo. "Man, I *hate* it when he says stuff like that." He slapped the manual shutoff on the arm of the seat, but the engine rumble continued. Rick threw the gang-switch for Fuel Pump Shutdown and the engines starved black.

"We got yaw," Chooch supplied helpfully.

"Yeah, yeah, yeah." Chase hunkered forward from his seat and took the small, console-mounted joystick in his fingers, nudging it this way and that while he focused on the simulacrum in the attitude threedy tank and Chooch sang out rate of drift against a reference star. His world narrowed to the image. Fingers and joystick were one. He was the ship and the ship was him. It was during moments like this that Chase came fully alive. He knew he was in the zone when his inner ear began to react to the tumbling image. Just another nudge and . . .

"Attitude stabilized," Sung-yi announced.

"Zero drift," Choo-choo confirmed.

Chase released the vernier controls and slumped in his seat, drifting slightly within his harness. Chooch handed him a towelette and he wiped his face. "Goddam simulator practice sure comes in handy," he announced offhandedly.

"Now 'n' then," Honnycott agreed just as casually. They didn't quite look at each other.

"Well"—Chase clapped his hands together and rubbed them—"break's over. Situation?" The longer burn meant a longer transfer ellipse, reaching apogee above and behind the chase. But he needed numbers, not adjectives. The upcoming planar change was a fuel hog. If the overburn used too much, they could arrive at Leo Station's orbit, but out of synch with the station and its propellant tank farm. They'd have to scrub the mission, and Chase was far too aware of what was riding on this flight to relish the thought. Especially if the rumors were true and a second asteroid had been sighted. And there was always the small matter of his own reputation.

Rick told off the fuel remaining—dorsal and ventral tanks dry from takeoff and the starboard tank just under half empty. Chase nodded satisfaction. Not much under the flight plan nominal, thanks to Chooch's quick action on the pump switch. Enough for the planar change, if they timed it right. The steering jets were low, but held enough reserve for close approach and docking—if they didn't have to work out of another spin.

Chase rubbed a hand along his jaw, contemplating. Chooch threw the new orbit on the monitor. Yeah. Longer burn, higher apogee. They wouldn't synch with Leo Station this time around.

"I have three burn options," the bunny said, "to correct our orbit."

Chase spun his seat around and stared at her. "You what?"

It was Professional Rosario. She tucked her chin up just a little. "As soon as I realized we overburned, I queried the deeby and Clarence gave me a list of maneuver options from his library. What Mr. Sung-yi and Mr. Honnycott just said about our fuel and orbit eliminated all but three."

Chase gave her the Eye, but she didn't flinch. "Chooch?" he asked.

"Three options is what I get, too." He unbuckled himself and floated across the deck to the fourth station. A moment later, he said, "Same three." He and Chase exchanged glances. Chase said, "I think I'm in love."

"Not with me, I hope."

"You wish. Cadet, which of the three burns do you recommend?"

Rosario's face tightened and she pulled her lower lip in between her teeth. "Option B is do-able, but it leaves us low on fuel," she said after a moment or two. "Option A is fuel-conservative, but the transfer time's pretty long. You may not want to spend that many hours cooped up in here with Mr. Honnycott. I'd recommend Option C," she concluded.

"You're wrong," Chase said. "Now tell me why."

Rosario seemed nonplussed for a moment. Then her eyes lit. "Mr. Sung-yi, what the hell malfed back there?"

Chase nodded. "Very good, Rosario. Except, *I'm* the one who gives orders on the flight deck. Rick, what the hell malfed back there?"

"Already working on it," the F/E announced.

"Yeah," Chase continued to the cadet. "Until we know what went wrong, we can't commit to *any* of those options. If we burn a correction and an engine fails to cut off again, we'll overburn a second time. Stopping another spin would deplete out steering fuel. So—"

"Number five initiator valve failed open," Sung-yi announced.

"Yeah, I thought it sounded like just one engine. Fixable?"

"Lemme check the FMEA."

"We can fly with one engine dark," Chooch pointed out.

"Sure," Chase said. "But if Five went down because of a common-cause failure mode, we can't trust the other four, either. Same thing could happen." And Number *Two* had burned long on takeoff, he remembered. Just a little, but . . . "Get on the horn with STC and see what they think. Rick, can you waldo the main engines and do a visual?"

Sung-yi unshipped the virtch helmet from its lockdown. "I'll try."

"Don't try. Do."

Sung-yi paused. "Malf could be inside, you know. Command fault. There's a relay junction inside the engine room that the fault tree taps as a hi-prob cause." His fingernail indicated a line item on the Failure Modes and Effect Analysis, now displayed on his diagnostic screen.

Chase nodded. A command fault there could affect any of the five engines, at random. They weren't in deep doo-doo, yet; but he could catch a whiff of the odor. If the other initiator valves began sticking . . . A cutoff failure during landing would tip the ship over . . . But that wouldn't be a problem because a cutoff failure during the de-orbit retrograde burn would shed too much delta-V and they'd come down steep and tumbling and do a credible imitation of a meteor, complete with flaming through the atmosphere and punching a hole in the ground. Chase glanced at his copilot, who returned a grim look. Yeah, Chooch had thought it through, too. Chase unbuckled his harness. "I'll suit up and check the command circuits in the engine room. Start nitro purge and pressure reduction."

Sung-yi paused with his virtch helmet half raised. "Vacuum work in the engine room is a job for the engineer."

Engineers. Playing with the toys was all that mattered. Rick was a bean dude, but he probably didn't yet realize what had happened. Chase pointed to the virtch helmet. "I need you for the outside work, because you're the best teeper we got. And I need Chooch for navigation and making smoke with STC. That leaves me to do the vacuum work."

"You're the captain."

"That's why they pay me the big bucks."

Chooch looked up from his console. "Traipsing through the passenger module all duded up might get the otters upset."

"They're big boys. They can handle it. What about that nitro purge, Rick?"

The F/E set his virtch helmet in place and fastened his chin strap. "Check your boards. I started the prep cycle as soon as we malfed. I figured there was a good chance *somebody'd* have to EVAde."

Chase clapped him on the shoulder. "Good man. That's why I love you."

"Fickle," said Chooch.

The cadet also unbuckled and floated out of her seat. "Captain? If you don't want to upset the passengers, I can suit up, too, and you can tell them you're taking me aft for training."

"Not to mention you get some unscheduled suit time under your belt," Sung-yi commented. The virtch goggles covered his eyes. Chase couldn't read how good-humored the gibe was.

Rosario took a stance just this side of defiance. "I've had suit drill in the Academy's hypobaric chamber; and I've had forty hours in the Neutral Buoyancy Tank at the Academy. But if you don't think I can handle it, Captain, just take me through the passenger deck suited up to keep the cargo quiet and I'll wait by the airlock to the fuel bay."

Chase rubbed his jaw again. She sure as hell sounded confident. And Johnny Sedgwick's NBT training was the best you could get groundside. And what the heck. Sure, the engine room wasn't pressurized, but it wasn't like he was taking a bunny Outside. "Chooch," he said, "we got any, uh"—he checked out her figure—"size-A suit fittings?" Rosario nearly bounced across the flight deck and Chase had to stifle a reprimand. They were in a fairly serious situation, but, hell, if you couldn't enjoy yourself when the shit hit the fan, when could you?

In cross section, a Plank was much like a rugby ball, though one that was seventy feet on the long axis and fifty on the short. When you factored in the hull thickness, the conduits for air and other utilities, the storage lockers that lined every bulkhead—including the nominal floor and ceiling—plus the two large suit bins, the utility deck aft of the flight deck became a great deal smaller on the inside.

At least, it seemed so to Chase when he shared the space with the cadet. The Liquid Cooling Garments were spandex, which hugged the body's contours, and Rosario had rather more contours than most. Chase showed her where the breathing masks were stowed and helped her with the fittings. The more pure oxygen they breathed, the sooner the nitrogen would be purged from their blood. They had to bump and push by each other. Rosario tended to flinch at the contact, but by the time they were done, Chase was breathing hard and not just from ziggy.

Rosario indicated the space suit that was already spread-eagled in its rack. "Do you have to EVAde often?" she asked through her oxy-mask.

"Not very often." Chase anchored his Velcro slippers to a stay-put pad, opened the suit locker, and pulled out a small hard torso, which he and the cadet maneuvered into the second rack. Then he located the size-A fittings. "The SOP is you always keep one suit prepped and ready. Same reason we wear the LCGs. You never know when an unplanned EVAsion might come up."

One day, Chase knew, someone would have to wriggle into that suit without adequate prebreathing or depressurizing and the nitrogen would bubble through him while he did whatever desperate deed had compelled the move. And afterward, Delight Jackson or Styx Carson would sing a song about him.

A pure oxygen atmosphere would eliminate the possibility of the bends, but it would increase the chance of an uncontrollable fire. The new fabrics were supposed to be oxygen-impermeable; and fibrops and plastics had replaced most of what might once have caused a spark; but the lessons of Apollo One had been graven in stone.

Chase wondered if the cadet had thought ahead to de-orbit or landing. He glanced her way. She was pushing the inserts into her gloves and the inserts were pushing back. Well, you had to learn the right touch. A small knot wrinkled her forehead just above her nose. "Worried?" he asked.

She looked up from her task. "Should I be?"

An interesting response. He wasn't sure how much to tell her. He didn't want to terrify her with what, for now, were only possibilities. Time enough after they diagnosed the malf. Yet, she was cadeting for his job and if a bad scenario could scare her off, best that it happen now. "It's never routine," he said, postponing the moment. "Fear's no good—it paralyzes; but complacency's no better. They'll both kill you. So, worry. Yeah. Worry is a good strategy."

She gazed at him a moment longer before bending back to her task.

The Rector knew something was wrong. Chase could see that in the man's eyes as he led Rosario through the passenger module and gave the construction boss the yee-haw about training the cadet in vacuum suit techniques. Bensalem pursed his lips tight enough to draw wire. "You could have warned us," he said after a strained moment. "First I knew you were going de-press was when our ears began popping. And I suppose all that hokey-pokey earlier was your cadet learning the steering jet controls. Three guys needed their blow bags, which does not give this room a sweet perfume."

So Bensalem would play along. Chase couldn't tell if he bought the story; or simply bought that there was the need for a story.

Behind the passenger module, on the cargo deck, the otters' personal baggage and equipment were stowed in small numbered bins. Rosario paused at the airlock to the tank and engine modules. "If you want," she said, "I'll wait here."

Chase sighed. "Put your helmet on, Rosario. If an otter comes aft to rummage in his duffel for reading material and sees you hanging around out here, he might wonder about our cover story."

"Yes, sir." Rosario tried to look serious as she settled her helmet into place, but she couldn't hide the grin that broke through. She was young enough for the enthusiasm. Eighteen or nineteen, Chase guessed. He was almost twice her age. Had *he* been that twitchy the first time Forrest took him up? Probably. Some days, he felt freaking *old*.

The fuel train and engine room were not pressurized because they were not normally manned during flight. Chase remembered the storm warning and grew acutely conscious that they were aft of D-Deck. This was not a user-friendly part of the ship.

Facing aft, he could see the forward pressure walls of the four LOX tanks. The dorsal and ventral tanks were tangent to each other. Since the tanks were circular in cross section, this left two spaces between the outboard tanks and the dorsal-ventral pair. The passages were only wide enough for one otter in a suit, so the informal practice had evolved of going aft down the port opening and returning forward up the starboard. One of the ship's former masters had painted a Do Not Enter circle on the forward pressure wall of the number four LOX tank. Someone else had graffitoed number two with an arrow and an admonition, "This way, you twit!" Chase figured that two Kensington otters had once met halfway down the starboard passage, forcing one of them to wriggle out backward.

Chase led the cadet down the passage to the rear of the ship. When they emerged, he looked around to orient himself. The "engine room"—more of an open space between the tanks and the aft hull—was a maze of equipment: injectors, pumps, valves, conduit, fibrop relays for the activator switches, even blinking lights on control panels that no one would ever normally see. Well, he was here now; and no doubt the panels were there for that very reason. Just in case.

"We're in the engine room, Chooch," he told the flight deck.

"Roger that, Chase," the copilot replied. "STC says to de-orbit in two hours if we're not satisfied with the status of the equipment."

Chase pondered the tone of voice. "What do you say?"

A snort of derision in his earphones. "I'm not going to fire up those engines unless I know what they'll do. Whether we go for de-orbit or go for rendezvous is all same-o, same-o. Wait one . . . Rick says the remote module is entering the exhaust bell and is inspecting the injector nozzles from the outside. You might feel some vibration from Uncle Waldo banging around outside."

"I'm hip." Chase played his suit lights along the main bus. "Okay, bunny, look for anything that could block the cutoff signal from here"—he highlighted the main fibrop trunk—"to here." He played the light along the valve connectors for the five engines.

"Engineer here," Rick announced through the radio. "Confirm, the valve is stuck open. I can see it. The waldo's arm can't quite reach in there and unstick it; but . . ."

"But that doesn't make it not happen again, anyway. Right. Keep looking for any other visuals out there." As he traced the fibrops, Chase could feel the vibrations in the hull from Uncle Waldo. Rick was top-grade when it came to telepresenting; but Chase was sure he'd rather have done the vacuum work personally.

He suddenly realized he was alone. "Rosario!" he called over the suit-to-suit. "Location?"

"Here, Captain."

Now wasn't that something helpful to hear over a radio link? He was about to make a sarcastic comment when he noticed a blinking light coming from inside a mare's nest of conduits. Rosario was flashing her shoulder spotlight to mark her location. "Playing hide and seek?" he asked.

"No, sir. Just following the fibrops. It's a tight fit here, but I'm small enough to make it."

It was a violation of protocol. Never leave your partner without warning. He would ream Rosario later, however.

Right now, there was a job to do. "See anything?"

"No. Wait. Yes. Maybe."

"Are you *sure* about that?"

"Captain, can you come in here?"

Chase approached the opening. There was not enough space in the engine room to hop, so he had to pull himself along with handholds and footholds, each motion forward being checked by a countermotion. That was why work in ziggy was so tiring. All effort was doubled. The opening was not all that narrow, he saw, unless you were wearing a suit; otherwise . . . wide enough for a dog mechanic in his skivvies to access the equipment there. Suited, Chase could put his head inside, but his shoulders were a tight fit. There was Rosario, pointing toward her feet, close by Chase's face.

Following the gesture, he saw a fibrop bundle with several strands frayed and cracked. "Bingo!" he said. He turned on his suit camera and relayed the images to the flight deck. "Rick, take a gander. This is the . . . uh . . ."

"S-45-double ought-7-slash-72 fiber-optic harness," said Rick after a moment. "I see one line completely severed. Probably got frayed like the others, then parted from the vibrations during our burn. Two of the others look like they could go, too, the next burn."

"Fix?"

"Forget number five. We only need four engines. It'd take too long versus mission timing to replace the fibrop. The others you can field-repair, and we do the fixee-fixee after docking with Leo—when we don't have to worry about timing a rendezvous."

"Okay, Rick. You the Man. Rosario? I can't get in there. I'll hand you the materials and talk you through it." He pushed away from the cul-de-sac, jackknifed and retrieved the fibrop repair kit from his right leg pocket. He stuck his arm through the opening. The cadet took the kit from him and Chase stuck his head back inside.

"Duct tape?" he heard Rosario say. "We're going to fix a space ship with *duct tape*?"

"It's not 'duct tape.' It's a flexible, adhesive overwrap, rated for vacuum, cold, and radiation."

"It's cold-and-vacuum-resistant *duct tape*!"

"Laugh all you want, but we still gotta repair the fibrops."

One tiny little tube, smaller than a soda straw . . . It wasn't right for success to depend on something so inconsequential. Failure ought to be a grand affair. Dammit, a pilot ought to be able to depend on his own mojo and not be betrayed by his hardware. Technical malfs meant that failure was never quite something within your own control.

"How on earth did those cables get abraded anyway," he growled. Stupid, to float here with just his head sticking inside the work area; but he had to walk the cadet through the repairs. And wasn't *that* a piece of luck that he'd had someone as small as Rosario along. He'd have something to say when he filed his Squawk List, that was damn sure. Never put a malf where no one can reach it.

How "on earth," indeed . . . Under gravity, *those* fibrops would drape across *that* flange; so the scuffing and abrasion meant . . . "God damn!"

"Sir?" Rosario, having brushed the abraded section smooth on the first fibrop, paused before rubbing it against the epoxy swatches.

"No, carry on, Rosario. I just realized. Some herbie dust bunny with his thumb up his toot stepped up on that flange and crunched the fibrops against the edge with his goddam boot!" The Mark VII Planks were the cream of twenty-first-century technology—parameter engineering, robust design, simulator validation, micron machining, with failure modes analyzed and contingencies planned—and then you threw people into the mix; and people, you didn't buy to spec.

While Rosario mended the fibrops, Chase meditated upon the failings of groundlings in general. Maybe it was the gravity that made them so heavy-handed and clumsy . . .

"Done, Captain."

"Okay. Chooch, you in circuit? Give me a command check. Rick, tell me what Uncle Waldo sees."

"Fuel flow off. Number one initiator valve command open," said Chooch over the circuit.

"Confirmed," said Rick.

"Number one initiator valve command closed."

"Confirmed."

They worked their way down the checklist. Chase had Rosario shake the harness to make sure the repair held up under vibration. When they were done, there was only one task left.

"Number five is still stuck open," Choo-choo reminded them. "Maybe Rick can reach in there and jiggle it."

"No go," said Rick. "Waldo's finger isn't long enough."

He sounded offended. But then, no one ever thought Waldo would have to go inside an exhaust bell and jigger a valve by hand. One more thing to add to the Squawk List. Still, if they couldn't get the sucker to close, number five would fire and keep firing at the next burn.

Honnycott interrupted. "Emergency Response Team's prepping *Janet Bragg* groundside, in case we need a pickup," his copilot told him, "and Yvgeny Zaranovsky has the *Princess Shakhovskaya* moored at Tsiolkovskigrad. Soon as he can off-load his otters, he'll co-orbit with us. Two hours until rendezvous, either way."

"They can come by if they want to; but I plan to get my bird flying." Chase switched over to Rosario's channel. "Okay, Jacinta. Wriggle out of there and join me at the afterlock."

"Sir?"

"Which word didn't you understand? I'm going to have to EVAde and reach up into the bell with my own personal hand. SOP says I need a lifeline and a baby-sitter. You stone?"

Chase climbed his way through the piping to the access hatch in the center of the aft hull. It was not an airlock, since the engine module was kept at vacuum, but the crew called it the afterlock anyway. It was a simple lever-and-bolt arrangement and slid easily when Chase worked the mechanism.

The circular opening framed a starfield of infinite depth and impossible multitudes. On his right, a slice of Earth spread a luminous blue blanket. Chase was still for a moment at the sight. It was different from the view through the forward ports or the viewscreens. It was more immediate somehow; as if he could reach out and grab a fistful of glittering gems. Rosario came to his side and hesitated.

"Watch the first step," he said. "It's a doozy."

"You could fall a real long way." There was something approaching awe in her voice.

"Three hundred miles or so, as the crow falls. Atmospheric drag and Earth's gravity would pull you in. Here." He pulled cable off his belt reel. "Let's find a place to hook on. You, too. Rules say if I can't get back, you gotta haul me in, which means you gotta dog yourself down."

"Why wouldn't you be able to get back—"

"Do you really want a catalog?" he snapped impatiently. "Let's make this happen." He wrapped the end of the tether around a strut and clipped the end of the line. There really ought to be an eyebolt here, in case anyone had to go out the back door. He tested his own line, then Rosario's.

"Now. You Stay Here. Understand?"

"No offense, sir; but I don't think you can get inside the bell, either."

"I don't have time for an argument, Rosario. If we can't get the valve closed, the chamber will charge when we start the other engines and the radiant heat will ignite it."

"Captain. With the suit on, how wide are you at the shoulders? Wider than Uncle Waldo, I think. You won't be able to get far enough up the bell to reach the valve."

"I got long arms. If not, I can use the screwdriver to extend my reach. And besides . . ." He didn't want to say it because saying it made it real. "If the valve *is* stuck open, there's likely to be fuel and oxidizer vapors in the bell, from residuals left in the lines. If I make a spark with the screwdriver, it could ignite the fog and . . ." He paused, searching for the right words. "And I'd be exhausted."

Rosario's question was a while in coming. "So why are *you* volunteering?"

"I'm not volunteering. I'm the goddam captain."

"Which doesn't mean you do the job yourself. Which means you pick the crewman best suited." When Chase made no answer, she continued. "And—" A longer pause while the circuit hissed and crackled. Chase could hear the cadet swallow a deep breath before going on. Then, in a voice almost a plea, "And I'm the best choice for this job. I'm the smallest and the most expendable in the crew. I can fit up in there and maybe reach the valve without using the screwdriver."

"Rosario, no beautiful woman is expendable."

"That is a goddam sexist remark. Sir." The joke came out ragged; the laugh, a trifle forced.

"So, sue me." His response was equally strained.

Rosario twisted her head to look at Chase. Her face, obscured by the bright external helmet lights, seemed pale and drawn. "Ever since I came on board," she said, "I've wondered why you and Mr. Honnycott rag on each other so much. It's because it's always like this, isn't it? I mean, even when it's routine, it's always on the edge. So you crack jokes to—"

"I don't know what you mean," he growled. But he did. Forrest Calhoun had summed it up one time. *A million things have to work and work together and work all the time.* It wasn't a thought that bore dwelling on. It was easier to crack jokes.

Silence again, only this time a more peaceful sort. The decision had been made and there was a certain inevitability about the future, however it turned out. This was the nasty part, Chase decided. Sending someone else into risk, then standing by in safety. "All right," he said, opening the command channel. "Let's do it. Chooch? You have the conn."

Over the copilot's channel: "Chase, do you think . . . ?"

"I try not to. It upsets the digestion. Chooch, she's never been in the Big Empty before. I gotta go out with her."

"But if there *is* a fog, and it *does* ignite . . ."

"That's too many fucking 'ifs' to worry about."

Rick logged on. "Sounds to me," the flight engineer said, "like our cadet wangled herself a virgin EVA."

"She volunteered to stick her head up the ship's anus, which it may or may not fart. You stone for that, Rick?"

"In a New York minute." The engineer's voice held the absolute assurance of someone not actually faced with the task. Yet, bravery is more easily imagined than found. Chase had never thought of himself as particularly brave; only someone who had it to do.

"Yeah. Look. Rick. If we'd known up front it would come down to this, I'd've given you the gig; but—"

"Tell the counselor. Just . . . Shit, just be careful out there, okay? She may be a snot, but she's *our* snot."

"Sure. I'm in love with her, too. Out." He tugged again on the tethers, looked at Rosario, and—since you couldn't see nods clearly through the visors—curtsied. He stepped into the hole, giving himself a little push so he would float clear. The tether spun from its reel. He could feel the vibration through his suit. When he judged he had the right distance, he chocked it.

"Okay, Rosario. Your turn."

The cadet came out a little fast and jerked into a slow tumble when she chocked the reel, but she grabbed the tether in one hand on the first spin and stopped her motion with it. She hung free for a moment and Chase waited for her to compose herself. "All set?"

"It's . . . weird. The way everything looks. I can't decide if the ship is 'in front' of me or 'above' me or . . . It keeps shifting around, like those optical illusion drawings. I tilt my head 'up' and there's the Earth; but the Earth is 'below' us, isn't it?"

"Depends on your definition. Your brain can't make up its mind. It's easier if you keep your eyes fixed on the same object."

"Captain? Which engine is number five?" There was an edge in her voice; but only an edge. The afterlock opened in the center of the ship's stern, and the five engines circled it. To a bunny, they must all look the same. Chase, with his more practiced eye, noted the subtle asymmetries in the ship's configuration and picked out their destination with only a moment's pause.

"Check out Uncle Waldo. See where Rick's mobile is hanging out? Now, watch how you move. There are handholds in a couple of places. No, don't try to soar; because stopping isn't as easy as it sounds. You'll find that getting a grip or a foothold is more difficult, too. Keep in mind that you and the *Latham* are both *falling*."

They made their way carefully across the stern of the ship, pausing frequently. Rosario discovered how difficult it was to take steps. Her feet kept sliding away from her. In free fall, you could never actually *stand* on anything, and the least step could become a leap with only a moment's carelessness. Chase kept a firm grip on her tether, a wearying task, since he had to brace himself against each move. When they reached the bell of number five, Chase called a rest. No wonder Cernan had almost not made it back inside Gemini 9.

"The hardest part is coming up," he said over Rosario's protests. "Inside the bell it's relatively smooth. No handholds. So just relax and catch your breath. How's your visor?"

"Clear."

Chase could hear her breathing, harsh and ragged over the commlink. One part nervousness; one part fear; one part eagerness. Who knew what else was in the mixture? He glanced at the waldo floating in space and waved to it. Rick flexed its manipulator arm in acknowledgment. Split personality.

Rick was on the flight deck wearing a virtchat; but he was hanging back here with the away team, too.

"I never knew my father," Rosario said over the private suit-to-suit channel.

"What?" said Chase. "What was that?"

"Even my mother didn't know; because—not to gloss things over—there were so many possibilities to choose from. Likely, whoever it was, he stopped by only that one time. She might never even have caught his name."

Chase said nothing.

"There was a long succession of men, in and out. She called them 'boyfriends,' which when I was a little older struck me as absurdly coy. She always seemed upset when one stopped coming around; though it never took her long to find another. She didn't fool me with the 'boyfriend' talk. I don't know if she fooled herself or not. Sometimes they would . . . I still don't like to be touched.

"There was one man—Javier was his name—who actually did care about her. Maybe he only cared about having a woman he could show off like a Rolex; but he paid Mama more than the barest attention. Only, his plans, they didn't include any stepdaughters, you know. 'You ain't my blood, girl,' he said to me one time. 'You nothin' to me.' That was the night, under my blankets, listening to them argue in the next room, that I decided I didn't ever want to be nothing."

"I don't think you'll ever be that," Chase said gently.

"And you know what, Captain? Mama was never a very good mother . . . I had to dress myself from the time I was four, make my own lunches. As soon as she could get away with it, I was my own baby-sitter while she stepped out all primped up night after night with people she thought were her friends. She had no notion what to do with me besides shout or play—she wasn't much past childhood herself. So, I can't say she was much of a mother . . . But she gave up Javier because he wouldn't have me." She paused while her thoughts fled elsewhere. The glare of helmet lamps, hers and

Chase's, had made her visor a dark, impenetrable screen. "I didn't know it at the time. She was angry for days after Javier left, and she took some of that out on me. So, I left home and joined the silver apples. And Mama, she and I, we never had much to say to each other after that."

"That's tough breaks," Chase asked.

"I wrote her a letter last year when I heard about the asteroid coming and all; and she wrote back, and I wrote back again. That's how I found out about Javier; and that when she had to choose between us, she chose me."

"It must have busted her up when you walked out right after."

Chase regretted the comment the moment it left his lips; but there was no calling it back. Rosario was silent for a while. Something like that, the reminder had to hurt.

"Captain?" she said.

"Right here."

"If this doesn't go right . . . Mama and me, we were going to meet after this flight. I was planning to fly to New Jersey, and we would get together and we'd have dinner and . . . talk. So if things don't go right, would you . . ."

"You're setting me up for a blind date with your mother?"

Rosario sputtered into laughter. "No," she protested. "That's not—"

"Don't worry," he said, "you'll tell her yourself."

"I guess we better get this over with."

"Yeah, that's enough lollygagging." He switched back to the common channel. "Look, I figure you can get up the bell easier if Rick gives you a push. He's got jets. You hear that, Rick? You give Rosario a shove on her butt."

"That's a roger."

With only a little fuss and bother, he and Rick managed to stuff the cadet up the engine bell. After that, it was just hang around and wait. Chase wondered what sort of retrofit they would do on the Planks after this flight. The Rule was "If it happened once, it can happen twice." A longer arm on the repair waldo seemed logical. How had they decided on the original length, anyway?

"Okay, I'm in," Rosario reported. "Spotlight's on. I can see the valve."

"Turn on your camera so we can all watch. Rick, send her a picture showing the valve in closed position, so she knows what she's supposed to do."

"He already did, Captain. I have to push it to my left . . . if I can squeeze my gauntlet in there . . . Captain? There's frost on my visor."

"Fogging up?"

"Negative. It's on the outside. I think you were right about vapor in the combustion chamber from the open valve. I can see it on the bell walls, too. It looks like snow."

"Be careful, Rosario. Your cuff rings and elbow rings are metal. If you strike a spark—"

"I'll find out why they call it a combustion chamber. Right. Don't distract me."

The popper screen on Chase's visor wiped open and Chase saw Rosario's arm, extended toward the valve. Chase caught his lower lip between his teeth. Hell of a thing, to risk crew on something the waldo should have handled. The forefinger found purchase. He could see the gauntlet flex; but the valve didn't budge. Another try. He heard her grunt. Still nothing. Rosario was practically hissing; her breath coming through clenched teeth. "I felt it move, a little," she reported. "Once more . . ."

This time the grunt was more of a yell. And the valve clicked over to the off position. Chase could hear cheering through his flight deck link. From Rosario, an extended silence, broken only by her ragged breaths. Finally, she said, "Get me the hell out of here."

Later, after Rick had extracted her as neatly as a cork from a wine bottle, and she and Chase had slid out of their suits on the utility deck, Rosario threw her arms around Chase and clasped him tight. He could feel her arms, her legs, her whole body twitch, as muscles held long in tension found sudden relief. Despite the closeness, despite the feel of her body trembling against his, Chase felt nothing the least erotic in her embrace. She said nothing, and neither did he, but her breathing verged on sobs.

After a time, they parted—slowly and awkwardly, as if they had suddenly become strangers.

"You're wet," he said foolishly and unnecessarily as he tugged a towelette from the dispenser in the supply canister. Despite the LCG's best efforts, perspiration sheened like glass on her forehead and cheeks and the circle around the base of her neck where the garment did not cover. Small droplets had broken loose to float suspended in the air.

"I don't like to be touched," she said; but she made no move to take the towelette from his hand and after a moment Chase put his left hand behind her head to hold her steady and slowly patted her face and neck dry. When he was done, she returned the favor. Chase found this mutual grooming oddly erotic where the earlier tight embrace had not been.

Their faces hovered an inch apart, lips almost touching, and . . .

Chase teetered uncertainly over the abyss. Silence ran between them until, staring into her eyes, Chase realized with a frisson of self-awareness that *this was the woman,* and if the cadet were to give the least invitation he would succumb, and do so gladly.

But no signals passed. Parting after a moment, he turned away and sought his coveralls, dressing in fumbling haste. He pulled the zipper up, turned, and saw Rosario's eyes a-brim. Tears broke loose with each movement of her head. "Hey," he said, pulling another towelette, "you're crying."

She might not have known. It can sneak up like that, and exhaustion has its own command of the body. Chase reached out with the absorbent paper, but the moment had passed and Rosario took it from him and dried her own eyes. "I'm sorry," she said. She straightened her body and crossed her arms over her chest in an odd ritual gesture. Her lips moved as she recited something. Then, dry-eyed and composed, she turned to the flight deck hatch and undogged it.

"Rosario?" The cadet paused with the hatch open, about to push through, and gave him a questioning look.

"You pass."

7.

Honor

Ellis Harwood had been a friend of Phil Albright longer than almost anyone except Simon Fell. As such, he had a proprietary attitude toward Phil's legacy, the People's Crusades, and indeed, toward everything Phil had left behind, including Roberta and her child. He had entertained grave doubts about Phil's dalliance with "the Carson girl"—Roberta remembered the night when Phil had told her that—but ultimately, seeing what a boost it had given his old friend, Ellis came to tolerate her and even to see her as something more than another of those dedicated but naive compassion-groupies that walked into the Crusades and burned out after a month or a year. He was never quite affectionate, never avuncular. It was not in him to be that way. But he had become something approaching a friend.

He was a broad-shouldered man, with grizzled hair that peeked sometimes from the cleft of his open shirts. He preached a "muscular progressivism" and complained from time to time that the "good guys" seemed to attract all the wimps and weenies. Impatient with careful studies and position papers, he declared, like Phil and all his generation, that they ought to pursue goals because they were *right,* and not because some sociologist found a correlation coefficient of 0.20, significant at the eighty-five percent level. Boomers, in Roberta's opinion, too often confused "right" with "what I want," and her personal preference was to pursue goals that *worked*, though sometimes she longed for the absolute moral certainty that informed Phil and Ellis—and Mariesa.

By common but unspoken consent, Ellis had taken up the reins of the Crusades from Phil's hands. Yet, the young college footballer had become the old college professor, and he tended to lecture where Phil had inspired, and to give assignments where Phil had led. Donations had fallen off—no one cares to be lectured at, least of all people you are asking for money—and even some of the Cadre had drifted away. But it's the same message, Ellis sometimes said plaintively, as if it were the public's fault somehow that they did not listen to him as raptly as they had to Phil.

Roberta had always considered Ellis more than a little arrogant and egotistical, but she could not refrain from pity over the man's bewilderment. It was not given to every man to speak the words that stirred hearts. Phil had had that skill; McRobb, too, curse his guts. And Mariesa, to judge by the reception her recent speeches and webdresses had gotten. Perhaps, Roberta admitted to herself, even good, old Styxy could play the magic flute when the planets were properly aligned and the rats of Hamlin were in a dancin' mood. After all, she wrote most of those speeches Mariesa gave. But Ellis Harwood, good-hearted though he was, could be heard wagging an admonishing finger even when his hands were still.

Though she still lived in Washington, Roberta did not make it to Crusades' headquarters as often as in the past. She spent half her time at the Silverpond Nature Preserve, of which she was director, and half her time with the "Lucky Thirteenth," of which she was administrator. The other half of her time, she spent with Carson, helping him grow. And if that made three halves, it was a measure of how full to bursting her life had become.

You ought to come over more often, Ellis had told her once. *We really miss your talent for organization.* Translation: he needed an office manager, bad. Roberta felt sorry for him, she really did. All too often, progressives had their vision so firmly fixed on the future that they neglected the petty details of the present. Affect counted more than effect. Or, as Isaac Kohl used to say at the end of interminable Cadre meetings, Talk plus Action equals a Constant.

But what drew Ellis Harwood to Silverpond Nature Preserve in the hot July of '18 was nothing so quotidian as logging whistleblowers or balancing bank accounts or organizing a door-to-door.

The Dip had not much affected Silverpond. Nature had its own seasons, much like the economy—only in a more predictable rhythm. Fuzzy-knobbed fawns scampered along the margin of the meadow in the springtime without a thought to the Dow. The Queen Anne's lace filled the grass with billows of white when summer was high, heedless of the quarterly dividend. Hawk and mouse acted out their age-old dance despite the unemployment rate. As for the staff at the center, most were volunteers; and for those on salary the income had been steady. The drop in Crusades donations had slowed one funding conduit to a trickle, but the senior financing was from the Van Huyten Trust, and the Dip wasn't made that could dry that up.

Roberta showed Ellis around the grounds. He nodded over the scale-model diorama in what used to be the ballroom—trees and shrubs made cunningly from bits of stick and lichen, plaster of Paris simulating the swells of the land and the flank of Skunktown Mountain, real water driven by a silent "hush-pump" bubbled down a mock Runamuck Creek into a miniature Silverpond. Even tiny deer, driven by MEMS micromotors, gamboled on the lichen lawn. She led him through the exhibit rooms, with their pressed leaves and computer images; the four "succession" rooms that showed how different ecosystems followed one another after a burn-off;

the VR room, where you could watch the seasons roll past in quick-time, and zoom in or zoom out from the microscopic to a LEO lookdown. If Roberta enthused a little too much, it was because she felt genuine pride in what she had accomplished with Mariesa's gift. School trips from the local area were frequent, but the occasional charter bus pulled in from Pennsylvania or Connecticut and once even from Maryland.

Throughout the grand tour, Ellis nodded and said the right things. He patted little Carson on the head, like he was a pet; but Roberta put that down to his own childless life. She could tell, however, that there was something else gnawing at him; so she turned the front desk over to Roy, the field director, and took Ellis and Carson into the library, where she shut the door for privacy.

"Okay, Ellis, what is it?"

Harwood's countenance, none too cheerful on arrival, fell another notch. He walked the room, glanced cursorily out the windows on the meadow behind the mansion, ran a finger across one of the bookshelves. Roberta seated herself in one of the reading chairs and set Carson on her knee.

"I knew Terry McRobb a long time ago . . ." Ellis paused, scowled to himself, clasped his hands behind his back. "Even before his first election, when he was a union organizer. Phil, Simon and I, and Terry, and Solomon Dark and a few others that I've lost track of over the years. Phil and Simon had just started the Crusades. Hell, we were kids. Well, they were, anyway." He smiled faintly and an absent hand passed across his waning hair. "Terry wanted to clean up his local. They were all mobbed up back then. Goombas sucking off the pension fund . . . As long as I've known him, Terry wanted what was best for the workingman and -woman. Bad enough when your company doesn't give a shit—and most of them don't—but when your own union . . . So he wanted to take them down; but he didn't want to wind up floating in the Chicago River, either. He came to me, because I was teaching labor law back then, and I asked Phil and Simon to come out west and we rapped a bit and came up with a crusade."

Roberta bounced Carson gently on her knee—a horsey ride. She couldn't imagine Ellis "rapping" and thought the word must have meant something different in his generation. She wondered what his point was and how long he would take getting to it. "You never said you knew McRobb."

He grimaced. "I never mention my crazy aunt, either. We used to meet at Butch McGuire's down on Rush Street, banging pints of Ballantine Ale and dreaming up a better future than the one Nixon was laying down. Things were different then. We had hope, not irony. But the Terry McRobb I knew is dead. Seduced by the dark side . . . I don't know everything they did, he and Simon and the rest. I wasn't full-time in the Crusades yet. Simon set it up. I think they . . . planted evidence that made the goombas think they were shafting each other. Nothing that pointed to Terry, you see. The cops had been content to pocket their share and close one eye, but they couldn't ignore it when bodies started turning up. The Feds moved in and cleaned house and held supervised elections. We contributed enough to the Party's campaign chests to make sure the Reform slate won; and afterward Terry, he ran a clean local."

Carson wriggled. He wanted freedom. Roberta set him on the floor to totter and explore. A year old, she thought. Remarkable how fast the time went past. "Cut to the chase, Ellis. Why'd you trek up here?"

Ellis stopped his interminable pacing, fell silent for a while. Then, sighing, he sank into a soft, high-backed chair opposite Roberta. He rubbed the palms of his hand together. Back and forth. Back and forth. "I don't know where Terry went bad. He always had a suspicious bent and thought every setback was a countermove by the 'Establishment.' He saw agents provocateur everywhere. He began calling greens 'job-killers.' Well, okay; I could see that. But when he started blaming immigrants and foreign labor for every ill since Noah's Flood, it bothered me, a lot. He began to sound more and more like a . . . like a socialist Republican. Dammit, that's forbidden by Leviticus."

Roberta smiled. "Populist," she said.

"What? Yeah, I guess so. He's toned that down some, recently. Had to, if the American Party's to be anything but a footnote. Over in Europe, any single-interest whacko can corral enough dittoheads to get a slice of parliament; but here, you need a broad-based party to stand a chance, and there just aren't enough whackos on any one issue to let that happen. That's the genius of our system." He looked up at Roberta and drew a long breath. "Felix Lara called."

"Felix!" A short, tense man with a broad, darkly curled head and eyes that burned with an inner fire. When Phil had expelled Simon from the Crusades, Felix Lara and a few others had gone with him and formed the Direct Action Faction. For a while, they had played bad cop to Phil's good cop; but their actions had grown increasingly erratic, sliding from pickets and demonstrations, to bomb threats and stalkings, to assault and battery with paintballs and other nonlethal weapons, to direct sabotage. Last fall, a vice president at a logging company had died from injuries sustained in a nighttime beating. No one had proven the Faction's involvement, but it was widely assumed in the Movement, to the tune of much clucking and tsking and a few "we oughtas . . ."

Ellis nodded. "Felix told me . . . You know how the population growth people and the anti-immigrant people have been working together?"

Roberta nodded. " 'The world doesn't need another little brown baby in a mud hut,' " she quoted.

"Well, that's why Felix called me. After all, he was once a 'little brown baby' down in Chiapas. He says Simon and Terry are meeting."

Roberta sat up straighter. "What? Simon Fell and Terrance McRobb? Those two? That's oil and water."

Ellis shrugged. "Simon has drifted so far out on the left, and Terry so far on the right, that they may have met somewhere, in some dark, ugly antipodes of the mind. Felix wasn't entirely sure what they've been talking about—he thinks he's been deliberately cut out of the loop, another reason he called me—but they may be trying to sabotage Damocles."

"Damocles?" Roberta stood up. "I can't believe that! Simon may be a little extreme, but—"

"But a couple of asteroid whacks may topple our patriarchal, racist, materialist Western technology. Simon always had a problem with babies and bathwater. He used to wish for some disaster to send us back to the Stone Age. 'So we could live in our valleys,' he'd say, 'with our localism, our appropriate technology, our gardens, and our homemade religions. Close to nature and guilt-free, at last!' " Ellis shook his head. "That's where he and I butted heads. Try selling *that* program to the unions . . . Then he would back off and say that he was only describing a hypothetical ideal."

"Simon was never so herbie!"

"And Terry never believed every government action was part of a vast conspiracy." Ellis spread his hands, helpless, begging. "Sometimes, if you snuggle too deeply into your ideals, and wrap them around you like a blanket against the cold, they grow twisted. I only know what Felix told me. He thought they had already tried one bit of opportunistic sabotage—crushing some control relays on one of the orbiters last month."

"Why have you come to me? What can I do about it?" She waved her hands around the room, around the nature preserve, showing the vast magnitude of her power. Carson, misinterpreting, waved back. Roberta stepped across the room and scooped him up. Sabotage an SSTO? Madness!

"You know where I stand," Ellis said. "I was skeptical, at first, about the asteroid. But Darryl Blessing, he was solid, and he convinced me. Now, some people are saying it could miss us; and others are saying it's too small to do much damage except right where it hits; and others are saying most of the Earth's surface is water and there isn't anything *to* hit.

But a big public works project—building the ships and the solar power satellites and all—is just what we need to get employment back up to normal. Terry, for once in his life, is going against the workingman's interests."

A remarkable manifesto, Roberta thought. For the Planetary Defense Committee, building the civil defense projects and the battle lasers and the deep-space vessels were the means to an end. Ellis Harwood saw them as the end itself. "Okay," she said, "but . . ."

Ellis's eyes were unfocused. He seemed not to have heard her. "Phil and I, we had no idea what would happen when we began stirring the pot back in Chicago. But I think Simon did, and Terry. I think they *knew* there would be bodies."

"But I still don't know what you want *me* to do!" She nearly cried in her frustration. Carson, his arms around her neck, squeezed. Mommy was upset.

Ellis stood, too. "I keep forgetting. You didn't know them in the seventies. You don't have to struggle with memories of laughter and hope and comradeship and cold beers." He braced. "What you have to do—You're our rep on the PDC. What I just told you, I want you to tell Solomon Dark."

Roberta blinked in surprise. She rubbed Carson on his back and held him tight. "Solomon Dark? Why?"

Hands clenched tight, Ellis whispered, "Because, back in Chicago . . . I think he knew, too."

It wasn't easy, getting to see Solomon Dark. The People's Crusades was a member body of the North American Planetary Defense Committee, but neither Ellis nor Roberta were held in as high a regard as Phil had been. Still, like Harwood, Dark had been an old associate of Phil Albright and he found a few minutes on his busy schedule for his friend's widow.

A measure of how busy that schedule was could be seen in the meeting time. At ten in the evening, most government buildings were dark and abandoned. Yet, Dark's office on the southeast corner of the Executive Office Building glowed in the night. Only a short jaunt on the Blue Line from her home to the Farragut West station, yet Roberta emerged from the underground into another world, as if the Metro were one of those interplanetary transport devices Jimmy Poole liked to read about. This was a world not of snug row homes with postage-stamp yards, but of cold, monumental buildings. Aloof, indifferent architecture. This was not a neighborhood where people lived.

Not exactly true, she noticed as she hurried down Seventeenth. There were lights on in the White House, too. Second floor. Rutell, watching a late movie on the tube? Or worried sick over the responsibilities that history had dumped so unexpectedly in his lap? This was his 'hood. Problem was, there were no homies to share it. No next-door neighbors where he could walk over, kick some brewskies with his skillets, and bitch his troubles around.

She paused before entering the Executive Office Building to gaze at the sky. You couldn't see the Bean, of course. It was much too small and much too dim and, for the moment, much too far away. But there by the Washington Monument, only recently risen, was red Mars; and higher up and to the right, the brighter spark of Saturn. The night sky had never been anything more to her than a host of anonymous lights; but Chase was fascinated by it and would occasionally point out planets and stars when work at the Lucky Thirteenth took them into the evening. She remembered Mariesa lamenting one time that people did not know the names of the trees and flowers. Neither did they know the names of the stars and planets. There were those who did not know even the names of their own neighbors. It was a lonely and alienated world when nothing around you had a name. *That* was how names gave power. They connected you.

Solomon Dark showed signs of wear. Some of the sharp edges had rubbed off his facets. He was no longer seen of evenings in all the hot places, unless you counted this office as one; and while he was seldom less than perfectly dressed in public, as he had become more solitary, so he had become more casual. A sports jacket hung from a coat tree in the corner; a red tie with small blue spots was draped over it. His sleeves were rolled up, his eyes were tired and distant.

He was on the phone when she entered, but he waved his hand to indicate a leather chair beside his broad desk. "*Hai,*" he said to the phone. "*Takamiga sono* E-mail-*o-oyomi.*" He nodded. "*Wakarimasu.*" An attentive silence, then, "*Hai.*" He hung up the phone and rubbed a hand across his face, giving Roberta an apologetic smile. "It's the middle of the day over there," he explained. "Makes for a long workday here."

He came from behind the desk and took another chair beside her, next to a small table. There was a pot warmer on the table, with a coffeepot, but Roberta refused the offer when Dark made it. They passed a few moments in small talk. He asked how she was getting on and how little Carson was, and she told him a neighbor was baby-sitting, but she had a message for him from Ellis Harwood. Dark sat back puzzled and she could almost see him list and sort and discard possibilities; so she told him straight out everything Ellis had told her about McRobb and Simon.

Dark swiveled his chair and stared out the window, where the Washington Monument stood tall and brightly lit. "Simon Fell and Terry McRobb . . ." His voice was soft, his gaze distant, as if he were not seeing the obelisk, but something else much farther away. "Simon Fell and Terry McRobb," he said again. A smile curled his face, but there was no humor in it. He said nothing else for a long time, until Roberta silently rose, intending to slip away and leave him to whatever memories now occupied him. But he started at her movement and focused on her once more.

"Most people," he said, "don't believe in anything in particular. They go to work, raise their kids, fiddle at some hobby—maybe a boat, maybe woodworking, or tracking down ancestors. Maybe they read some popular novels or watch whatever's In on the threedy. But ideas?" He shook his head and his gaze turned once more to the window. "Opinions, sure. Everyone has opinions, and sometimes at the bar or the card club they can get pretty worked up over them. But *ideology* doesn't drive them. It's not why they get out of bed in the morning. But there are always those for whom the Great Abstraction *is* real and everything they see or hear they stuff into its procrustean bed. Some—call them idealists—are willing to die for the idea. The problem, Roberta, is that there are others—ideo*logues*—who are willing to kill for it." He turned and stared at her and slowly, in his basilisk gaze, she sank back down in her seat.

"Yet, I think," he continued, "a sense of kinship crosses the gulf of ideas, much like soldiers who face one another across no-man's-land. A feeling that they share something that others can never feel; that the enemy is, in some fashion, also one's brother. When you hold something dear, you expect to make sacrifices to achieve it; but sometimes the price . . . The price is something you never expected." His lips curled slightly into a wan smile. "You don't know what I'm talking about, do you?"

Roberta shook her head.

"Good."

Silence grew until Dark broke it by slapping both hands on his knees. "Well . . ." He rose from his desk and Roberta rose with him. Over his shoulder she could see the world map hanging on the wall. A bright, yellow band stretched in a great-circle arc across half the world, from Khartoum to Tulsa. The orbital plane of the Bean. East and west of the band, the asteroid would skim the Earth, skip off the atmosphere.

She pointed to the map. "I'd hate it if my portfolio was heavy into Azores real estate."

"What?" Dark turned to follow her pointing finger. "Oh. You aren't supposed to see that yet. That's just best guess stuff. The 'point estimate,' the statistical types call it. The rest of the band—north, south, east, west—is uncertainty. The 'interval estimate.' We don't have the plane pinned down exactly and we don't have the hour and minute of impact. Not until it comes back into the eastern sky and we can get more fixes."

"Still, I guess the Asiatic PDC is breathing a lot easier."

"There's a second one coming."

Roberta's heart faltered. She jerked her head to look at him. "A second one?"

"We've been tracking it for a while and confirmed it just last week." Dark's lips had settled into a thin line. "Who knows where that one will strike? And don't forget, these *things* have engines. They can shift trajectory. Guangdong and China and the rest are breathing, but not easy. And Roberta?" Stepping to the wall, he laid a finger on the track in mid-Atlantic. "Don't tell anyone about this estimate. Not yet. A mid-ocean strike . . . They might think there was no reason to prepare. Play into McRobb's hands. But if the asteroid is only a few hours behind where we think it is, and the Earth turns just a little bit more before it hits . . ." His finger ran left across the "interval estimate." Across New York, Pittsburgh, Columbus, St. Louis. He turned to look at her. "And even if it is the Azores, who are we to write them off? Do you want to be a citizen of a country that can stand idly by because it's *someone else* that's going to get whacked? I don't. Neither does Blaise. A country like that *deserves* an error in the estimate. What it doesn't deserve"—and he slapped the wall map with the flat of his hand in a sudden fit of uncontrolled anger—"are assholes who don't give a shit how many people die as long as they can validate their own ideas."

"Sol?" His face had closed down and his gaze was directed now, not at some distant vision, but inward toward something closer to hand. "Sol?" she said again. And this time, Dark blinked and looked her way. "Something I don't understand," she said. "Why did Ellis come to *me*? You and he were friends together in the old days, in Chicago." Chicago lay north of the risk zone. Old Town, the Loop, Diana's in Greektown, safe. Unless the L-waves from the impact made the ground ripple even that far off the track. "Why didn't he come straight to you?"

In two paces he was by her. His arms dangled and for a moment she thought he was about to embrace her and hold her tight against some horrid threat. But he only reached out to hold the door for her. "One thing you must know about Ellis," he said. "He likes to keep his distance. He can talk the talk, all right; but he always preferred the lectern to the street."

He eased her out the door and the last thing she saw before he closed it on her was that wall map with its impact zone glowing in fluorescent yellow. And she remembered afterward thinking, *What is it you hold most dear, Solomon?*

And at what price?

They also serve who only sit and shuffle.

There was nothing glamorous about Roberta's job at the 13th Deep Space Wing. It was mostly administrative and organizational. She juggled assignments, processed travel vouchers, arranged work schedules, approved purchase orders, sweet-talked subcontractors . . . She was constantly on the phone de-snaffing snafus or on the Net seining deebies. Billie Whistle had taught her to use an induction cap, but Roberta found the beanie irritating to wear, and besides a mouse was good enough for her.

Colonel Eatinger would sometimes comment that although he was commanding officer it was actually Roberta who ran the show. And only fair, because the whole operation, as blue-sky as it might be, was as much her child as was Carson. Hobie might have had the vision, but he could not have brought this collection of one-time slackers together in Building 400 at NASA's Goddard Spaceflight Center. "The Lucky Thirteenth," they all called it, flipping the bird at Fate.

Although it was a rare day when they actually all did come together. Jimmy Poole, his cheeseheads and code monkeys and script kiddies teeped in from half the states of the Union and five foreign countries. Hobie and Ladawan were on orbit more often than not, doping ceramic paste and drawing wire. Meat Tucker's crew was building the X-ship at Goddard City Free Port. Even the Principal Researchers on the subprojects were more likely to be at Lewis or Cal Tech or MIT as on the NASA campus in the rolling Maryland countryside.

In principle, Roberta could have teeped from home, as well. After all, the Thirteenth was a nexus of tasks and activities, not a physical plant. Yet, there was something symbolic in having a live human being at the zero coordinate; and it gave everyone a handy point to check into when they were in town. The facility had a day-care center just down the hill from Building 400, where Carson could play with other ankle biters. And the cafeteria was just as likely to be a spontaneous meeting hall as a refectory. When you came right down to it, it wasn't as *lonely* as teeping.

Chase Coughlin was on-site more often than anyone else in the unit because the magsail simulator was set up in one of the laboratories there: a full physical mock-up of the flight deck—at least as envisioned by the Rev. G prints. Every now and then, Chase identified an ergonomic issue or testing located a potential malf. The design team was saving up the changes for Rev. H.

Sometimes Roberta sat in the control booth while Billie Whistle thought scenarios at the system. Billie's software simulated the solar wind from models generated by the Solar Explorer team years before. The internal software, running off a second drive, simulated a sail with magnetic field properties derived from Hobie's latest tests. The simulated wind would impinge on the simulated sail and simulate lift. Jimmy Poole's evolving shiphandling A/S—growing and learning on the third system—would respond by adjusting simulated current in the loop or by reeling in or out on the simulated shrouds to torque the angle of attack. Chase liked to joke that he was the only element in the training that wasn't simulated. Jimmy said that could be fixed.

It all looked very high tech, until you realized that none of the models—not the wind, not the sail, not the navigational interface—was well understood. So the computerized version reacted the way theory said it ought to; but in the end, someone would have to take the real thing out and find the gap between theory and practice. And that was why, although Hobie could think his long thoughts and Jimmy could weave his intricate skeins of code, it was for Chase Coughlin, who had once squeezed her breasts in high school, that Roberta found the most empathy. Because when the time came, he would take it out. And maybe he would bring it back.

"No!" Uncle Waldo shouted. "Too close! You'll quench the loop!"

Roberta, standing with her arms crossed in the back of the control booth, noted on the monitor that it was Jimmy's link that had spoken; but she could have guessed that anyway.

"Sure," said Chase from the simulator room, "but *how* close?" He was concentrating on a screen readout somewhere above the optical pickup. His right hand nudged a lever forward. "Okay, babe," he said to Billie, "let's make it happen."

The cheesehead nodded and looked thoughtful. Menus extended and scrolled on her screens. Sometimes Billie—paralyzed below the waist, lacking most of one arm, head shaved the better to plant electrodes into their skull sockets—made Roberta profoundly uneasy, as if the woman were an alien creature. Scientists had learned to translate neural impulses into electronic images back in '99—Roberta remembered visiting the Cat's-Eye View web site—yet it still seemed strange that those same neural impulses could be translated into computer system commands.

But Billie had replaced the laser cup on her arm stump with some new sort of prosthetic, one that behaved remarkably like a natural arm and she was training its embedded neural net to respond to old commands for gripping and bending. It was as if she were being slowly reassembled . . .

"Current doesn't matter as much as loop radius," Jimmy said. "Run out the secondary sail and change the field shape."

"Stop twitching, herbert. Takes two hours to circularize a sail. I want to catch the wave."

"Real world, Chase, you'd get advance word of the wave from Helios Light."

"That's only half an hour lead time when you're eight hundred out from LEO. Time and tide, good buddy . . ."

"Quenched," announced the operator overseeing the sail simulation. "Zero field."

Everyone in the control room groaned, except Roberta. Billie Whistle said, "That'll do it for today." She began shutting down the sun, making her log entries.

"Great. Now gravity takes over," Jimmy said, "and you fall into the sun."

Chase shut down his panel, paying the waldo no attention. He worked his way down the checklist, just as if the simulator were a functional " 'chine." *It's never just "pretend,"* he had told Roberta one time. *Never just a computer game.* Roberta couldn't tell if that was prudence talking, or habit. Or just method acting.

Or maybe an offhand put-down of Jimmy Poole.

Roberta went to the simulator room to wait for Chase. "I *told* you," Jimmy Poole's voice was saying as she stepped inside the simulated flight deck, "that you were too close to the quenching current."

Finally, Chase slapped his cliputer on the copilot's chair and put his hands on his hips—a curiously feminine gesture, Roberta thought. "Your job," he told the empty air, "is to make sure the navigational software does what the pilot expects. It's *not* to make piloting decisions."

"Into the sun," Jimmy pointed out.

"That's the point of running sims, herbert. You gotta poke the edges of the envelope. Besides, why'd your software even *let* me max the current past the quench point?"

You could tell Jimmy Poole that he was a fat dweeb, Roberta thought, and he would regard it as nothing more than a rhetorical flourish. You could tell him that his wife was chubby and his son had Dumbo's ears, and he would consider it a matter of "different strokes." But tell him that his code was faulty, and that was a slap in the face.

"Because," the teeper explained in the measured tones reserved for children and the slow of wit, "*pilots* insist on having a manual override, because they *think* they can think faster than a neural net. Or because they always have to show how big their cock is."

Chase scratched his chin and frowned in thought. "Tell you what, Jimmy. Why don't you fly out here and we'll run a test to see which is bigger: my cock or your mouth."

Roberta didn't think there was anything in the world that could shut Jimmy Poole up once he got rolling; but Chase proved her wrong. She and Chase left the simulator before Jimmy could think of a reply and walked together down the long corridor of the space physics building. Most of the office doors were open and Roberta waved to Yoji and Charles and the other researchers as they walked past.

"He's right, you know," she told Chase.

Chase shrugged. "He's always right. Plus, he always gotta let you know it. Drives me crazy. Always has."

"I don't think he likes you, either."

"That tears me up. I'm weeping."

"Is it smart to honk your programmer like that?"

"You mean, would the little weenie bogey the cheese so I do drop into the sun? Not a chance. The guy takes too much pride in his work to release a defective product. He don't gotta love me. He only gotta love himself. Which he is very good at, seeing no one else wants the job."

She held the door open for him and they walked down the steps to ground level. "He has his good points."

"Then he oughta let 'em show." They followed the path to

the cafeteria. Chase shoved his hands into his jeans pockets. "Yeah, I know. I'm no prize, either."

"It's not that, Chase . . . I'd rather everyone on the team got along. Things go smoother if everyone gives everyone else their space."

"You want me to swallow my pride."

"I'm not asking you to kiss him—"

"And a good thing, too."

"—But cut him some slack. He's a key player on this team; just as you are. The rest of us—Ladawan, Billie, the colonel, me, Meat and his crew—we're all replaceable. But we need Hobie and we need you and we need Jimmy to make this thing work."

"You need Jimmy's money."

Roberta grabbed Chase by the sleeve and jerked him to a stop. She pushed him in the chest and he staggered a step backward. "You're damn right, we need his money." Another shove. "Otherwise, the hotshot pilot doesn't get paid." A third shove and Chase was off the path and in the grass. "And the magsail doesn't fly and maybe we miss the extra shot we might need to reach the Bean. *Comprendez-vous?*"

"Hey," said Chase. "Easy. Message received. Coddle the weenie. Yes, ma'am!" He saluted. "I just wish he wouldn't always point out everyone else's mistakes."

"Everyone needs a hobby. Besides, your life may someday depend on him pointing out a mistake."

"Sure, but he doesn't have to *enjoy* it."

"Look. 'Just Do It.' Okay?"

"Yeah. But I won't go down on my knees to him. Back in school, he came on so know-it-all that it drove me up the wall. I never had the words to argue back, so I used my fists . . ." He balled his hands and turned them this way and that, studying them. He looked at Roberta. "Not proud of it. It's what I learned from Dad, you know. But, Jesus, if he'd've been in the room just now I might have waled on him. You know what I mean? Just for old times' sake."

"He can come through," Roberta pointed out. "Didn't he do the seat-of-the-pants flight programming for you and Ned when you barnstormed the Moon back in '09? And the *flocker* debug during the Skopje Rescue in '10 . . ."

"Sure," said Chase. "As long as helping means showing how clever he is." He fell silent for a while and they resumed their slow walk toward the cafeteria. "You know," he said as they crossed the parking lot, "no offense, Roberta, but whether this project flies or not, there'll be regular ships that go out to meet the Bean; and there aren't many dudes with deep space time. Calhoun and Krasnarov, they're too old; so they'll be looking at us lunar pilots, and Karen and Li'l Chase'll be waving bye-bye no matter what. What I'm trying to say is that I'm down with you not because it's a chance to get my name in the books. Hell, my name's already there. But I think you and Hobie are right. If it gives us a wider margin, it's worth trying." He colored slightly. "Not that I'm a hero or nothing . . ."

Roberta laid a hand on his arm. "I know."

"It's just that I could be risking my neck out there and S. James Poole acts as if this were one big computer game."

"It's how he thinks," Roberta pointed out. "When your only tool's a hammer, every problem looks like a nail. The Lucky Thirteenth isn't just about flying hot 'chines, either."

She had thought that Chase might take offense at that; but instead he laughed. He was inherently a man of the moment and it took little to restore his wonted humor. Chase in a rare talkative mode was quite capable of yakking Jimmy Poole under the table, though Roberta forbore from pointing this out; but his tales were also inherently more interesting and he tended to make himself the butt more often than not. Roberta didn't know whether this was a genuine humility, or a persona he had assumed because this was, by God, how test pilots behaved. And yet, what did that signify? One's thoughts shaped one's words and actions, but also in large measure words and actions shaped one's thoughts. The ur-

Chase was not a boy worth knowing. Had he grown toward his natural bent, he would have become a man to prudently avoid.

Certainly, Styx had felt that way. She had imagined Chase-then as a pair of hands with legs and hormonal urges, and found his occasional "accidental" touches repugnant. Now, she found she rather enjoyed his company. Not that he had become a soul mate of any sort. He was far too lighthearted for that and lacked the faculty of introspection; so there were fields on which they could never meet. Yet, he was pleasant and possessed of a ribald wit that she found a welcome respite from the arch and subtle—and often malicious—humor of her literary peers. He still touched, but his hands were more innocent—brief hugs or a friendly arm around the shoulder, shared with both male and female companions. Finding words a difficult thing, he used his own way of connecting.

After dinner, they crossed to the day-care center, so Roberta could pick up Carson. Chase tickled the boy under the chin and spoke to him man-to-man. On the way back, he used the opportunity to talk about his own son, named (inevitably) after himself. Layered between the brags, Roberta heard genuine affection and tenderness, that special bond that developed only between fathers and their sons, different in kind, if not in depth, from that between herself and Carson.

"It tears me up sometimes," he said in a rare moment of revelation, "when I have to be away from the little guy. Like on a flight. But it's important to be the kind of man he can look up to. A guy who does what he has to do and does it the best he can. I seen what happens," he added, "when it's the other way."

"You must have had some bad moments on your flight last month."

He flashed her a wary look. "What do you know about that?"

"Oh . . ." She waved her hand in the air. "I talk to people."

"Yeah? I don't. Not when I been told not to."

Told by whom, she wondered. "There was more went down than training that cadet."

"If you say so, Styxy."

"Way I heard it, some control wires got severed and you *had* to EVAde to fix them. Wasn't just a training exercise."

"Someone has a big mouth." He stopped and put a hand on her shoulder. "Look, Styxy. I mean, Roberta. People gotta have faith we can do what we're trying to do. There are always fuck-ups, but you can't make a big deal out of them. Blow 'em outta proportion, people could lose hope. You hear what I'm saying? Something heavy going down, there's only three things you can do. Cry for help. Cringe and stick your head in the sand. Or brace yourself and face it head-on. Now I got nothing against praying for help. Mom was a churchgoer, and I've offered up a prayer or two myself now 'n' then. But God helps those who help themselves, right? You and me, we both know there's a lot of people out there who'd just as soon throw in the towel and party down till the Bean squats 'em flat. You hear what I'm saying?"

Roberta not only heard what he said, but she heard things he hadn't said. Chase had been told not to talk about "the malf," but he hadn't been told that it was sabotage.

Chase's flight had been the only one to deviate from profile, and the official explanation—cadet training—had sounded thin, since cadets had ridden on all four flights. And how would Felix Lara have overheard Simon Fell talking about "crushing some control relays" unless Simon knew about the malf on board *Latham*? Chase's response was the next best thing to confirmation of Ellis's information, and that meant it had to be the true quill.

Chase dropped them off at the Greenbelt Metro station and she rode the Green Line into D.C., where she changed to the Blue Line. She wondered if she should call Solomon Dark and tell him. But then she realized that it had most likely been Dark who put the lid on Chase and the others. That was before Ellis came bearing tales. Which meant either Dark really didn't want discouraging stories spread about—or that he had suspected sabotage from the very first.

Two weeks later, a drunk driver forced the Honorable Terrance McRobb (A, Ill.) off the ramp where the Dan Ryan met the Eisenhower, and the leader of the American Party landed in Northwest Memorial with a tube up his nose.

A week after that, Simon Fell died when a device he was preparing exploded prematurely.

And a week after that, Ellis Harwood placed a bullet through the soft part of his mouth and made an ungodly mess of it.

And Roberta Carson, reading the news, realized what the price was that Solomon Dark was willing to pay.

8.

Neither Day nor Hour

Mariesa van Huyten hated to fly. It was bad enough in a jetliner, where she could pretend that the plane coasted just above a soft, fluffy surface of cotton and she could, if need be, sit in the center, well away from the windows. In a small plane, it was worse. And it was in small planes that Charley Jim Ffolkes would take her in and out of the equally small, private airfield atop Jugtown Mountain. Though closer to the ground than jetliners, such flights seemed paradoxically higher. Perhaps because she could see scale-model towns below, not cloud layers or abstract geometries of light and color, and this drove home to her hindbrain how high up she really was.

And yet, she could conquer fears when the need arose; or, if not conquer, suppress. Sometimes, she could immerse herself in her work and forget where she was; but for the most part, her hands gripped the armrests with fierce determination and a series of nervous jokes.

She could make her speeches and commercials and web site interactions from the comfort of her home at Ridgeview. Heimdall Communications had set up a mini-studio in an unused bedroom. But such videos had a tendency to look like videos shot in one's spare bedroom; so more often she had a car drive her to the A/V facilities at VHI or even into the City and one of the major studios. She reached more people that way, to measure by viewer counts and web hits; but viewers were passive and surfers detached. For pumping up the blood, her producer told her, there was nothing like an old-fashioned live rally.

And so, she flew about the country, making personal appearances: on local talk shows, in stadiums, in public parks and squares. An exhausting schedule that often left her numb and confused in generic hotel rooms puzzling out the name of the city outside the window. Headaches had become a nearly constant companion, and she consumed several bottles of aspirin in a month. Once, her MicroMotion implant signaled its network, which summoned a nearby neurosurgeon over his tracey and it took all of Mariesa's powers of persuasion to convince the earnest young man that it was only a migraine brought on by jet lag and the stress of travel.

Heimdall Communication's advance team would set things up for her. They laid out schedules, hired venues, engaged entertainers, built the temporary stages and bleachers. Sometimes Mariesa spoke alone, but usually she shared the billing with other celebrities she had recruited. Athletes like "Lightspeed" Bikolu or Nancy Hughes: entertainers like Yoli Nemensky or Bond & Seal. There were governors and mayors, congressmen, a few lofty senators. Mostly diehard Democrats and Republicans, she noted. Once, she shared a stage with Azim Thomas, one of "her" children. Though most of the audience had forgotten his fifteen minutes of fame, Azim made a splendid appearance in his dress blues with the medal of honor draped around his neck.

Patsy al-Zoubaidy, her producer, had deliberately targeted towns in American Party swing districts. A good turnout there, she said, might shake loose a congressional vote or two. And, indeed, after the first few rallies, Mariesa was startled to find Tom Gaythwaite, a pillar of the local Party, sharing an uneasy hour with her on a Gary, Indiana, stage. His speech was supportive, though tepid, and Mariesa could tell that he still regarded Damocles as largely a government stunt. Yet, he could count rally attendance as well as votes, and his taste of Washington had been savory enough that he wanted to lap up more. Thus does power corrupt. Mariesa wasn't sure whether she was glad for his reluctant fellow-traveling or sad over his loss of innocence; and by his countenance, Gaythwaite wasn't sure, either.

In Denver, she spoke from a stage on the back side of the Museum of Natural History. A wood and aluminum affair, it creaked alarmingly when she climbed the steps. But it was a grand vista, with the park spread out before her and the towers of Denver glittering in the crystal air behind it, and behind those the grander, white-capped towers God had built rising into the sky. A thin, ocher band hovered in the air over the downtown, the dust kicked up by a million feet in a semi-arid bowl valley. It had been worse in the old days, the mayor assured her, before electrics had come into widespread use; and the new Baleen aerogel filters were now cleaning up the residue.

The other speakers this time were, for the most part, the usual Important Strangers. Mariesa smiled and shook hands down the line. Behind the stage, a giant banner hung on the museum's facade: Earth encircled by mythic figures. John Bull, La Belle France. The Bear That Walks Like a Man; a Zulu warrior brandishing an assegai; a long, frilled, snakelike dragon breathing laser beams; Ali Baba strewing sparkling magic lights along High Earth Orbit; and others as well. In the center, Lady Liberty stood with her shield up and her spear poised for throwing. In the right background, a fleet of angry, defiant ships soared outbound while, on the left, a string of Conestoga wagons did the same. Across the top, the old motto that was fast becoming the world's: *Ils ne passeront pas!* They shall not pass.

Mariesa found Ned DuBois near the end of the row of chairs and she negotiated a change of seat with a congressman in order to sit beside him. Ned slouched, with his legs stuck out and his arms crossed. He seemed to be asleep. Mariesa touched him on the arm.

"Ned, it's good to see you again."

He grunted and opened one inquiring eye. "Good to be seen," he said. They shook hands and Mariesa offered her cheek to be kissed. Down on the sward, a roller band was finishing its set and the lead singer thanked his audience and told them "the speechifying" was about to start. Mariesa expected the younger crowd to drift away—they had come for the music—and she was pleasantly surprised when most of them stayed to listen. "Maybe there's hope for the future," she told Ned, pointing them out.

"There's always hope," he said. "Sometimes, there's not much else."

"Congratulations, by the way. Solomon told me you've been named to the manpower committee for FarTrip II."

Ned grimaced. "Yah. Me and a couple of other high-profile Old Farts. We get to pick the kids who'll go out on the flight each of us would give a testicle to take ourselves."

"A testicle? My." Mariesa was used to Ned's ways and could no longer be shocked. "Surely, a great sacrifice."

Ned laughed. "Not as great as it would have been ten years ago. And you'll notice I didn't say 'both.' "

Open venues like Denver made Mariesa nervous. Cerberus Security, which afforded her personal protection when she traveled, could not screen access like they could in a closed studio. Twice, Schwar's agents had turned people away at metal detectors; and once they had apprehended a lunatic outside Mechanics Hall. Here, mixed with the Denver police, the sheriff's posse, and the FBI agents guarding the federal politicians, the Cerberus people were like a dozen Dutch boys facing a dike with a thousand leaks. The crowd barriers kept people far enough from the podium that knives were not a worry, and handguns grew notoriously less accurate with distance. There were few positions where a man could unlimber a rifle unremarked by his neighbors. Still, all you needed was one man obsessed enough not to care about his own safety. The air was cool at this altitude, and a bulky sweater could hide a remarkable panoply of explosives.

And yet, the cruelest weapons were not made of metal or gelignite.

Her speeches came more smoothly now, the words well worn with practice, and she hardly ever resorted to her notes. The danger in giving the same speech in venue after venue was that the words would fall mechanically, without the spark the heart could give them. Repetition might be the mother of learning, as the Russian proverb had it; but it was also the father of slumber. So, she alternated a half-dozen set speeches, and had taken to extemporizing between blocks of boilerplate. As the months had gone by she found that it was in these intervals that she most moved her audience.

The shout stopped her as she turned away from the microphones.

"Wasn't for you, we wouldn't need this!"

She couldn't see who had spoken, and most of the audience had not heard the words. A few in the front were craning their necks to find the heckler. Mariesa barely checked her stride. She had adopted a policy of not responding to such catcalls. She could hardly change their minds when she could not even change her own.

But one such voice gave rise to others. They were scattered thinly among the crowd, and their objections—those Mariesa could hear—were not all of a piece. Some were party shills for McRobb, still riding the hoax theme. Others were fatalists. "It's the judgment of God!" one man in front hollered. "You've brought God's wrath on us."

Perhaps that registered on her face, because she saw Ned DuBois glower, rise to his feet, and stalk to the podium. His eyes searched the crowd, fixed on one man. Whether the original heckler or not, Mariesa did not know. "Son," he said gently, so gently that even with the loudspeakers, the crowd had to quiet to hear him. "Son, that sounds like blasphemy to me. Seems to me, you oughta get on your knees and pray the Man's forgiveness. 'Cause, Mizz van Huyten, she's pretty damn rich and all, but I don't like hearing you say she can order Almighty God about like He was her flunky."

A ripple of laughter spread through the crowd. Mariesa slowly resumed her seat. Ned in his aw-shucks mood was unstoppable.

"It's blasphemy to block God's judgment on a sinful world!"

Was that a different voice? Why did such people come to a rally like this? Simply for the opportunity to ride their hobby horse?

Ned repeated the comment for the benefit of those who hadn't heard it, and elicited a few boos—and some Amens! too. "If it is God's will, we *can't* block it. Nothing wrong with keeping ourselves busy in the meantime. But why do you say it's God's will, brother?"

"Says so right in the Book! Not the water, but the fire next time!"

"And if the Bean hits the ocean? I guess that'll be a flood to beat all. But I remember my mom reading from the Book, and I recollect it says that God's judgment will come 'like a thief in the night' and we'll know 'neither the day nor the hour.' " He paused and glanced about the audience, gathering them in with his eyes. "Well, friends, the *day* is 17 October 2023"—some woofs and fists pumping the air—"and the *hour,* I hear, is sometime between ten in the morning and ten at night." Another pause. "Eastern standard time." A burst of applause. "Which doesn't sound like any thief—or any night—I ever heard of. But I've got a question for you, now, brother." He scanned the front rank of the audience. "You see that woman there in the yellow dress? To your left, brother. The one with the baby in a carry-sling. Raise your hand, ma'am. Thank you. Brother, I'd like you to go to that woman, introduce yourself, and then . . . tell her what horrible crime her child has committed that God intends to wipe him off the face of the Earth." He waited expectantly, but received no answer. Instead, the heckler shoved his way out of the crowd, helped along by others.

When Ned resumed his seat, Mariesa leaned close to him and said, "I never knew you were a religious man."

"I'm not. At least, not like Forrest. But I know a sight who are; and they aren't anything like that clown out there. Anyone else rags on you, you just call ol' Ned and I'll give them a whup upside the head."

"Thank you, Ned, but . . ."

"Though we really ought to pray," he said, his face grown more long and serious. "Not for miracles. The way I figure this God thing is, He's no performing monkey to do tricks on command. No, we need to pray—you, me, everyone—for the strength to see this through, whether that strength comes to us as God's grace, or whether we find it inside ourselves. Because this is not going to be easy. Fellow I know at SkyWatch told me there may be a third one coming."

"That's not confirmed."

Ned settled back in his chair and stuck his legs out again. "Not yet."

Sometimes, when she woke up in the night, Mariesa felt disoriented. The bed faced the wrong way; the windows opened on an alien landscape. The smells and sounds were all wrong. When she lay still under the sheets, she thought she could hear Harriet stirring about, but it was only the pipes or the air conditioner or some other inanimate object playing the ghost. The thought occurred to her one time that Harriet's spirit might have been unable to find its way to Ridgeview.

She had dreamed this time of Ned DuBois. Standing on the catwalk at Silverpond outside her rooftop observatory, Ned beside her, watching the nighttime skies. A cold night, she remembered, when, shivering, she had accepted Ned's sheepskin flight jacket around her shoulders. His hands had draped it, straightened it, touched her. Warmth enveloped her, spread to her throat, her lips, her loins. Their faces turned toward each other, eyes searching, asking permission and granting it. Lips hungry. Pressing against him, feeling him strong and hard against her. His hand inside her blouse; his tongue in her mouth. Her eager fingers unfastening his trousers, bringing him forth.

How much of that was real, she wondered in the still cool of an October night. They had stood there, yes. A long time ago. Ned had been young and at the top of his form. As young then as some of her "kids" were now. She remembered the feel of the soft fleece and the assurance of his arm around her shoulder. But the kiss? She wasn't sure. Probably not. Certainly not the rest of it. Not the eager probing and caressing. Not the passionate conjoining. She had been a cold fish then.

And now she was an old lady who slept alone.

She rose from bed and made her business; but, returning, she stood by the tall double window that opened on the private deck. On cue, a meteorite scratched a line of fire across the western heavens. She followed its track. God was mocking her.

Stepping outside, she found the night cool. The crickets and the fireflies had long packed it in; but occasional rustles in the surrounding trees told of possum and owl and other nighttime creatures. She unfastened the front of her nightgown and invited the breeze under the flannel. Invisible fingers caressed her, raised goose bumps on aged skin.

How could she remember so vividly a kiss she had never gotten?

In the car; on the go.

"No, Marcel," she said into the tracey. (Terribly awkward, holding your wrist in front of your face. The old-style cell phones were better, she thought; but try to find one anymore.) "No, Marcel. Keep the production going. The bill is on Rutell's desk. Some of the Liberty congressmen finally came over, 'government program' or no. And with McRobb still in the hospital, we had enough defections from his party, too. No, I don't know how soon. Next week, at the latest. Stockpile them. If I have to, I'll pay for them myself. Yes. Thank you. End call."

She slumped in the seat. Her arm felt like a dead weight. A line of fire ran down it to her fingertips, which tingled as if she had slept on them. She rubbed the muscles. The driver glanced at her in his rearview mirror. "You all right, Ms. van Huyten?"

"I'm fine, Laurence." Every few heartbeats, she felt as if she were rising from her seat, as light as a feather; as if she were floating gently on the swells of an inner ocean and the tide of her heart were going out.

"The name's Volodya, ma'am."

"What?" Broad Slavic features looked back from the mirror. "Oh. Sorry." Laurence had been a black man. He had grown his business to the point where he no longer drove cars himself. "Do you know Laurence Sprague?" The driver shook his head.

"Sure don't, ma'am." And what lilt was that in his voice? Atlanta? It was certainly not St. Petersburg. Did that mean that Laurence had retired, or that Chris used a different livery service? She had fallen out of touch. What was Zhou Hui about these days? Or Belinda Karr or Steve Matthias?

Or Barry Fast?

It was strange that she never dreamed of him. They had

shared a bed for five years, shared dreams, shared love. Of course, Barry had shared his love a little too much.

Barry's just what you need, Tracy Bellingham had told her one time. *He makes you glow.* And when had she last spoken with Tracy? Not since Harriet's funeral.

Glowing had not been high on her daily To Do list back then. Perhaps it should have been.

The car pulled into the driveway at Silverpond. It felt odd to be coming home, and coming home a beggar, at that.

It was her home no longer. It would be important to remember that. Old habits were hard to break, and she might thoughtlessly send Roy on some errand. But she had grown up here, and it *felt* like coming home. Ridgeview had not been hers long enough to earn the emotion and so its loss did not affect her so gravely. At least, its mortgage had been sacrificed in a good cause.

Oh, she was not really beggared. The income off the Trust was more than sufficient to keep her off the street. But her liquid assets and most of her real property were gone. The futuristic "clamshell" house overlooking the Oregon coast, she had never cared for; but the lodge above Jackson Lake held poignant memories of her flight from Barry's infidelity. The others, in Hawaii and Catalonia and elsewhere, she had used so seldom she hardly thought of them as hers. Piet . . . yes, her father had stayed in them often in his eternal chase after sun and good times; but their cash value in support of Damocles had counted for more than any memories.

And so she had pled the clause in Silverpond's charter that entitled her to living quarters there. She had never envisioned that clause as anything more than an overnight stay when work kept her late at VHI; but still, it was there. Roberta had stretched the point and said that Trish, her valet, could live there, too. Mariesa thought Roberta would have stretched the compact to include all of Ridgeview's staff. There was plenty of room in the old mansion. But Armando and the others had found other positions. The economy was moving haltingly;

but it was moving at last. There's important work to be done, Armando had told her apologetically, and off he had gone, to do what Mariesa wasn't sure. Still, if he couldn't weld a seam on a vacuum-tight hull or program navigational code, he could mother hen those who did.

If you had only waited, Norbert told her. The bonds will be floated and moneys loaned to Damocles would be repaid with interest on maturity. Poor, dear Norbert still did not fully understand. It had taken very nearly a year to get the bond issue passed, in the face of economic paralysis, suspicion of "international bankers," and political posturing. It was a year the world could ill afford to lose, and thanks in part to her efforts—and Ed Wilson and Nathan Rothschild and Prince al-Walid and the others who had joined her quixotic cause—the world had not lost too much of it.

The LEO stations were operational again. Many of the tenants had moved back in and a certain air of determination had begun to take hold. A magnetic X-ship was a-building at Goddard Free Port. Two Planks were undergoing refit for deep-space work at Leo and Tsiolkovsky, as was the experimental nuclear ship, *Jackie Cochran.* A Russo-Khazak-Japanese consortium was fabricating Salyut living quarters. The Three Cities were building solar power lasers in geosynchronous orbit. A pair of giant battle lasers—too powerful to place anywhere in line-of-sight of Earth—were planned for Mendeleev and Korolev craters on the Moon's Farside. Acting on his own initiative, Ed Wilson had popped a supply pod into orbit with the first of many equipment caches, to be fitted with strap-ons and sent ahead to the Bean on long-orbit rendezvous.

God bless Ed Wilson. Wilson Enterprises was teetering on the verge of bankruptcy. The Kilimanjaro ram had passed to the Union of East Africa for debt, though Wilson continued to operate it under the Pan-African PDC. She would give him a kiss on the lips, if she didn't think he would misconstrue it as an offer.

And maybe even then. Wilson was good-looking, fit; they shared many of the same visions; and he was between wives at the moment. They had gone through so much together that it seemed right to share a little more. She smiled faintly. She was a bit older than the usual targets on Ed's radar screen, but she wasn't looking for burning lust anymore. At her age, companionship meant more.

She saw Roberta waiting by Silverpond's front door. How their roles had been reversed! Once, it had been Roberta seeking refuge here. Roy was waiting, too. She could remember when he had been a gangly boy, sent to clean the stables by a juvenile court. Now he was an accomplished horse-breeder and field director of Silverpond Nature Preserve. In a way, though she had never thought of him so, Roy was one of her "kids," too.

Trish Niederman, who had overseen the moving, hurried down the steps to open the limo's door. Mariesa smiled at her and waved to Roberta, who stepped forward with her hand outstretched and pleasant words upon her lips.

Mariesa said, "Robera, so gradoo see-oo." A bright flash, then the sharp sting of a slap across her face and her vision turned red. *I've bought you one year,* she thought as she fell. *Use it.* The world spun around her, and just before she struck the paving like a wave on a rocky shore, she heard a tide of voices that made no words.

Voices: Lamentations

Testing, one, two, three . . . Be quiet, Carson. Okay, I guess this thing is working. Damn digital recorders . . . I hope it downloads okay when I squirt it to you . . .

<pause>

I don't know what you want us to say, Tani. I know we're supposed to keep diaries of some sort about the project, and you're going to use them for your new book; but I don't know what you think is important and what isn't. So I guess I'll do what I always do and wing it.

<pause>

. . . and stay out of there . . . Because Mommy says.

<laughter> No flubber, Tani. I swore when I was a kid that I would never say that to *my* children. God, I wish Beth were here to see this. You know what? I think we could understand each other now, a little. I keep thinking that we could have become friends.

I spent the day at the hospital, so I'm really down. Oh, Tani, you should have seen her . . . She looks like she'd been drained and there's nothing but a husk wrapped up in blankets and tubes. I know they say it was a stroke; but that head wound . . . Maybe it was when she hit the pavement, like the doctor said; but maybe it was a graze from a bullet. I don't know. Roy says he thought he heard a sound, but no one else did. And maybe it doesn't matter. She's lying there with tubes up her nose. Does it matter what put her there?

We've always had a love-hate relationship, the Rich Lady and me. At least, I thought we did, until I realized the hate was all on my side. God, what a revelation that was. I couldn't be with Phil for a week afterward, and he thought it was something he'd done. That was, oh, years ago.

This is all a digression. I know you said not to erase anything: but that REVERSE button is awfully tempting . . .

Oh, well. You'll take what you need, right?

I sat in the ICU as long as they let me, but I couldn't think of anything to say, except maybe I didn't hate her anymore, but I think she already knew that. Words would have been wasted, even if she could've heard me.

Tani, *what if she never recovers?* First Phil; now Mariesa. Who's going to lead us? You and me and Chase Coughlin?

* * *

Wonderful, now we get a fucking fascist for Speaker. Have the people lost their collective mind? Why is *he* out of the hospital and not Mariesa? Chase thinks McRobb is okay; but Colonel Eatinger over at the "Lucky Thirteenth" gets purple in the face every time he hears McRobb's name. And Hobie, I swear, doesn't even know there's been an election. That's how we wind up with the McRobbs of the world. I'm afraid I yelled at Hobie, the poor, puzzled dear; and that made Ladawan mad at me, and that's one lady I don't ever want mad at me . . .

Funny, how it's me and the Air Force colonel on the same side here. I'd always thought of the military as McRobb's peanut gallery; but they're like everyone else. Eatinger says he doesn't like military airs from "someone who never wore stripes."

At least, we finally have the Planetary Defense Bonds. I don't know if the third asteroid is what finally convinced McRobb, or whether he just needed to horse-trade the last couple of votes for the Speakership. Nothing's official until January 3, but thank God Rutell kept the old Congress in emergency session and the bonds are on sale now.

Damn him. Not Rutell, McRobb. What if he dragged his heels too long?

Oh, Tani, do you really think anyone will be around to read your new book? Four asteroids? And maybe that fifth one, but they're not sure. I don't know what we've done to deserve that kind of punishment, Tani. I really don't. I know it's not "God's Judgment." If this is what God does to children because their parents don't go to church, then it's not a god that *should* be worshiped. "The fire next time . . . ?" That's not a promise; that's a threat, and their god is a thug!

But the Visitors . . . What sort of empty, soulless *things* would hurl asteroids at my child? Aliens, yes. But *that* alien? I guess deep down we always thought they'd feel the same kinds of emotions as we do. They might look like giant spiders, but they'd still be stone for peace and love.

Four of them. No, five. I don't believe in false alarms anymore. I—

<pause>

I'm sorry, Tani, but this latest news really has me on the canvas. I wake up and I think. What's the use? They'll just keep coming and coming and maybe we'll stop one or two and maybe three, but some will get through and people will die, maybe everyone will die, and something that used to be a cockroach will dig up our fossilized bones in a couple ten million years and put us on display.

Even Chase is a little less cocky than usual. He talks about "going down fighting." And Hobie . . . All he cares about is drawing superloops and plugging Ladawan. I know he wants kids, he's told me so; but he also told me he can't bring a kid in just to die, and it's tearing him up. And Jimmy Poole, who knows what he's thinking? But he looks grim all the time.

You're the exception, Tani. I don't know if you know that. But planning this novel may be the most life-affirming act of anyone on this planet.

Or else, Tani thought, playing back Roberta's recording, *it's a shield of my own devising.*

9.

The North Magnetic Poole

From Phoenix to LEO a-roving I went,
To stay in Earth orbit, mon, was my
intent.
Free fall and close spaces got under my
skin;

An' so I departed for groundside again.
Singing, fly!
Fly, otter, fly!
Those orbital willies will strike by and by.

He had called himself "Meat" for so many years that he sometimes forgot he had been born with a different handle. Every now and then, when he had to sign a document or cash a check, he would remember that he was "Morris Tucker" and shake his head. How far did names make the man? He had dropped his birth name because who ever heard of a metal singer named "Morris"?

But then "metal" had gone in the toilet and "goofball" made him puke and now they played "roll," with its regular BAM-bam-BAM-bam beat like ocean waves, gaggy tunes sometimes so soft you couldn't even hear them. If the walls didn't shake, man, it wasn't *music.*

If he had gone by "Morris," would he be an accountant now? Or an ad exec? Or just a weenie with a funny name. He would probably not be construction boss on Project Lariat, that's for sure. Not be floating about in God's backyard with the whole wide world above his head. Not that he was stone for poetry or nothing, though sometimes he read Styx's verses, but there was a feeling that came over him whenever he was ziggy and he could never quite find the words for it. Maybe Styx had found them, though that was hard to believe 'cause she'd never zigged. It was Delight Jackson who had found the real words, and if they were not words of deep emotion, they held those emotions inside themselves like a secret code; and every otter who heard them knew what he meant. The times when "out" became an infinite, dizzy "down." When directions scattered six ways and you didn't know your which from your what. When you slipped and slid and found no traction even when you could force your feet into place.

I lifted on Quimby *standing out on the pad.*
When I t'ink on it, mon, it was not so much bad.
When de torch lit I t'ought it was all for de best;

Till a big honkin' rhino she sat on my chest.
Singing, rise!
Rise, otter, rise!
Those orbital willies sneak up by surprise.

Flaco Mercado, Meat's *segundo,* poured another cup of juice. The red stream curved out of the bottle and Flaco held the cup a little to the side to catch it. The *Lariat* crew had taken over the lounge on Goddard Station's Diamond-13, where spin gravity ran about one-third Earth-normal, but the Coriolis effect gave everything a funny twist. Delight sat in one corner of the room and tickled his uke singing "The Orbital Willies" while the rest of the crew kicked. It had been a tiring day.

"Not like the ol' days, *'mano,*" Flaco said, looking around the lounge. " 'Member that? Building the Hub for Leo station? We didn't have no spin-up then. Slept in little honeycombs lining the walls."

"No flubber," said Uncle Waldo after the usual bounceback delay.

"Oh, go away from me, Uncle," cried Aedh McCracken. "As if you'd be knowin' ziggy."

"Proton's lifting a new vessel next week," Meat said. "About seventy-five percent rigged out groundside. It's what they call a fixer-upper—if puking in ziggy is what you want."

"A whole tank to ourselfs?" That was Sepp Bauer, a welder. "Goot. I wass getting tired of sleeping in d' bed wit' you."

"Been meaning to talk to you about that, Sepp . . ." said Meat, to general laughter.

One day I decided to go for a walk
With suit, boots, and gauntlets. I thought 'twas a lark,
I slipped loose de tether and turned on de strobe
And all by myself, mon, I circled d'globe.
Singing, float!

And they all broke off talking to shout: "FLOAT! OTTER, FLOAT!"

Those orbital willies are no cause to gloat.

"I heard from Jimmy Schorr over on Leo," Flaco said. "Skinny says the three ships in the yards there and at T-grad are all for Operation Intercept. Three otters each in *Mitchell* and *Sikorsky*, and four in *Jackie Cochran.* Primary mission is—"

"To blow up the fucking Bean," said Bird Winfrey; and the others pumped woofers in the air.

Flaco shook his head. "No. They taking a shitload of explosive, that's for sure; but first they gonna try and rig engines on the *cabrón.* No shit. That's what Jimmy Schorr said an' he heard it straight from the Rector. You ever know the Rector to get it wrong?"

"Only vunce," said Sepp with a secret grin and he refused to elaborate, though Svetlana Lupoff blushed a satisfying crimson.

"So," Flaco continued, "I figure: three ships means three pilots. Prob'ly three engineer-copilots, too; cause in case something happens, you know? Don't want to be stuck with no driver. So that leaves four slots. Figure one is a scientist, 'cause they sure want to study that Bean. Well, the engineers, I guess they gotta know how to do real work; but I think they gonna need a rigger, a 'lectrician, and an NDT tech." He tossed back his bug juice; looked around the assembled group. "Who you think they gonna pick?"

Sepp said, "We start a pool?"

Meat looked around the group. *Me?* he thought. *Get my name up there like the others. Right up there with hot pilot Chase Coughlin, or war hero Azim Thomas, or big-time poets and writers like Tani and Styx. Rich, like Jimmy Poole; or important like Jenny Ribbon and her silver apples. So what am I? Meat Tucker, Big Deal. Ain't nobody ever gonna remember my name; except maybe someday Jilly tells her grandkids about her dad and shows 'em a scratchy old TIFF file and says that's your great-grandpop, Morris, and one day he—*

One day he what? He nothing. Unless she takes them by the hand out into the yard and points at the sky. But who remembers the names on the gang that raised the Brooklyn Bridge or dug the Panama Canal? Leo and Goddard, they won't be no different. Take pride in your work; but the important dudes in their suits still push past you in the crowd and don't even look down their noses.

Well, that's life. If you don't like the hand you get, you can always cash out. The exit is no farther than the nearest airlock. Meanwhile, you do your job.

He wouldn't go out. They wouldn't ask him. Too much a-building in cis-Luna. Transfer ships; power satellites; dockyards. Maintenance and repair. So people like the Rector and Tiny Larsen, or Izzy Mac and Jimmy Schorr and himself, they'd keep here to organize and run things. To build what needs building. For Operation Intercept, they'll pick a dude who knows what he's doing and can think on his feet, even when his feet are floating away from him. Meat's gaze lighted on Eddie Mercado.

"Twenty on Flaco," he said.

Flaco blinked and drew back. "Not me, 'mano. That's a dead man's flight. I got two kids." Meat grinned and said nothing, and after a moment, Sepp made a notation on his wristpad.

And now I live groundside. I sit by d' fire.
Life is more simple once you drop and retire.
I fish and I golf and I t'ink now and then:
If it weren't for de willies, I'd go back again.
Singing, soar!
"SOAR, OTTER, SOAR!"
Those orbital willies can't get you no more.

Meat pulled a sheet of paper from his coverall pocket. "Okay, otters, listen up. Tomorrow's assignments . . ." A chorus of groans. "Now, you know the Thirteenth didn't put us up here to goof. Bird, the shroud motors were welded in place today. You get the router from Sepp? Good. Those are double-star points on the print, so check 'em good. A shroud tears loose and that's all she wrote for keeping the sail set. Sepp, the mast gets stepped tomorrow. That's one long honker, so get a couple of Flaco's dudes to help you. *Hambleton*'s supposed to lift a shipment of motherboards for the *Lariat*'s computers. Vivian, that's electrical work. There'll be a hot-shot software dude lifting with the package, but he don't know shit about hardware. He'll run the debugs, but you do the installation and connections. If he touches a tool, shoot him. Flaco. The guy's a bunny. You baby-sit. Wipe his chin if he pukes. You know the drill. Now"—he unfolded a set of drawings and flattened them on the table—"the loop housings go on the Salyut's forward bulkhead. Waldo, we need alignment with the vessel's centerline . . ."

Meat glanced at the manifest a second time and chuckled to himself. Jimmy Poole in orbit . . . who'da thunk it.

Certainly not Jimmy Poole.

Things in orbit were supposed to float gently, gracefully. All the videos agreed on that. They were not supposed to rotate slowly while your eyes grew crossed. Jimmy clamped down hard with his jaw. The meal he hadn't eaten wanted to come up on him, but he refused to show weakness before the experienced spacehands. He'd read that one person in three experienced vertigo in free fall; so the odds were fair that the grinning spacer waiting for him had ralphed his cookies his first time up, too. By what right did he laugh at Jimmy Poole?

Jimmy extended his hand and the other man shook it vigorously and before he knew it, Jimmy was floating in midair, out of reach of any handhold. "Hey," he said, flapping his arms. But all that accomplished was to send him into a mild spin, which did little for his equilibrium. The guy who'd welcomed him had passed on and was doing the grip-and-grin with Red Hawkins, the Baleen operative who had come up with Jimmy on the *John Hambleton.* Jimmy noted that the two men held on to spars while slapping fives.

"Chico, my man!" Red said. "How're they hanging?"

"*Que pasa, 'mano.* Long time."

"Excuse me," said Jimmy.

"Come up for the harvest, mate. You know Baleen Aerogel Filters?"

"Excuse me," said Jimmy.

"Baleen? Sure. I use' to run this plant, back before the Dip."

"That was you? The whole thing was so hush-hush I didn't even know there *was* a second plant."

"You're Eddie Mercado?" asked Jimmy.

The crewman turned finally. "Do I know you?"

Red Hawkins wagged a thumb. "That there's Jimmy Poole, one of Baleen's partners. Bankrolled number two his own self, Billie Whistle told me."

Jimmy Poole splayed his arms and legs to slow his tumble. "Can you guys give me a hand?"

He should have known better. They clapped.

The nausea passed after a day or two. *Normal,* said Mercado. *Means you'll ralph again groundside, because the solid ground will seem to rock and spin.* He probably meant to be helpful.

Yet, after the initial disorientation, Jimmy found free fall exhilarating. Maybe it had to do with the way the blood pooled in the body without gravity constantly sucking it down out of the brain and into the legs. Or maybe it was just the sense of freedom in three-dimensional movement. Certainly, he felt his weight less; though that he still had mass was brought painfully home several times.

"I'm a natural-born otter," he told Meat and Flaco at dinner, ignoring the look they exchanged. "I should have come up years ago." So far, no one had asked him the obvious question: namely, why didn't you teep this gig? He wasn't sure himself. The debug didn't need bonebag, except for the installation tech. It didn't need his own personal fingers tapping keys or speaking cues shipboard.

They put him in a hard suit and taught him safety routines and clipped his tether to Flaco's suit. Mercado did everything but hold him by the hand when they took the giant leap from the east end spacelock to MSX-1, *Lariat.*

He had feared that stepping into the Big Empty might lead to the Big Barf. The ultimate vertigo. Instead, sudden terror chased all nausea from him. He stopped, frozen, in the open airlock. The stars—there were trillions of them—filled the void with infinite depth. He stared down and down and down until Flaco tugged on his safety line and brought him to. Flaco was waving him out. Jimmy raised a foot from the airlock rim and . . .was surprised to find that it hadn't moved. He was supposed to step out into *that*? Where there was nothing to support him?

"Hey, 'mano," said Flaco over the suit-to-suit, "jus' look straight at the *Lariat.* Don' look away."

Jimmy found that fixing his gaze on the refitted Salyut module changed the perspective utterly. It seemed huge and far off. Then it seemed smaller, but closer. He grunted, closed his eyes, and pulled himself out along the cable. He couldn't fall, not really. Not tied to Flaco like he was. His breath came in pants and his heart thudded against his ribs. By tomorrow, this story would be all over Goddard; within a week, every otter in LEO would know how Jimmy Poole froze up in the airlock. Sooner or later, Chase would hear it.

This was Chase's milieu and he must have EVAded countless times, but he had never mentioned the ecstasy of free fall or the feeling in his gut when he teetered over an endless precipice. Chase had no more depth than paint. If he saw stars as anything, he saw them as points of light; and the void, as no more than a place to cross. Jimmy, more sensitive, naturally felt both the awe and the terror more keenly.

But his superior sensibilities were small comfort as Flaco pulled him along—like a dog on a leash!—through the cold, hard vacuum. He could close his eyes and the fear of falling would lessen, but he could not banish the knowledge that death enveloped him like the waters of an ocean far from land, probing his suit for leaks, waiting for his thermoregulator to fail. He glanced toward the sun. Was it brighter than before?

Flaco cycled him aboard *Lariat* and if Jimmy could have wrapped his arms around the composite and aerogel structure and kissed it, he would have. He had always had a touch of agoraphobia, but the intensity of the attack surprised him. He tried to forget that when his job here was done, he would have to cross the void a second time.

Flaco led him to the control pod, which was set in the forward three-quarter frustum aft of the observation blister. Jimmy started to tell Flaco that he already knew the way. He'd been studying the prints and layouts for more than a year and now that the prototype design was frozen, the control room wasn't likely to have moved somewhere else. But free fall was disorienting and he approached features from random points of view. Only when he figured out which way was nominal "down" and, by grasps and turns, had oriented himself to the remembered prints did everything click into place.

The shields were closed, shuttering the view from the observation blister. That disappointed him at first; but then he reflected that he'd never get his work done with that infinite distraction spread out before him. Odd, that looking out at the void filled him with nothing but rapture; while stepping into it paralyzed him with fear.

The ship was pressurized to facilitate inside work, so both Jimmy and his guide removed their suits, all but the LCGs. Flaco made him promise not to touch anything but the computer panel; as if Jimmy were herbie enough to tamper with the artifact that kept his head from exploding. The rigger needn't have worried. Jimmy probably knew more about the innards of the ship than anyone else. Sure, Hobie knew the magsail principles. And the design team knew the overall configuration. And the engineers knew their individual sectors and modules—electrical, mechanical, HVAC, and so on. But Jimmy's navigational programming interfaced with most of the systems on board, and his curiosity had led him into every nook and cranny of the plans. He had even cat-birded a few times when Chase flew sims. In a way, it was his ship more than it was Chase's, and perhaps even more than it was Hobie's.

"Vivian installed the motherboards yesterday," Flaco said. "Continuity checked out."

Jimmy nodded. "Okay. Let's teach James some tricks." He unsnapped the goat-case and pulled a RAM pin from the foam holdfast.

"James?"

"The name of the A/S. You know, like the chauffeur? Home, James." He didn't tell Flaco that he had given the A/S his own persona and voice, and had even included some conversational flexware. Something to keep Chase company on his test flights. Jimmy swallowed a smile at the thought. At least a part of him would be making the flights with Chase. He found the thought oddly exciting.

"How fast will this thing go?" the rigger wondered.

"Depends on current density, orientation, and a bunch of other factors programmed into the RAM pins here." He flourished the goat-case, careful not to shake it. "If you're sailing large before the wind, your acceleration is about a thousandth of a gee."

"That don' sound so fast, my friend."

Jimmy grinned, having said almost the same thing to Hobie last year. "Not compared to an SSTO main engine, right. Get a couple gees squashing your bag during a lift, right? The sail gives a gentler push, but *it keeps on pushing.* You don't run out of fuel unless the sun goes out; in which case fuel is not your major concern. Bottom line is: a magsail can get you to Mars in about the same time it took the *Mayflower* to cross the Atlantic."

Flaco looked impressed. Jimmy had gotten most of the information from Hobie's friend, Otul Ganesh; but you couldn't give attribution to every factoid you repeated or your conversation would be nothing but footnotes. "What that means is," he concluded with a flourish, "is that when sailing ships come into regular use, Mars is no farther from LEO than Massachusetts was from Europe."

A pilot's seat had been installed. It was really more of a rack where a pilot could strap in. This ship would never experience enough acceleration to need a padded chair. If it ever entered a gravity well, it was dead. So the rack was mainly to give purchase and leverage. Jimmy pulled himself into it, shoved his feet in the stirrups, and snapped the waist and shoulder belts in place. He tested the reach of his arms against the keypads. Satisfied, he rotated the pilot's teep helmet into place and positioned the induction cap on his skull.

Chase would sit here someday and pilot this crate for real. *But I got here first.*

He paused. That couldn't be the reason he had bonebagged!

Jimmy considered, then dismissed the possibility. No. Nothing so juvenile had motivated him. All he wanted was to make sure everything was right. Not for Chase's sake. Screw Chase. But because it was S. James Poole's reputation on the line.

He activated the display and his virtch goggs gave him a view of a starless void within which blinked a tiny cursor. *And the spirit of Jimmy moved across the face of the void, saying, Let there be Light.*

And there was light.

"Lord!" said Delight Jackson. "Would you look at that!"

The other otters jostled for a view of the doid screen in Goddard's lounge. Jimmy finished his checklist and looked up. "That my ride home?"

Meat said, "I don't know what it is."

Jimmy studied the vessel on the screen. "Hydrogen tank," he said, knowing that somehow the obvious answer would be wrong.

Meat grunted. "Hydrogen tank with docking handles on the sides and two LTVs latched on."

"Tugboats," Sepp declared after getting his glimpse. "Dey're taking the tank somewheres."

"But where, mon?"

Sepp assumed an air of authority. "Where do Lunar Transfer Vessels go?"

"Is that a riddle?"

"That," said Svetlana, "is New Hope. How do you say it? Apartments and workshops? Fifteen colonists going to live on Moon. *Gagarin* and *Titov* will be towing it to site in Smythe Sea near Artemis Mines. They have dug trench in regolith and lunar lighters will bring it down."

"Need the whole bleeding fleet for that," said Nigel Long.

Meat looked troubled and pushed away from the viewscreen. He sat with Jimmy. "What is it, otter?" Jimmy asked him.

Meat shook his head. "Just trying to see six lighters hooked up to that tank and taking it down easy and level. They could lose a boat."

And its crew remained unspoken.

"How do you know dis t'ing, Svetlana?" Sepp asked.

The Russian welder pointed to the screen. "Master Pilot Feathershaft came over to clear with Port Captain Takashi. We talk in ladies' facility. Luna Settlement Company bought tank dirt cheap when North American Pressure Vessels was going bankrupt. Module was fitted out groundside and lifted by cargo shuttle. Colonists are coming soon in *The Ninety-Nines.*"

"Fifteen outbackers crammed into *Gagarin* and *Titov*? Those buggerlugs'll be chockers." Red Hawkins, having finished his harvest and replenished the aerogel and biocultures in Baleen No. 2, was also planning to drop with Jimmy in *The Ninety-Nines.*

"They'll put three each in the LTV cargo holds," Svetlana said. "The rest will be riding in habitat itself."

Hawkins shook his head. "Hope they don't just bung it down, moonside."

Jimmy shuddered at the thought. Moon was low grav, but that didn't mean you wouldn't hit hard if you fell from Low Lunar Orbit. *Good thing they dug out the crater ahead of time.* A bad joke and he knew better than to voice it. It wasn't his problem, though. A bunch of crazy people moving to the Moon. He hoped they weren't bringing their kids. "What're they planning to do up there?" he asked.

"Pilot Feathershaft was not sure," the Russian electrician said. "She thought some will be dryponic farmers, or mechanics, some tailors for space suits. They sell to the miners for oxygen."

"They'll die," said Jimmy flatly. "Some of them. Maybe all of them."

"Oh, Luna Settlement Company sends supplies first year. But, tovarich, are many graves in Siberia and also in your American Wild West and Chinese New Territories. Fifteen is not many, but Earth tells these aliens who attack us, *You don't get us all.*" She turned and scowled at the screen. "No matter what, you don't get us all."

Jimmy waited at the west end docks with Red and the Lariats and Goddard City cadre whose shifts were up while the citizens of New Hope disembarked from *The Ninety-Nines* with their personal gear. Some of Takashi's cadre were waiting to escort them down the length of the Hub to Eastport to ferry them over to their new home. None of the waiting otters gave the colonists the DuBois Handshake, which annoyed Jimmy somewhat. *He* had floundered in ziggy; so it was only fair that these bunnies pay their dues. Instead, guide ropes had been deployed on which they could tug themselves along. The otters actually applauded, which surprised and puzzled the "pilgrims" as much as it did Jimmy. It started as a single, rhythmic handclap—Jimmy did not see who—that spread exponentially through the watching crowd until it was a continuous roll punctuated now and then by a shout or a fist pumping the air.

A passing woman checked herself on the rope and twisted about to face him. "Jimmy?" she said. "Jimmy Poole?"

He didn't recognize the origin node, so he ran on autoreply. "The one and only." With a big smile.

She laughed. "You haven't changed."

Changed? Since when? His puzzlement must have reached his face, because she slipped out of the line and took hold of a guy rope. "Leilah," she said. "Leilah Frazetti. Remember? Witherspoon High?"

What he remembered was a bimbo with long, silken hair who sometimes appeared to him in his sleep. He remembered large breasts in a blouse too small to hold them; bright red lips; and a willingness to use them in a variety of ways. USS Leilah, the submarine, going down on Greg Prescott under the bleachers. Ah-oogah. Dive, dive! Fire torpedo!

And here she was, pale-faced, her lustrous hair chopped

away; the come-hither gone thither; the bazookas big enough to take out an M-1 Battle Tank, hidden away behind baggy white coveralls. So it was only natural that he ask . . .

"Why?" she answered. "I'm a teeper. I was Uncle Waldo on this station." She tapped the guy rope. "So, I'm teeping some of the robot mining equipment up at Artemis and I figured if I lived in New Hope it would cut down on that annoying commute."

"Commute?"

"Yeah. That's what teepers call the lag time between signal-out and signal-back."

A flippant answer, and not, he guessed, the true one. "It doesn't seem . . ."

"Like the Leilah you knew?" She touched him. Fingers whose imagined touch alone had once been enough to rock him off. "Jimmy. These days all of us find that we have to go beyond ourselves and become people we never thought we'd be. New Hope is important. Regolith. Mix it with zeolite and it makes a terrific soil. The mining crews, they'll pay for fresh vegetables. We'll make a go of it. It's important to learn self-sufficiency. So here I am . . ." She laughed and gestured at her body. "Leilah Frazetti, farm gal." She gave him a brief kiss on the cheek. "You drop in to see us sometime, okay? I'll leave the strobe on in the porthole."

He watched her scramble awkwardly out the guide rope and wondered if he would ever see her again. New Hope? More like Slim Chance.

The passenger module of *The Ninety-Nines* consisted of two rows of couches circling a hole in the floor. At least, it would become a hole when the ship was under acceleration. Just now, it was simply an opening and the ladder that ran through it nearly the entire length of the ship was little more than a series of handholds to pull yourself along.

Jimmy located his assigned seat in the "orchestra" row. Permanently reclined to accommodate the brutal acceleration of a lift, the seats reminded him of psychiatrist couches. He grinned at the image of twenty patients undergoing simultaneous Freudian analysis. The notion of mass therapy tickled him. Economies of scale . . . *Okay, bring in all the manic-depressives . . .*

A trio of Gyricon screens attached to the "ceiling" displayed a view of the New Hope module. Most of the otters were gawping with at least half an eye while they settled in for the drop. "It's not going anywhere for another twenty-four," Jimmy offered as he pushed his flight bag into the space under his seat. The bag insisted on pushing back. The otters all turned and looked at him and Aedh McCracken, one of Meat's riggers, groaned theatrically.

"An' it doesn't look like we're going anywhere for another twenty-four, ourselves," he said, "until bunnies learn how to shove it." A couple of the others laughed with him and Jimmy reddened.

"I only meant," Jimmy said, wrapping his dignity around him, "that you were watching that tank like it was about to light a shuck and I just thought maybe you didn't know when departure was scheduled."

"Light a shuck," McCracken repeated. "Now who's after saying you could talk like that?"

"Well," said Jimmy, "I heard the other otters say—"

"The *other* otters, is it?" McCracken rolled his eyes. "*Other?* Sweet Jaysus, how many lifts you got, Flopsy?"

"Well, just this one, but—"

"And half a lap makes you one of us?"

"Ah, leave the little dag alone," said Red Hawkins, "he's not the worst boofer floating."

McCracken eyed the other space-rigger. "It's gotta be earned, Baldy."

Jimmy closed his teeth on the words that boiled up. He ought to be used to the ragging. People like McCracken—people like Chase—the years of mockery. He ought to be used to it by now, able to shrug it off. Why should he care what such louts thought of him? Yet, it still cut.

Maybe it was some sort of pheromone he gave off—some advanced gene of his—that made the monkeys uneasy in his company. Even Red had been lukewarm in his defense—if it was a defense. Dag? Boofer?

"I've been Outside," he said—and then cringed to hear himself. Stupid, to wave credentials at this crowd. How would he feel if one of them said *I logged on* as if it proved they could hack the cheese?

"We heard," Tiny Littlebear answered.

Was he grinning? Jimmy waited for the snide remarks about freezing in the airlock or about Flaco leading him by a leash; but oddly enough they didn't come.

He tried to tune the chatter out as he struggled with his buckle. He had learned that strategy years ago. Retreat inside your head and no one could get you. Except physically, but he had no defenses for that.

The seat belt refused to cooperate. Groundside, it had been just a seat belt; now the straps floated and writhed like snakes. Worse, his body refused to stay put, drifting out of its seat. He was used to that after a week on the station, but that didn't make it any easier. He yanked on one of the shoulder straps and that pulled him entirely out of the seat and put him into a slow tumble. It also twisted the straps.

No one offered to help. They simply watched. Sepp Bauer, sitting two seats to his right, grinned. "During max-Q," he said, "you go flying like a bounce ball, vit' your harness unfastened." At that, he was the most sympathetic of the lot, because the others only looked thoughtful, as if they might enjoy the sight.

Vapid, Jimmy thought. Dull, prosaic, insipid, stupid, simple, uneducated, ignorant . . . He was smarter than anyone on board. He was smarter than anyone he knew. Yet they made him feel foolish and inept. He had done well enough programming the *Lariat*'s computer. He'd had no trouble—well, only a little—eating and drinking on LEO. So, how was he unable to perform so simple a task as buckling in?

Leilah Frazetti had flustered him. That must be it. The unexpected encounter . . . the memories of unrequited lust . . . the move to Luna . . . He'd never been with any woman but Tani, and every now and then he wondered if he might be happy and content only because he had no standard of comparison; like a man who loved meat loaf because he'd never tasted filet mignon. And there had gone prime rib, off to the Moon . . .

The Moon was a frontier, and frontiers attracted loose women. Leilah Frazetti, farm gal and teeper? Miners would pay a lot more for nookie than for fresh veggies. How stupid did she think he was to fall for that "we have to go beyond ourselves" crap? People did not really change. Not that much. Not like that.

A dull thud aft as the lock to the station just closed. The ship was about to cut loose and drop. He snatched at the end of the buckle just as a small, lithe form sailed like a dancer up the ladder from the cargo bay.

A girl, he saw, blessed with dark, cropped hair and even darker eyes. She was as small as Tani, but lighter complexioned and (Jimmy couldn't stop from noticing) with a better mass distribution. Her powder-blue uniform bore two dark stripes on the cuff. She looked around the room. "Any bunnies?"

Every eye on the deck turned to Jimmy, who surrendered to the inevitable by raising his hand. "I can't seem to get this seat belt straightened out," he admitted. "I don't know if it's twisted or what."

"Let me take that." The girl—the name strip over her breast pocket read ROSARIO—anchored her slippers on a Stay-Put mat and straightened the shoulder straps across him. That put her name strip, and those parts of her anatomy directly underneath, very nearly in his face. "Here's your problem," she said. "The straps are all shortened up." She unclamped the straps and lengthened them while the other otters looked as surprised and innocent as circumstance or conscience allowed. "There"—the girl inserted the shoulder and lap flanges into the padded buckle—"keep it snug, but not tight."

Aedh McCracken unfastened his harness and let it float loose. "I'm needing help, too, *a cuiscle*."

"Sure, Mac," the girl said without looking. "Just wrap it around your neck and I'll snug it up good in a minute." Then, while the others hooted McCracken, she continued to Jimmy. "Okay, they probably briefed you groundside before you lifted, but pay attention. A drop profile is different from a lift."

Aurora B&O used cabin attendants on their ballistic flights, which had a much higher rate of business and holiday travelers; though with the longest lob no more than forty-five minutes from antipode to antipode, it was hard to see what job duties they had. He hadn't heard of flight attendants on the orbitals, but . . . "Are you a stewardess?" Jimmy asked.

"Uh-oh," said Sepp Bauer.

"Dead man," Red agreed.

Someone made bugle sounds. Taps.

The girl, Rosario, considered Jimmy for a moment; then gave him a smile that was at once friendly and dangerous. "What do you think?"

What Jimmy thought was that he had just stepped in it. Aurora wore purple. This gal wore powder blue. That meant a different organization. Okay, sometimes ships lifted with mixed crews. Energia wore blue, too; but a darker blue—*síniy*, not *galubóy*—and she didn't sound Rooskiy. Her patch was not Pegasus's famed winged stallion or Aurora's sunburst but a sixteen-pointed star, white on black. So, two plus two equaled . . . Duh.

"Space Academy, right?" Rosario nodded and a sense of reprieve filled Jimmy's soul. "And the two stripes means . . . ?"

"Ensign. I'm a pinned cadet on my midship year. I'll be landing the ship today."

After she had instructed Jimmy on what to expect during initial descent, max-Q, inversion, and final approach, she dogged the hatch to the cargo module and jumped through the manhole to the next deck. A gentle sigh ran around the seated otters.

"Landing the *Nines,* is she," McCracken said.

"No worries, mate. Everybody's jackaroo sometime or other."

"Choo-choo vould not permit it," said Sepp, "if he did not t'ink she vas ready."

Jimmy blinked. "You mean she's never done a landing before?"

Red grunted. " 'At's wot I said, wunnit?"

How many tons of aerogel and composite traveling at how many klicks, and they were letting a teenager land it? Okay, maybe she was twenty, but . . . "They practice a lot on simulators, right? I mean before they do the real thing."

The otters all looked at each other. "The real thing," said McCracken, "is always different."

"No vun is an expert." Sepp pronounced, "who vas not vunce a bunny."

"You're not wrong, cobber," said Red. His glance rested a moment on to Jimmy. "You're not wrong."

The moment of vertigo that Jimmy felt was due to the ship firing her brakes and going into drop. It was different from the endless feeling he had had standing in Leo's open airlock. Different, yet somehow the same.

10.

Check Flight

The first thing Jacinta Rosario saw as she climbed the companionway ladder onto the flight deck of RS 178 *Bobbi Trout* was Chase Coughlin slacking and grinning in the supercargo seat.

"The circle is now complete," Chase said, basso profundo. "When last we met, I was the master and you, the student. Now, *you* are the master."

Jacinta did not understand why the line was supposed to be so funny, but that might have been her own nervousness. Looking around the circular deck, she saw the copilot and flight engineer already busy at their boards at the ten o'clock and two o'clock positions. The flight captain's seat at "high noon" stood empty. Jacinta stared at the seat for a moment, took a deep breath, then climbed the last few rungs onto the deck, dogging the hatch behind her.

"Captain on deck!" Chase called out sharply, causing Jacinta to jump and the other two crew members to glance across the room. Jacinta leaned toward Chase.

"I'm only 'master' for one flight," she said. "After this, I revert to pumpkin."

Chase's grin turned serious. "But you *are* the master. Says so on the articles. Don't you dare forget it, even for a moment. I downchecked a candidate last year because he kept looking over to me for confirmation. For the duration of this flight, Ms. Rosario, 'You the Man.' Me—" he kicked back—"I'm just along for the ride."

"Yes, sir."

"Don't 'yessir' me. I'm not here. Get on with it, *Captain*."

Jacinta swallowed, nodded, then walked around the donut to the captain's position. She turned the padded chair and ran her hand over the cool leather. How long had she dreamed of sitting here? As long as she could remember. She had spent twelve months as Captain Honnycott's midshipman, executing lifts, rendezvouses, dockings, and landings under his meticulous and often sarcastic supervision. Her flight schedule had been grueling but it had also been exceedingly thorough.

Today the training wheels came off.

She lowered herself into the soft, contoured seat. Live fire exercise. Legally in command. Responsible for the cargo. But passing would entitle her only to a third stripe and a left-seat billet. Only time and experience would win her the center seat.

She turned to the copilot. "Do you have the manifest, Ms. Meredith?"

Total Meredith handed her the Gyricon thinscreen, contriving to touch hands as she did. "All stowed and inspected. Captain," she said with a smile.

Jacinta's answering smile was fleeting and nervous. She remembered how kick Chase had been on her first flight—"laid-back," as her gramma used to say. But how could anyone relax when she was responsible for—she scanned the list—three multimillion-dollar satellites, the lives of twenty otters headed for Goddard City, and supplies for the mysterious Project Lariat? She thumbed off on the list and handed it back.

"Relax," Total said. "Just another sim. You made it through the written and the orals. This part should be easy." Then, in a softer voice, she added, "You're looking good, 'Cinta."

Totally Awesome Meredith was looking good, too. She had been a pinned cadet during Jacinta's nooboo year at the Academy. Hard-muscled and lean as a whippet, with her short-cropped hair aggressively spiked, she moved with the tightly leashed grace that only years of practice in the martial arts could bestow. The huntresses, the sisterhood to which Total belonged, emphasized physical culture in the way Jacinta's own silver apples emphasized communication and body language. Both paths led to mastery of the self; both paths had kept them safe from the predatory streets until they had gotten command of their own compass.

After the accident in the Neutral Buoyancy Tank when Jacinta had nearly drowned, Total had breathed life back into her. Yungduk had lifted her from the depths and Total had lifted her from the darkness. A twofold debt, never repaid: and Jacinta suspected the two payments would preclude each other.

"Nice to see you again," she said in the Voice of Comradeship, carefully keeping intimacy from her tones. Jacinta had always admired the huntress's poise and confidence; the way she had found and maintained her own center; her willingness to take a risk and the confidence that she could meet it; her comfort in her own body. But Total wanted more than admiration from Jacinta.

Jacinta turned her seat to face front—outboard, actually—and activated the preflight checklist on her chair screen. "Flying commercial now?" she asked in the same abstract, friendly-but-distanced tones. Unlike Chase and Flight Engineer Yoshimura, who wore Aurora purple, and Jacinta, who still wore Academy blue, Total was sheathed in the midnight-black coveralls of Air Force Space Operations, with the trim, the three bands at her cuffs, and the spaceship-and-planet AFSO logo done up in silver. She flew with the Emergency Response Team, the AFSO-managed civilian volunteer pool that stood ready for on-orbit rescues.

"No, ma'am," the other sister answered. "Just logging some proficiency hours. The flock doesn't fly every day, so ERT ready crews spend most of their time compressing butts."

Jacinta turned to the flight engineer on her right with not a little relief. "Hi, Yoshi. Ship check out?" Midshipmen stuck with their captain-instructor like moss to a bureaucrat, but crew assignments were "mix 'n' match," so she and Kenji

Yoshimura had crossed orbits a few times during the past year.

Yoshi handed her his own thinscreen. "There was a malf on the number three standby computer, but I have addressed that."

Chase laughed and spoke for the first time since Jacinta had taken the command seat. "He whacked it with his shoe."

Jacinta raised an eyebrow to the engineer, who shrugged. "It's working now," he pointed out.

"Anything else?"

"We replaced the number three diverter valve and an airflow recirculation control relay that wouldn't calibrate."

Jacinta nodded. "Thank you, Yoshi." She scanned the rest of the report, thumbed it, and returned it to the F/E.

"You read that engineer's report damn fast," Chase said.

Jacinta turned her seat to face the check-pilot. Was he hinting that she had done something wrong? Or was he complimenting her on her efficiency? "I have an F/E ticket," she said. "I sat for the exam a few months ago—under Yoshi, as a matter of fact."

Chase showed surprise. "I thought piloting was the itch you wanted to scratch. What's the flight engineer certificate for, a fall-back position in case you wash out?"

And what did that tone of voice mean? Disapproval? "I don't wash out," she answered him. "But a silver apple *always* acquires more than one skill. It makes me more marketable, adds reliability to normal flight crews through skill redundancy, and—if they ever mount a crew with a need to double up on billets, I've got a better chance of making the cut." She spun back forward, wondering if she had revealed too much of herself. She knew it made her seem standoffish, but she did not like talking about her inner desires.

"Doubling up on billets," Total murmured. "Now, what flight could that possibly be?"

"Just thinking ahead, is all," Jacinta answered; then, in normal tones, "Departure window?"

"Opens in twenty," Total reported. "Closes in fifty."

"Weather report?"

"Terrestrial weather . . . low pressure center over the Carolinas. There may be some turbulence on the ascent path. Solar weather . . . seventy percent chance of flare with charged particle sleet."

Jacinta was not too concerned with the flare warning. Her flight plan was below the Van Allens, but the folks on Upabove Station and the other twenty-fours might have to button up. Most ships and habitats were equipped with hobartium belts—loops of superconductor—whose magfields would divert the sleet, but ionizing radiation could still be a problem.

She worked her way methodically down the checklist, activating systems, checking status. Cabin pressure. HVAC. Air and water regen. Radars. Outside view pickups. Fuel load. Radio frequencies for Skyport Allentown and Recife STC. At some point, she knew, it would all become second nature; but she had *never* seen Captain Honnycott make a lift without using the checklist. Each model ship was a little different, he had explained. Planks, Black Horses. Rotrons, Lock-Mar cruisers . . . not to mention the OTVs and LTVs and Luna Lighters. Even the different Planks. *Chkalov* class handled differently from *Quimby* class, for example. Preflight, Choochoo had told her, was the most important part of the trip because a screw-up in preflight could mean an unrecoverable malf later on. Jacinta thumbed each item as it was confirmed. Chase said nothing the whole while, but she was acutely aware of his eyes on her while she worked.

The background whine of the LOX and LH2 compressors, which had been barely audible through the plated aerogel hull, ceased, and a few moments later Yoshi announced that the ground crew had cleared the pad.

"Fuel pump status?" Jacinta asked.

Yoshi flipped some switches. "Function verified."

"Set active standby mode."

"Active standby mode, aye."

"All the otters buckled up?" The engineer reported everything nominal on the passenger deck. Jacinta took a deep breath and called on her Inner Strength. Then she opened the link to Space Traffic Control. "Allentown Tower, this is Aurora 238 requesting clearance to lift."

"Acknowledged. Climb bucket is clear of air traffic. You are number two after Kelly 46."

"Roger." The climb bucket was a cylinder of restricted airspace sixty thousand feet tall and five miles wide to accommodate the circular "noise footprint" of vertical lift and landing. Spaceplanes—which employed horizontal flight—used a much broader noise field west of the spaceport. Yoshi hit the klaxon once and Total got on the horn to alert the "cargo." Every otter knew what one blast meant, but the regs said you had to tell them anyway.

Shortly, the fuselage shuddered and a faint boom sounded without. That was Kelly four-six lifting for the SPS-4 construction site in geosynch. She tried to follow Kelly's flight path in her mind, counting off the seconds. Climb. Climb. Begin gravity turn. Alignment check. Torch and . . . Depart. Bucket clear.

No squawk from the tower. Jacinta tried not to bite her lip. Was something wrong? She clenched her hand over the ABORT button. The computer handled the lift once they'd programmed it, but the pilot had to be ready to abort if anything malfed on the upstroke.

Then the radio spoke. "Aurora, Allentown STC. Cleared for lift. Climb unrestricted on flight plan as filed. Passing Flight Level Six Zero Zero, contact North American Space Control Center. Have a good flight. And good luck, Rosario."

Jacinta grunted. There were a lot of otters, dogs, and bunnies in the space-flight community, but it was still small enough that everyone knew what was going down. Still, it was nice to know folks were pulling for you. "Acknowledged," she said. "Climb unrestricted per flight plan. Contact North American SCC at FL Six Zero Zero. And I will have a good flight, but only since you insist." She cut off just as the laughter erupted in the tower. "But luck," she added, turning to Total, "has nothing to do with it . . . Yoshi, activate fuel pumps." The faint vibration came to her through the seat. "Ignition." She threw the gang switch for all five engines. The ship bucked and trembled as the torch lit.

"We have function," Yoshi announced. "Board is green for go."

"Full throttle!" Yoshi hit the klaxon three times. Jacinta watched the dynes climb on the status board, felt the shaking build in the frame. Then, before her throat could close up on her, she announced, "Up ship!" and RS 178 *Bobbi Trout,* Acting Captain Jacinta Rosario her master and commander, broke the sky.

It was a heavy lift and the "Flying Fish" hit LEO as dry as the alkali flats near Glenn Academy. Jacinta had noted the mass on the manifest, but was surprised to discover that she could *feel* the difference in the way the ship handled during the lift. Well, this might be her first lift in command, but she had taken up a half-dozen ships under Choo-choo's tutelage. After a while, you started to notice little things.

Yoshi confirmed the fuel usage—enough to close with Goddard Free Port—but that didn't bother her. There was a gas station in Goddard's sub-orbs. The habitat fell in orbit twenty-eight-slash-thirty, while an Allentown lift put the *Trout* into orbit forty-slash-thirty; so there'd be a planar change, but a relatively minor one. She told Total to verify their position with NASCC and tweak the burn schedule for the close approach accordingly. Then she double-checked the calculations herself, not because she didn't trust Total's skill, but because a dry-tank approach left little room for error and an independent verification was a reasonable precaution.

Once they were in the slot, Jacinta and her crew relaxed. Closing with Goddard City was just a matter of waiting until chaser and chase fell to the same point. When she turned her seat around. Jacinta saw Coughlin making notes on a Gyricon thinscreen. The supercargo seat at the six o'clock position had a full set of readouts, though no controls, so her examiner knew every move she made. She thought about asking how she was doing, but didn't want to get downchecked for lack of confidence. Besides, a flight captain *knew* how she was doing (which was "damn good," in her case). Everything was nominal—fuel usage, longitude of ascending node, argument of perigee, time of perigee passage, velocity relative to the chase, distance to the chase—and she didn't think you could go too far wrong bringing the flight in on schedule.

Though, speaking of distance to the chase . . .

She studied the check-captain covertly. Coughlin shaved the sides of his head and kept the center short and spiked, much like Total. Late thirties—but with his sidewalls shaved like that, you couldn't tell if the temples had grayed. Which was maybe the whole idea. He wasn't *old* exactly, though his career spanned the divide between the early flight test days and the routine commercial era. Back in '09 he had helped Ned DuBois take the old *Glenn Curtiss* to the Moon, which had led to a minor fad for "moonstorming" ships that were about to be decommissioned.

Chase noticed her and sent a sly grin and a cocked eyebrow in return. Jacinta turned hastily away. Chase was narrow-faced and pale and his eyes were set a little too close together for her taste, but there was no doubt he was an attractive man. She remembered how his arms had felt, holding her tight after those terrifying minutes inside the nozzle of the *Hubert Latham.* He could have taken liberties then and pleaded misunderstanding after; but he hadn't, and that counted for something.

They dropped off the otters at Goddard Free Port and picked up a work crew that was rotating Earthside. They also loaded a sizable consignment of Rodriguez-Baker nanofibers, which were used Earthside to make fuel canisters for electric cars.

Nanofibers were related to buckyballs and absorbed up to sixty-five percent of their own weight in hydrogen, even at room temperature, a storage method that made fuel cells not only economical but also acceptable to a public nervous about "exploding cars."

Before leaving Goddard, they topped off. The LOX and LH2 tanks at Goddard's tank farm were painted bright white and orange, respectively. Bold black lettering on one tank announced: LUNAGAS: *Finest LOX moonrock can yield.* Jacinta snorted, as she had the first time she had seen it. "Oxy is oxy," she said.

"Sure," said Chase. "It's the impurities that can screw you. Trace elements and contaminants can gum up your rocket engines with weird by-products. Wheezer Hottlemeyer topped off with contaminated LOX one time and wound up with yoorz in the fuel injectors."

Jacinta turned in her seat and frowned. "What's 'yoorz'?"

"Single malt scotch. What's yours?"

Jacinta took off her gimme cap. "A moment of silence, please, on the flight deck."

Now it was Chase's turn to frown. "What for?"

"That joke was dead on arrival. We ought to show some respect."

Chase barked laughter, and for a moment, the two of them locked gazes and something passed between them. What that something was, Jacinta could not guess, and she turned away from her examiner before she was tempted to find out.

"All hatches sealed," announced Yoshi as he returned to the flight deck. "Cargo is stowed and battened."

"C of M?"

"Nominal."

"Good." Jacinta pulled her harness closed. "Mild boost. Compressed gas. Retrograde. Prepare to disengage."

"Orbiter, six o'clock, low," Total reported as they backed away from the tank farm. "Closing and rising."

"Trajectory?"

Total studied her boards for a moment. "Closest approach, two point three kilometers. Looks like a docking approach."

"Heavy traffic," said Yoshi, shaking his head.

"I feel your pain," Jacinta told him. "Put the comm laser on that ship, Total. Let's say hello."

Total set target and frequency, then thumbed her mike. "*Hóigh,* approaching ship, this is RS 178, *Bobbi Trout* out of Port Allentown, bound for 10K-zero-zero with a load of satellites. Where away?" Total had cited the first three parameters of their destination orbit: argument of perigee, eccentricity, and inclination.

The responding hail followed close on. "*Bobbi Trout,* this is RS 204, *Carlo Piazza,* out of Prague Skyport, bound for the LEO circuit with R&M and life-support supplies for Goddard, Leo Station, and Europa; Acting Captain Yungduk Morrisey, master and commander."

If ziggy had allowed it, Jacinta would have bolted upright in her seat. Yungduk? Here? And they had missed each other by minutes! She toggled her own mike, cutting in on Total. "Duck, this is 'Cinta!"

" 'Cinta?" The delight in his voice was palpable and not, Jacinta suspected, only to those trained in Voices and Postures. "Coming or going?" he asked.

"Going. We just topped off at the tank farm."

Pause. Then, "That's too bad. Ships passing in the night. Maybe next time we can dock together . . ."

Jacinta flushed. In otter slang, "docking" could mean something else, not involving ship and port. She flipped her comm to *private.* "Duck," she whispered, "you were on the flight deck PA."

"What, you afraid your crew will learn I'm in love with the smartest and most beautiful ensign that ever won her pin? I don't care who knows . . .

> *"Oh, beautiful for spacious eyes,*
> *For raven locks of hair.*
> *For—"*

"Duck!" The Voice of Total Embarrassment was not one of the canonical Voices the sisterhood taught, but she used it nonetheless. "If the next line has any reference to 'mountains,' I'll never speak to you again."

How could you hear a grin over a microwave laser commlink? Yet she did. "What say we meet at Miguel's in Tehachapi after we get our stripes," Yungduk suggested. "Kenn Rowley is going up tomorrow. The three of us can celebrate together."

"Set it up and let me know by voice-mail. But if Kenn can't match orbits, that's not a deal-killer." That was as close as she dared say out loud that she didn't mind going out alone with him.

After they had signed off, Jacinta became very busy at her board. "We have to set up for the planar shift," she said after a moment. "Our birds have to be dropped in equatorial orbits." When she glanced up, Total's gaze was unreadable.

"Yungduk Morrisey?" she said, making it a question and perhaps an indictment.

Jacinta wouldn't quite look at her. "We began seeing each other during the recession, when the Academy shut down. We helped each other maintain proficiency." Then, almost in protest, "He's really a bone charlie. The sisters approve of him."

Total turned back to her own board. "Confirm apogee at three hundred kilometers," she said, suddenly all business. "Hohmann transfer to destination altitude, burn at ascending node. Calculated delta-V to enter Hohmann transfer is"—she consulted the ship's orbital deeby—"twelve hundred meters per second. Total delta-V is twenty-two hundred meeps. Estimated transfer time, one hour twenty-three minutes."

Jacinta was just as happy to drop the subject. "We'll gyro as we ascend," she announced, "and combine the horizontal burn with the apogee kick. A planar change of twenty-eight degrees thirty needs fifty-two percent of our velocity, so we might as well do it when we slow down at the top of the loop." She didn't know why she was babbling like this. To show Chase she knew her stuff? But nervous chatter might actually count against her. The transfer was already programmed into the flight plan and neither the copilot's report on orbital position nor the engineer's report on fuel usage and equipment function had given her a reason to modify the preset plan. She took a deep breath. How many candidates had washed out because they had tried too hard?

"So you've got a boyfriend now," Chase Coughlin said after the orbital change had been executed and the crew was once more standing down. Space flight was like that. Meticulous calculations, split-second timing, then nothing but waiting. "I thought you didn't go in for that sort of thing."

Jacinta kept her back to her examiner. Was he *trying* to rattle her? "What do you mean, Captain?"

"Don't call me 'captain.' This flight deck only has room for one of those. I'm 'Mr. Coughlin' for formal purposes; 'Chase' at all other times. And what I meant was, I thought your sisterhood was into celibacy or something."

"Chastity," she told him. "It's not the same thing." She didn't ask him what the "or something" was and she barely glanced at Total when she thought about what other somethings there were.

"So," said Coughlin, "you're chaste while I'm Chase." He seemed to think that was enormously funny and Jacinta said nothing to correct him. The older generation as a rule found chastity and self-respect amusing. The Boomers were even worse than Chase's generation—they seemed to regard sex as a sort of sacrament and acted as if being "uptight" and "Victorian" was worse than leaving unwanted babies with young, abandoned mothers.

"Too damn bad," Chase said, and this time Jacinta did turn to face him.

"What is?" she said in the Voice of Contention.

"You having a boyfriend. It means you're off the market."

Market . . . how like Exers to compare something so deeply personal to a cash transaction. "So are you," she pointed out. "You're married."

"That's the theory, anyway," he said with a grin.

But the falsity in his voice startled Jacinta into momentary silence. It was all an *act*? The Punk Pilot of the Spaceways was straight edge? She tested him by asking in flip tones, "What, your wife doesn't understand you?"

His grin widened. "Heck, *I* don't understand me." And the deft way he had dodged the question was all the confirmation Jacinta needed. This guy was *married*. In the true meaning of the word, he was as chaste as she was.

And yet . . .

There was something in his eyes when he looked at her.

They had already launched two of the satellites and Yoshi had gone aft to load the third one in the slinger when the call came in. Total suddenly stiffened and put a hand to her ear clip. She listened a moment, then said, "Captain, you better listen to this," and flipped the switch for the speakers.

". . . say again, this is OTV *Harry Stine* at SPS-5. There has been an accident during docking. Both the ship and the habitat have been breached and are losing pressure. Three confirmed dead and one missing, all of them powersat personnel. Mayday, mayday. All ships and stations. This is OTV—"

"Harry Stine," another voice broke in, "this is GSO STC at Upabove Station. What is your situation?" Jacinta, still listening, bent over her boards and began feeding queries to the navigational deeby.

"Upabove, this is Lieutenant-Captain Adrienne Coster, piloting OTV *Harry Stine*. Our attitude jet malfed during docking and we corkscrewed the lock, hard. The whole structure's twisted out of alignment. Our nose is breached and the first interlock is misaligned. Won't seal properly. Command module is losing pressure. Powersat—they tell me their receiving module is open to vacuum. Three dead, one missing—but the missing otter wasn't suited up, so . . . Adjacent modules are also leaking. Wait one . . ."

Jacinta could hear the tightly controlled panic in Adrienne's voice; yet she worked through the emergency as methodically as if she did it every day. *You go, girl.*

"*Harry Stine,* Upabove STC. Be advised. GEO Shuttle *Graham* is on its way."

Silence from Adrienne. Everyone knew how many otters a GEO Shuttle could carry. Then: "Acknowledged. I am informed that SPS-5 is currently unsustainable for life support. Construction gang numbers twenty-four. Correction, now twenty. Five workers report being trapped in pressure without access to suits. Two others were suited and outside at impact and are currently on suit air and power. Remainder of construction gang has taken refuge in two intact modules. They are suiting up, but have nowhere to go. All modules are slowly leaking. Be advised: Time is not our friend."

And that, thought Jacinta Rosario, would go down in history as the greatest understatement of the twenty-first century. She studied the readouts her search engine had collated. Scratch *Carlo Piazza.* Yungduk was still refueling. *Henri Farman* had cast loose from Europa for an Earthside drop just before the mayday and could not abort to orbit. *Lotus Blossom* had just lifted for Tien Tao, but would hit LEO nearly as dry as Jacinta had and would also need to refuel. *Princess Shakhovskaya* was moored and fully fueled at Tsiolkovskigrad, but would not have a launch window to SPS-5 for another forty-five minutes and their minimum-time trajectory required a fuel-slurping planar change. What else was up? What else? The OTVs . . . But they were basically tugboats and couldn't carry any more people than the *Graham.*

"Attention . . ." It was a third voice. "This is Jason Ulundi, Emergency Response Team, Nairobi Spaceport. The flock is flying. RS 217 *Claude Grahame-White* departed Nairobi at ten-oh-eight. RS 76 *Santos-Dumont III* departs Recife at ten-thirteen."

"Acknowledged," said Adrienne Coster. And Jacinta could have recognized *that* voice without any training at all. The voice of despair concealed. She cut off the speaker and turned to Total.

"Lieutenant Meredith, lay in a course for Solar Power Satellite Number Five. Minimum orbital transfer time."

"SPS-5, aye." Total leaned over her board and began searching for trajectories in the deeby Jacinta toggled her mike and said, "Yoshi, secure all equipment and return to the flight deck immediately. Wait, who's senior among the cargo."

"Crew chief named Mercado," the engineer's voice said over her headset. "What's going on?"

"Bring him with you. I'll tell you when you get here."

"Ensign Rosario!" It was Chase Coughlin and Jacinta turned her seat to face her examiner. "May I remind you that you have a satellite in your hold worth one-point-two million federal dollars." Coughlin said. "If you fail to insert it into the proper orbit, it becomes one-point-two million dollars worth of electronic lawn ornaments."

"Mister Coughlin . . ." She had not missed his use of "ensign" in addressing her. "There are twenty construction workers and two OTV crewmen up there slowly losing air and power."

"The ERT is on it," Chase said, "and Upabove is sending *Graham*."

Jacinta could not decide if he was serious. It was a test—but what was the right answer? "Total, when's our window?"

"Fastest arrival? Engage transfer ellipse in twelve minutes. Transfer time to rendezvous, three hours twenty-four minutes. Next window in thirty-seven, but that's a slower ellipse and we wouldn't rendez' until . . ."

Jacinta nodded. Until it didn't matter anymore. She had

surmised as much from her own quick search of the deeby. But . . . twelve minutes for a decision that could make or break her career? She faced the examiner again. "What would you do, Mr. Coughlin?"

The older captain seemed to withdraw from her. The six o'clock seat was as far from her as the deck allowed, yet he had somehow become farther still. "Are you asking me for orders?"

"No, Mr. Coughlin," she said in the Voice of Command and was surprised to see him flinch. "I am the master of this bucket and *I* will decide our course of action. But a captain uses *all* her resources; and those include the instincts and judgment of Aurora's senior pilot. I'm asking for your advice, not your orders."

"Eleven minutes," said Total. Yoshi climbed up through the companionway with one of the otters. "Brief them, Total," Jacinta said. Then, to Chase: "Well, Mr. Coughlin?"

"Can the ERT handle it?"

"Negative. It's a gesture. They can't reach geosynch in one bump. They'll have to refuel, either at LEO Station or T-grad. *Carlo Piazza* and *Shakhovskaya* will be climbing to GEO before the ERT can top off. Bottom line, no one can get there before the guys in the suits run out of air and no one but the *Trout* can get there before the five in the leaking module suffocate."

Chase rubbed a hand over his chin. "Guessing, or did you suss the deebies?"

"What do you think?"

"The *Stine*'s service module can hold three people in a pinch," he pointed out.

"If they're real skinny. That's Adrienne, her engineer, and one of the suits. The other guy's SOL. You want to tell him?"

He shook his head. "He's SOL anyway. You can't get there before his suit gives out, and neither can the *Graham*."

"That any reason to give up on the others?" She didn't wait for an answer, but turned to Meredith. What was Chase's problem, anyway? Gone suddenly shy of risk? "Total?"

The copilot shrugged. "It's Adrienne," was all she said.

"You know Coster?" Chase asked.

"She was in the cohort between Total and me at the Academy." Jacinta saw no reason to tell Coughlin that when she was recovering from her near-drowning in the Neutral Buoyancy Tank, Adrienne had visited her and had prayed over her. It hadn't done any harm that Jacinta could see, and maybe it boosted her Inner Strength just a little bit. "She's charlie for live theater," Jacinta remembered.

Total turned to look at her and her mouth twitched. "Among other things."

"We went down to L.A. once," Jacinta went on. "To see Ntebele's *Helios* at the Space." She grinned a little as she remembered. "Adrienne is so intense. So focused. I thought she was going to climb up on the stage and start giving directions."

"Flight plan entered," Total said.

Jacinta turned to her engineer. "Yoshi?"

"It's your decision."

"I know that. I want your input. You've looked at the trajectory. Can we do it?"

The engineer pouted and looked at infinity. Then, he checked the indicators. "I can coax what she doesn't want to give."

Jacinta turned to the construction boss. "You heard what's going down, Mercado? Good. This isn't a democracy. You don't get to vote. You get to tell me what you think. When we get there, can your people do anything? Can you rig an airtight passage between the station's intact modules and the ship?"

"Lemme see the manifest. See what sorta equipment you have on board. Maybe we can jury-rig a temp lock, jus' last long enough to take some suits inside."

"You'll help, then?"

Mercado snorted. "Maybe I got friends up there."

Jacinta nodded. "Maybe we all do." She checked their orbital position, then flipped the horn. "Atlantic STC, this is RS 178 *Bobbi Trout*. Request permission for orbital transfer in"—she glanced at Total, who held up five fingers—"in five minutes. Destination, geosynch orbit, SPS-5. Purpose, rescue. Please advise of intersecting flight plans." She nodded to Total and the copilot squealed the flight plan to the STC. "Tell Adrienne we're coming."

"Can't," said Total. "They've abandoned the command module and bunkered up in the service module."

"Checklists, people," Rosario said. "Briskly, please."

They went down the critical items for an orbital transfer against the amended flight plan. Jacinta reminded Yoshi of the solar weather warning. GEO flight rules required activating the hobartium shields when passing outside the Van Allens during a storm watch. Another reason, she thought, to get to those otters fast and get them inside a magnetic field.

"One minute," said Total.

"Mr. Yoshimura," Jacinta said, "the long horn." The flight engineer sounded the emergency klaxon—a single extended blast. Total looked her way.

"Aren't you going to wait for clearance from Atlantic?"

Jacinta shook her head. She tried not to think of Chase Coughlin grading her performance. *Ensign Rosario did willfully neglect her assignment and flight plan and execute an O/T on her own authority and without authorization from STC.* "By the time they make up their minds," she said, "we'll be past the window. Those otters up above can't wait for the second window."

"They'll let you commit yourself," Chase said as the second hand swept toward ignition. "Then they'll second-guess you. What that second guess will be depends on how things turn out."

Jacinta's hand moved toward the ABORT button . . . but not over it, lest the sudden acceleration bring her hand slapping down on top of it. She didn't turn her head to look at her examiner. "Then we better make damn-all sure it turns out right."

Space was the ultimate pro-active environment. What you did *right now* fixed precisely what you would be able to do later on. So: "Think, then Act." But don't take too long thinking or your window would pass. Total had set a minimum transfer time orbit—overboost, rotate on gyros, then a fuel-slurping combination radial and posigrade burn when they crossed geosynch. If they foo'ed that maneuver, Jacinta would have to wait until the transfer ellipse apogee'd way the hell up and fell back to GEO for a second try.

Not that it would matter by then.

So, while she in theory had nearly three and a half hours to kill, Jacinta found herself sweating the minutes as she and Total worked out the angles and the timing for the insertion burn. Total verified their location in the J2000 coordinates through Geosynch STC on Upabove Station while Yoshi pondered fuel usage and center of mass and Jacinta worried over the thousand ways in which she could still get them all killed. Once, she glanced over her shoulder at Chase, and wondered if the fatalism he and Honnycott and the other senior pilots shared was nothing more than a shield for the awful oppression of responsibility.

Then there was the small matter of what they would do once they matched orbits with the station. The fate of the two otters caught outside would be decided well before the *Trout* could arrive; and the thirteen suited up in the two modules could hang tight until Mercado's people cut through. Adrienne and her engineer would be cramped in the *Stine*'s service module, but at least they'd be in pressure.

So, the critical path was the rescue of the five workers isolated in the third module. No suits and losing air and pressure . . . Total established a link with Wong Li, the SPS-5 construction boss, and Wong and Mercado worked out a strategy. The problem was how to open the misaligned interlock without turning a slow leak into an outgushing of what air was left.

"Simple," Mercado told Jacinta as he displayed the schematics Wong had downloaded. He tapped a finger on the throat between the ruptured receiving dock and the cul-de-sac where the five were trapped. "We take five empty suits in there, then Tonio—he's our smallest welder—he spot-welds a metal disk across this passage. Cork in the bottle—with the suits welded inside. Then the trapped otters come out, get the suits, and put them on."

"If they can," Chase Coughlin said from across the deck. Jacinta and Mercado looked up from their study of the schematics.

"What have we overlooked?" she asked.

"Slow leak," the older man reminded them. Mercado slapped his forehead.

"Ay yi! Anoxia . . . Right. They could be delirious. Okay . . ." He studied the dimensions of the shaft more closely. "Okay. Tonio welds in five suits and two otters. That'll be me and . . . Bird Winfrey, I think. I'll ask him. This is strictly a volunteer gig."

"I'll do it," Chase said. "I'm a spare wheel here, anyway."

"You know anything about rigging, *'mano*? 'Cause that twisted lock, she might not be so easy to open, now that I think about it." He frowned at the plans again. "Maybe Tonio welds us in from the inside, 'cause he might have to cut through . . ." He shook his head. "Five suits, two otters plus Tonio and his welding rig. 'S getting very crowded in that little passage. Just me an' Tonio, then."

"And you're not volunteering for anything, Mr. Coughlin," Jacinta said. "You are to take the conn of this ship while Total and I enter the *Stine* and rescue Adrienne and her engineer."

Coughlin's face narrowed in disapproval. "Don't try to be a hero. The captain doesn't go out with the 'away team,' " he said.

"And I wouldn't go," Jacinta answered, "except for two

things. One: I've got you taking up space. You wanted to volunteer a moment ago? I'm volunteering you for this."

"And the second thing?"

"Adrienne is a friend of ours."

Chase pursed his lips and nodded. "All right." Then, after a pause: "I hope she has talent. I mean as an actress or director."

Jacinta turned her seat around. "Interest," she said. "Not talent."

"Too bad. Because she'll need another career after this."

His offhand callousness angered her. "We don't know that the accident was pilot error," she snapped. "It sounded like an engine malf to me."

Coughlin shook his head and snatched his cliputer, which had been floating beside his seat. "You still don't get it, Rosario. Responsibility isn't about *fault.* Coster's the captain of the tub. It doesn't matter if she screwed up or the ship malfed. It doesn't matter if she was off-watch and asleep, or even medically incapacitated. Her name is on the articles. *Response*-able. That means she has to *answer* for whatever happens. The Board of Inquiry—and trashing one of the powersats means the mother of all boards will be sitting—might clear her of any wrongdoing; but she'll never get another plum assignment."

"That wouldn't be fair . . ."

"Fair? When did fair come into it? No one will ever see Captain Coster's name on the duty list again without thinking about the *Wreck of the SPS-5*—and people would rather not think about bad news. That's why—"

He stopped suddenly and pushed himself back into his seat.

Jacinta finished for him. "That's why you reminded me that I wasn't *obligated* to fly to the rescue."

Chase shrugged. "A ship's captain can get away with a lot of crap, as long as it comes out all right in the end. And if it doesn't, then it doesn't matter if she did everything by the book. STC didn't come back with your authorization because if they'd *ordered* you to SPS-5 the outcome would have been *their* responsibility. You're a cadet on her check flight, an unknown quantity, and they couldn't bring themselves to order you into something they didn't know you could handle."

"They sure let me volunteer, though," Jacinta pointed out.

"Sure. That's different, though you notice they didn't recall the two ERT flights. You can grab all the responsibility you can handle. But not one gram more."

Jacinta pondered that in silence; then she asked quietly, "What would you have done?"

"Me?" Chase snorted. "Just what you did. Not that I'm a hero or nothing, but they *expect* that kind of stunt from me."

Jacinta spun to face her screens. "Just living up to expectations, right?" she said lightly over her shoulder. He didn't fool her for one minute.

Flaco Mercado was a bone charlie. He and his crew knew ziggy, so Jacinta had no qualms about seeing them jet off into the twisted entry to Solar Power Satellite Five. Or at least not many qualms. You sent the best you had, she realized, but bottom line, it was *you* that sent them. So whatever happened, it was you that shouldered it. Chase had been dead right about that part.

But he had been wrong about not being obligated to make the attempt, and not only because Adrienne was a friend and you didn't leave friends to die. It was because every otter in ziggy—from the Guangdong powersat crews who could not forget the asteroids their lasers were designed to burn to the pleasurers on FreeFall SkyResort who did their best to make them forget—was a "sister under the skin," and she could not stand by, just doing her job, and watch when she could have made a difference. Failure didn't matter—except maybe to the Board. The one true failure was not to try. STC had had to *order* Yungduk Morrisey to stand down and had ordered Captain Zaranovsky in *Princess Shakhovskaya* to abort to LEO after he had already departed in Jacinta's wake.

When they entered the *Stine*'s service module through the sidelock. Jacinta and Total found three otters huddled there already suited up and waiting. There was frost everywhere. The module had been powered down and the pressure lowered to the barest tolerable to conserve heat and oxygen. It was not until they had escorted the three across to the waiting *Bobbi Trout* and they had removed their helmets and taken a breath of reasonably fresh air that Jacinta realized that none of the three were Adrienne Coster.

She and Total sealed up their helmets with more haste than the situation required, yet less than their hearts demanded. They jetted across to the derelict *Stine* and squeezed into the command module and there she was.

Adrienne Coster had not even bothered to suit up. There was frost in her hair and her eyes and streaks of black blood had squeezed from nose and mouth and ear and around the edges of her ice-crusted eyes to float in small globules about the cabin. And all of a sudden, as if frozen words had slipped from those bloodless lips, Jacinta understood what it meant to accept responsibility for a ship.

"She could have suited up," Total protested over the suit-to-suit. "She might have made her suit air stretch. Dammit, why couldn't she have waited?"

Jacinta had no answer to that. It might have been that the *Stine* had lost too much air to begin with and there was not enough for four people to breathe. And it might have been that, having room for only three, Adrienne could not—or would not—choose between the two Guangdong otters in their nearly exhausted suits. Or it might only have been the Board of Inquiry, where she might be found negligent or she might be found faultless but the one place she would not be found was back here among the crystal stars.

Jacinta tried to imagine herself faced with the choices Adrienne had faced and felt something cold and hard and heavy form within her. Something so cold she knew it would never,

ever melt. "Did she leave any family behind?" she heard herself say. "Any loved ones?"

"Yes," said Total in a voice of distant grief. "Oh, yes."

Afterward, when the ERT ships with their med-techs had rendezvoused and taken away the living and the dead, and Jacinta brought the *Trout* down, down, down to LEO once again and they docked at Goddard Free Port to the glare of websters and newsgroupies, she was asked again and again about her "heroic rescue mission." And again and again she tried to explain. How there had been no choice, really. And it was Flaco and his friend Tonio who had rescued the four trapped otters still alive. And Chase Coughlin and Kenji Yoshimura had juggled the complex logistics of bringing the others across. But try as she might, she could not explain that the real hero had been Adrienne Coster, who, whether she had blundered initially or not, *had* been faced with a choice and had taken the harder path. But it was not only responsibility for disaster that a captain must learn to accept. Unearned praise must also be borne. In the end, she found her refuge in a phrase she had heard to the point of self-parody from the lips of the man who had somehow become her mentor.

"I ain't no hero."

The newsgroupies went wild over it. The public likes their heroes in aw-shucks mode. No one seemed to notice what she really meant—that someone else had been the hero—and they wouldn't have believed it anyway. They had a paradigm to fill and Plucky Neophyte Rides to the Rescue was just what their readers and viewers and scrollers demanded. But Total knew. And Chase knew. And so Jacinta understood that—regardless how the Board of Inquiry or even the Board of Examiners might rule on her performance—she wore the four stripes on her soul. Whether she ever wore them on her sleeve seemed somehow and suddenly a matter of no importance.

11.

Taking a Chance

Jimmy Poole so seldom made a personal appearance at the Lucky Thirteenth that Chase could not let the occasion pass uncelebrated. He waited until the weenie was away from his desk, then slipped into the room and put a barf bag in his center drawer. It was a real, no-foolin' zero-gee barf bag with the Aurora sunburst logo embossed in purple on its face. Chase did not want to reflect on the sort of mind that felt blow bags ought to be decorative, nor that a company's prestige was enhanced by the appearance of its logo on such an item. He spent much of the rest of the day waiting for Jimmy to notice.

Zubrin, the simulator program manager, took him around the revised flight deck. Revision H was not that different from Revision G, but Chase paid careful attention, because you never knew which detail could wind up biting you. He was pleased to find that most of his own suggestions had been incorporated in the rev. A designer who listened to the user was a pearl beyond price.

Billie Whistle, the cheesehead who ran the simulator room, stopped him in the hallway later that morning and congratulated him for the rescue of the powersat workers. Chase told her it was entirely Rosario's show. "I was just along for the ride." But he didn't think it sank in. Being famous and being involved was all that mattered. Ned DuBois had laughed when he complained about it the week before.

"Hell, Chase," The Man Who had told him over dinner at chez Coughlin, "I didn't do half the things I got credit for."

Ned and Betsy had stopped in Phoenix on their way back from visiting their daughter at Glenn Academy and Karen had insisted on entertaining them at home.

"I just don't want people thinking I'm some kind of hero," Chase explained.

Karen cut off a piece of her enchilada with her fork. "As long as you don't start trying to live up to other people's expectations." She didn't look up when she said that.

Chase wasn't sure what she meant. "Some people," he said, "their opinions matter. Yours, for one." And that did bring Karen's head up. "And Little Chase's. Even Ned, here. I care what he thinks."

"Lord knows why," said Betsy. "Even *he* doesn't care what he thinks."

Ned chewed thoughtfully and took a sip of his Corona. "What other people think shouldn't bother you, one way or the other. It's what you think of yourself that counts." He looked at Betsy and some secret glance passed between husband and wife. "Trust me. I know."

After dinner, Chase took Ned and Betsy outside to show them his cactus garden while Karen got dessert ready. Ned had seen the garden before, of course, but it was new to Betsy. Spring in the Arizona desert could be cool when night came on. The crimson and umber bands in the western sky cast long shadows across the hardpan. The cacti, spaced irregularly about the grounds, ranged from short, broad prickly pear and chollas covered with their downy leaves and needles, to tall, imperious, wickedly spiked saguaro and organ pipe. Betsy gasped.

"Why, they're beautiful!" she said. "I never expected that." The flowers were a riot of scarlet and lavender and yellow and white. On some plants, the funnel-shaped flowers completely hid the plant itself. Their fragrances wafted in the evening breeze.

"It's the spring rains," Chase explained. "They only bloom for a short time. That one over there"—he pointed—"it only blooms on a single night. I think it'll be Friday. The rest of the year, they look just like you expect cacti to look."

Betsy put an arm around Ned. "That's a lot of days of ugly for a single week of beauty."

Chase shrugged. "Oh, it keeps me occupied."

"Why don't you grow—oh, roses, instead of those—pincushions?"

Chase folded his arms. "Roses have thorns, too. A cactus is more honest about it."

Walking back to the house, Ned held Chase back. "I ever tell you I met your Lieutenant Rosario? Back at the Academy, oh, three years ago, I think. I dropped in to see Forrest, and Rosario and a friend of hers snuck aboard my plane and started running dry sims in the cockpit."

Chase grunted. "Sounds like something *you* would have done."

Ned laughed. "Or some others I could name. What's your opinion of her?"

Chase stopped. He turned and ran a hand through his hair. He stared out over the darkening cactus garden. So beautiful for so short a time and all the more beautiful for the brevity. He hadn't known how to explain that to Betsy. He pondered Ned's question, wondering, too, at the man's interest. "Rosario's a little green, but she'll ripen right up. She thinks fast and isn't afraid to accept responsibility. She's got an engineer's ticket, too—"

"And she's a licensed electrician," Ned added. "A regular jack-of-all-trades. I read her file."

"Jill," Chase corrected him. "Jill-of-all-trades, because she is, sure as taxes, female." He gave Ned a second look. "And you were reading her file because . . . ?"

"I'm an old retired fart. I gotta read something. But not everything's on paper, if you know what I mean."

"Yeah. I know what you mean." He thought about how Rosario had handled the rescue. And earlier, as a cadet, how she had volunteered to climb inside the *Latham*'s exhaust bell.

"You maybe gotta sit on her sometimes. She's willing to take a chance, but maybe too willing. A year or two under an experienced hand is what she needs."

Ned grinned. "You want to take some sweet, young pilot under your wing."

"Like you took me under yours."

"Well . . . you weren't all that sweet."

Karen called from the kitchen. "Dessert's ready!" and Little Chase hollered, "Cherry pie, Daddy!" Chase grinned and hollered back. "Two shakes, slugger!" He turned and sat on the stoop. He cast a shy glance at Ned. "Kids."

Ned leaned against the newel post for the handrail and folded his arms across his chest. "Yeah, tell me about it."

"Your Liz turned out okay. Professor at the Space Academy and all."

"I guess I wasn't a total failure as a father. She's gonna make me a grampaw next year. Her and Zach. You imagine that? Me, a grampaw?"

Chase rubbed his hands together. "Look, Ned . . ." He paused, uncertain. "I don't think I ever told you this, but . . . you're like a father to me." There, now how hard was it to say that?

"I'm way too young to be your dad," Ned replied in mock offense.

Pretty damn hard. Chase kicked the gravel. "You know what I mean."

"You must have been hard up for a dad if you picked me to be one."

"I was." And his flat tones were enough to blot Ned's grin.

"Okay. Sorry. I never knew."

"Understand, Dad wasn't a *bad* man. Just . . . weak. He drank too much and he fooled around and he used to hit on us. Weren't for you . . . Well, weren't for you, I'd be him."

Ned grabbed his shoulder and squeezed. "You turned out okay."

"He's dried out now. One day at a time, like they say. We

see each other sometimes, and he's almost the guy I knew when I was five. So, well, I owe you that, too."

Ned raised his eyebrows. "For that? How?"

"Because I had to pay you back somehow for what you did for me. So I got him the help he needed and I saw to it he took it. Pay debts forward, not back. Isn't that what you always say?"

"And Rosario is another payment forward?"

Chase made light of the whole thing. "Passing on the torch, Ned. You to me to 'Cinta. 'S like parent to child, only different. Passing on the torch."

Roberta Carson called a meeting for noon. Technically, Colonel Eatinger called the meeting, but everyone knew that Roberta took care of all the nuts and bolts. Chase sidled into the room and tried to take a place in the back corner, but Roberta put him right up at the table with the other department heads, across from Zubrin and Hobie and—the gods being in an antic mood—right next to S. James Poole.

"Hey, Jimmy," he said as casually as he could.

The geek looked at him over a pair of reading glasses. "How beneficent of you to grace us with your presence."

There it was again. Did Jimmy carry a thesaurus up his butt just so he could fart words that Chase might not know? Chase dropped his portfolio to the table. "Well, I'm a beneficient kind of guy, is all. Besides, aren't I talking to Mr. Telepresence himself? I haven't seen your bonebag in quite a while. Though I gotta admit, there's not so much bag as there used to be. Working out?"

Jimmy grunted. "That wasn't my allusion."

"What *is* your illusion?"

"*Al*lusion. Learn English, for crissake. I meant your taking off from the project to go haring off into space."

"It's my job," Chase said, keeping a straight face. "I'm a Rocket Man."

"Besides which," Colonel Eatinger interrupted, "there

aren't that many senior captains to supervise check-flights. Chase's leave had my approval. Now, Morris Tucker is teeping from Goddard and will only be in line of sight for twenty-five minutes, so let's take X-vehicle construction status first on the agenda. Roberta?"

Carson glanced at the screen embedded in the tabletop before her. "Timeline says the ship is ready for unmanned orbital transfer tests by midsummer. Meat, how do we stand on that objective?"

Chase drifted into a state of benign inattention. He knew such periodic head bumping kept everyone's piece of the action in synch, but it never seemed to him as if anything *happened* at meetings. He'd rather be in the sim room or—better yet—taking the *Lariat* itself out beyond the Moon.

Zubrin reported on the status of onboard HVAC design and Chase went back in the zone.

Ned had asked him about *Lariat,* too, that night in Phoenix. Chase had put it down to the older man's wistful desire to fly a new sort of 'chine, but now he wondered. Ned had seemed almighty curious. When would the X-ship be ready? In time for the upcoming asteroid rendezvous? Just starting flight test by then? No backup pilot? Do you think that's wise? But it wasn't like the project had unlimited funds, and most of that was going into the hardware and the software. Chase might have a high opinion of himself, but he knew he was just about the cheapest component in the stack.

What had Ned meant, *do you think that's wise?*

Hobie reported on the magnetic properties of the latest version of the superconductor. *Everyone* went into the zone. Except Billie Whistle, Chase noted, who took detailed notes. Well, change the sail and you had to change the simulator code.

Jimmy was the software department. Chase knew he had a team of top programmers scattered around the world and working together on-line. Roberta had told him that a cracker had tried to winkle the cheese and Jimmy's friends had come down on him like God's hammer. Some goof kid pranking or some doom-kisser planting sabotage, it didn't matter. There were people out there who *wanted* the Bean to hit, who looked forward to it. Because it was God's will; because it would reduce "Man's footprint" on the planet; because they thought they would be Big Dog in the chaos after the strike. For some it meant a chance to scold others; for some it meant an excuse to party hearty; for some it meant a reason to stockpile food and weapons.

It was hard to wrap his mind around that kind of thinking. Though sometimes he wondered whether Project Lariat—and Operation Intercept and Project Sabre and Project Redoubt and all the other pieces of the planetary defense effort—were much different. Party hearty while the hammer fell. Just a different kind of party. Just a different way of keeping busy.

Jimmy reported on successful validation of a revision to the navigational code.

This time, Chase did not zone out. He straightened from his perpetual slouch. "How could you validate it?" he asked. "I was tied up with the Board of Inquiry hearings over the *Stine* Incident."

"I ran the sim," Jimmy said.

"You!" And suddenly everyone was looking somewhere else. "*You* ran the sim?" The image of Jimmy on the flight deck was so preposterous that he very nearly laughed. That he did not was only because he knew Eatinger must have approved the assignment.

"It wasn't like it was a real flight," Roberta Carson pointed out. "And we didn't know how long you would be tied up."

Chase tugged on his lip. "How'd it go?" he asked finally.

"I didn't drop into the sun," said Jimmy, "if that's what you mean."

Chase looked at him. "That's not what I meant."

"You can review the logs," Roberta told him. "Now that you're back, we can start pushing the envelope on the new revision."

He did review the logs after the meeting, and he found that Jimmy had been running sims for a couple of months. "We all have," Roberta admitted when Chase shook the copies under her nose. "Just for fun, you know. After hours. Colonel Eatinger has; Bob Zubrin; Billie Whistle . . .even me. Sometimes we just want to test the simulator itself. Or the solar model. Or quality control test on the software. Not every sim needs a *pilot*."

Chase wasn't sure why it bothered him so much, unless it was that everyone else seemed to think it was a game. Maybe that was the other half of the reason why he'd jumped at the chance to proctor Rosario's check-flight. The need to get out into the Big Empty, where things were real and mistakes mattered and you didn't put a bunny at the yoke.

Chase put in some tough sims over the next few days. The revised software was not radically different. This deep into the project, concept changes were expensive; so the basic architecture was frozen, just like the X-ship configuration. The time for free play at that depth was way back in advance quality planning. But there were just enough differences to keep Chase interested. The edges of the envelope had been moved and he had to find them again.

"Tell the weenie," he told Roberta after one session, "that his new cheese doesn't stink."

"Tell him yourself," the program administrator answered. "He's taking us out to dinner tonight at King Arthur's."

"Whoa! Big Spender . . ."

"Can it. It's convenient to the hotel. Last time we tried anything out of the way, Hobie got lost. He has a flight to Houston in the morning—Hobie does—and Jimmy's heading back to California, so tonight's the last chance to get together."

"And celebrate? Well, if Jimmy's leaving town, that's reason enough to celebrate."

* * *

King Arthur's was done up in pseudo Olde English decor. The tables centered around a substantial salad bar, and though the hot entrees were decent, many came to the place just for the salads. Jimmy co-opted a large round table so they could spread out. They were ahead of the after-work dinner crowd, so there were few other diners present; and those that were talked among themselves in subdued tones. Chase had noticed that a lot lately. With five asteroids headed Earthward, there wasn't a whole lot of call for cheerfulness.

"I don't know why they're waiting," he heard one diner tell his companion as he passed by with his salad plate heaped high. "They should go out to that Bean *now* and not wait until the last minute." Chase didn't linger to hear the response. *Pay attention, dude,* he thought in the man's direction. *Can you say, "Launch window"? Hello?*

He told the others about it when he sat down, and even Jimmy Poole rolled his eyes. Hobie began to say how the *Lariat* would be more flexible and they all told him to put a sock in it because it wasn't as if they didn't know that already. Roberta asked Jimmy how Tani's new book was going and he told them how much Tani appreciated the recordings they were sending and that the new book was progressing just fine. "She likes to get the characters straight first," he explained, "then she sets them loose in a situation to see what they do."

"Wait a minute," said Hobie, loading mushroom onto a bed of spinach. "She's the freaking *author*. She *knows* what they're going to do."

Jimmy shrugged helplessly. "I'm just saying what she told me."

"You haven't listened to any of those recordings yourself, have you?" Chase asked.

Jimmy, too, had gone heavy into the salad bar. He directed his attention to the lettuce. "She won't play them for me," he said.

Which did not exactly answer the question, but Chase did

not press the issue. "Hey, Hobe. Remember when you and me were on Leo Station a couple years ago and I said I wanted to fly something no one ever flew before; and you said—"

Hobie cocked his head. "And I said, if I ever designed a new sort of ship, you'd be the one to fly it."

"Tell me straight, otter. You already had the *Lariat* in mind."

"Well . . . something like it." The project scientist grinned and Chase shook his head.

"Couldn't let me in on it then, could you . . ."

"Let you in on what? My wet dreams?"

"Why not? I let you in on mine." Yeah. Out on the edge. That was his dream. Out where there were no footprints. Where you couldn't just go by the book because there *wasn't* any freaking book. And there might never even *be* a freaking book.

"Want to hear *my* wet dream?" said Jimmy, and Hobie and Chase both turned to him and said, "No!"

"This is too much sharing," said Roberta.

"Think flight test will clock on schedule, Styxy?" Chase asked her. They called it flight test, but it was really the pilot that was tested. Measured against chance and the cosmos. The 'chine was only the instrument for conducting the test.

Roberta had ordered herself a Maryland seafood platter. "Everything seems to be coming together," she allowed. "Ship's nearly ready. Software's nearly ready. How about the pilot?"

Chase laughed. "I've been ready for years."

Hobie grunted. "This is a little different than what you're used to."

"Tell me about it. Who's been running sims for the past year and a half?"

"The sims aren't like the real thing," Jimmy said.

Chase snorted. "As if you would know."

Jimmy colored. "I know as much as you about the ship.

My cheese interfaces with every system on board. I've gone bone deep into each module. It's the software that flies. The ship is just the enabling hardware."

"Hey," said Hobie.

"What you know," Chase told him, "is 'book learning.' You don't know jack about the *ship*."

Jimmy's chin lifted. "I've been aboard her—a couple of times."

"Yeah? And I visited the Louvre. Doesn't make me an artist."

"Chase is right," Hobie said. "Installing the RAM pins and the updates since then isn't the same as *flying* the ship. Hell, you didn't even have to go aboard to do that. You could've teeped."

"It was my money for the lift ticket. What do you care whether I hack the cheese in San Mateo or Low Earth Orbit. I happen to like ziggy."

"Yeah," said Chase, "I heard."

Jimmy must have heard the subtext and shot him a glance both embarrassed and angry. Chase wondered if he'd found the space-sick bag yet.

"Well, mister hotshot pilot, maybe I did fly your ship a little."

Chase scowled. "What are you talking about?" Hobie said something, too; but it was Roberta who imposed silence, laying a hand on Jimmy's arm so that he couldn't lift his fork to feed his smug, self-satisfied face. "Yes," she said in a voice like a knife, "what *are* you talking about?"

Jimmy turned sullen. "It wasn't any big deal. Last time I went up, I tested the interface on the loop controls, is all."

Hobie's jaw dropped. "You powered up the loop?"

"I had to make sure the interface worked," he protested.

Hobie said, "Jesus Christ! You could have put drag on the loop and dropped the whole ship out of orbit. Jimmy, are you *fucking nuts*?"

Roberta once again sliced through the babble. "Who authorized that?"

"It was just a quick electronic function test, and the ship is fine, Hobie."

"Who told you that?"

"Chase."

Chase had been listening to the confession with blank astonishment. Now he found his voice. "I didn't tell you jack."

Now the smug smile returned, defensive, proud, and even a little triumphant. "Sure you did. All those sims you flew? Well, every time you solved a navigational or operational problem in the simulator, my neural net learned the solution. It's an evolutionary system. Harbor Master—that's the module that pilots the ship in the magnetosphere—reacts just the way Chase would. That's how I know the loop wasn't powered up long enough to affect the ship's orbit."

Chase shook his head to clear it. "Let me get this straight. You're programming *me* into the software?"

"More accurate to say that you're *teaching* the software how to fly. You may not be the best pilot there is," Jimmy said, "but you're the only one we have, so I had to make-do. Basic notion of reliability is redundancy. I'm making the human pilot redundant."

"You wish," said Chase. But Artificial Stupids already did a lot of routine work and controlled a lot of simple processes. Maybe Jimmy was writing the next step in their evolution. "I don't believe the human pilot can ever be useless. I don't care how hard geeks like you work at it."

Jimmy stood up and threw his napkin on the table. "Try not to be any stupider than usual, Chase. I said 'redundant,' not 'useless.' " Heads turned at nearby tables. "Why do designers put redundancy into a system in the first place? To have an alternative when the primary fails. What's the ship supposed to do if something comes up that's outside the freaking envelope? Thinking fast is what an A/S does best, but thinking outside the box, on its feet, when the shit hits the fan, it needs a backup system. If you can't see that, I'm outta here."

"We won't miss you," Chase told him.

"You'll miss me five minutes after I'm gone." And with that he stalked off. The other diners nearby pretended that they had not been gawking.

Roberta hit the table with her fist. "What Jimmy did was reckless and irresponsible! If I ever find out he pulled another stunt like that, I'll see to it he's grounded. Chase, what's so goddam funny?"

"I wish I knew if he done it on purpose."

Hobie frowned. "Done what on purpose?"

"I just realized . . . When he said he needed me on board to back up his software, he laid down one of the finest compliments I've ever gotten."

Hobie thought about that one for a moment. "I don't think he knew. But you know what's funnier? I already miss the little geek."

Roberta was still boiling. "What are you talking about?"

Hobie wagged a thumb at the approaching waitress. "Son of a bitch stuck us with the check."

Chase planned to fly the project's jump jet back to Phoenix for the weekend. One of the privileges he was granted, to compensate for the long weeks away from home, was the frequent long weekends back. His locker at the Center had a digital combination lock keyed to a passcode only he knew. Not that there was anything particularly irreplaceable in his flight kit.

Except a powerful reek.

Chase held the satchel at arm's length. Then, holding his breath, he zipped it open.

And there was the barf bag he had stuck in Jimmy's desk drawer to remind the weenie of his vertigo and fear of the

Big Empty. Only it was a used barf bag now. In spite of everything, he grinned.

The boy showed promise.

He always came home like a hurricane. Door flying open. Flight bag hurtling across the room. Karen scooped up in his arms and whirling about. Little Chase running around them, laughing and dancing. Daddy's home! Daddy's home!

They would all go out to eat at a Hunan Wok or a Tandoori Kitchen or a Taco Bell and get some good American food, and Chase would tell them all about the latest simulations or the bugs in the software or the argument between two of "the professors" about the proper modeling of this, that, or the other. Karen would laugh with him, brushing back her long black hair, watching him with eyes bright with promise.

Afterward, he would play a game with Little Chase or read him a story—or tell him one, real or made-up, about the troll named Jimmy. Whenever he deviated from the set plot line or dialogue, the boy would laugh and correct him. No, no! That's not how it goes! And later still, he would lie with Karen, with his hands caressing her tawny body, his tongue tasting her honey, taking things slowly, reining in the urgency built by absence, until everything burst forth and one or the other of them would pounce like a tiger, and the need would spend itself.

"I should fly out to Greenbelt more often." he said, "because the welcome home is so tasty."

Atop him, Karen pressed her lips into his neck. Her long hair spread over them both like a protective cape. He squeezed her buttocks, then ran his hands down the backs of her thighs. The damp of her skin was fading in the dry Phoenix air. She raised herself up on her arms, and the hair cascaded tentlike over his face, tickling where it touched. "If you were underfoot every day," she said, "I'd maybe take you for granted. What's so funny?"

Chase shook his head. "Nothing. I was just thinking that

Jimmy Poole would probably write a program or something to try to maximize ecstasy by optimizing the combination of the frequency and durations of absences."

Karen snorted. "What's the trade-off?" A teeping accountant, she often phrased things in economic terms; even love, with talk of inflating assets, mergers, market penetration. Not to mention double entry. Pillow talk at the Coughlin household could be strangely erotic.

"Getting it on less often," he said, "in exchange for—uh—greater return on ass-ests."

She shook her head, brushing him gently with her hair. "Your skillet must be one dude lover," she said sardonically.

"He ain't my skillet," Chase said. "I just gotta put up with him."

Later, at breakfast, he approached The Topic. Karen had whipped eggs into a fluffy omelet rich in cheeses and onions and mushrooms—just the sort he liked. Bacon just short of crispy. It was as much a part of the welcome home script as the fervid lovemaking the night before. Karen wore a thin, pearl-white negligée and soft pseudo-fur slippers. *Old married couple*, he thought. Not so old as all that, but Chase knew a couple of guys who'd been in and out already. So how long before the dazzle fades? And what took its place? He knew some couples in their forties who spent their time hissing and scratching each other; and others in their sixties who held hands on park benches. There was a secret there, he was sure; one that made the difference between the two futures, but when would they let him in on it?

"Selection Board started meeting," he said in as casual a voice as he could muster. And then, in case she didn't know what was what, he added, "They're picking crew for Intercept."

Karen chased a piece of omelet across her plate. She glanced for a moment at their son. Pretty soon, he'd be too old for Mommy to wear sexy nightgowns to breakfast. "You didn't volunteer, I hope."

He didn't say anything for a while; long enough that Little Chase looked curiously from Mommy to Daddy. Karen, too, noticed the silence. "You did."

He put his fork down. "It's not a question of volunteering. The Board will do the picking. They'll look at everyone's skill profile and they'll do the old mix and match to optimize mission success. If they want me, they'll ask for me."

"You could say no. I scread that on the public site."

Chase balled his hands together, the way he used to when Sr. Mary Liguori had made them keep their hands on their desktops. "I could. I don't think they'd shoot me for planetary treason. But the word would get out and everyone would know and . . ." He looked up and met the anguish in her eyes. "Being away from you tears me up, but you knew when we married that my job would take me away from you sometimes."

Karen picked up her plate and carried it to the sink. "Yes," she said over the running water. "For Moon runs or up-and-downs. Ordinary, scheduled flights. I always knew when you'd be back. I'd mark it on the calendar." She rubbed the plate with a scouring sponge. Back and forth; back and forth.

"The Intercept flight profile has a return date, too."

"Nine months down the road."

"That's less time than Forrest and them spent going out to Calhoun's Rock and back."

"And they almost didn't make it back."

"Karen . . ." He carried his own plate and Little Chase's to the sink. The water was still running, though Karen's plate was long scoured clean. Mechanically, she took the others from his hand. "You go to the supermarket," he told her, "there's a chance you won't come back."

She threw her arms around him. The hands were wet from the sink, but he didn't mind. "Oh, Chase. I guess if the world wants a hero, they know your phone number."

"I ain't no hero," he told her. "Besides, I just wanted you to know. Intercept probably won't pick me, because I've been training with the Thirteenth."

Karen shook her head against his chest. "No, they'll take you. You told me so yourself. Didn't you say they were going to pick the best?"

Little Chase grinned ear to ear. "Mommy's kissing Daddy! Mommy's kissing Daddy!"

Voices: Psalm 23

She drifted through a world that never seemed entirely solid or permanent. Forms and shadows came and went, glimpsed between periods of darkness. They seemed strangely distant, indistinct and sometimes surrounded by a pale rainbow of colors, like objects viewed through a very thick prism. They were never the same twice. Sounds were slippery, never quite grasped, running like quicksilver through her mind. Each time the darkness lifted, the forms and shadows had changed, as if she were but catching intermittent glimpses of an ongoing drama.

Once, there was a solidly built man sitting beside her, his head lolling on his shoulders, eyes closed, gently snoring. For some reason, the sight filled her with both a warm comfort and a vague distaste. Another time, it was a smaller man with fine hands and feet, pacing tigerlike by the window. He turned at some motion of hers and she saw eyes of a pale green that she carried with her into confused and lustful dreams. Still again, she saw a slim, black-haired woman with eyes like still waters over bottomless pools.

She thought that they must have names—indeed, that she herself had a name—but they did not come. There were other shapes, too. Boxes with blinking lights; tubes and rails; men and women garbed in the colors of angels. There were names for them, too.

Often, she felt a nagging urgency, a sense of things undone—though what things, she could not tell—and of consequences most severe; and so her dreams were often troubled by inchoate menace creeping ever nearer. Sometimes the urgency was sister to guilt, the knowledge that she had done something awful and would be called to account. She was pursued in those dreams, running through a formless darkness, seeking shelter or protection or simply an end to feeling.

Gradually, she realized that she was alone in her world, the single creature of an inept God, one Who had neglected to finish what He had begun. The universe was one vast darkness because the light had not yet been separated from it; and things had no names because there were no names until she chose to bestow them. She toyed with the notion for a timeless interval, and names like "Barry" and "Ned" and "Roberta" occurred to her, though to what objects they might be applied she could not decide; and names without objects were only sounds her mind gibbered to itself.

To name names meant engaging the universe, and it was not the sort of universe she cared to engage. Lonesome, dark, haunted, abandoned by its God . . . The occasional glimpses she had were an irritation and a distraction. There was greater comfort in drifting through the nothingness and hoping that it would never end and the darkness would go on undisturbed forever.

12.

Lives

Ned DuBois felt like a ceremonial object, a relic of bygone days trotted out from time to time for important occasions. His presence on various boards and bodies was meant to induce awe and nostalgia; but like poor, old Chuck Yeager on the Rogers Commission, he wasn't expected to actually *do* anything. And yet this one time, his position as Chief of Crew Operations for Daedalus raised him a notch above hood ornament.

He was "The Man Who." An appellation usually followed by a string of firsts, from the sublime to the absurd, many of which he had actually done. In some—first to take an SSTO to orbit and back—he took the quiet pride of a craftsman in a job well done. In others—the invention of ziggy bounce-ball—the amusement of a man who disliked the pompous. Still others—first to boink a femm in ziggy—he could not shake with any number of denials or even knowing winks from an earlier generation of "astronauts" who better deserved that honor.

The Selection Board was large. Too large, in Ned's opinion, to accomplish anything useful. But most of the members were on for show. When it came to making the pick there would be only a dozen or so on the "working subcommittee." And even in that smaller group, there were four who mattered more than any of the others.

It was generally, though silently acknowledged whenever the subcommittee met *in corpora*. There was a space defined by a boundary of mojo that the others seldom crossed, and then with deference. Not that Ned and his friends were demigods in their eyes. They had all rubbed elbows too closely during their cockpit careers to maintain any illusions of divine ichor running in anyone's veins. Yet, there was clearly an attitude of "first among equals" that gave them if not leadership of the group, at least a Supreme Court sort of status.

For old times' sake, Ned hosted the May meeting at the flight test facility on Fernando de Noronha where the original cadre had tested the first Plank SSTOs. Most of the subcommittee attended in the flesh, largely for the sense of pilgrimage. In a fit of nostalgia, Ned even managed to locate Claudio, whose roadside cantinha had once served the finest feijoada north of São Paula. Age had slowed the old man down, but he still made one mean stew. Ned considered for a moment looking up Claudio's sister, who had played the guitar back then, but decided not to press his luck. Guitars had not been the only instruments her fingers played on.

"We don't do much training out here anymore," Ned told the others when they had seized a booth in the lounge of the tourist hotel that had replaced Claudio's ramshackle shed. It was the sort of hotel for people who, when they left home, insisted on taking home with them.

During flight test, secrecy had mattered, and Daedalus had selected the island as much to keep its R&D under wraps from competitors and governments as because of its position near the equator. A pile of rocks in the middle of an unfriendly ocean, Fernando had never been a favorite landing site. Recife was the prime spaceport now in this corner of the world.

"Por favor!" Forrest Calhoun signaled to the waitress and wagged four fingers horizontally about a foot over the table. *"Tragam-nos quatro."* He wagged a thumb at Ned. "My friend here's buying." The waitress smiled professionally and brought four bottles of Xingu and waited while Ned counted out the *tarif,* then waited some more until he had peeled off a more generous tip.

"So," said Katya Volkovna, lifting her bottle, *"Na zd'rovye!"*

A clank of bottles, a cold swallow or two; then thoughtful silence.

Katya said, "What did you think of the plenary session?" After fifteen years in America her English was nearly unaccented. She and her husband, Valeri, had flown ballistic for Aurora for many years after the original SSTO flight test program wound down. Now she was Aurora's Chief of Operations and Valeri was Director of the Orbital and Ballistic Pilots Board of Examiners. Between them, they knew the profiles of nearly every space jock practicing within Canada and the USA. Valeri was laid up in the hospital, courtesy of a double-black ski trail in Idaho; so Katya had come down in his place.

Ned had lusted after Katya in flight test days; but then, it was hard to find the woman Ned had not lusted after back then. Tall, hard-built, with steel eyes and a crew cut, Katya owned the sort of build that had once given Olympic judges bad dreams. She was possibly the most muscular woman Ned had ever met. Flirtatious, as long as you didn't take her seriously.

Forrest snorted. "You mean that presentation about the neural net? I'll believe in a pilot selection neural net when I see it; though I bet Senhor Machine here may find it right up his alley."

Mikhail Krasnarov, the Iron Mike, smiled. "In theory, neural net can sort and arrange all factors we look for in crew."

"In theory," Forrest said, "bumblebees can't fly."

"Oh, I agree, my friend. Are always intangibles. No A/S can know pilots as we do." The Iron Mike chaired the Board of Examiners for Russia and its associated states. "Databank can say how many years this man has flown and on what flight profiles and in what equipment. But they cannot say what is in here." And he tapped his forehead. "Or here." His heart. "For that, one must know the man." He nodded to Katya. "Or woman."

"So," said Forrest, "do we have a vision of what we want here?"

"An older pilot for mission commander," Krasnarov mused.

"Like you, good buddy?" Forrest asked.

Krasnarov sighed and a wistful look came over him. "A few years ago . . . But, no. None of us."

"Why not?" said Forrest. "Maybe *you're* over the hill—and besides you 'n' me, we had our little trip back in '10—but maybe Katya here or Ned deserves a shot at deep space."

"If we were eligible," Katya pointed out, "the UN DeepSpace Commission would not have named us to the Selection Board. To select ourselves would be . . . unseemly."

"She's right," Ned said. "Our punishment is to send others out."

Forrest gave him an odd look, but Ned did not elaborate. He took another drink of Xingu. "Okay," he said. "We get a forty-something as mission commander. Someone with deep space experience. That means—Forrest and Mike being out of it—someone from the Lunar run."

"Feathershaft," said Forrest. "She's good. The younger pilots look on her as a mother."

Ned recalled looking on Alexandra Feathershaft in another way entirely—which was itself a measure of his own years. "What about Kilbride or Eustis?"

"Not enough deep space time."

"Coughlin?"

"Too young for mission commander. But pencil him in as a maybe for one of the other two ships."

"What about Yablokov? He handled that little problem on *Gagarin* last year."

Krasnarov pursed his lips. "He has five children. Maybe we consider that."

"Zaranovsky, then. He's the best there is for orbital docking."

"As good as Singh?"

"Better. There's Ng Wu-hsi. He doesn't talk much, but he knows ziggy."

They batted a few more names around. Ned noted that Krasnarov, with his usual efficiency, was jotting the names on a paper napkin with the stub of an old pencil. Ned didn't even know pencils could get that small and thought they should change Mike's nickname to Senhor Frugal. They were just beginning the selection process, but Ned had a feeling they had already named the three ship commanders. He trusted largely to instinct and figured the ones with the best mojo would be among the first few names to pop into their heads.

"So," said Katya after a few minutes. "Now what of backups? For each ship?"

"Unlikely," said Krasnarov, "that all three pilots will need replacement. Perhaps one spare pilot will be sufficient."

"Jesus, Mike." Forrest emptied his beer; signaled for another. "That's a damn cold-blooded way to look at it."

The Russian shrugged. "Another rigger may be more useful than another pilot."

"The other subcommittee's working on that end."

"Young," Katya laid out the requirements. "Good pilot, but also sound in engineering; and can assist in the work on-site."

And expendable, thought Ned; but he said nothing aloud.

Forrest sighed. "You're talking about my babies . . ."

"Is Sulbertson," suggested Krasnarov. "Number two on *Yeager, Cochran's* sister ship."

"Actually," said Forrest, "*Cochran* is the sister. *Yeager* the brother." His grin was brief, however. "Okay, 'Lonzo knows nuke engines. Plenty of deep space, too. Who else?"

"We thought you would know the younger ones better than we," said Katya.

Forrest sat back and looked toward the ceiling with his lips pursed. "Meredith," he said.

"The ERT pilot?"

"That's the one. Lightning reflexes. Top physical shape. She practices karate or something."

"What will she do," Krasnarov wondered. "Break asteroid into pieces with hand chops?"

Forrest grinned. "You're getting better at it, son. Keep practicing, and someday you'll come up with an actual joke."

"I defer to master. I know of Chernovsky and Nieves."

"Rosario," said Katya. "Very good on electrical systems and she has a flight engineer ticket. Her pilot-instructor—"

"Coughlin."

"Yes. He gave her high ratings on her check-flight."

"Can't send Rosario without sending Morrisey," Forrest pointed out. "Wouldn't be fair to break them up like that. Ned, old son, you've been powerful quiet there."

"Should we even be sending husbands or wives or fiancées?" Ned asked. The other three fell silent and regarded him soberly.

"You want to explain that, good buddy?"

A brief shake of the head. "You know what I mean. Some of them won't be coming back. Mike"—he pointed to the napkin with the list of names—"that's a death warrant."

Forrest reached across the table and seized Ned's wrist. "So's the Bean, good buddy. So's the Bean. This is our first and best chance to knock it aside. I don't want to lose any of them. They're my kids. I know 'em up close and personal. But that's why we're picking the best. They'll be the ones who come back."

"Then why not send all senior people?" Ned asked quietly. After a moment, Forrest released his wrist. "Yeah," Ned continued. "Got to save some of them for the next rock, and the one after that. Christ, FarTrip barely made it back in one piece, and they don't come any better than you and Mike. What's Total Mission Reliability for a single ship . . . about eighty percent? So the probability of all three coming back is—"

"Fifty-one percent," said Mike, "and two-tenths."

Ned drank the dregs of his beer. It tasted flat and bitter. "Yeah. So, it's a coin toss whether all three ships make it; which is the same as saying three or four of the people we name won't come back." He placed the bottle on the tabletop and pushed it into the center with the other empties. "Sure, I know how the song goes: '*Between their loved homes and the war's desolation* . . .' They'll be heroes, even if they fail. Falling stars. And, yeah, it's not a war, exactly; but that doesn't make counting the body bags any easier."

Forrest winced and looked down at his reflection in the table. "Counting three or four bags is a sight easier than counting three or four million."

"And it is 'expedient that one man die for the whole people.' Never mind. The medicine might taste like crap, but I can swallow it."

"Each one we nominate," Mike pointed out, "has right to refuse."

Ned shook his head. "Anyone like that, we'd never put him on the list."

The band returned from their break and, in a rattle of tall drums and maracas, opened with a lively samba. Forrest signaled for another round, but there were no toasts this time when they raised their bottles. *Dead Man's Flight.* Ned had heard the whispers. But if so, why had so many already dropped their names in the hat? There was no volunteering, but there were ways of making one's willingness known. For that matter, why were he and his colleagues so wistful? Because, being old geezers in their fifties, they had nothing to lose? Maybe that was why the mission needed younger hands. Softening in the gut, eyes growing dim, Ned was too aware of mortality. On a Dead Man's Flight, you wanted those who didn't believe in death itself. Plus an older hand to watch over them and be the voice of caution.

God, Sandy. Take care of them. Feathershaft had had flaming red hair and a body like Eve's a half an hour before the Fall. She'd been the first woman to make herself available that Ned DuBois had ever turned down. Among The Man Who's titles was The Man Who went back to his wife and never regretted it.

And Chase. The rest of the committee might not know it yet, but Ned thought he could name half the crew already. Chase was almost his son. They had slipped into Skopje together to rescue the peacekeepers, and Chase Coughlin had stood in the open cargo doors of the old *Calbraith Rogers* with one hand on a strap and the other on an M-16K while they plucked Gunnery Sergeant Azim Thomas from the center of a circle of death. He and Chase had skylarked the Moon back in '09: the first human footprints there since the bean-counters killed Apollo. Had anyone ever looked less promising than the kid Ned had met in the machine shop at Thor Tools that summer long ago? Sullen look, head shaved on the sides, enough ear studs that he'd never make it through an airport metal detector. He'd been miking a change part for one of the experimental SSTOs, and Ned had dared him to finish the machining in the absence of the master. Chase had shown two redeeming traits then: a willingness to take on a challenge; and the intelligence to take one he knew he could meet.

Chase knows his way around a machine shop, Ned recalled. Ship an omnitool with the mission and enough feed-stock and he could fab about anything the mission needed but forgot to pack. Another plus mark to chalk up beside his name.

The samba band was bouncing and some wild evolutions were taking place on the dance floor. Ned and Forrest and Mike and Katya leaned closer together over the table, and they wrote more names on the napkin.

13.

Duty Calls

Yungduk Morrisey was waiting at Tsiolkovskigrad when Jacinta returned from the Moon. He had a bottle of vodka and a "reservation" in Komorov Spoke at Mars equivalent spin gravity. Jacinta regarded the vodka, the room, and Yungduk with equal suspicion. "What's the occasion?" she asked as they kicked off down the centerline of the Hub. Captain Rustov had gone off with the port captain to handle the paperwork and the LTV *Titov* was as snugly buttoned up as a flight engineer could make it, so officially she was "paid off" and at liberty until her next booking. Theoretically, she should check in at "pilothouse" to see where she stood in the rotation, but the morning was soon enough for that.

"I hear you landed on the Moon," Yungduk said as they soared together across the receiving bay to the interior manlock. "That's quite a milestone. I thought we'd celebrate."

"And you just happened to be docked here at T-grad when I came in?"

They both jackknifed and landed feetfirst by the aperture to the stockroom bay. Yungduk bowed her through first. "I don't trust to coincidence when I'm trying to meet up with you," he said when he'd joined her on the other side. "I checked all the flight bookings, found a ship that would dock here just before you came back, and did a little horse trading."

"Intercept orbits, hunh? Yungduk, people are starting to talk. Even Captain Rustov asked me if I was going to be meeting you here." And he'd grinned like a grampaw when he did.

"So, save me the aggravation of juggling assignments. I'm

a pilot and you're a pilot *and* a flight engineer. Let's fly together."

"Okay. Let's!" And she sprang hard off the bulkhead and sailed down the length of the bay. She used her hands and feet to fend off from the storage bins lining the walls until she was oriented right down the centerline of the Hub. The interlocks, from what she could see, were open all the way to *Peredni Levi.* She heard Yungduk whoop behind her and knew he was following. A grin split her face. It was always good to get together with the Duck. He was smart, lively, solicitous of her feelings; and she liked the way his arms felt around her. Sometimes, when she made port and Yungduk was *not* there waiting for her, she knew a profound and illogical sense of loss. Not that she would ever tell him.

Like most of the LEO installations, T-grad was built on the pinwheel design. Each of the spokes as well as the spindle itself was a stack of modules based on the old U.S. Shuttle external tank. The Hub itself remained in ziggy while the Pinwheel of eight spoke-pairs spun around it.

When they passed through the second module, a station cadre working on some zero-gee experiment or manufactory paused in his labors and waved. *"Nye byespokoityes, tovaritch!"* he shouted. *"Ty yeyo lovish!"*

Yungduk must have sprung off harder than she had, because halfway through the next bay, he pulled up level and reached out a hand. She took it and they went into a slow lateral spin due to their different velocities, but a few kicks and nudges against the passageway walls brought them into synchronization, and they flew on side by side.

"Superman and Supergirl!" Yungduk shouted.

"Super*woman,*" she corrected him.

"Whichever," he said. "You're super, either way."

Okay, he was mushy; but it made her tingle anyway.

When they passed through the last interlock, it suddenly seemed as if they were spinning. In fact, the Hub's center module was mounted on a pair of giant Romanov magnetic bearings, so that it was the station that was rotating around them. A riot of pastels in red and gold and white and blue; of solemn-eyed men and women in ritual poses; of intricately twisted vines and strange stylized birds. Mosaics and icons spun around them—slow enough to be seen, fast enough to give her vertigo.

"How do we stop?" Jacinta said. That was their spoke entrance coming up on the clockwise turn, sure enough.

The face Yungduk turned on her was full of mock terror. "Stop?"

Grab hold of something, obviously. But what? The only thing she *wanted* to grab was sharing her acceleration frame of reference.

Their problem was solved for them by the unexpected emergence from the second traverse spoke of a short, thickset man. Jacinta had time for one brief glimpse of pale eyes widening in surprise and of an unruly thatch of straw hair, then they were all three tumbling and spinning and grabbing handholds, in the course of which the Russian grabbed more than a handhold. As they disentangled themselves, Yungduk's arm wound up around her waist and Jacinta let it stay there for a few heartbeats before pointedly removing it. The removal—and the delay preceding it—both being messages.

She had expected the Russian to be angry, but the man was laughing. *"Spéshitye?"* he said to Yungduk. *"Búdet oná kholódnaya?"* He seemed to think this was even funnier. *"Kto pobyeditl?"*

"Sorry," Jacinta said. He seemed friendly enough and Jacinta wasn't *entirely* sure the grope in the confusion was intentional. His coveralls were bright, *krasniy* red with gold trim and bore a golden sunburst with the numeral one over his right breast. Over the left, Cyrillic letters spelled out 3APAHOBCKI. Jacinta judged his age to be mid-thirties, a captain-pilot by his cuff stripes. Jacinta took an immediate dislike to the man, though she could not have said why. It might have been the "hands on" experience she had just had, or it might have been only the cocky look on his face, as if he were not only the Master of the Universe and knew it, but he wanted everyone else to know it, too.

"Amerikanskii . . . Govoritye pro-russkii?"

It was sometimes hard to tell when a Russian had asked a question, since the tones and rhythms were different from English. Yungduk spoke up. "*Ochen nyemnogo.* My friend doesn't speak it at all."

"Hey," Jacinta protested. "I have a few words. Gar taught me on the mooner. Uh . . . *'zdrasti'* and *'poka'* and, uh, *'yolki-palki.'* "

The Russian guffawed and said. "Very useful, that. Very Russian saying." He wiped an eye. "Yvgeny Pavlovitch Zaranovsky," he said when they introduced themselves.

Jacinta took the proffered hand. "I've heard about you. You fly for Vostok, don't you?"

Zaranovsky tapped the sunburst and its numeral. "First in space," he said, quoting the corporate slogan. "For docking and pod-snatching, is no one better than Zaranovsky."

Jacinta was willing to bet that he carried the "docking" and "snatching" into other activities, as well. Yungduk tugged at her hand and she said, "Well, it's been nice bumping into you . . . I mean—"

But the Russian laughed again. "Comes now safety lecture." He wagged a finger at them. "Not to be flying through Hub in future. Is dangerous. Lecture ends. Now come with me to restaurant and we are celebrating."

"Celebrating what?" Jacinta asked.

Yungduk said, "We were sort of planning our own private celebration."

"Oh ho!" Zaranovsky wagged an open hand in front of his chest. "Very private, hey?"

"Not *that* private," Jacinta said as much to Yungduk as to the leering Russian. Still, she did not let go of his hand.

But Zaranovsky was not to be dissuaded. "Come," he insisted. "First, you are helping me celebrate. Then, you may . . ." He made a fist and pumped it. He kicked off across the Hub to an accessway on the farther side. Jacinta and Yungduk followed. Each of the spokes was named after a dead cosmonaut and bore an icon beside its entry with his image and the instruments of his valor. The spoke they entered was named КОМОРОВ and the icon included an image of a tumbling Soyuz capsule trailing a hopelessly tangled parachute. Just before he turned to enter the spoke feetfirst, Zaranovsky kissed his fingers and touched the image.

"For luck," he explained. "Was pilot with greatest . . . What is American expression? Power? Skill?"

"Mojo," said Yungduk.

"Bone," said Jacinta.

Zaranovsky nodded. "That is expression I heard. 'One bone charlie.' No power, motors malfunctioning, ship tumbling and spinning, fighting atmosphere turbulence with no controls but these"—he held up his two hands—"and no computer but this"—a tap to the head, this time—"and *still* he was bringing his capsule down 'in the groove.' Had his parachute only deployed properly . . ."

That didn't sound much like a patron for luck to Jacinta, though it did sound like one hell of a pilot. "What are you celebrating?" she asked again.

Zaranovsky patted a zippered breast pocket. "I am to pilot *Sikorsky*."

It was a beat and a half before Jacinta realized what he meant and why a routine ship posting could create such excitement. It wasn't a routine posting at all. "You're going to the Bean!" she said. "Oh, my God, the Selection Committee's announced its choices!" And she had received no notice. And that had to mean . . .

She tried to mask her own disappointment. "I'm happy for you, Captain Zaranovsky," she said with as much enthusiasm as she could muster. But disappointment was a pale word to name the pang she felt. "Who else was picked?"

Zaranovsky rotated and pushed himself feetfirst into the

spoke. For the first few levels, the spin gravity would be negligible; but a few levels down the ladders turned to stairs and you had to be real careful or the Coriolis would have you banging into the walls and each other. "Is private notification," he said, "so one has choice to refuse without public . . . notice." His voice revealed what he thought of anyone who would refuse such a duty.

Much of the station cadre was in the refectory on Komorov-12—and not a few of the transient otters just passing through. A FedEx parcel ship on a fractional orbit was in port and its hapless pilot had been carried bodily into the celebration, shouting, "But I gotta be in Guangdong in twenty minutes!" It seemed as if everyone wanted a chance to pound Zaranovsky on the back and drink a glass of vodka with him. Jacinta wondered if the man's spine would withstand the punishment it was taking. She had never seen grown men kiss before.

Gar Rustov spotted Jacinta across the room and wound his way through the pack to her side. "A great honor," he said, pouring from a bottle into a cup held at a slight angle. He thrust the cup into Jacinta's hands. "Yvgeny Pavl'itch is—how do you say it?—'hot pilot.' "

"That's how we say it," Yungduk agreed. Rustov did a double take, looked from him to Jacinta, saw their hands clasped tightly together. "Ah! You must be 'The Duck.' " He shifted hands, tossed his bottle straight up, gave Yungduk a quick handshake, then snatched the bottle before it had fallen more than a half a foot. "But I must say you disappointment me."

Yungduk frowned. "Why?"

"From descriptions I have heard, I was not expecting mortal being."

The Duck shot Jacinta a sardonic look and she felt herself color from chin to crown. "Gar!" she said in anguish.

"Your woman," the lunar pilot continued to Yungduk in a voice that would have been confiding had it not carried to most the room, "excellent pilot. She was flying with me as engineer, but I taught her LTV controls and Jørgen Andersson of Selene was showing her how to land lunar lighter. So I am thinking no one knows more ships than this young lady."

"Yeah," said Yungduk—and there was a very strange tone in his voice when he said it. "She's one all-round pilot-engineer." What was it: Fear? Disappointment? Yungduk could not possibly be jealous of her! As gently as she could, she disengaged her hand. Just as well. The Duck was in danger of becoming a permanent growth attached to her.

Komorov-16 spun at 0.36 gees, just shy of Mars equivalent. Though only four floors below the refectory, the "barracks" were in the Outer Spoke, somewhat insulated from the noise and vibration of the party above. Each floor of the spoke was a disk 8.4 meters wide with—discounting the stairwell—46.6 square meters of usable floor space. Cadre residents in the other spokes shared their floors in pairs, but transients didn't need spaciousness—or at any rate were not given spaciousness—so the floor space was halved again. Eleven and a half square meters. Enough room for a bed, a dresser/desk, and a small closet. There was a commode as roomy as an airliner lavatory; and the shower—on the next level down—was communal, thank you very much.

Jacinta threw herself on her bunk. She seemed to fall in slow motion and lay with her arms outspread. "My head," she complained. "I feel like I'm spinning around and around."

"You are," Yungduk pointed out. "Spoke revs at two per minute."

She didn't need a reminder of that. Her brain couldn't take spinning in two different planes. "Is that really the Russian custom—eat one course, then drink one course, then repeat until you pass out? Or was Gar pulling our leg?"

Duck staggered and sat on the edge of her bed. His own bed was in the adjoining cube, but the door between them was open. She ought to ask him to shut the door. "I'd ask him," he said, "but last I saw him he was on the floor with the others."

Jacinta giggled. "The Russian national sport." It wasn't that funny, but Yungduk laughed with her.

He was lying beside her. She couldn't remember him reclining and she wondered if she had had a momentary blackout herself. "I hope he wouldn't take this wrong," she said carefully, because the vibration of her own voice made her head tremble, "but I really hope Zaranovsky never has another need to celebrate. At least, not while we're around, the lucky bastard."

"You think he was lucky?" Duck said. His face was awfully close to hers. She could look deep into his dark brown eyes, feel the feather of his breath on her neck.

"Goin' t' th' Bean . . ." Now she did let her frustration show. "Wish I was lucky."

"Depends on what sort of luck," he said and his lips were on hers.

It wasn't the first time they had kissed nor the first time his touch had lit her soul. Yet, there was something electric on this occasion and she responded with a sudden, inexplicable hunger. Her arms went around him and then they were pressed together, with kiss following kiss—lips, neck, throat—and his hand caressing her. She shivered and stroked his back. "Oh, Duck . . ." And he said, "I love you, 'Cinta . . ."

There was a fire in her belly that seemed to swell. Did his words mean so much to her? It was absurd, a part of her realized, but she felt weirdly *safer* with his arms around her, though his embrace could do nothing to protect her from vacuum, endless cold, or solar flares. She only knew that she didn't want him to release her.

Somehow, he was on top of her. He weighed surprisingly little. But then Jacinta remembered they were not quite at Mars-level spin gravity. His hands began to explore. "Duck . . . ?" she said in the Voice of Caution. But the station was not the only thing spinning, and she couldn't quite form the thought. Danger! But what was the danger? How could there be danger when she felt so good?

In the brutal, pounding morning, of course, she saw the danger all too clearly. Jacinta woke to find her coverall disheveled and unzipped to her waist. Groggy, she could not exactly make out the significance of it. She tugged a little at the zippered edges, because she was cold. Then it all came crashing back: Zaranovsky, the party, unlimited vodka, making out with Yungduk, and . . .

She sat bolt upright in her bed. A mistake, as her head threatened to come off entirely. She gripped it between her hands and bent over, groaning.

The call of the wild. An answering groan from the next cubicle. Yungduk.

"You bastard!" she shouted.

There were inchoate sounds from the other room. Then, the Duck staggered into the open doorway, banging into the frame as if he could not quite find his balance. Jacinta reached out with her foot and swung the door closed on him. "Don't come near me!"

This time she was answered by a fist banging on the other wall and a muffled voice shouting something in what she guessed was Russian and guessed further would translate as Shut Up!

The door hadn't closed and latched. Yungduk was in the way. It swung open. He rubbed his shoulder and stared at her. "I'm sorry," he said.

"Sorry?" This time she hissed; low, so the other rooms would not hear. She realized one of her breasts was exposed and she twisted to straighten her halter; but there was not enough room to turn her back on him and she had to do it in front of him. "You could at least look away." she said bitterly. Surprisingly, he did.

She tucked and zipped but felt no better for it. "This time," she said, kicking again, "don't let the door hit you when it slams."

But he would not get out of its way. "I said I was sorry, and I really am. We were drunk. I need to know how to make it right."

"Make it right?" She could not believe she was hearing right. "Make it right? Can you put Humpty Dumpty back together? I was saving myself for when it was right, and a drunken grope was not exactly the magic moment I was looking forward to."

"Will you marry me?"

That deserved dead silence, but didn't get it. "What, now you feel *obligated*? Fuck the drunken slut, then marry her out of pity?" It took an effort to keep her voice down so others would not hear. The words wanted to spit out and the pressure of keeping them in started tears in the corners of her eyes.

Yungduk's face dissolved in astonishment. "What? But we didn't—You didn't—'Cinta. Love. You could never be a slut." He tried to take her hands but she pushed him away. He pulled a wrinkled handkerchief from a zippered pocket. "We didn't," he said. "You passed out. I fell asleep beside you, woke up later, and crawled over to my own cubic. And, Jacinta, I mean *crawled*."

"We didn't . . ." She searched for her Inner Strength, found it, and knew somehow that he had spoken the truth. "I thought you . . . I thought we . . ." She didn't know how to say it, couldn't find the words. Maybe there were no words. Convulsively, she wiped at her eyes. She shuddered. "I'll *never* get that drunk again."

"Jacinta," he said gravely, "if we'd been any less drunk, we would have kept on going and ruined everything, even friendship."

"I wanted to," she remembered. "It felt so good being with you." And which of them had pulled down her zipper? Which of them had unfastened hooks? She had reached for him as he had reached for her. But there was no memory, only a black hole.

"I've always felt good being with you," Yungduk said. "Even just sitting on the quad at the Academy doing nothing but picking out planets in the night sky. The way I felt waking up beside you last night . . . I want to do that every day."

"Duck, you really need to work on your marriage proposals. You haven't got the romance part quite right."

He ran a hand across his scalp and lowered himself cross-legged to the floor. "I'm no good at this sort of thing. My head hurts. My mouth feels like the bottom of a bird cage. I don't know which way the shower is, or even what day of the week it is. All I know is that I love you and I want to be with you always."

Jacinta fought a moment of vertigo. "Why the sudden rush?"

"Rush?" He lifted his head and laughed. "We've known each other for three and a half years and we've been seeing each other for most of that. Your mom seems to like me, and I *know* my mom and dad like you. They keep asking when I'm going to bring you by again."

"It's just that most boys think a 'long courtship' is a dinner and a show."

Face creased in agony, Yungduk whispered, "Does that mean 'No'?"

"Just last week when our orbits crossed at Europa Station, we talked about everything under the sun, but you never said anything about getting married. Why now?"

He closed his eyes. "Private notification makes damned good sense. A public refusal would be devastating."

Jacinta started. Was he talking about his proposal or about Project Intercept? Or only using the one as a metaphor for the other? "I haven't refused," she said, "because I haven't been properly asked."

Morrisey's smile was almost grim. "Yeah, let's sober up first."

"Or at least shower. And, no, not together." That would come later. That, and other things. Maybe it was wrong to make the Duck toe the line, but she would always remember the day he asked her, and wanted the asking itself to be worth the memory. She knew what her answer would be, too, because she had heard the question coming for several months already, possibly before Yungduk himself. She had seen the resolve building; but neither of them wanted to force it. It had to be the right moment, the right setting. There had to be something almost ceremonial about the moment. Duck knew that, too; which made this headlong proposal all the more puzzling.

"You were planning to ask me last night," she said with sudden clarity. "Before Zaranovsky hijacked our evening. That's why you said we were going to celebrate."

His eyes dropped and he looked away. "My brain is on hold this morning. Wait here." He disappeared into his room and reappeared a few moments later with a micro-CD packet. His lips parted, then closed, and he held it out as if it would do in place of words.

Jacinta saw the logo in the corner—the shield-and-globe. The Planetary Defense Committee—and her heart sank. They had picked Yungduk and not her? Yungduk was good, a careful and meticulous pilot, but she knew she was better. Certainly better for FarTrip II, where careful and meticulous might prove less important than flexible and multiskilled. She had pursued a flight engineer's license with just that thought in mind.

"Congratulations," she said, and even she could hear the flatness of her voice. Blame it on the headache.

"No," Yungduk said. "It's for you. Sergei, in the radio shack, gave it to me when it came in yesterday. He knew I'd be seeing you as soon as you arrived."

The moment was a rope bridge suspended forever over a deep, deep chasm, swaying in the wind. The packet formed the focal point of a series of concentric circles. In the first band: his hand; and hers, trembling slightly as it reached forward. And surrounding that center, Yungduk himself with a look of profound apprehension and loss. And surrounding that the anonymous clutter of transient quarters in a T-grad spoke. And beyond that, in successive bands: the Komorov Spoke, T-grad Station, Low Earth Orbit, the Earth itself, Luna, stretching out farther and farther into the void until, in the very last band, she saw a small, gnarled marble of a worldlet tumbling faster and faster toward the center.

"You'll need your private key to read it," Yungduk said.

Her hand touched the packet—and moved a fraction beyond it to touch his. "It might be a rejection," she said.

The Duck laughed. *"You?"* was all he said. A single word, but so full of love and admiration and . . . yes, he had complimented her before on her skills, but never before had she received praise as sincere as that one word.

"You're disappointed," she said. "You wanted to go." Everyone she knew wanted to go. For hearth and home. To stand between their loved ones and disaster. For the adventure or the glory. Because they never imagined not going. Because it was there.

But Yungduk shook his head. "Not especially. I don't want to go to the Bean. I want to go with you. Wherever you go. The destination doesn't matter. Am I disappointed? Yes. Because you'll be gone from me for . . . nearly a year."

"Oh, Duck . . ." She was crying again. She took the packet from his hand. And laid it beside her on the bed. Then she reached out and took his own hand in hers. He had finally managed to do it right. "Yes," she said. "You can go with me, wherever I go, for the rest of my life."

However long that might be.

And she knew with abrupt, frozen certainty why Yungduk had proposed so precipitously when he learned of her new assignment.

* * *

Chase got the word on a slow Tuesday when, back at Goddard once more, he was running a sim on LEO-GEO transitions. It was a slow process, requiring a perigee kick at north magnetic with each turn of his orbit. "Like a kid pumping her legs on a swing," explained Zubrin, the project manager. Personally, Chase thought they should use strap-on boosters to pop the ship up to geosynch, where she could catch the solar wind and really show her legs. But part of the magsail's potential usefulness lay in fuel-less lifts from low to high orbit for construction of the orbital defenses; and so Hobie and Zubrin, not to mention Eatinger, insisted on testing those capabilities. Jimmy Poole's programming team had devised an Artificial Stupid named Harbor Pilot based on the physics developed by Zubrin and Ganesh. It was all engineered with unmanned cargo shuttles in mind.

Too well engineered, in Chase's mind. As if the pilot were an afterthought. Jimmy Poole and Adam van Huyten had capitalized a virtual company, Mesmer-Rise, to exploit unmanned orbital transfer magsails. They had posted a public Review and Comment site and were interviewing subcontractors to conduct different aspects of the business.

"A perfect run," Billie Whistle said from the control booth as Chase finished his checkdown. "Jimmy said to tell you 'you didn't screw up.' "

Chase gave a sharp glance at the glass-enclosed booth and saw the half smile on the cheesehead's face. He finished the post-op and thumbprinted the pad, tossing it onto the chair for the next sim. Yeah, Jimmy had probably thought he was giving a compliment. Cut the weenie some slack, Roberta had cautioned him. So Chase smiled and gave a Cub Scout salute to Whistle and made no response.

Stepping outside, he found Colonel Eatinger and Roberta waiting for him with grave looks on their faces. Bob Eatinger handed him a disk packet. Neither of them said anything. Bad news, Chase thought. Something's happened back home. But when he glanced at the cover and saw the shield-and-globe of Project Damocles he knew immediately what the encrypted message would be.

A cold hand gripped his heart as he inserted the diskette into the closest machine and plugged his dongle into the decrypter. Nine months in deep space with the fate of the world on his shoulders . . . The notice had been signed by Valery Volkov for the North American Board of Examiners and countersigned by Krasnarov, Delacier, Ling, and Abreu for the other regional boards. At the very bottom was a note from Ned DuBois. *Congratulations, Chase. I know you'll do the right thing.*

Sure he would; but what was the right thing here? To stay with the Thirteenth and the team he'd been training with for the past year? Or to accept the call and take the Long Orbit? On the one hand, he'd be leaving the Thirteenth without a trained pilot just as *Lariat* was nearing her trials. On the other hand, on Intercept, he'd probably contribute more to the planet's defense. Hobie's magsails were a long shot as far as diverting the Bean went. Of course, Operation Intercept was a long shot, too, both in terms of its likely success and, literally, its distance; but at least FarTrip II would be more than going along for the ride in an A/S-controlled pod. The work would be too far out to be preprogrammed and "well engineered." Decisions would have to be made by those on the spot.

He looked up from the letter and caught Roberta's eyes on him. It was some trick of the lighting playing off the angles of her brow and cheeks, but it seemed to him for a moment that Roberta had no eyes at all, only tunnels endlessly deep.

"What do you think I should do?" he asked her; and not until that moment did Chase ever imagine he would go to Styx Carson for advice.

"What do you *want* to do?" she answered, which was not a big help. Chase looked to Eatinger, who only held out his hand and said, "We'll miss you."

Chase accepted the hand, although he said, "I haven't decided whether to accept the assignment." Eatinger looked shocked, but then he was a military man and the invitation from Project Intercept must look to him very much like an order from headquarters. Hell, it *was* an order from headquarters, except that Chase did have the right to decline. "I mean, I don't want to leave you guys in the lurch."

"What's going on?" Whistle and her two operators had come out of the control booth. Jimmy Poole, looking impatient, had booted up on the desk monitor, teeping all the way from California. "Hey," said the weenie. "The debrief? I got a pile of notes . . . ?" He made get-on-with-it motions with his hands.

Roberta glanced at the monitor. "Chase just got drafted for FarTrip II."

"Oh, that's great," said Jimmy—and for a single instant Chase thought he was offering congratulations. "That's just great. Who's gonna validate my software now?"

Later, Chase actually laughed. Of all the people whose advice he might have taken, it was Jimmy Poole, who hadn't offered any, who had showed Chase the right decision.

FarTrip set up a block of rooms in the Nassau Bay Hilton on NASA Highway One outside Houston and installed the Intercept crew and such of their families as could relocate with them. Fancy digs, Chase thought when he and Karen explored the suite behind the howling whirlwind that was their son. But then, the Intercept crew was lionized as no other group of space explorers since the original Mercury and Vostok test pilots. Their pictures had graced webzine portals; they had been interviewed on threedy. Politicians jostled to be seen with them. They "wore the robes of the world's hope," according to news-star, Broder Hart.

Chase thought that was an overstatement. They were the world's first, best shot, but it was still a long shot. Of course, even slim odds were orders of magnitude higher than doing nothing. If you don't play, Chase had told one interviewer who insisted on stressing the long odds, you *can't* win.

Karen pulled the drapes aside and the summer sun of Houston poured through the tinted glass. "At least you'll have a nice view," she said. "You don't see that much water around Phoenix. Hey, Chasey, come to Mommy. Look at all the boats down there!" She bent and scooped the whirlwind into her arms and pointed. "See?"

"Boats!" the kid said. "I want one!"

"Maybe there's some that hire out," Chase allowed. *They must look like toys to him,* he thought. Across Nassau Bay sat the gleaming bronze glass of Argonaut Labs. Hobie and Ladawan would be practically neighbors—when they were not out in Greenbelt or up on LEO. They could keep him briefed on *Lariat*. He still felt bad at leaving them without a pilot and wondered if they had found anyone yet. A tall graceful bridge arched in the distance. The town of Kemah lay on the other end. Real stompin' nightlife, he'd been told. Kemah Therapy. "I wish you were staying," he said. "More than two weeks, I mean."

Karen shifted their son to her other arm. "You're getting too big for Mommy to carry, you know that?" She lowered Little Chase to the floor and he took off in a random direction. Karen rose, brushing long black hair from her face. "Me, too."

"You could teep your accounting practice from anywhere. You don't have to stay in Phoenix."

"I don't like leaving our home empty for so long. You'll be training here for what, a year?"

"Eighteen months. Boost-out's in January of '21."

"Okay, and the Disaster-on-Legs just started first grade. He's in a new school, meeting new friends. That's a lot of strangeness for him. It's best if he has a familiar home ground to come back to. And besides, that's *our* house; everything about it is the two of us. This place"—and she swept her arm around the hotel room—"this isn't a *home*. It's not a place to come back to."

Chase sighed and put an arm around her waist. "I know, babe. But I'll miss you, anyway."

"You'll be too busy to miss me."

He kissed her. "Never too busy for that."

Little Chase ran up to him and grabbed him around the legs. "Daddy? Daddy!" Chase pulled him up and sat him on his hip.

"What?"

"How come you're always not coming home?"

Chase swallowed. "Not 'always,' " he said. "But sometimes my job takes me real far away and it takes a long time to come back."

"All the way to the park with the swings?"

Chase smiled. "And even a little farther."

One problem with fame was that strangers thought they knew you. That was okay when what they wanted was to buy you a drink, but sometimes what they wanted was to sell you an insurance policy, or even a nice bridge. And sometimes what they wanted was just to get in your pants. That was okay, too; though Chase never took up their offers. Flattery never hurt, and it was the thought that mattered.

Karen had taken the Human Tornado to a local park to blow off some steam. She was right, Chase thought, about the hotel room. It was an impossible venue for a six-year-old boy. His legs needed a backyard for the stretching, not a hallway or a lobby. Chase was sure the other hotel guests would enthusiastically agree.

He drifted down to the hotel lounge just to see what was what. There was a roller croaking against recorded music and a handful of drinkers trying not to listen. Most of the clientele, Chase guessed, were there for happy hour, though most of them looked pretty grim. Hassles from a hard-nosed boss or hard-assed girlfriend. Hassles with money, or customers, or traffic. Fear of flying out that night to another strange town to meet with other strangers. Maybe even, in the depths of their hearts, the lurking presence of the Bean spiraling ever closer.

Chase perched himself on a stool by the bar and ordered a Skull Mountain lager, then studied the room with the tall, cool bottle in his hand. Come Monday, the Intercept crew would report in at NASA; meanwhile he was free to kick.

There was a drunk at a table across the room hassling a young woman. He was leaning over the table, both fists planted, jacket open, tie loosened. The woman had her back to Chase, but he could tell from the set of her head that she was looking away from the drunk. Black, short-cropped hair. A colorful scarf draped across her shoulders. Chase grinned and slid off the stool.

"C'mon, honey," he heard the drunk plead. "Just one teensy drink, is all. 'M honored to buy one for you."

"I told you, I don't drink with strangers."

"You don't have to come all high 'n' mighty, Miss Stuck-up. Think you're so special, just 'cause—"

"The lady says she's not drinking with you," Chase told him. Jesus, it was only three in the pee-em. What business did a guy have getting drunk in the middle of the day?

"Butt out. This's a pribit, a pribit—private conversation. Who do you think you are to—"

But his bleary eyes had found Chase's face by then and perhaps he saw something there, because pale as he was, his coloring faded a shade or two. He stood away from the table and looked off. "Didn't mean nothing," he muttered.

"Good." Chase clapped him on the shoulder; a friendly gesture, but one that propelled the man toward the bar. "You look like you need some solid food in you. Go on have a sandwich at the bar. My treat." Chase shook his head as the other man weaved through the tables in the lounge. He made a sign to the bartender and pointed toward the drunk, and the bartender nodded. Chase sank into an empty chair at the table.

"I could have handled him," Jacinta Rosario said.

"Sure, and the charge wouldn't have been much more than

manslaughter two; but it still wouldn't look right in the publicity releases. Someone told me you made the team. I always knew Ned had good taste."

Jacinta smiled briefly. "Nice to see you again," she said.

"How does it feel to be a three-striper, now?"

She was wearing civvies, but her eyes dropped to her wrist and the smile this time was broader and longer-lasting. "I thought it would take forever. I've been flying out of Allentown on the LEO circuit; but last month I took an F/E billet and moonered with Gar Rustov."

"Gar's a good man. He knows ziggy."

"He let me bring the ship into LoLO, and then one of the lunatics—I mean, Moon-based otters—showed me how to land a Luna-Lighter at the Selene catapult head."

Chase smiled at her enthusiasm. He saluted with his beer. "Easy lifts . . ."

". . . Soft landings," she answered, lifting a water tumbler. Chase offered to buy her a drink.

A brief, clouded look. "No thank you," she said.

"I know. You don't drink with strangers, and they don't come much stranger than me."

Jacinta laughed. "It's not that. I'm meeting my special friend here. We're going out to dinner later."

"Hey, great. Karen and Junior are here, too. Maybe we could make it a group?" His mouth felt suddenly dry and he took a swallow of Skull.

Jacinta regarded him with wide, serious eyes. Her hand went to the silver apple pin on her scarf and one finger traced its outline. "That would be . . . nice." But she had hesitated.

Chase chuckled. "Rather be alone with your 'special friend,' right?"

Jacinta straightened in her chair. "We're not married yet," she said severely.

"Well, then you'll need me and Karen for chaperones . . . ?"

"I don't *need* dueñas. 'I am my own mistress.' "

Chase kept his sigh to himself. He had forgotten how Jacinta had burned part of her sense of humor on the altar of chastity. Of course, on the plus side, she was headed beyond the Moon and not nursing a baby off a skimpy welfare check and wondering where the father had gone, so maybe the trade-off had been worth it.

His wrist phone warbled, and when he looked at the "who-he?" saw the ID for the Thirteenth. Though officially detached from duty with the 13th Deep Space Wing, he still felt an obligation to help out with the loose ends his sudden departure had created. "Speak to me," he told the logic.

"Chase, where are you?" It was Jimmy Poole's voice and Chase rolled his eyes skyward in mute accusation of a prankish God. He had never known Jimmy to start a telephone conversation with a simple "hello." The social amenities were beyond his ken.

"I'm right here," he told Jimmy.

"Ha. Ha. Wait one." Then, "Okay." The connection went dead.

Chase frowned at his wrist. What was that all about? "A guy I know," he told Jacinta when she asked. "Don't know what he wanted."

But he found out a few minutes later, when Jimmy Poole entered the hotel lounge and squinted through the dim light. "Houston," Chase muttered aside to Jacinta, "the Ego has landed." Chase slouched in his seat, but Jimmy noticed him anyway. The dweeb crossed the room, followed, Chase now saw, by the silent mass of Leland Hobart. Jimmy pulled a chair from another table and sat by Chase. "Told you he was here," he said to Hobie. The black man shrugged and set a fourth chair at the table. He held a hand out to Jacinta.

"Hi, I'm Leland Hobart. People call me Hobie."

Jacinta took the hand, but pointed with the other. "Hey! You're the Master of Cool, aren't you?"

Chase began to hum the theme song, but Hobie glowered at him and he grinned and flagged the waitress, raising three fingers. Jacinta introduced herself and Jimmy said, "If you ever need anyone to fiddle with your seat belt, she's the one."

Chase couldn't figure out what Jimmy was talking about, but Jacinta's nostrils flared and before she could say anything, Chase turned on Jimmy. "If I ever orbit into the Big Empty, there are damn few folks I'd want in the right-hand seat more than Lieutenant Rosario, here; but I want her because she's smart and she's quick and anything electrical she's bone. And yes, she's easy on the eyes. But I can shake her hand without wanting to pull her pants off."

Okay, that wasn't entirely true; but it was true enough. Chase didn't look directly at Rosario, suddenly afraid of what he might see.

Jimmy mumbled something about joking and changed the subject. "Don't you want to know how I found you?"

"It ain't a secret the Intercept cadre's being put up at the Hilton." Chase growled, certain that Jimmy had a more self-congratulatory reason for posing the question.

Hobie hooked a thumb at Jimmy. "GPS. Knocked on your door upstairs. Thanks," he added to the waitress who dropped off the bottles Chase had ordered. "No answer, so Jimmy calls. When you acted cute, he ran your location. Satellite said we were right on top of you."

Chase scowled at his wrist band. "I liked it better when *houses* had phones instead of *people.*" Come to think of it, did Jimmy have legal access to trace people through the GPS? Not that it would have stopped him, either way.

Hobie grunted philosophically. "That's why they call it a tracey. So they can trace you."

"Okay," Chase agreed. "You were looking for me. You found me." He waved his bottle in a circle, inviting them to fill in the blank.

Hobie pursed his lips, glanced at the cheese-hacker, and with a shrug said, "He's got an idea."

Chase kicked the beer back. "Sure, that's a fine habit and I wouldn't want to discourage it. I had an idea myself, once."

"Same one, actually," Hobie said.

"Eh?" The smile at his own joke faded into puzzlement. "What do you mean?"

"About flying *Lariat.* Jimmy thinks he can hack it."

Chase put his bottle of Skull on the table. "He what? Just like that?" Chase traded a glance with Rosario, who looked profoundly skeptical.

Jimmy leaned over the table. "No fooling, Chase. I can do it. Who knows the software better than me?"

"More to flying than software," Chase suggested.

"Not when *I* hack the cheese. Maybe when pilots were constantly jiggling rudders and flaps with their hands and feet . . . but this is different. The cheese does all the work; the pilot just decides which cheese."

"Then it ain't piloting," Chase announced. He raised his bottle to Rosario, who returned the salute with her water tumbler.

"Lieutenant," Jimmy turned on the younger pilot, "how should I angle the magnetic field against the solar wind to achieve an effect of negative solar gravity."

"Not a clue," she said cheerfully.

Jimmy spread his hands, as if he had proved something. "See?"

"See what?" said Chase.

"Trick question," said Hobie. "Need amps and mass."

"She still wouldn't have known."

"Big deal," said Chase. "She hasn't been through the training on that particular 'chine."

"But that's my whole point," Jimmy insisted. "Nothing she knows about *rockets* would prepare her to run a magship any better than me. And I *do* know the software and the theory."

Chase set his bottle on the table. " 'Scuse me. I gotta go express an opinion." He left the lounge and sought out the men's room off the lobby, where he selected a likely urinal and pretended it was Jimmy. Who did that arrogant bastard think he was that he could waltz in off the street and do a job that had been Chase's profession for years? How wide of an ego did a man have to have to think he could pick up another man's expertise *on the side*? That was one of Jimmy's problems, he decided. He always thought he was better at anything. Even back in high school, he remembered, Jimmy had tried to show off in chemistry and history and the rest, always raising his hand, always squeaking "I know! I know! Call on me!" until the weary teachers caved. He read all the books. Not only the mind-numbing, sleep-inducing textbooks; not only the *assigned* reading; but even books that he didn't *have* to read, just for the chance to tell you something you never asked about or wanted to know.

Chase made a fist and struck the wall above the urinal, then he sealed up and stepped away to the sink, where he stuck his hands under the autofaucet.

But he was all out of the books, Jimmy was. He could read a story and tell you what color eyes a character had in chapter ten; but he could not *write* a story to save his life. Tani wrote the books. He could recite the periodic table; but it was Hobie who was the chemist. And he knew the *Lariat* inside and out; but could he make her dance?

Chase rinsed off and raised his eyes to the mirror and saw Danny Coughlin there. Hard-faced, eyes narrowed into a squint, lips tightened to a point. The way Dad used to look just before a swat to the head. Chase bent over and cupped the cold water in his hands, then splashed it onto his face and rubbed. Then he looked into his own eyes once more.

Okay, who debugged the flocker program when you and Ned were flying into Skopje?

Who worked out the flight program back in '10, just so you and Ned could make footprints on the Moon?

A long time ago, before the Bean, before the Dip, Chase had kicked with Hobie in the lounge up on Leo Station. *I'm not cut out to be a truck driver, Hobe,* Chase had said. *Flying damned Lunar Transfer Vessels like some damned FedEx droid. Know what I'd like to fly? Something no one's ever flown before. Something that doesn't have any damned manuals; something where you don't know where the edges are.*

And Hobie had waved his cup of fruit punch and said with a secret smile on his face. *If I ever invent a new kind of spaceship, you'll be the first to fly it.*

Yeah. Except now he wouldn't.

Nuts. You made your choices and you lived with them. Yet, if not Chase Coughlin at the yoke, then who? Kilbride? Schmidt? Ng? Jimmy was right. *Lariat* was so new that except for ziggy and suit discipline and storm drill and all the crap that was *not* piloting, *anyone* who strapped into her rack was starting from scratch.

He jammed the paper towel into the mulcher and shoved the door open.

Some of Danny Coughlin must have still been on his face when he returned to the lounge, because Rosario looked alarmed and Jimmy shrank in his seat, and even Hobie, the old Doorman, blinked his eyes. Chase pulled out his chair and dropped into it. His bottle of Skull Mountain was empty. He sighed. He was taking Karen and Junior over to Frenchy's later, and two was his limit on nights like that. "All right," he said.

Jimmy blinked. He looked from face to face. "All right, what?" Jacinta looked curious and Hobie, thoughtful.

"All right," Chase said. "Fly the freaking *Lariat,* if that's what you want. I've got a date with an asteroid." He pushed himself to his feet. "You and Eatinger wanted my blessing? Fine, you have it." He sketched a cross over Jimmy. "In nominy hominy, pack no biscuits. Stand and receive, nooboo."

Jimmy looked uncertain, but Rosario, her lower lip caught between her teeth, waved him to his feet. Then Chase braced him on the shoulders and kissed him three times, on the left cheek, on the right cheek, and square on the lips. Jimmy jerked away, startled, and wiped his mouth with his sleeve. "What the hell—?"

"Go away," Chase said. "Or I'll teach you the secret handshake." He made a clutching motion with his right hand and Jimmy jumped back.

"Did you mean that?" he asked.

"About the handshake?"

"No, about flying the *Lariat.* You don't mind if I do it?"

"Mind? Of course, I mind. But I'm off the project. You don't need my say-so. If the colonel and Hobie let you play with their toy, I don't have no veto."

Jimmy turned to Hobie. "You heard him. He said I could do it."

Hobie, who had said very little the while, nodded. "Heard him. Didn't hear him say exactly that. Let's go back to the lab, now." He gave Chase a curious look as he ushered Jimmy out. "Eatinger might call you."

Chase shrugged. "Fine. I'll tell him what I told you."

When the other two were gone, he pulled another chair closer with his feet and propped them up on it. "I wonder why they felt they had to ask me," he said.

"I wonder why you said yes," Rosario answered.

"Yeah, me, too." He signaled to the waitress for another round, and to hell with the two-bottle limit. "Hell, maybe they're right and a nooboo like that can do as good a job as you or me on that kind of ship. On the other hand, maybe he'll screw the pooch royal. I heard tell he wets his pants over stepping into the Big Empty; so maybe he'll never even get back aboard the *Lariat,* let alone fly it."

"Then, why . . . ?"

"Why'd I say go for it? Easy. Someone like that, he doesn't have to do it and he ain't rightly cut out for it and he pisses his pants, but he wants to do it anyway so bad he comes to me for permission . . ." Chase shook his head. "Win, lose, or draw, a dude like that *deserves* a shot."

It would never happen, Chase told himself. Jimmy would freeze up or something. On the downside, that might damage the prospects for the Thirteenth. On the plus side, he'd never have to listen to Jimmy bragging on it. Still, he could not help think that he may have in effect signed Jimmy Poole's death warrant.

He probed his soul to find how he felt about that.

14.

Lucky Thirteenth

The Year of Grace 2020 ran like water through open fingers. It was an odd phenomenon. Roberta Carson thought, and not one that physicists could explain. It was as if the rate of time were proportional to the number of events packed into it. As if activities consumed chronons. Her days sank into the Thirteenth as if into quicksand, but the world was entitled to them, even if the world did not understand how grateful it ought to be and what it would someday owe to her little crew of misfits. She believed that the magship project was far more important than either Solomon Dark or General Sapper seemed to grasp; but that was always the way of it. One always regarded one's own puddle as the almighty ocean itself. Meanwhile, her son grew in strength and wisdom.

The country had shaken off the aftereffects of the Dip like a fighter coming off of the canvas and growing vaguely aware that another, harder punch was coming. Only four years to Impact, she noted one chill October day, and shivered not entirely because of her efforts to conserve heating oil.

Roberta had always hated waiting in lines. More often than not she would shift queues looking for the fastest one; sometimes she would roam from restaurant to restaurant seeking the most immediate seating. The result was usually a later dinner, but at least the tedium of waiting was replaced with the sense of motion.

It was bad enough waiting in line to get *into* something: a movie, a concert, a restaurant. There was at least the promise of enjoyment at the end. What really frosted her cookies was waiting in line to get *out* of something, and supermarket checkout lines were the worst of all. Scanners had been meant to speed the process, but managers had cleverly countered the engineers by reducing the number of lanes, a ploy she had immortalized in "The Conservation of Inconvenience," in her *Ars Domestica* chapbook.

For a while she had used the scan-it-yourself lanes; until Carson had turned two and demanded both her hands when *he* was bored with waiting—which, at two, was very nearly always. Roberta had realized as well that "self-service" meant she was doing the supermarket's job for them without getting paid; so she went on strike.

The one compensation to waiting was the chance to observe H. sapiens in its native habitat. Two slots ahead of her in line, Man the Hunter placed his kill on the conveyor belt, having by various wiles tracked the mighty pot roast to its lair. Men in supermarkets, she thought, often did resemble hunters in the way they vaguely wandered the aisles in search of their prey. Women were the Gatherers. They *knew* where the berry bushes were and went straight to them.

"We ought to nuke that Bean," Mighty Hunter said. "Blow it to rubble."

"That's right," the youngster behind the scanner said. "Use all those ICBMs they stockpiled during that arms race."

Strangers at the grocery debating strategy with all the wisdom of those neither responsible for the outcomes nor privy to the inputs. Roberta maintained a discrete silence.

"*If* they still work," said a gray-haired man, the Tribal Elder, behind Roberta. His red handbasket bore sixteen items and his deep brown face, a look of righteousness. The express lane next to them had a limit of fifteen. "They stopped testing nukes decades ago," he added. "Who knows what kind of shape they're in by now? Innards all chewed up by their own radiation."

"They can fix 'em, can't they?" asked the checkout girl, blissfully unaware of the actual capabilities of moribund ICBMs.

"Nuclear missiles in space?" demanded a chunky woman at the bagging end of the lane. She was stuffing her Perma-Sacks™ with canned goods and dehydrates. Roberta wondered if she were stockpiling. Impact was still years off, but, hey!, why not Avoid the Rush? The woman brushed hair from her face and stood erect for a moment. "The whole idea's immoral."

"So's the idea of letting the Bean hit us," said a taller, darker woman with close-cropped hair. "If we can blow it up before it comes, then I say let's do it."

A couple of others in line woofed her, pumping their fists in the air. The first woman scowled, then turned and presented her rationing card to the checkout girl, who ran it through the scanner.

"Anyway, Inter-*Continental* Ballistic Missiles can't hack it," said Mighty Hunter. "We need Inter-*Planetary* Ballistic Missiles."

"We don't even need that," said an intense, serious, twenty-something woman. "I heard they have new superweapons they haven't told us about. Some sort of magnetic ray gun. Just wait and see. McRobb knows what he's doing."

"McRobb's a sellout," griped a middle-aged woman in a sweater vest. "One taste of Washington and he's the same porker as everyone else." She and Serious Woman exchanged glares.

It was sad, Roberta thought, how few people mentioned Rutell anymore. And yet the president had worked with the PDCs from the beginning, while McRobb had dragged his heels and obstructed. Yet, somehow McRobb had become a Leader, as if asteroid defense had been American Party policy all along. Perhaps the auto accident had knocked some sense into him. Perhaps being privy now to inside information had convinced him that it was all on the level, after all. Or perhaps, like Sweater Vest had said, having gotten a fingerhold on power he intended cynically to play the game. Whatever the reason—a bird in the hand; a disinclination to be in charge when the Bean hit—McRobb had announced his intention to remain as Speaker and not run for president this year. Roberta had damn near written him a thank-you note.

Oddly, no one seemed much excited by the upcoming election. All three candidates were decent sorts; all three were committed to stopping the asteroids. The Fusion candidate was favored. Even McRobb had said he could work with Barnes—which Roberta thought a mark against.

Carson found a rack of puzzle magazines within his reach and Roberta patiently took the booklet from his grasp and replaced it in the rack. When he seized it again, she took it from him again. Carson quickly conceived the routine to be a new game and went into what Jimmy Poole called an infinite DO-loop, laughing each time Roberta pried the book away.

"You're all talking about *war,*" said a quiet young man who Roberta recognized as an occasional hanger-on at the Crusades. The way things had been going since Ellis's suicide, he might even be leading the Crusades by now. "War is the wrong paradigm. We ought to be opening negotiations."

With an enemy ten thousand years gone? Roberta shook her head. Believers in super-secret technologies to be revealed Real Soon Now were not the only ones guilty of wishful thinking.

"It might hit somewhere harmless. I read that. You know, like in some remote area. Like that one in Canada a couple years ago."

Cans-and-Dehydrates had gone and Mighty Hunter was presenting his card. "I'm sorry, sir," the clerk told him, "but your recycling account is below the limit."

"I've got a box of aluminum cans in the trunk. I was going to the 'cycler after I finished here."

"I'm sorry, but the computer won't accept your purchase of any new cans until you've recycled your old allotment. It's the Defense Effort, you know."

"I scread on the Lattice where the Bean might actually miss," Tribal Elder announced.

Mighty Hunter looked indignant. "It better not. All this scrimping on rationing cards for no good reason . . ." Taking his time, he set the forbidden six-packs aside.

"Better not let the Planning Board hear you say that," said the Crusader. He cast a nervous glance at the McRobb supporter.

"We need the materials," the Serious Young Woman said. "For converting ships to deep space; for constructing Impact Shelters and stockpiling goods for After; for building those deep space lasers and missiles. Petroleum's needed for rocket fuel, so we have to cut back on gasoline and heating oil and stuff."

"Yeah, right," said Sweater Vest. "Like it's all really going to happen."

"I still don't like it," Hunter grumped. "Government shouldn't be telling me how much soda I can buy."

"You can buy as much soda as you want," Serious Woman told him, "but you've got to return the metal, can for can."

"Recycling is a good in itself," the Crusader assured him. He looked uncomfortable at agreeing with a McRobber, even if for loftier reasons.

It was partway a sham, Roberta knew. Damocles didn't really need this sort of rationing. Most of the high construction was using lunar materials— transport costs were less— but the rationing program encouraged a sense of participation among the public of far greater value than the materials themselves and helped them accept the fact that the subsidies and payments and price supports they had gotten used to receiving were being diverted into the defense effort.

And there were other motives. McRobb had used the crisis to implement his platform of "rational economics." Planning Boards consisting of government, academia, labor, and industry allocated resources and markets. Rationalize the economy, he said. Protect American jobs. Focus, focus, focus. And the heavy fist came down on the podium.

"You youngsters don't know what sacrifice is," said Tribal Elder. "When I was in 'Nam—"

" 'Nam, hell," said Mighty Hunter. "I was in the Mack."

"Macedonia?" The old man laughed. "How long is *your* wall, son?"

"Well, I'm sacrificing plenty," said Serious Woman. "I've got a shoebox full of PDC bonds."

Roberta finally gave up and handed Carson a crossword puzzle book. He threw it on the floor.

"I've got a niece working as a space-rigger on Goddard," said Tall, Dark Woman. "I worry about her all the time. Vacuum work, you know."

"I'd go up," said the teenager behind the counter. "Build those laser platforms and deep-space ships. I put my name in." She stuck her chin out and dared anyone to laugh. "Anything's better than this." Her gesture included the checkout lane, the griping line of customers, the rationing, perhaps her entire life.

Mighty Hunter was gathering his things into Perma-Sacks. Roberta began unloading her own cart onto the conveyor. Hunter looked at her as if she had just materialized from nowhere. "What about you?" he demanded. "You've been almighty quiet. What are you doing for the defense effort?"

Roberta didn't answer him; but when she lifted the milk cartons from the cart she made sure he could see the patch of the 13th Deep Space Wing on the shoulder of her jacket. It was manipulative as all hell, but it shut him up in a most satisfactory manner.

When she was finished a few minutes later, the seventy-something behind her touched her on the arm and, when she turned to look, saluted her. Roberta ducked her head and left the store as quickly as politeness allowed. That a man who had faced enemy fire should salute her seemed somehow wrong. *She* would not be riding the Long Orbit, to take this not-quite-a-war to the not-quite-an-enemy. That lot would fall to people like Chase, who better deserved the salute. She was only one of those who would make it possible.

All her life Roberta had hated uniforms and the regimentation they implied. Group-think. Just follow orders. She had stood alone in proud isolation, needing no one and, more tragically, no one needing her. Until first Phil, and then Carson, and now the entire world had fallen into her care, and she discovered not regimentation, but community; not following your orders, but doing your duty. Her sense of stand-alone independence was a price she had willingly paid; yet she could not help but think that, like McRobb, she had surrendered some of her old ideals in the process.

She confessed as much to Mariesa when she visited the older woman in her apartments at Silverpond. The Rich Lady smiled with half her face and replied in a slurred voice. It was difficult to make out the words, and sometimes Roberta thought that like the *awenyddion* of pagan Wales or the oracle at Delphi, Mariesa uttered random sounds to be interpreted at will by her listeners. *I, too, learned the secret,* she seemed to say one winter's evening when the Moon coasted through naked treetops against a cobalt sky. *The Goal can eat you up if you let it, and turn you against yourself. Purity is not to be found in this world; but there is a line in the sand which, if you cross it, you lose yourself.* And the withered, parchment hand had crawled from under the sheet and grasped Roberta by the wrist. *You must learn where you have drawn your own line.*

At other times, Mariesa was not nearly so oracular. It depended on what drugs she had been given that day.

* * *

Meat Tucker had submitted a purchase requisition for additional supplies for *Lariat*'s construction. Roberta reviewed the line items on her MRP screen and noted that all were within budget and plan for this stage of the build. A little early, but then Meat liked to stay ahead of the key dates. She entered her private access key and typed her name in the approval block.

I just approved the spending of three million federal dollars, she told herself, a little awed that she had the authority; and—for the same reason—a little appalled.

She worked the PERT and saw that Jimmy's projected flight test had slipped by another month, so she began backsearching the critical path to locate the bottleneck and found it in an altered flight schedule for June's SSTO lifts. The new schedule meant a late delivery on air and water regen equipment and a consequent idle time for the riggers.

That won't hunt, Chase liked to say. Meat and the others wouldn't mind a few days' kick, but Rotation Day was coming and Meat's gold crew would be dropping while Izzy Mac's blue crew lifted. There was always confusion at shift change. That would not be the optimal time to receive a critical new shipment. So . . . either delay the delivery still more to let blue crew settle in; or . . . find a way to rebump the schedule.

The revision had an Asia-PDC icon and that meant restoring the original path would involve negotiations not just with Big Hats, but with foreign Big Hats. Roberta didn't have the patience for that; and—who knew? Asia-PDC was coordinating powersat laser construction and might have an urgent need for the lift capacity that the revamped launch sequence freed up. Priority was: first, FarTrip II; second, lunar and orbital battle lasers; third, civil defense. Somewhere below that horizon were blue sky projects like *Lariat.*

Too much to lift in too little time with too few lifters in service. Daedalus, Energia, Boeing, Salyut, Ariane, YoshiSpace . . . The equipment makers were turning ships and modules out as fast as safety and reliability could churn them. Two Planks and a nuclear DSV were in Sky Dock being modified for Operation Intercept, taking them out of commercial service; and others were being prepped for missions to Rabbit Punch. Two-by-Four, and the later asteroids. If anyone noticed that no one counted on re-using the same ships for the later missions, they were too polite to mention it.

There was even a program for cheap up-and-down recoverables. "Liberty Ships," they were called, named after an earlier program. Not quite re-usable; but a whole lot cheaper for the short term. As for the long term, the world would worry about that when it thought there would be one.

Roberta picked up her stylus and began to noodle the screen, looking for alternatives. *Lloyd's Register* popped a list of ships and cargos, which she sorted by available dates and lifting capacity. She found a tramp SSTO squatting groundside in Prague for two weeks without a cargo. The old RS-135, *Neta Snook*, ex-Pegasus; U. Kitmann, captain and master. Roberta checked the Dun & Bradstreet database and the Deeby-deeby came back with an A+ credit rating for Golden Arm, the holding company that owned the ship. *Jane's Commercial Lifters* gave the "*Snookums*" a Good for on-time performance and an Excellent for ship-handling, even though the tramp's master was not an Academy grad. The current status log listed no maintenance downchecks and no safety citations from port captains where the *Snookums* had called. Roberta launched a 'bot to check security clearances, but she already suspected this Kitmann would rate high. Golden Arm didn't seem the kind of outfit to skim off a cargo.

Roberta pulled up a standard contract from the template file and plugged in the required delivery dates and the bill of lading for the regen equipment, adding the NAPDC premium to the fee schedule. She doubted that a tramp waiting for a cargo would turn down any job, but it never hurt to sweeten the tea. Then she downloaded the contract, the schedule revision, and the bottlenecked PERT to Eatinger for his approval, adding a note: *If we toss the shipment from Allentown to Prague on a ballistic run, Golden Arm can put it on orbit by the ninth, three days ahead of the* original *schedule!*

She felt the same glow of satisfaction that she so often felt after wrangling with a particularly difficult poetic line, when the meter and the cadence and the images all came together in a kind of rightness. There was a kind of poetry to this work, as well; and the intricate dance of orbital lifts and drops, of launch windows and carefully coordinated deliveries, had a satisfying rhythm of its own.

"You know what bugs me?" said Jimmy Poole.

Roberta slapped her stylus on her desktop and glared at the screen. "I wish you would stop doing that!"

The screen swiped and there was Jimmy in all his glory, a puzzled look on his face. "Doing what?"

"Hacking in uninvited. It's rude. I was in the middle of something."

"No you weren't. I waited until you were finished."

She stared at him a moment. Not only did Jimmy Not Get It, but there were times when she thought he would Never Get It. "What do you want?"

"Tell Whistle to fire up the boilers. I'm coming out for another round of sims."

"Been a while," she said suggestively. Every now and then she had noticed a slippage on the "Pilot Readiness" track, but somehow the slippage always disappeared within a day. Roberta suspected that Jimmy was hacking the schedule rather than admit that his stepping into Chase's shoes had delayed things.

"No way, Charlie," he said. "I've been practicing out here. I cloned the system onto a super-salamander and set up an A/S to toss scenarios at me. I've been working the sims every night. The only thing I don't have here is the physical layout of the ship's cabin, so I need to come out and practice with the hardware. Does Whistle have Rev. J running yet?"

Roberta looked at her side screen, where she kept the status log permanently displayed. Billie and Dr. Zubrin had installed the revised model of the solar wind nearly a week ago and she suspected Jimmy knew that as well as anyone. He should have been practicing here at Greenbelt on the real equipment instead of playing with a computer game version at home. She told him so, if not quite so bluntly.

"I got better things to do than fly back and forth across the country," he said, but his eyes dodged hers across the screen. Used to be that teleconferencers never looked you in the eye because they were looking at the screen and not at the camera; but the new models had the optical pickups embedded in the screen itself, and of the few things of which Roberta was absolutely certain, that Jimmy Poole had the latest equipment was one.

"I'm E-mailing the scenarios I want to practice," Jimmy said. "Make sure she has these."

Roberta glanced at her mail log, then back at the screen. So that was it. "You got these scenarios stoned?" she said.

Jimmy's head bobbed like it was on a spring. "Righteous beans."

"Then maybe while you're here you should practice some other scenarios instead." Jimmy's sudden look of fear confirmed her suspicion. "After all," she continued, "the whole point of practice sims is to discover potential problems. That's how we perfect the flight plans. What's the point of a sim that goes smoothly?"

"I don't make mistakes," Jimmy said.

Like hell. And maybe Jimmy had already made the biggest mistake of his life; and Eatinger and Hobie, too. What on Earth had possessed Chase Coughlin to give his okay? Sure, this was the most thoroughly programmed command-and-control system any spacecraft had ever gotten; but there was something more to space flight than playing with your joystick and giving voice commands to an Artificial Stupid. Roberta didn't know what that "something more" was, but she was sure that Jimmy Poole didn't have it.

The little weenie was scared. She knew that as certainly as if he had told her. Not scared of space—he rhapsodized over the beauties of infinite space—but scared of not looking perfect in front of the rest of the Wing. His ego never could stand a ninety-five. It always had to be one hundred. "Jimmy," she said, because for better or worse, the Lucky Thirteenth was committed to Jimmy flying the *Lariat* and *that* would need more Luck than was ordinarily available, "this is not high school or college, and a simulation is not an exam. I don't score it, Billie doesn't score it, the colonel doesn't score it. If the sims you run out here run *too smoothly*, I'll recommend we replace you with another pilot and eat the delay time."

Jimmy was pale complexioned to begin with, but Roberta thought he lost color. "You wouldn't do that!"

"Try me."

"Look, I've *got* to do this!"

" 'Got to'? Why?"

He looked off-screen again. "I can't tell you."

"If piloting *Lariat* is too much—"

"Chase can do it; and his IQ they measure in imaginary numbers."

Roberta stared at the screen. "It's not a question of IQ. It's a question of drill and reaction time and 'feel' for the ship. Piloting isn't your gig. It's no shame if you can't handle it."

His lower lip protruded slightly. "I can handle it. I know I can."

"Jimmy, it's not a game. If the scenarios have been hacked so the pilot always 'wins' . . . that could *kill* you, later on."

And that just *couldn't* be what Chase had intended when he gave the go-ahead. Could it?

Jimmy's mouth settled into a rigid line and his lip trembled. "You think you're so fucking smart!" And he cut the connection. Roberta grimaced in irritation. Sure, run *these* scenarios. It wasn't that Jimmy thought she was gullible enough to think Jimmy hadn't bogied the sims to make himself look good; it was that Jimmy had tried to fool *Jimmy* into making a game of the sims.

The next week, Billie ran a whole new suite of scenarios and, unprepared for them, Jimmy crashed and burned each time.

The election came and went and Barnes won in a walk away. The victory, long assumed—the Fusion ticket combined Democrat, Republican, Liberty, and even some American behind the former engineer and project manager. Perhaps these are the skills, the public seemed to say, that the world will need in the coming years. Accepting the victory, Barnes had galvinized the nation with a simple declaration, spoken with quiet force and determination.

"I did not run for this office to become the last president of the United States."

That the president-elect wore a skirt, a red bow, and a string of pearls seemed unimportant. The world had more important matters to occupy it.

From the Greenbelt station, Roberta could take the Metro all the way home, with only one change—to the Blue Line at L'Enfant. So after she picked up Carson from the Center's day-care facility, she usually took the shuttle van to the Metro. Sometimes, when the winter turned cold, she regretted her choice; but wrapped up warm, she stuck with it. Besides, gasoline was being rationed, too.

It was December of 2020 and it was raining. Not cold enough to freeze, but cold enough to chill to the bone. Cold enough to make the waiting passengers on the platform huddle in on themselves in solitude under the overhang. The rails gleamed in the dusk as if from an inner light. Down the track, a column of lights glimmered green and red.

Carson, bundled into a thick, down-filled parka, clung to her leg. To him, this was life. Mommy dropped him in the day care, played with him at noon; then later, they waited together on the rail platform for the train ride home. Not for the first time, she wondered what it all meant to Carson. Did he know that another life had been possible? Safe and snug at home all day, with his scrapes and boo-boos kissed away by a mother, rather than by a paid professional. Roberta shook in the cold. It was how she had been raised. Beth had always been gone; always came home too tired. Roberta remembered how, in later years, not understanding the sacrifices life had forced on her mother, she deeply resented that disconnection; that, during years when she hungered most of all for love and security, she had not been fed.

I'll make it different for you, she promised the child; promised the young Roberta. *When this crisis is over. When things are normal.*

"Hi."

Roberta turned at the voice and saw a man in his high thirties. Soft and vulnerable eyes with a look of desperation around their edges. He wore a long cashmere coat and a plaid scarf. A fedora like the ones Solomon Dark had worn years ago crowned his head. From his shoulder hung a laptop case. Another harried worker bee heading home.

"You take this train a lot? I've seen you here before."

Roberta considered the line. That it was a prelude, she did not doubt; but a prelude to what? The others waiting ignored them; everyone huddled into their own chill misery. It was the sort of day that people drowned themselves, or swallowed too many pills, or hooked the hose up to the old exhaust. "Yeah," she said, volunteering as little as possible to a man who, so far, had done nothing but offer polite conversation.

"Me, too." He nodded, but said nothing else. Roberta had concluded that he meant only to share that bit of useless trivia, and was beginning to toy with the notion of "*useful* trivia" as a theme for a comic poem, when he spoke again. "That your boy?" At Roberta's nod, he added. "I have a girl. She's two."

"Three," Roberta said automatically.

"The 'Terrible Twos.' " He flashed teeth in a fleeting grin. "I live in Cheverly."

The revelation invited a confidence she was reluctant to share. "The City," was all she said.

"Long commute."

"Yeah."

"Look . . ." He looked away from her, down the long line of track. "There's a hotel near the Minnesota Avenue stop. We could stop there, you and me; and—"

"No," she said distinctly and she bent and lifted Carson to her; held him between her and this importuning stranger like a shield. The ring Phil Albright had given her flashed in the halogen lamps of the overhang. Phil had worn its twin and it now lay buried with him; as this would lie with her.

He ducked his head, turned his own hand so she could see the ring there. "Me, too. But the Bean is coming, and there are things I've never done; and now I'm afraid I might never do them. I'm not asking for much, not for a relationship."

"You're asking for more than you'll get."

"I'm sorry. Really, I am. I saw your eyes before, and I thought . . ." He began to turn away, then turned back. There was pain in his glance, and Roberta, briefly, felt pity. "After the Bean hits," he said, "no one will care. None of it will matter."

"You," she said coldly, more coldly than the sleeting rain, "are too scared of dying."

"You may be right," he admitted. "But I don't want to be scared of living, too."

"The chances are the Bean won't hit Washington."

"It will if there's a God."

Roberta gave him the shoulder and walked to the other end of the platform. A while later, she noticed him talking to a pledged virgin. The younger woman's scarf flapped in bright pastels, the only color in a gray, grizzled day. It was as if the entire scene—tracks, station, people—had been done in black-and-white, save only the scarf with its lamb-and-cross and the distant signals near the bend in the track.

Lots of luck, she thought sardonically, then paused wondering if she really did wish him luck. Impact was less than three years off, a little too early for the eat-drink-and-be-merry thing; but there were already some who saw their own mortality on the horizon, or thought they did. She had seen them in the strip malls with their Perma-Sacks full of liquor bottles. Her petitioner was no predator; only a frightened man who wanted someone to embrace him for a few moments of oblivion.

But she decided she did not want to ride the train with him and when the long silver cars coasted to a whispering stop and hovered above the rail on humming magnets, Roberta held Carson back and let the platform empty of life. Carson didn't know train schedules, but he knew a break in the routine and gave her a look half puzzled, half frightened. Roberta stooped to his level and brushed at his face, a comforting grooming gesture. "There'll be another train soon," she said.

Over his shoulder, she saw a brightly colored scarf sodden in a puddle on the concrete platform. The wind barely stirred it and the water it lay in already had the black, turgid look of incipient ice.

Mariesa had come to live at Silverpond and Roberta visited her whenever her duties brought her to the nature preserve that the estate had become. Some modest remodeling of the upper floor had created an apartment. It was a quieter and more subdued Mariesa than the one Roberta had once known. The stroke had slowed her down. She spent much of the day sleeping or reading and her nights in the observatory making meticulous notations. Doing something useful, she explained one time, now that she no longer had such enormous masses of money to leverage events.

When it came to money, Roberta suspected the two of them had different definitions of "enormous masses."

Mariesa took a certain joy in Carson, whom she regarded

as a sort of grandson; though it distressed her that she could not keep up with him and that she often had to repeat herself because the boy could not make out her words. "I suppose it is hereditary," she said about the stroke when they had settled into the soft chairs of the living room. "Though my mother was so much older when she had her first."

"Your mother didn't work herself so hard," said Susanna. Susanna Blackstone was something of a valet, a companion, and a visiting nurse, and fell somewhere between Mariesa and Roberta in age.

Mariesa said nothing for a moment, though Roberta saw the momentary impatience in the set of her lips. Susanna was pleasant enough, but had a nurse's inevitably domineering manner toward patients. Her attitude combined compassion with scold and she seemed, Roberta sometimes thought, to regard Mariesa as a child placed in her care. How long had the Rich Lady searched to find a nurse with the attributes of Harriet Gorley?

Mariesa smiled faintly. "It is a chore, though, waiting for the next one."

"Nonsense," said Susanna. "You've completely recovered."

But they all knew she was speaking pro forma. It would be boorish to say, *Yes, and the next one will probably kill you*; though Roberta could tell from Mariesa's precise way of speaking—always a sign that she was stressed out—that the woman knew there would be a next one.

When evening fell and Roberta had put Carson to bed in the suite she used as director of Silverpond, Mariesa asked her to come upstairs and help in the observatory. So she followed the other woman into the elevator cage—the same, old, gilded grillwork elevator that she remembered from so very long ago. It had been a part of the old Hudson Valley mansion, Roberta remembered being told. Willem van Huyten had kept it as a sort of souvenir when he built Silverpond. Visiting as a teenager, Roberta had often played with the disconnected control handle.

"I don't get Jimmy Poole," Roberta said as the elevator slowly rose. "I mean, he's doing okay on the sims now. Tani tells me he practices constantly. Almost obsessively. But I don't know *why* he's doing it."

The old woman placed a hand lightly on Roberta's forearm. "Does it matter why?"

"I don't know if he's up to it."

"Perhaps that is why."

"To prove something to himself? That he can pilot a spaceship? We're trying to save the world, not boost the Ego's self-esteem."

"That may not be what he is trying to prove."

Roberta gave her a sharp glance. "Then what?"

But Mariesa only shook her head. "He was never one to plumb his own heart, like you or Tani. Perhaps he needs to know only that he is capable of making the attempt."

Inside the dome, Mariesa pulled on a heavy sweater and gave another to Roberta before sitting at a computer keyboard and entering some information. The turntable on which the telescope was mounted rotated through its arc while the barrel itself altered its inclination. The dome slid open. Roberta looked around the room at the photographs and digital images that lined the walls. One plate had a small smear of light—an asteroid—and a label bearing the name "Harriet." One of Mariesa's personal discoveries.

"Do you want to look for yourself?"

Roberta glanced toward the telescope, where Mariesa had seated herself. "Sure."

The eyepiece was cold. January air spilled into the observatory from the slit in the dome. Roberta clutched the edges of the sweater tight around her neck.

The viewfield was spattered with stars. And planets and galaxies, she supposed, though she wasn't sure how you told which from what. "The one in the crosshairs," she heard Mariesa say.

A point of light no different than any other point of light.

She heard the hum of the motors and felt the ground turn under her a minute fraction. "And that is the . . . ?"

"The Bean, of course."

So that was it. Roberta nestled closer to the eyepiece and cupped her hand around it. That piddling little point of light was going to splash into the Sohm Abyss and wash away all the ticky-tack from the Jersey Shore. "You don't look so tough," she said.

"Oh, it's somewhat larger up close. The Hubble has mapped it. But it does make me wonder."

Roberta raised her head from the eyepiece. "About what?"

"Why the Bean? Big enough to hurt, bad; but small enough to survive. Six years' advance warning. If the Visitors were simply the Galactic Bug Exterminators, there are asteroids out there that would squash us flat."

"Maybe this is just the big buildup. They like to play with their victims first, like a cat."

"You could be right." Mariesa walked to the side, where another chair stood, and lowered herself into it. "I thought at one time they were just trying to get our attention. Like a young boy tossing pebbles at his girlfriend's window."

"Tossing bricks, more like it. Besides, if all they wanted was to get our attention, a big sign on Mars with a smiley face saying YO! would have worked pretty well."

Mariesa smiled briefly. "It's foolish to second-guess alien psychology. But I think they have thrown these missiles simply to learn what we will do."

Roberta raised her eyebrows. "You mean like those Pan-Galactic whackos who run around saying that the whole thing is a test of our faith; and that Galactic beings would be 'too advanced' to wish us harm?"

"So to demonstrate our faith, we should do nothing. No, nothing so foolish as that. I do think it's a test; but it is an IQ test."

"An IQ test?"

"Yes. They threw a rock at our head, and they want to see if we're smart enough to duck."

Roberta laughed. "And if we don't?"

"We flunk."

"That seems a little . . . drastic."

" 'Inhuman' is the word you want. I have no proof, but I am morally certain."

Roberta crossed her arms and shoved her hands inside the sweater. "It's as good a theory as any."

"I've gone to see Dr. O'Neil."

For a moment, Roberta tried to connect the sentence to the conversation and it made no sense whatsoever. She started to ask, but Mariesa spoke before any questions formed.

"He has the most marvelous device. Spartacus, he calls it. A remote-controlled—I/R, I believe he said—a remote-controlled sphere no bigger than a dust mote. It is inserted into a blood vessel and microscopic scythes emerge to trim away plaque and other buildup. The surgeon wears a telepresence hat and operates as if he were inside the patient's arteries. Can you imagine that?"

"And this will . . . ?"

Mariesa motioned with a hand and looked away. "Reduce the chance of another stroke."

"This Dr. O'Neil, he's a brain surgeon?"

"Oh, no. He's an engineer."

"You're going to let an engineer cut open your brain?"

Mariesa pressed her lips together. "Certainly not. A qualified surgeon will perform the operation; and very little cutting is involved. Just a slit to introduce the device, once they have identified the target vessels. Dr. O'Neil has another device for that. You swallow it and it collects and analyzes blood and tissue samples in situ. The doctor reads the results by telemetry. It eliminates the possibility of contaminating the specimen, and you don't have to wait days for the results to come back from the lab. Dr. O'Neil has been supplying MEMS—

micro-electromechanical devices—to the medical community for years."

"And this arterial Roto-Rooter, it actually works?"

Mariesa's eyes went elsewhere again. She rubbed her left hand with her right. "That is what we hope to learn."

Roberta stood up from the telescope's chair and crossed the floor to where Mariesa sat. She knelt beside the chair and put her arms on the old woman's shoulders. "Could it . . . ?" Mariesa nodded, but said nothing. Roberta felt a cold wind run through her soul. Undoubtedly, a stray draft of night air. "Are you sure you want to take the risk?"

"Roberta, I watched my mother fail. I don't want the same thing to happen to me. I want little Carson to unnerstan . . . to understand me when I speak. If the operation fails . . . well, the worst that can happen is I go a bit earlier than if I did nothing. If it works . . . I'll have a great many more years. I want those years, because . . ."

"Because . . . ?"

"Because there's so much yet to see and do. Carson growing up. Tani's next book. Whether Chase can tame the asteroid. But most of all, I want to find where the Visitors come from; and then . . ."

"And then, what?"

"And then we'll see how smart they are."

Voices: Ecclesiastes

Well, Tani, today's the day. The *Lariat* is all ready; I'm all suited up; Hobie and the others are waiting . . .

I know you're nervous, but the teep flights—the remote control flights—all went smooth. This is just a little longer. Out to Lunar orbit, skate around to the Moon, then back home. No ballistic ship could ever do that, but I'm going to do it. Me, Jimmy Poole.

It's a beautiful ship, Tani, in a Japanese sort of way. Spare, lean. No big fuel tanks or engines. Just the life-support module—a standard Salyut module like everyone uses—and a mast stepped forward from its prow. Aerogel rings support the superconducting cables, and spokes and shrouds tie the rings to the mast and to Salyut's body. That's how I steer: I use the shroud motors to angle the magnetic fields.

Well, you've seen all the pictures, hit the web sites. I know you have. And I know you'll be watching this on threedy just like everyone else Earthside. You don't want me to describe what I see, but how I feel.

Everything's been planned and programmed, but Jesus, Tani, I'm scared enough to wet my pants. Just the idea of stepping out into the Big Empty freezes my gut. I guess that's why these suits come with diapers. <laughs.>

So why am I doing this?

I'm not really sure, myself. All year long—ever since I stepped into Chase's job—you never asked me why; so I figured *you* must know, and you have your own reasons for not telling me.

There's a feeling I get when I'm ziggy, a feeling of peace; but I'm scared all the same. I spent a lot of years inside a box that I thought was the size of the universe; and now I've seen the real thing and it's . . . Tani, it's beautiful.

But that's not the whole reason; 'cause I can get ziggy starfield in the Galaxy Room at FreeFall SkyResort—and have you with me, beside. I don't have to put my hide in a can that doesn't have any engines . . .

I keep thinking about what I told Chase one time: if the loop quenches—maybe the cooling fails or something—the current goes and I lose the sail, the ship will coast on forever, or arc into the sun, depending on the final velocity vector.

Oh, I know the risk is small—I calculated it myself. I've ballparked *all* the risks—from crossing the street to getting all three Intercept ships back safe—and this little skylark is *not* the most dangerous thing anyone has ever tried . . .

I think I have to do this for myself.

I know . . . I think . . . that when you married me, all you wanted was to pick my brain; and the sex . . . Well, close your eyes and think of plot lines, right.

Well, fair is fair. All I wanted at the time was to get laid. So, who's to say we both didn't get what we wanted. But, Tani, it's been eleven years now and you're still here; so you must have seen someone inside this bonebag besides that "Duncan Orb" character you created.

I want to find out who that someone is, and I don't think I'll find him in my computer sanctum. Because the more I think about it, the more it seems to me that a parting remark last year by a woman I hardly knew is the real reason I need to go.

I want to be a better character in your next book.

<Knocking, followed by Hobie's voice:> "Showtime, dude. Two hours for the hoop stress to circularize the loop. Time to get aboard."

Okay, Hobie.

<Hobie:> "Remember when you approach the Moon—"

The Moon's got no magfield to brake against. And I gotta watch my α setting: negative to get net repulsion from the sun; positive to fall toward it. Zero to move in a straight line. Jesus, Hobie, you're like an old woman. I wrote the flight programming, remember? There's plenty of margin. Don't worry, I won't break your toy. I've been practicing the sims now almost as long as Chase did. And you have to admit, things went a lot smoother once he was out of the loop and I was hacker *and* user.

<Hobie:> "Ready?"

Let's make it happen.

<Hobie:> "Good luck, man."

Luck's got nothing to do with it.

* * *

Chase caught the news on the threedy in the Hilton's lounge. Jimmy Poole had taken the *Lariat* out to the Moon and back. Smooth flight, no hassles. He wasn't sure which bothered him more: that someone else had taken the *Lariat*'s cherry, or that the someone else was Jimmy Poole.

But, still . . . Maiden flight. New machine. Hell, a whole new set of principles. Something new under the sun. You came right down to it, the little weenie done okay. No two ways around it; and he'd probably have to buy the guy a beer or a Coke or whatever the next time they met. If only he didn't brag on it in Chase's ears.

Yeah, the little weenie, he done okay.

15.

Bean Stalkers

Pitted, rough, as hard as endless night and cold could make it, the asteroid's surface hovered in the dark just beyond Chase's outstretched arm. Black and barely visible in the night, easy to run into if you misjudged the distance with no familiar references. That was one of his jobs. Chase Coughlin, Human Yardstick. His other job was to keep the lights aimed at the selected anchor points while Flaco and Bird maneuvered the booster rocket into place. "Not too fast," he cautioned. "It only weighs a few grams on the Bean, but it's still got the same mass."

Bird Winfrey said something about grandmothers and eggs, but Chase pretended not to hear him. Flaco jetted closer to the asteroid's surface, where a fixture had already been installed to align the motor. "Move it toward me," he said. "Half a meter. Easy. Easy." He wagged his hands, but must have realized Bird couldn't see the signals. "Down, now.

Now. Engaged. Forward end has engaged." Flaco shoved the cotter pins through the aligned holes.

"Bad news, Pancho," Bird told him. "Back end doesn't line up with the rear mounting fixture. It's short maybe an inch."

Flaco commented at length on the shortcoming. Chase moved in with a cable and threaded it through the eyebolts on the motor and the matching holes in the mounting flanges. At least the motor wouldn't torque off before a workaround could be devised.

Lights flared around them like the sun had gone nova and everything turned white. Chase grabbed instinctively for his dosimeter. Then Krasnarov, the program training manager, spoke over the radio link. "Exercise is terminated. I am sending cage down to bring you up."

"I think we ought to stay on it," Chase said. "On the mission, we won't get to restart if a fixture's been misaligned."

"Negative," said Bennett, the safety officer. "You've been down long enough. My divers need to rig things for tomorrow's exercise."

"Let's pack it in, guys," Chase told the other two. In the bright underwater lights, the asteroid had become a mock-up and the rocket motor a dummy cleverly balanced with embedded weights and floats. NASA's Neutral Buoyancy Tank outside Houston was damn big, but the walls, floor, and wavering surface overhead were now clearly visible.

They climbed aboard the elevator platform and it began its measured ascent. There would be several stops on the way up, to let their blood chemistry adjust. Time enough for recriminations.

"I don't know how that rear fixture got out of place," Bird said, anonymous in his white buoyancy suit.

"Meters. Inches. You got mixed up, *'mano.*" Bubbles swirled as the suited figure swirled his arm through the tepid water. " 'Member that Mars lander, years ago? You wanna smash like that?"

"Well, I'm real fucking sorry, *compadre.*"

"Sorry won' do us no good when we're at the Bean."

"Button up," Chase told them both. "We'll discuss it at debrief. Whole point of rehearsals is to find every possible foo and figure out workarounds ahead of time. When we're in Beanland, good buddies, I don't want *any* surprises. I want that whatever happens, we'll know what to do."

"Long day," said Flaco.

"Yeah," said Bird. "Look, Flaco, I really am sorry. I'm an NDT tech, not a rigger. I'm learning the craft because we all gotta do triple duty. Chase, here, he's got even more to learn than me, since he don't know squat about any of the crafts."

"Thanks for that vote of confidence," Chase said.

"I think better lighting would help," the tech suggested.

"Let's bring it up when we teep with Sandy and the others tonight. But there's not much window left for launching supply pods. Any pods launched between September and November won't reach the Bean until *after* we've been there and gone."

"That don' make no sense to me," said Flaco.

"Trust me," said Chase. "It's a question of delta-V and time of perihelion passage. With ballistic ships, every now and then 'you can't get there from here.' At least, not without taking the long way 'round. Constant boost ships, now that would be different."

Like *Lariat.* But he didn't like to think about that.

The booster engine had not kicked loose. Jacinta studied the scenario on the screen and contemplated. A glance at the rendezvous clock to check her time. Have to make some sort of decision, and soon. Abandon the pod? EVAde and try to disengage the dangling motor? That was an explosive bolt. Had it malfed, or was it waiting for some happy idiot to come along and jiggle it so the firing circuit could complete its appointed task. That would solve one problem: removing the engine so she could latch on and drag the supplies back to the Bean. But it would raise a second problem: a pilot with a bolt-hole drilled through her.

"What's in the pod?" she asked.

"Macht nichts," the simulator supervisor told her.

"Sure as hell does. If it's life-or-death supplies that's one thing. If the pod only has crap we already got enough of, I say let it go."

Her board froze and she heard the murmur of distant voices. A veritable flotilla of supply pods had been launched toward the Bean over the last few years. The very first ones had been lifted to LEO by Wilson RAM at its own expense, very nearly bankrupting the very company that had invented supersonic orbital guns. Once in orbit, the pods had been fitted with external engines powered by beamed microwave from Helios Light, which eliminated the need for an onboard power plant. Once insertion velocity had been achieved, the pods were supposed to shed their external engines and coast to the Bean. Lacking a kick motor to match velocity at rendezvous—and at any rate, considering the margin of error in the trajectory—the pods would need to be snagged and towed to the Bean by one of the three ships.

"Let's say the pod has vital supplies." That was Total's voice. She was sitting in the control booth, making notes; creating a decision tree. "Let's try solving this without an EVAsion first."

Total knew as well as Jacinta the dangers of an unsupported EVAsion. But there were way too many jobs to do at the Bean in too short a time, and so some of the work had to be done solo. "Roger." Jacinta reviewed her control panel status. "Okay. Resume." The clock began running again.

She had to remind herself that she was not being tested. She—and Total and the others—were trying to develop SOPs ahead of time for dealing with foreseeable glitches. That way, on the Bean, they would only have to worry about the unforeseeable ones. The planning team had developed a long list—a Failure Modes and Effects Analysis—of Things That

Could Go Wrong. Jacinta had seen the list. Some wag had signed "Colonel Murphy" to it, the legendary program manager at Edwards AFB who had enunciated the first great law of project management. Now it was the project team's job to figure out what to do about each item on the list that had been flagged high prob/high impact.

She tickled the steering jets to nudge her simulated ship closer to the simulated pod. The approach in her screens looked real. The VR was down to the bone. If it weren't for the gravity, she might almost think she was Out There.

Okay, if she couldn't go out to the pod, what were her options? She could flip the ship and try docking to the prow, instead; but that would mean a retrograde burn and in this scenario she needed to lift the pod to a *higher* orbit. Eventually the pod would rise higher than the Bean, due to the eccentricity of its ellipse. Problem was: it was a sun-focused ellipse and maneuvers that you could try in LEO every ninety minutes would here have to wait over a year. So that was a nonstarter.

There was the magnetic grapple, which she could fire like a harpoon; and there was "John Law"—Chase's name for the remote manipulator arm. "As in 'the Long Arm of . . .' " he had explained one evening. Was there a third option? "Fire phasers," she muttered under her breath.

"We'll try nudging the engine with the harpoon," she decided. "If the explosive bolts are armed, that might set them off and finish the disengage. If there's damage, we can replace the 'poon a lot easier than the robo-hand."

"Go ahead," said Total.

"Thar she blows," Jacinta announced and launched the grapple. The head was a powerful CORE magnet—cobalt and rare earths—made of directionally solidified metal and superconductors. If it got anywhere near the engine it would latch on like a used-car salesman. "Contact." She paused to study the situation. "Negative. The impact did not knock the sucker loose. I'll try jerking back." She set the tether reel at high speed and hit the on and off switch. Nothing happened to the simulator, but she was sure that in a real ship she would have felt a powerful shudder.

The engine was still attached to the pod, she saw; and now the two vessels were approaching each other. She nudged the ship with the attitude jets to maintain distance. "What if I just tow it in at the end of my line?"

"Negative," said Total. "Think 'crack the whip.' You'd pull ahead of the pod and the pod would swing around behind your engines . . ."

"If I time the burn right, I'll get engine cutoff before that happens."

". . . and keep on swinging. Conservation of angular momentum. Your ship will swing, too. Opposite sense."

"Damn. Scenario clock is expired. My big problem now is getting back to the Bean. Total, reset the clock to the decision point. I want to try something else."

"What?"

"Firing my phasers."

"Your what?"

"The microwave laser that we use for communication and power transmission. Crank it up high enough and I've got a cutting torch. I'll slice that sucker off."

"Umm. Wait one." There was a pause and Total came back on the line. "Heinrich says that's beyond the laser's envelope."

"Shoot, Total. You know the answer to that. We got a couple months yet to retrofit the shipboard lasers, don't we? Remember, 'Whatever we forget to take/We do without or learn to make.' "

"Lonzo's a better pilot than he is a rapper."

"No argument on this end."

"Okay, Heinrich says he'll override the program. If the scenario works, we'll put in an ECN to modify the shipboard lasers."

The workaround worked less well than Jacinta had hoped,

but better than some of the engineers had expected; so they all agreed that the propeller heads would find a more potent laser—something off the shelf because who had time for clean sheet these days?—and carve the cheese to fit the revised capabilities.

Afterward, Jacinta and Total decompressed in a booth in the Otter-wise Lounge on NASA Highway One. Jacinta wanted iced tea, but Total wheedled her into something stronger. "Anything but vodka," Jacinta said in capitulation and found herself faced with gin.

"This is awful. It smells like turpentine."

"Tastes like it, too," Total agreed. "Has a lot of the same uses." She turned the "gibson" glass in her hand. "The lonely girl's friend . . ."

Jacinta's lips parted, but she hesitated, then took a sip to cover. Setting the glass carefully on the table, she said, "You still miss Adrienne, don't you?"

Total wet her lips with her tongue. "Some days." She took another drink. "She would have been picked for this mission, you know. She was that good; especially at the kind of close maneuvering you were practicing today. If she hadn't . . . If only she hadn't . . ." Total drew a shuddering breath. "Ah, the hell with it." And she finished her drink in one swallow.

"Should you be throwing them back that way?"

Total set the glass down hard. "What, is little 'Cinta concerned? When I'm on duty, I'm functional. 'Sall that matters. Why can't girls be hard-drinking spacemen, like Chase and them?"

Chase was rather abstemious, Jacinta thought. He rationed himself rigorously and confined himself mostly to beer. He enjoyed drinking too much to get drunk. "You and Adrienne . . . you were"—Jacinta searched for a word—"an item?"

Total snorted. "We were lovers. Go ahead, you can say it. This is 'The Decade of Vision,' after all. The 2020s. Everybody says so, so it must be true. You don't approve?"

"No, it's not that," Jacinta protested. "Only I wasn't sure . . ."

Total placed her hand over Jancinta's and brushed the hairs on her arm. "Have you ever tried it?"

Gently, Jacinta pulled her arm away. "No."

"That's right. You're engaged. How's Yungfuck these days? He get into your pants yet?"

Jacinta clenched her fists on the table. "You've no right to say that!"

"Why not? All the boys want that. They can't help it. It comes from carrying their genitalia on the outside. Way too easy to get it rocking."

"The Duck's a gentleman."

"Only means his technique is slicker."

"Total, you don't mean that . . ."

"Don't I?" She leaned over the table and grabbed both of Jacinta's hands in her own. Jacinta tugged against the grip, but Total was a black belt and Jacinta was unable to break her hold. "God, Jacinta, I've been so lonely, and I—" Then, abruptly, she released her. Jacinta sat back in the booth and rubbed her wrists. Total looked down and brushed imaginary dirt from the table. "No, you're right, 'Cinta. It's just my own pain talking. I shouldn't let jealousy get in my way. Or yours. I wish you the best of luck. Both of you. I hope he knows how to do it without hurting you, because you won't have that much time together before we leave."

"He'll wait for me. I'll only be gone nine months."

"Just another flight, right? Except it's not. Shoving that Bean aside is important. It's the most important thing anyone's ever been asked to do. And that means that this is the first flight ever, since Gagarin rode a tin can, where the recovery of the crew is not the most important objective of the mission." She picked up her empty glass and held it up so the waitress would see it. "Are you sure you don't want another, dear; because I do."

When RS 74 *Artie Smith* lifted from the Phoenix desert, it was the first time in a great many years that Chase Coughlin had lifted as a passenger. Operation Intercept had decided in their wisdom that the FarTrip II crew did not need to maintain proficiency inside gravity wells; and it could be that they were right. There wouldn't be much in the way of gravity, to and from the Bean. Choo-choo, the pilot captain, had seen him on the passenger deck and insisted on giving him the straight bunny lecture, much to the puzzlement of the nooboos and the amusement of the otters who knew Chase from of old.

Choo-choo did promise him a hand on the controls once they reached ziggy. Docking practice, the big hats agreed on. There would be much docking and snatching on FarTrip. The copilot was a cherry named Rowley; but he gladly relinquished the left-hand seat to Chase when Chase came forward to play. Chase asked Honnycott why the ship's nickname was "Bird Boy," and Chooch filled him in on Artie Smith, "the Bird Boy of Fort Wayne," who had been the first pilot to fly at night.

"And I saw a repro of the 'chine he flew," Honnycott told him. "Hanging in the airport there. A modified Wright Flyer. No better'n a box kite with a motor. What're you up for?"

"Checking out the living quarters on *Mitchell*. The Salyut is mated up and ready for residence. I'm going up to see if they speak sooth. Zaranovsky's checking out *Sikorsky* and Sandy's clucking over her baby. They had to cut into *Cochran*'s nose to attach the Salyut module."

Honnycott shook his head. "Won't get me aboard no nuke. What if the bottle fails?"

"Reaction shuts down would be my guess," Chase said cheerfully. "Or maybe just lose power. It's the orifice of the magnetic field that gives Chang-Diaz drives their specific impulse. If the bottle goes spritz, you don't have a nozzle anymore."

"Just high-speed ionized gases going every which way."

"Didn't say there wouldn't be a downside." Chase wasn't

sure chemical rockets were much safer—at least when you thought about things that *might* go wrong. But OTV-X2 *Jackie Cochran* was a larger ship and gave them an extra body on the Bean as well as a poke more supplies. Intercept probably would have sent the *Yeager* as well, but word was they were saving the only other nuclear X-ship for FarTrip III's voyage to Rabbit Punch.

Choo-choo dropped him off at Goddard Free Port and wished him luck. Chase checked in with Port Captain Patel and made arrangements to take the shuttle over to *Mitchell.* Then, since he couldn't do jack until the shuttle returned from Vulcan Furnace, he repaired to the lounge.

Goddard's lounge was level fifteen on its number four spoke and featured a wraparound pixwall that doided the entire surroundings of the station. When the lights were out, it seemed as if the lounge was floating out in the Big Empty itself.

Chase found himself a foo-brew and a chair and let the Coriolis plant him gracefully in the seat. He'd popped the lid and tilted his head back and the first gulp of cool refreshment had headed gutward when he realized he was staring realtime at MSS *Lariat.*

It didn't look like much. An oversized Salyut with a honking long mast on its prow. The mast was festooned with aerogel support rings and shrouds and stays that transmitted the thrust to the vessel. No engines visible, except the little attitude jets. If an otter didn't know better, he'd suppose it was some sort of mini-habitat. Maybe a small manufactory, or a research station. There were plenty of those about in Goddard's sub-orbs.

What was it like to fly her? No thunder, no punch; just a slow steady pressure, starting slow and building, building. Free. To sail anywhere at any time. Free of gravity—if you trimmed your α right—but also at its mercy if the system failed. He wondered if Jimmy knew that, deep down inside where it mattered. It was easy to do something brave if you didn't know what you were doing.

The hell with it. That was DSV *Billie Mitchell* on the far side of *Lariat*. It looked funny with the Salyut mounted forward; like a boy pushing a peanut with his nose. Not to mention the strap-ons mounted aft: boosters that would be powered by beamed microwave from Helios powersat in its sun-synchronous polar orbit. Boost to a delta-V of fifty percent, burst free of the gravitational arms of the Earth-Moon; hurtle outward into the lonely, empty abyss of translunar space. No fallback; no pickup; no reboot.

He took a long ragged breath and slugged back his near beer. He glanced at the clock. They'd promised him the shuttle would be back in twenty minutes. Maybe he ought to find a suit and prep himself. Anything was better than sitting here and staring at broken dreams and nightmares.

The shuttle dropped him off at *Mitchell* and Chase booked his return flight for two hours. "Don't sweat it," the shuttle driver said with a knowing wink. "I got a regular round, like a bus route. I can stay away as long as you want. You need some hang time, you got it." Chase contemplated that remark while he cycled through the lock on the cargo deck. The man had spoken knowingly, as if they shared some great secret; but it was a damn good secret because Chase didn't know it.

Using the gangway ladder to propel himself toward the nose lock, Chase had the sudden, odd thought that it might never be used as a *ladder* again. In ziggy, it was only a series of regularly spaced handholds. Only in a gravity well, would you have to *climb* up to the flight deck. And the poor, old *Mitchell* had been worried at enough with cutting torches and weldments and all what have you that a drop through the atmosphere would probably kill it. Max-Q could rip it apart.

When he emerged on the flight deck, he was startled to see Jacinta Rosario sitting in the flight engineer's seat. She was wearing headphones and a look of intense concentration and

Chase checked his forward progress by hooking a rung with his feet when he was halfway out the interlock. Jacinta's brow was knit and her lips were parted and pouting slightly. "Coming into range now," she said to her mike. Then another long silence while she tracked a blip on the radar screen. "Targeting . . . I've got lock. One thousand. Nine-fifty. Energizing . . ." She flipped two switches and pressed a button. "Bounceback. I have contact echo. Power up." This time she moved a handle and lights flickered across her console. "Let me peep a close-up." Teep goggles flipped into place over her eyes. "Telescope view shows a good burn line . . . You getting the feed? Good. Okay, done! Got it. Sliced like a salami! Automatic power cutoff. . . . Let me verify that." She flipped her goggles up and played the keyboard. "Okay. Confirm shutdown. I'll see you guys at the debrief tomorrow." One last switch thrown. Then she pumped her fist twice in the air and said, "Yes! Yes!"

Some noise or movement must have caught her eye then, because she turned, saw Chase in the interlock, and shrieked.

Chase rubbed a hand over his chin. "I guess I should have shaved."

"You scared me half to death!"

"Sorry. I came up to check out the Salyut. The shuttle driver didn't say anything about you being on board." And he could have quietly ducked out of sight while she was still distracted and come back making more noise. But he had enjoyed watching her work. Or just watching her. "What were you up to?" he asked.

"Field test on the new cutting laser."

"I guess it worked. If sound carried in vaccum, they'd know it in Goddard, too."

She flushed deliciously. "I was excited. It was my idea. In the sims last month . . ."

"I know. Well, as long as we're both here and you've finished your test, why don't you help me check out the Salyut."

Jacinta picked up her flatscreen cliputer and an electric stylus. "Gotta finish my checklist. I've already been up there."

The shuttle wouldn't be back for two hours. Chase didn't mention that. Maybe Jacinta had made other arrangements. Or maybe the shuttle driver figured Chase's directive included Jacinta. The wink-wink, nudge-nudge made sense all of a sudden. The bastard had assumed Chase was after some docking maneuvers. Some people had dirty minds. Chase didn't mind a fantasy or two, and before Karen he hadn't been exactly celibate; but he didn't like it when others fantasized about him in the third person. People like that should get a life. At least their own fantasy life, if they didn't have a real one . . .

The Salyut module was mated to *Mitchell*'s nose by a small frustum that Forrest Calhoun used to call "the foyer." Chase passed through into the first cylinder, which was three meters wide and four long. Looking it over, he remembered something Forrest had said about his own year-long jaunt with Mike Krasnarov and Nacho Mendes to 1991JW—"Calhoun's Rock." *We had to get real friendly,* Forrest had told him. The engineers could tell them all about the equipment and the life support—the zeolite plants, the water and air regenerators—and the scientists could tell them all about orbits and transit time; but only the crew of the old *Gene Bullard* could tell them what it was like to *live* in one of these things for month after month.

What'd you do for fun, Forrest?

We had us a contest, son. Who'd be the first to kick off from the nose lock and sail all the way to the observation blister without touching any of the walls along the way.

Chase propelled himself forward. The smaller cylinder was to be the "recc room" though he didn't see much space reserved for a tennis court. There was a fold-away stationary bike and a set of spring-loaded weights, as well as the usual giant elastic band. Chase hated those things. He felt ridiculous inside one, stretching it out with his arms and legs; but it was supposed to help preserve muscle tone in ziggy. The μCD library was slated to contain copies of thousands of works of art and fiction. *Hope you like to read, son,* he heard Forrest's voice, *'cause the jogging facilities are a tad limited.* Chase opened the bin and saw that the CDs had not been stowed yet. Suppose they forgot . . . Nine months on the Long Orbit with nothing to read, no games to play. What would they find to amuse themselves?

"Chase?" It was Jacinta calling. He moved away from the interlock and the engineer copilot emerged from the opening. She looked around the vessel with a broad smile, as if she owned the place and was showing it off to a potential buyer.

"Definitely a fixer-upper," Chase said. "Maybe we can build an addition later."

Jacinta treated the remark like a joke. "Have you seen the kitchen? Come on." And she led him through the joining frustum—"the grand hallway"—into the living quarters. The second cylinder, four by four, contained their food and other stores, shower and water closet, tethered sleeping bags, and a bewildering array of equipment tucked and packed away in bins. Every surface was a chest of drawers. And why not? It wasn't as though there were ceilings and floors in ziggy. Chase pointed to the empty bins still awaiting the crew from Boeing Outfitters.

"Ever try to repack a suitcase after you've been on a trip? Seems like you can never get everything back in place again."

Jacinta's laugh was like bells. "Look at this. Not just a microwave, but an induction oven."

"Yeah, but what if I want to flip an omelette?" He made frying pan motions with his hand.

"You can't fry," Jacinta said seriously. "Heat doesn't rise in ziggy, it . . ." She trailed off as she realized he was joking.

"Come on," he said. "Let's check out the view."

The nose of the Salyut was a hemispherical bubble of syndiotactic polypropylene two meters in diameter. Just now the shields were open, flooding the forward reaches of the Salyut with Earthlight. The planet hovered enormous on the edge of their field of view. High, wispy streaks of cloud, like careless swipes of a painter's brush, over a canvas of blue and brown and green. Was that New Jersey there? Hard to tell. He was upside down with respect to conventional maps. Barely glimpsed through cirrus and stratus, crusted with white, dreaming of a white Christmas. He and Karen and the Tornado were spending the holidays at his folks' place in old North Orange. Last chance to visit before departure. The limb of the Earth was pale, almost luminescent, where the atmosphere thinned into the vacuum of space. There was no boundary. There were molecules of Earth's atmosphere banging around even up here, which was why orbits in LEO eventually decayed unless periodically corrected.

It looked thin, the atmosphere did. Thin and fragile, until you realized how large the planet was beneath you and how many millions of tons of air blanketed it. Drop a rock through that soup and it would vaporize before it hit the ground.

Unless it was a very big rock.

On the way back to Goddard, he stopped at *Lariat.* He couldn't not stop there. Jacinta was curious, too, having heard about it from Chase and having seen the stories of Jimmy Poole's test flights. The shuttle driver shrugged off the unscheduled stop and said whatever the "Bean Stalkers" wanted, they got. The media were lionizing the FarTrip crew as "heroes" and Chase figured what the hell good was celebrity if you didn't cash in once in a while. And if they hadn't exactly done anything heroic yet, it made no sense to wait until afterward. Soldiers received their bounty money *before* reporting for duty.

The driver engaged the prongs and the shuttle latched on to the *Lariat*'s man-lock. Chase and Jacinta cycled through. No one ever locked doors in LEO. It was not so much that petty theft was unknown, but that an otter might need to get into pressure in a hurry and didn't have any time to pat down pockets looking for a key.

It was a day for surprises. Jimmy Poole was up.

He had turned to look at the sound of the lock and when he saw Chase, he froze up pretty solid. There were two otters with him—electricians, by the look of them. One was honey blond, or would have been had he let his hair grow out; the other was a pale, wispy thing who would have disappeared entirely had she turned sideways. They were working at some installation or other. Chase couldn't see what it was. A clamshell covered it to contain the vapors and searing droplets of the soldering tool. The two techs both wore white with the Lucky Thirteenth patches on their shoulders. After a single glance in the newcomers' direction, they bent back to work. Periodically, an actinic flash would make itself seen through the seams of the clamshell.

Jimmy wiped his hands on a rag and hung it precisely and motionlessly in the air beside him. "What are you doing here?"

Chase gritted his teeth and smiled. "Everybody gotta be somewhere. 'Cinta and me were on our way back from *Mitchell* and thought we'd take a peek."

"Weren't thinking of taking it out for a spin, were you?"

Chase ignored the smarminess of the accusation. Maybe the weenie meant it for a joke. It was hard to tell with Poole. He was also surprised, then disgusted, with the brief blossom of thrill he felt when, for a moment, his hindbrain thought Jimmy was making a serious offer. But the way the dogs had the access panels removed, the wiring spaghettied out, and the soldering clam flashing, the *Lariat* wasn't going anywhere soon. Engineering changes based on the last test flight, Chase guessed. He pointed to the techs.

"You didn't break it, did you?"

Jimmy scowled. "No. This ship is my baby."

Unaccountably irritated, Chase said, "I thought it was Hobie's baby."

Jacinta interrupted, "Can you show us the ship? We don't have that much time and I'm really interested," and there was something sweet in her voice that defused both Chase and Jimmy.

The geek bowed. "Certainly, ma'am'selle. If you would follow me . . ." Chase took the "you" as plural and went with them toward the prow.

The vessel was also a Salyut, though a slightly smaller one than *Mitchell.* The magship wasn't designed for year-long voyages. It was an X-ship, testing concept and feasibility. So while it had the usual bio-support systems, it was not packed so full to the gills. No greenhouse, no sleeping bags, no racks of drawers and bins. It was a lean, mean, stripped-down 'chine. Chase ached to buckle in and kick the amps.

But it was Jacinta who settled into the odd support rack. It fit her like an exoskeleton. "I'd love to learn to fly one of these things."

Jimmy waggled his eyebrows. "And I would love to teach you."

The innuendo bothered Chase more than it did Jacinta. "How does she handle?" he said.

Jimmy hesitated, then shrugged. "Like a dream. Literally. No shaking, no sound except the air pumps . . . Utterly silent. She's balky. Won't steer on a dime. And it seems to take forever to build up speed. You ran a few of the sims. I'd say they were eighty percent on the money."

"What was the twenty percent?"

Jimmy blinked like an owl caught in sunlight. "Being weightless."

Chase grunted. Jimmy had lost a lot of weight in the last year. There ought to be a joke he could crack—weight-less—but the precise words eluded him. When Jacinta was done playing pilot, Chase deliberately affected a blasé attitude. "Maybe after I get back," he said as Jimmy led them toward the lock. "Hey, remember I said I'd buy you a drink in honor of your maiden flight a couple months ago? Come on over to Goddard. We have maybe a half hour before the *Ruth Law* drops."

Jimmy closed up just a little. "I'll wait for the shuttle."

The shuttle was already waiting, but Chase didn't point that out. He and Jacinta were both suited from their outside inspection on the *Mitchell* and its Salyut. Jimmy probably figured they had spacewalked over and left their helmets in *Lariat*'s lock. Chase grinned. "Oh, come on. We'll jet over. I'll hold your hand."

Yeah, the weenie had definitely turned green. "I'll wait."

Jacinta had opened her mouth, probably to mention the waiting shuttle; but closed it now and gave Chase a puzzled look. Chase said, "You'll probably miss your drink. We'll be dropping before you walk over."

"So I'll die thirsty. Buy yourself a drink and pretend it came from me. That way it comes out even."

Chase blinked. "Why would you buy me a drink?"

Jimmy looked away, saw that his rag had drifted in the slight breeze of the air system, and kicked over to grab it. "Last chance," he said as he folded the rag. "Christmas is coming and you guys are leaving . . . when?"

"Just after New Year." As if the whole world didn't know the departure date on that one.

"Yeah. I won't see you after that. So. Good luck." He extended a hand, and after a moment's study Chase took it. Jimmy shook Jacinta's hand, too. "Kick that Bean's ass good."

Chase nodded. "I'll pretend it's yours."

Surprisingly, Jimmy returned a grim smile. "Whatever works."

"Okay," said Chase. "Buy me the drink when I get back."

Jimmy hesitated only a fraction. "Sure. When you get back."

In the shuttle once more, Chase folded his arms across his chest. "I can't stand that guy. He drives me up a wall." Jacinta said nothing and closed her eyes. She napped the rest of the short way back and Chase sat there watching her breathe and thinking of the long, hard task that lay ahead.

* * *

The honeymoon would be on orbit. She would have three days at FreeFall SkyResort before the crew of *Mitchell* would muster and depart into the hostile deep. But the ceremonies were on Earth—a small, private family affair, though one newscopter did manage to locate them at the last—and so her first night with Yungduk was at the hotel by Allentown Skyport. Jacinta's mama had cried, as much for what her own life had missed as for her daughter's "growing up." Yungduk's dad had given him all sorts of last-minute fatherly advice of the sort that men seldom discussed seriously among themselves, and Yungduk had listened gravely and thanked him as if he had never heard any such thing in his entire life.

They went traditional. The bride wore white. But a garland of wildflowers rather than a veil and adorned her hair. Greenhouse grown. It was winter, right enough; but the old god, Janus, wore two faces—one looking forward, one looking back. And so it was appropriate that such a change in her life take place in January, when she could look back at the twenty-two years of who she had been and forward to the unknown years of who she would be. The snow had melted off and a warm breath had wafted up from the south. Spring was coming, if reluctantly; a time of hope, as she was embarking now on a voyage of hope.

In two senses. Not only FarTrip II, but her life with Yungduk.

They gathered in a small meeting room at the Skyport hotel. Jacinta's mother had a bungalow in Hamm's Corner and Yungduk's folks lived in married enlisted quarters on Edwards AFB on the other side of the country. Neither locale was well suited for a wedding, but the hotel's management had been only too glad to donate the meeting space to one of the world's heroes. After all, as the newsreaders had portentiously announced, the upcoming wedding was "a symbol of confidence in the face of adversity."

Jacinta wished they had not singled her out. All during the

year, while trees back home greened and then turned gold and she had trained and trained, and then trained some more, newsgroupies had hovered around the margins of her life looking for bytes, looking for emotive gushes. All the ten crew members had to endure some of that, of course; and their spouses—those who had them—and their neighbors and friends and forgotten classmates from second grade. But what she and Yungduk shared was a very private thing. It was not a spectacle, neither for the public's amusement nor for their reassurance. She had always been an intensely private person and the groupies had at first taken her reticence for snobbery; but someone very high up must have leaned on them very hard, because as the wedding drew nigh they backed away, leaving her, as the venerable Broder Hart had implored his colleagues publicly, "her space."

Other hotel guests did glance at her from time to time—when she checked in, when she and Yunduk had dinner with their parents the night before, and most of all while she walked slowly in a cloud of white and gold and violet down the hallway to the meeting room. But they respected "her space" and confined themselves to smiles and whispers and a handful of well wishes. "She's so *beautiful,*" Jacinta heard one child say to her parents as she passed. But the girl couldn't mean her, could she? Beautiful? Yungduk had told her so, and often; but Yungduk was not a reliable source on that point. Happy, perhaps, was a better description; but how did an observer spot that? Unless beauty was only happiness that showed.

She entered the room wearing her Maiden's Shawl across her shoulders: the silver apple against a geometric background of light greens and yellows. She left it with her shoulders bare.

It was a warm night, with just enough of the desert cool in its breeze to take the edge off. In the morning Chase would leave for Goddard City, board *Mitchell,* then depart for the

Bean. He had spent the day packing and giving instructions to Karen. This bill had been paid; that magazine should be canceled. The screen on the back door needed replacement. Karen nodded and pretended to listen, but Chase knew she would run the house on her own terms, as she always did. Still, he needed to act as if his going made a difference.

And of course it did, though the differences did not lie in screen doors or magazines. "I'll miss you, so much," Karen said as they sat side by side on the bench in the cactus garden. "There's a part of me that's proud of you for being picked; but that doesn't mean the other part of me won't be hurting."

Chase had spent a lot of hours planting and tending those cacti. He would miss them, too. As a hobby, it was a prickly one and he had accumulated more punctures than a New York City junkie; yet there was a certain austere beauty to the result that made it all worthwhile. "I'll be thinking about you every minute I'm out there," he said.

She gave him a little shove. "Don't tell me that. You'll have work to do. I don't ever want to hear that the Earth got whacked because Chase Coughlin was daydreaming about his woman when he should have been down to business. Hear me? If they insist on making you a hero, I want the Jenuine Bean. You come back, but come back with your head held high."

"I ain't no hero," he said, wrapping an arm around her waist.

He raised his eyes to the sky. Hopeless to spot the Bean. Eyeballs weren't in it; and it was the wrong quadrant anyway. Still, it seemed to him as if a dozen pinprick lights were growing larger, heading directly toward him. The heavens had become more hostile in recent years. No longer romantic; no longer awe-inspiring; no longer an adventure. Instead, a dark and threatening vista, like an untamed forest within whose secret fastnesses lurked savage beasts and savage men. Or things that were much like men.

"You just come back," she said.

"It's in the flight plan," he answered lightly. "I made sure of that."

"I mean it." Her eyes glistened in the starlight. "If you don't come back, I'll hate you; and I love you too much to hate you."

It didn't make any sense, but Chase forbore from debating the issue because it was true in the only way that mattered. He drew her closer to him. The Long Orbit would be long indeed, and hard and lonely, far from home, with desperate work to be done. Dependent on dozens of supply pods matching rendezvous orbits. Handling explosives and propellants, heavy rigging. That was dangerous enough Earthside, where there was an entire world of emergency support, hospitals, and medical care. FarTrip had Peterson Ku, a cabinet full of medicines and surgical tools, and no practical experience in zero-gee surgery.

No one did. Yet.

Forrest Calhoun and Mike Krasnarov and Nacho Mendes had taught the three ships' crews everything they had learned the hard way about working on an asteroid; but FarTrip I hadn't had a fraction of the physical labor planned for FarTrip II, and like the Man said, there was always one more thing to learn.

Yet, Karen's part might be the harder one. She had to stay behind and wait.

A cool breeze whispered off the Sierra Estrellita. Karen shivered a little and Chase held her tighter. Funny. He had imagined this night of leave-taking as one of passionate love-making; yet here they sat holding hands, just being with each other, and he was content.

16.

Outward Bound

The gatekeeper at Allentown Spaceport was very patient, but Hobie could hear the edge in his voice as he explained one more time to the official why the lift was delayed. Hobie was more than a little anxious himself to get to LEO. The new slug would improve the current density in *Lariat*'s sails by twenty percent, once he had drawn it to wire; and he preferred to oversee the initial tests personally.

"You don't understand," the official said, distracting Hobie once more from his flatscreen. "I'm making a connection on Leo Station. I *must* be in Prague by two for an important meeting."

"I'm very sorry, sir," the gatekeeper said, "but as I've already told you, Space Traffic Control has ordered a stand-down until the Intercept fleet has left. The drop from Leo to Prague is delayed as well. To reduce the risk of an accident."

"That's absurd," the man replied.

Privately, Hobie agreed with him. Flight planners knew their job. The likelihood of a collision between routine traffic and the departing fleet was minimal. Ships docked and dropped from the stations all the time. But someone had spooked the herd in the European Parliament and the better-safe-than-sorry germ had infected the Congress and the Duma, as well. And so the pulse of the world would pause for a time while the Interceptors departed.

And maybe that was the right thing to do, Hobie reflected. Not because of safety, but because of respect—and a fare-ye-well.

"Do you know who I am?" the official shouted at the gatekeeper. "DO YOU KNOW WHO I AM?"

The gatekeeper picked up the microphone. "Attention in the gate area. There is a poor man here who doesn't know who he is. If anyone could help identify him, it would be greatly appreciated."

Hobie was still laughing when Ladawan returned to the gate area with a pair of cups: fruit juice for him, green tea for herself. She glanced at the functionary who had been harassing the gatekeeper, then turned a wry eye on Hobie, lifting one brow. Hobie shrugged and made a face. "I can understand his impatience," he said. "I'd like to get started on the refitting after the last trials. The *Lariat*'s my baby, after all."

Ladawan lowered herself to the seat beside him and patted her swollen belly. "Not your only one," she said. She leaned against him and absently Hobie laid his arm across her shoulder.

"Nothing to do but wait," he said. For FarTrip, for the baby, for the Bean.

Meat Tucker was playing ziggy bounceball in Hub 3 on Goddard City when the announcement came. It was the Thirteenth versus the Goddard City Grays and the score was tied at two-all. Olya Tsvetnikova, an Energia electrician, had taken the rebound off the C/D ring frame and deftly passed off to Bolislav Drozd; but Meat had anticipated the move and kicked from the longitudinal long-line to intercept it.

"Attention," the internal speaker system announced. "Power diversion in five minutes. Repeat. Helios Light will divert beamed power from our rectennae in five minutes. Please shut down any nonessential equipment."

Meat threw the ball to Sepp, who bounced it off the outer bulkhead; but the game petered to a stop by a sort of unspoken consent as the players turned and looked at one another or gripped a stanchion on the flyby and took up the Hub's rotation. Bounceball in Hub 3 was more challenging than elsewhere in the Hub because the module was under spin, which gave the ball rather peculiar english.

"Let's go down to the lounge and watch on the pixwall," someone said. Meat noticed that a few of the players had already departed.

"Nah," he said. "Too crowded down there." And besides, to show too much enthusiasm was not kick.

Time stretched until the very air seemed ready to shatter. Meat had begun to think they had missed it when the lights suddenly dimmed. It was only for a moment, before the on-board system picked up the slack. Leo Station had its own solar array, but used the beamed power for peak load times.

The bounceball players moved toward the starside airlock like iron filings pulled by a magnet.

Outside, the stars were tumbling.

It was a slow rotation—just over two revolutions per minute. Every twenty-seven seconds, a brighter, first-magnitude star came into view: the strap-on booster stages of the departing *Mitchell.*

"How long," Bolislav asked, "will they use the Lighthouse?"

"Twenty minutes," said Sepp. "A long boost. Dey must escape de whole Earth-Moon system."

"Tha's why the boosters use beamed power from Helios," said Chino Guiterrez. "They traded their power plants for more fuel."

Meat looked wistfully out the window at departing ships. *The first, best hope,* the news-sites had been calling it. The asteroid still didn't seem quite real to him. How could something you couldn't even see cause as much damage as they were saying?

"Vaya con Dios," said Chino, and Olya crossed herself right to left.

Roberta had watched the whole thing on threedy with Mariesa up in the Roost at Silverpond. The buildup to departure, with the hushed and excited commentary; the moment of ignition as first *Sikorsky* at Tsiolkovskigrad, then *Mitchell* at Goddard City, and finally *Cochran* co-orbiting with Leo Station lit their engines and moved out of Low Earth Orbit. Then the long, lingering view of the departing ships in echelon astern when, bereft of all words to fill the empty void, even Broder Hart could whisper only, "Godspeed."

Throughout it all, Mariesa van Huyten sat expressionlessly. Roberta wondered what occupied her mind. The asteroid she had always feared? The chances of the Intercept fleet? Or perhaps the upcoming surgery? Whatever the thoughts, they had kept her silent and looking inward. Roberta reached out and touched her on the forearm.

"Well," she said, "they're gone."

Mariesa roused slightly, focused on Roberta, then on the screen, and she nodded once, very slightly.

When Jimmy Poole concentrated, the rest of the universe faded to background noise. This was especially true when he was teeping a magship sim at home. With the goggles blacked and the headphones set, he was, for all practical purposes, aboard the *Lariat* out beyond GEO Ridge sailing large before the solar wind. So, when Tani entered his Sanctum and interrupted the run, his first thought was to wonder, *How did she get out here?*

It was a momentary fancy and one that amused him. He removed his teep helmet and blinked at her. "What?"

"STC just confirmed that the burns were successful and all three ships are on orbit to rendezvous with the Bean."

"Of course," Jimmy said. "Hyperbolic orbit. The Earth will slow them down as they climb, but they'll still have V when they hit the border. If you think people didn't check those burn schedules down to the last decimal place, think again."

"I thought you would want to know. After all, Chase is on one of the ships."

"As long as he's far away from me, and getting farther." He grinned at his own joke.

Tani was not amused. "He's doing something important. He's risking his life for all of us."

"*Lariat* is important," Jimmy pointed out.

Tani rubbed his shoulder. "It's not a contest."

"I know that. Just don't expect me to get all sentimental over him just because he's doing something dangerous. You didn't know him like I did."

In fact, Chase probably wasn't smart enough to realize how dangerous the expedition really was, Jimmy thought after Tani had gone. He lifted his teep helmet, but paused before putting it back on. He had calculated the probability of success for the mission. Component reliabilities for the ships themselves were supposed to be confidential—commercial secrets and all that—but few were the deebies that were dark to him. And DeepSpace had figures on accident rates on work in ziggy.

Jimmy had fingered the data and run the math. Assume that burn-in and painstaking inspection had eliminated early failures, and that the journey was not so long as to invoke wear-out failures. That put everything in the random failure regime, where the exponential model was appropriate and you could add up the component failure rates.

He was not so naive as to suppose that those who had planned the mission had not done the same. They had to know. Odds were, one of the ships would not make it back. What sort of person sent others out, knowing that some would never come back? It had to do something to you.

What if it was Chase who didn't come back? Jimmy had always thought the idea would please him. Not that he wished anyone harm, not even his old bête noire. But if it did happen, he never thought to waste any tears over it.

And yet, to his own surprise, he found the possibility oddly upsetting.

* * *

Somewhere in the Void, God had drawn a line. You couldn't quite pin it down, because God kept changing His mind, and so it shifted and moved with the Earth itself. But with every day they climbed closer to it. Up from LEO, past the Van Allens, pas GEO, past even where the Moon would have been had the Moon only been there. The Earth dragged them as they climbed, a distraught lover clinging to her beloved. *Mitchell* slowed, and slowed, and gradually its path bent until it seemed as if the greedy Earth would snatch her back regardless.

They seemed to have no velocity. No trees or fenceposts whipped past their viewscreens. No shifting of the background paralax. Certainly the stars did not move. The only indication of speed was the Dopplering of their contact with DeepSpace. With each passing day, replies took longer, as if DeepSpace had grown steadily more hesitant.

The first few days were filled with shakedown. They tested systems; inspected functions; ran diagnostics. Chase verified command and control; Jacinta checked engines and fuel and life support. Then they switched and checked each other. Even Flaco Mercado, the third of the *Mitchells*, pitched in. He might not be a pilot or an engineer, but he by God knew a cracked seal when he saw one, and every otter knew suit maintenance. They were rapidly approaching the point when "oops" would not be the most pleasant thing to hear.

Of course, everything had been checked down in LEO well before departure; but components often behaved differently under stress than when at rest. A lot like people, in that way.

They found several failures. There were millions of opportunities: components and connections and miles of wiring and lines of code. It wasn't plausible that *none* of them would malf. But those they found were not serious, and they could hope that those they failed to find were the same.

On day seven they crossed that fuzzy line in the void.

For the better part of the day, Earth and sun had been fighting like quarreling parents over possession of the ship and at the five-hundred-and seventy five-thousandth milestone the sun was awarded custody. All thought of apogee vanished from the ship's mind. Her orbit ceased to curl back and she hurtled on in what was very nearly a straight line. With grave solemnity and ceremony, Chase had Jacinta switch the navigational system from the geocentric to the heliocentric coordinate system. "Good-bye, Ptolemy; hello, Kopernick." And there was time for a little backslapping and hugging; and even Jacinta suggested they needed a new initiation ceremony for this new sort of milestone.

God rested on the seventh day; but God had not been piloting a hot ship on a hyperbolic orbit. There was the rendezvous with the first fuel pod to fine-tune. Insertion into Bean orbit required more fuel than they had remaining, so topping off en route would be required. An everyday maneuver in LEO and GEO—Chase and Jacinta were old hands at it—but fail at it here and the ship would coast outward forever.

Well, not forever. Until aphelion, well past the Bean's orbit. But that, from the crew's point of view, would be forever enough for anything that mattered.

So it wasn't as though any of the scheduled tasks were especially difficult; it was only that the consequences riding on them were greater. More than a certificate; more than a reputation. More, even, than their lives. Because the world had not sent them outward bound simply to test their mettle.

The mission schedule called for sleep, so they must have slept; though afterward Jacinta thought those first weeks a constant blur of activity. Perhaps she dreamed subconscious rehearsals of her tasks, so that even sleep was filled with activity. She barely thought of Yungduk and those frantic, urgent days before departure. When she did—his hands on her, his tongue in her, his body moving against her, moving within her—she thought no other days could ever be as sweet, and regretted—almost—that they had not been hers years earlier. On day nine she cried herself to sleep, she so missed his ready wit and gentle touch; but she wept close into her tightly held pillow, wrapped within her sleeping bag so that no one would know.

And, what the hell, the pod rendezvous went like clockwork. "What do you expect," Chase asked the universe in general, "when you send the very best?"

After that, things calmed down for a time. The initial crisis points on the mission time line were past; the next batch—a planar change and, later, insertion—was yet to come. They'd done the "hurry up," now they had to do the "wait." And the "wait" could prove a great deal harder.

Voices: Exodus

17 February, 2021. Deep Space Vessel *Billie Mitchell* calling Tani Pandya. Chase Coughlin reporting.

This is my first recording since the Great White Fleet left Earth orbit in January. First chance I've had to catch a breath.

There's really not much to say. Everything is nominal. Ship's in good trim. Flaco and Jacinta and me, we get along pretty good. The other ships have come within range—converging orbits. We talk with them, but we don't go visiting. EVAsion is serious shit, so you don't do it out of whimsy. Certainly not over the distances we keep between us.

We fly on suit atmosphere and pressure. That way we don't have to do prebreathing if we have to go out and snag a supply pod.

I see on the uploads that Jimmy made another flight with the *Lariat* to test out compound sails. Tell the jerk I said he done okay.

* * *

We had to do an orbital correction today. Radar said *Sikorsky* and *Cochran* were drifting toward each other. Probably minute differences in the initial parameters during departure. Mission Commander Feathershaft and Command Pilot Zaranovsky were behind the sticks and the whole maneuver went slicker than snot on a door handle. Us *Mitchell*s didn't have anything to do except watch. Flaco was bored, but Jacinta and I found it professionally interesting.

I'm not sure what you meant in your last message about me recording my "inner thoughts." I thought that's what I was doing.

Talked to Dr. Frechet, the physicist on board *Sikorsky*. He had a black eye, so I guess he finally figured out that engineer/copilot Total Meredith is also a total lizard. Serves him right. He thinks he's God's gift to women, which I know is not true because I am.

Anyhow, I thought it was pretty funny.

We rendezvoused with another of Wilson's fuel pods and found that the LOH had mostly leeched out through some microfractures. Had some bad moments over that, but it wasn't mission-critical and the next pod—air and water and food—was fine. I let Rosario handle the docking on that one.

Those microtech implants they gave us before we left are pretty creepy. I mean who wants a microscopic gizmo running around his innards? There. That's *inner feelings,* isn't it?

<uncontrolled laughter.>

Anyhow, Yvgeny Zaranovsky started running a fever a couple days ago, and Dr. Ku . . . That's Peterson Ku. Well, "Bay Deng" or "Pi-tsung" or however you spell it—but he goes by "Peterson." Anyhow, he was able to take blood and fluid samples and test them *and he wasn't even in the same freaking ship!* That was phat stoopid, I tell you.

We were worried for a while, because something contagious in a closed loop life-support system can be pretty damn serious. But things worked out okay. *Sikorsky* had the right medicine in stock, so Dr. Ku didn't have to make a house call and bleed him with leeches or nothing. Total and Alois took some precautionary doses and Yvgeny, himself, was back in the saddle in a day or two. Just in case, they purged their air and water completely when we rendezvoused with the next biosupport pod.

You wanted inner feelings?

I want to screw Jacinta Rosario in the worst way.

That inner enough for you?

Jesus, I hope you're right about Jimmy's encryption being unbreakable. I don't want any of those herbies back at DeepSpace listening to this.

Hell, *I* don't want to listen to this.

I think Ned should have cut her from the crew. Jacinta. I got nothing against her—except that *I'd* like to get against her. She's good, but there must be other engineer-pilots in her cohort who are just as good and wouldn't have to worry about their command pilot trying to get in their pants.

Karen, I miss you . . .

I know I must sound like your basic knuckledragger, but you know I'm straight-edge. So's Flaco, which is why I guess they put Miss Hot Bod of 2021 in the can with us. Flaco told me how he almost crossed the line back when he was building Leo Station and he'd only been up there three months. But those Hub modules are palaces compared to a Salyut-Plank stack. You could move around without all the time bumping and touching. And this freaking mission is *nine months long*.

I think Flaco must be feeling it, too, because I notice he tries to avoid Jacinta.

In fact, Jacinta asked me yesterday if Flaco was mad at her

over something. I didn't tell her what I thought, because what the hell can any of us do about it? Changing billets only moves the problem around—and I don't think Alois or Bird or the others have the same good manners as me and Flaco. She can't make herself unattractive, either—first of all, it would take too much work; and second, after a couple more months, it won't matter, anyway. Hell, by then, Flaco might start looking good to me.

That's a joke, Tani.

Jacinta was only married a few days before Departure Day. Just saw the guy the one time, at the reception in FreeFall SkyResort. Good-looking. Wiry build. A pilot, like her. I guess they were in Academy together, or something.

So Jacinta and Flaco and I were hanging and talking about our families and she's telling us about the silver apples and the vow of chastity and the way the sisters check out each other's fiancés. (No, I don't mean it that way.) And how there's usually a long engagement. So my big mouth asked her how come she tied the knot just before flying off for nine months, and she got real, real quiet and said finally that it seemed the right time to do it.

So call me stupid. I didn't figure it out until later. She meant if she didn't do it then, she might never, ever get to do it. Because she might die in the Big Empty, still a virgin.

We picked up the Bean on radar today. Marks another milestone, sort of. So there was lots of cheering and hugging and kissing. She doesn't even know what she does to us. Maybe when we reach the Bean and we're busy all the time, I'll be too tired to think about it; but there ain't all that much to do outbound, except measure the solar wind and shit like that.

I hope Jimmy appreciates that solar wind data, even though we ain't doing it just for him.

Closing in on the Bean from sunward.

The stern chase begins.

Last night, I turned *Mitchell* over to Flaco for his usual night watch. He doesn't pilot, but he knows what an alarm sounds like and where the button is that wakes me up. Usually we spend fifteen, thirty minutes on the debrief and the old yadda-yadda. But last night we wrapped it up quick and I went forward into the Salyut module and there she was. Jacinta.

I guess she'd been doing it ever since we left Earth orbit. The one time of night when both Flaco and me are aft in the ship and she has the living quarters all to herself. When I come through the rec room—that's what we call the aft frustum of the Salyut, the one that mates to the nose of the Plank—she was jackknifed over, tugging her shirt over her head and spinning a little because of it. That's why she didn't see me.

But I saw plenty of her.

We don't get to bathe too often—which is another problem—because we try to conserve water for drinking and stuff, so maybe once a week, we snuggle into the shower bag and turn on the trickle and the suction and take what Flaco calls a "dew-bath." When Jacinta showers, Flaco and me, we head for the *Mitchell* out of respect, where we float around playing computer games while we think about Jacinta all naked. I do. I haven't asked Flaco, but I don't think he's brain-dead, either.

What I didn't know was that Jacinta did a wipe-down with a damp towelette every now and then. I guess guys don't mind feeling dirty and sweaty as much as gals so.

By the time she got her top off, I'd backed up where she couldn't see me, but I was able to watch. Which, I'm ashamed to say, I did. She had just a few days with her husband, which is just long enough to find out how good it is, and then you have to go without it for most of a year. She rubbed off pretty good with that towelette. I won't describe nothing. You know what a woman's body looks like, Tani; though you might not know what it looks like to a guy. But you ain't writing a porno book; and nothing happened anyway except I watched and afterward me and Mr. Frisky had a long talk.

But Jesus, Tani. This is a nine-month trip. And the next nearest woman is a couple million miles across hard vacuum, not counting Feathershaft, who's too old, and Meredith, who's not on the table. If you're laughing at all this, don't. Back Earthside, whenever the water navy sent mixed crews out on long missions, they always came back with half the women pregnant.

We're going to learn a lesson from all this, I hope it's the right one.

You know what really scares me?

What if she knew I was watching and went ahead anyway?

17.

On Cold, Gray Shores

Jacinta watched the screens from the copilot's seat while they coasted sunward of the Bean, well clear of the ominous hole at the west end. A dark, craggy body, ill-lit even by the permanent sunlight. Shadows blacker than despair. No rotation or tumbling, she noted. Whatever the Visitors had done to it long ago, its stability had survived millennia of random impacts. She thought she saw a movement on the surface, possibly a micrometeor impact; more likely, an illusion caused by the three ships' own shadows dancing across the unchanging, sunlit face.

A small asteroid, everyone had said. Yet it dwarfed the three ships. How could there possibly be enough boosters in the supply pods to nudge that thing from where it wanted to go? Plan B was to fracture it into smaller pieces; but that didn't look so promising either, up close.

"Not a very attractive place," Chase said.

Attractive in two senses, Jacinta thought. Aesthetic and gravitational. But when she laughed at the joke, Chase turned away, and she wondered if she had made him angry somehow. For the last few months he had been growing steadily more tense and standoffish.

Flaco, sitting in what was normally the flight engineer's position, remained silent and stared out the ports with saucer eyes. He had never been farther from Earth than LEO. Jacinta, at least, had made lunar flights—and had even qualified on "cold" landings, setting a Luna Lighter onto the gravel of the Smythe Sea near the remains of New Hope colony. But even so, the Moon was a close and homey place compared to this desolation.

Dark and cold and lonely. She sighed. Yungduk had been left behind in a barely furnished apartment. The Selection Board moved in mysterious ways, but Jacinta could not decide if they had been motivated in this case by cruelty or by a misguided compassion. She missed him with a poignancy she had never dreamed she could feel.

They're saving me for a tougher expedition, Yungduk had said with his mock bravado, and she smiled at the memory of his voice. He'd put the best face on it, but he could not hide his disappointment from her. *Oh, my husband* . . . Sometimes, on the long flight out, she had closed her eyes and felt him with her. She was glad she had waited until it was right, because it had been so very right. Awkward moments at first, as they learned each other, but that very awkwardness had been endearing. Her sisters had wondered at the haste. Time enough when you return, they had cautioned. But Jacinta had seen the fear in Yungduk's eyes. And so she had made a gift of herself; and had taken his memory with her into the void to torment her soul with his absence.

"Yvgeny has the scooter out," Chase commented.

Jacinta did not like Yvgeny Zaranovsky, a brusque man

with the pale eyes and hair of the north. "About time," she said.

Chase would not look at her. "Remember the last time a spacecraft cozied up to 2004AS? Plasma plume? Vaporization?"

"That was at the west end, where the engines are."

"Sure. But who's to say there aren't other tripwires? Yvgeny, he's going over there to find out before we bring the ships any closer. You stone for that?"

There was no answer to that. The easy response—of course!—was easy precisely because it was undemanded. It was Yvgeny who had to face it. Jacinta could only hope that if she were ever called on to face the unknown, she would toe the mark without hesitation.

Landfall came without ceremony. No one even bothered to note which of the three ships was first to establish co-orbit, though Lonzo Sulbertson was later celebrated on Earth as "First to Set Foot on the Bean" when he planted *Cochran*'s tether. Websters often mistook milestones for news—as if the roadmarkers along the way were as important as the journey itself. *Mitchell* would be next to moor, and no doubt, they would anoint Jacinta Rosario as "First Woman to Set Foot on a Trans-Lunar Body." Jacinta didn't mind if her name went in a history book somewhere; but the FarTrip crew was here to do a job, not pose for pixures. Still, Yungduk would be among the millions watching, and that knowledge narrowed the seven-hundred-thousand-mile gap that separated them.

They had a schedule. Tasks and time lines and resource alloctions. With only a month to work their will on the asteroid, the whole thing had to be timed like a ballet. Supply pods would arrive at precisely calculated moments. Activities had been rehearsed and timed in the buoyancy tanks back home and fudge factors had been added to accommodate the unexpected; so that each task would be completed (and resources, tools, and people released) in time for the next task.

It was a brilliant and well-crafted plan and lasted intact for very nearly five days. After that, it was still a ballet, but more modern than classical, performed by an improv troupe.

"Some assembly is required," Jacinta said, looking over the structural parts for the Tower of Power and the oxygen plant. Recovered from a "slow boat" ram pod that had preceded them to the asteroid, the components hovered over the Bean's surface like the wreckage of some ship washing up on cold, gray shores.

Flaco floated beside her in a red and white checkered hard suit. "An' I know who gotta do the assembly," he said. You couldn't see a shrug in a hard suit, but Jacinta knew it was there. "Well, we gotta get this erected, or we don' get no light or power; an' I hate workin' in the dark." Total would harvest a kilowatt per square meter all day long and feed it to work-lights and power tools through the grid of cables, relays, and transformers that Jacinta was setting up. Chase had named the facility "Beantown Power and Light."

"Sorry, friend," Jacinta told Flaco. "You're the rigger. Me, I'm just a poor, simpleminded space pilot and part-time electrician here to make the power connections. But you tell me what you need and I'll help you with the erection as best I can." *Oh, God! She hadn't said that, had she?* "Hey, Total!" *Quick, change the subject!* "Think you can squeeze much oxygen out of this rock?"

"Yes, and don't distract me." The tall woman in the powder-blue pressure suit danced among the pieces, checking items off the screen on her wristcomp. Jacinta hoped all the parts were there. If they came up short, Home Depot was a long walk back.

"I don't like using up fuel," Jacinta said. The fluid bed for the oxygen plant used hydrogen to catalyze the reaction—and the only hydrogen sources at the moment were the ships' fuel tanks. Jacinta imagined Total siphoning slush hydrogen from the tanks with a rubber hose. *Don't suck too hard*...

Total punched a final entry on her wristcomp. "All present and accounted for," she announced in a satisfied voice, "including spares. Flaco, this one is the main spar. Let's get it positioned before it decides that there really is gravity somewhere around here. No, *that* end goes down."

"Okay, boss." Flaco floated to the butt end of the designated member and unclipped the stay-together line. Behind him, framing him, floated the eternally crescent Earth: a blue-green gem about a third larger than the sun as seen from Earth. The Moon would be smaller (once it came from behind the Earth) but still recognizably a crescent.

"We don't lose any hydrogen," Total said to Jacinta. "The catalyst gets recovered. When Chase tracks down the next fuel pod, we'll top off the ships' tanks. Meanwhile"—Total waved her gauntlet at the parts and subassemblies—"this baby will give us power, oxygen, metals, and even—if we do use some of the hydrogen—water." It was the Voice of Pride of Accomplishment. A little premature, but that was Total for you. She always came at you like she knew what she was doing. She was always faster, stronger, sharper; someone who at once both frightened and fascinated. If anyone really could suck cryogenic fuel with a rubber hose, it would be her. Jacinta always felt second-best around her.

Jacinta said, "I just hope that fuel pod Chase went hunting hasn't leaked out like some of the others."

"Word up," said Flaco. "Hate to run outta gas before we get home."

"Don't worry," said Total. "That's why they popped extras. We'll be rendezvousing with supply pods all the way home."

Jacinta said, "I still don't like the failure rates we been seeing."

"Hey, 'Cinta," said Flaco. "You grab the free end and take it up while I bring the butt end down. Turn it vertical. Total, how about you spread some pixie dust around so I can see the alignment laser? 'Less you want the Leaning Tower of

Beantown . . ." Using a cloud of fine, meteoric powder to make the laser beam visible had been Flaco's idea. You'd wait a long time for a plumb bob to tell you whether you had perpendicularity.

Jacinta followed Flaco's instructions and lifted off the Bean's surface. Abruptly, she seemed to be falling off the asteroid into a pit and fought the vertigo that resulted. The Bean didn't have enough gravity to establish a feeling of "down," so her perceptions sometimes flip-flopped. She was never entirely sure whether she was "above" the Bean or "below" it or "beside" it. For the first few days after arrival, her mind had played games with her; and even now she had the sensation that she was hovering *underneath* a massive millstone all ready to grind her bones.

Shortly, they had the long, thin pole balanced like a ballet dancer on her toes. "Let's see you do *that* in a gravity well," Flaco said with satisfaction.

"Okay," said Total. "Guys, next."

Flaco waited for instructions. Jacinta said, "Next, what?"

Total made an exasperated sound. "The guys. The cables to hold the pole in place?"

"Oh. Sure," said Flaco. "I knew that."

Jacinta's electrical work took her all over the Bean. There were the work lights to install, for one thing; but more importantly, the A/S that would operate the strap-on boosters needed power for ignition and control. Once the solar array had been unfolded atop "Total's Tower of Total Power," she ran feeder lines out to all the work areas. She also installed doid stakes, two-meter poles with digital optical input devices on their tops and a small umbrella of PV leaves to power their internal pea brains. The stakes, once installed, would give Commander Feathershaft complete optical oversight of the Bean.

Not quite as good as being there, but someone had to sit lifeguard. Dr. Ku, also confined to the ship, had his own monitors collating the medical inputs from the MEMS implants they all carried. Ku, Jacinta was certain, secretly hoped for an epidemic to break out, or at least a case of the willies, so he would have someone to treat. (*I am im-patient*, Ku had said one time with that lemon-sucking miniature smile on his barely visible lips.) Jacinta suspected that Sandy, too, yearned for some emergency—one that would require the mission commander to soar to the rescue like Wonder Woman. It must be frustrating, having come so far only to stay in the command ship and watch. Feathershaft had already bumped Chase and Yvgeny from a few pod roundups just so she could conn a ship for a while; but everyone felt more secure with the commander on watch.

Jacinta, especially, was bothered when Chase took a turn at the "guardian angel" board, because she rather suspected that he spent most of his time watching her. The rest of the crew could bounce off into space and he might not ever notice. She herself was used to being noticed. Ever since junior high, boys had suffered whiplash when she walked past. But there was a difference between a regard born of appreciation and one born of intention. Chase had strong drives—you could *feel* the energy just being near him; but he had channeled those drives toward Karen. He just liked to look at women. That didn't mean he planned to do something about it.

But lately, she had sensed a change coming over him, like a magnet about to flip poles. She could read it in his body language; hear it in his voice. He fought it. She could read that, too. Chase Coughlin, Straight Arrow, was part of his self-image. A year ago, she would have sensed that change without understanding it. Now, having bedded Yungduk, she knew. Because she could feel the same growing yearning in herself.

It didn't matter what the mind said; the body's answer—But I *like* it and I *want* to do it again!—was irrefutable. Just her luck, to be billeted aboard *Mitchell* with the two most bone charlies on the whole expedition. She could deny herself, for Yungduk's sake, for the remaining months. And so could Flaco, and so could Chase. But the combined system was reliable only if all three components worked. It would take only one failure, one slip, to crash the system.

She called on her Inner Strength each night that it would not be her that failed.

Jacinta waited with the control panel and cables while Flaco and Bird moved the next rocket motor into place. They had already fastened a rack into the bedrock with drills and bolts, and had installed three of the five motors into it.

According to the ballet, all five should have been in place and the rack ready for the electrical work. But number four, floating in space off the surface, bore bright orange Xs down its length. Bird had downchecked it and marked it so it would not be installed by accident. Later, he and Flaco would diagnose the malf and decide if it could be salvaged, but in the meantime, number five had had to be prepped, staged, and installed in its place and a replacement brought in from one of the cargo pods.

The schedule had allowed for defectives; but that was "on the average." The timing of a single random event is unpredictable and the downcheck, occurring when it had, had thrown off the whole dance—like the prima ballerina missing a beat just before leaping into the arms of the waiting prima electrician.

Bird chanted as he and Flaco moved the engine into place. Jacinta noticed that Flaco timed his own moves to the beat and supposed that was the reason for the chanting. Although Bird never needed a reason for sounding off.

> *"Set it in motion and give it a* lick*!*
> *A slow, careful pressure's as good as a* kick*!*
> *Easy it goes . . . then*

Yank! *on its chain*
And . . .

"Okay, Chico, we got match-up!"

Flaco blinked his strobes twice to acknowledge Bird's announcement. Jacinta was impressed. The motor had been brought to as neat a stop as anyone could ask and hovered half a meter off the surface, nestled between the guide brackets on the rack. Flaco threaded cables through the eye-bolts and opened up the splays. Then he took up the slack on the forward windlass, just enough to snub the lines without jerking the rocket engine. Bird had done the same on the other end. "Okay, Bird, wait for the word."

"Ready."

Simple and mechanical, the hand crank struck Jacinta as comically obsolete considering where they were. But the mission planners had made a deliberate decision to use the simplest equipment possible. Fewer things to malf.

"Feet in the stirrups? Together, now. Heave!" Flaco pushed the handle a half turn forward.

"Haul!" He completed the motion.

"Heave!"

"Haul!"

Jacinta had the odd momentary impression that the rocket motor was fixed in space and Flaco and Bird were cranking the asteroid *up*. Once the assembly was fully engaged on the mounting bolts, Bird sighted with the laser against the east and west benchmarks to check the alignment. He didn't need "pixie dust" for that because Frechet's benchmarks contained their own coordinate data in their pea brains and shook hands with the alignment tool.

Flaco torqued the anchor bolts in place with the electric wrench. "Won't do no good," he said cheerfully to Jacinta, "to light these torches if the rockets fly off the racks into space."

Bird chuckled. "Righteous beans, bro."

"Fire in the hole!"

The warning came across the All Suits channel. Jacinta glanced north across the barrel of the planetoid, where Lonzo was prepping the site for the next engine rack by leveling an inconveniently placed ringwall. The charge blew—Jacinta could feel the vibrations through the ground—but the "teepee" held and the debris was contained within the netting. Something small seemed to roll past Jacinta's foot, but that was all.

Bird brushed his hands, a useless gesture in a space suit, and said, "Shoulda brought some pick-and-shovel guys to lug the rubble over to Total's furnace."

Flaco grunted. "They did. What do you think is next on *our* To Do list, *'mano*?"

Bird sighed. "That's why I wish we'd brought some along. Seems a shame to waste our sterling talents that way."

"Total said the rocks have hair," Jacinta told them.

Bird tried to stroke his beard with his helmet on. "Now I gotta admit that I learn something new each day I'm here. Hair."

"When they bring the rubble over to her oxygen plant . . . She says the pieces have thousands of very fine hairs all around their edges."

Flaco grunted. "Wonder what *that* means . . ."

Bird chortled. "It means the asteroid is a freaking mammal, that's what it means." Bird was carried away with his own humor.

"Dr. Frechet suggested some sort of crystallization," Jacinta said. "He said something or other about fracture planes. But the threads *permeate* the rock like veins and he hasn't been able to separate the two to see if—"

"Jacinta?" That was Captain Feathershaft on the command channel.

"Yes, Captain?"

"Alois is venturing too far into the Forbidden Zone again. Go bring him back, would you?"

"Um, I'm supposed to install the control panel for this rack and test the connections back to Beantown Power and Light. Can you send Yvgeny?"

"You can't install your panel until the fifth engine is in place," Feathershaft snapped, "and that won't happen until they open the pod and assemble the stack. So, 'Just Do It.' "

Sikorsky's pilot should have been standing by with Lonzo, in case of an accident, but Jacinta had seen him jet up to *Cochran* a few minutes earlier. Jacinta didn't like to see procedures violated. They were there for a reason. She supposed Feathershaft had reasons of her own for summoning Zaranovsky, but Jacinta didn't think she'd be told what they were and knew better than to ask.

Downchecking number four meant idle time until Chase ferried over the replacement engine. So, either she could hang around sucking up oxygen to no good purpose or she could fetch the Maverick Physicist. Besides, Feathershaft sounded like her panties were knotted. "Yes, ma'am. Hey, Flaco. I have to go find Dr. Frechet. Try not to get into too much trouble before I come back."

A cordon had been set up near the asteroid's west end, to prevent anyone from going too near the Big Engine. No one knew how close you had to get before triggering the defense mechanisms, but no one wanted to find out, either. Except Dr. Frechet.

Jacinta couldn't really blame him. The geophysicist's mission task was to survey the asteroid, set the benchmarks, and select the best geological placement for the rocket engines; but he was also on the crew in case they found any alien artifacts, and he was not such a dullard as to find the former more exciting than the latter. (Dr. Ku, the fleet doctor, also had a "just in case" job, but finding any biological remains of the Visitors was regarded by everyone, including Ku, as a very long shot, indeed.) So far, the only alien artifact was the Big Engine itself—and no one dared get too close to it, let alone study it. So there was Frechet, like Moses atop Mt.

Pisgah. He could see the promised land, but he could not enter.

He had the long-range telescope images and sensor data, of course. But they were, as he had said, "As a picture of a woman is like a woman; enticing and, for some purposes, useful, but ultimately unsatisfying."

Jacinta found the physicist just east of the strobes that marked the No Fly Zone. Out of line-of-sight from all three ships, she noticed, which explained why Feathershaft had sent her in person. Frechet was crouched by a rock phone driven deep into the ground. He looked up when Jacinta's suit exhaust kicked up the dust at his feet. "Who is that? Ah, the lovely Jacinta. Come, my dear, this is interesting." He stood and beckoned, a rock-phone jack in his hand.

Jacinta pitched her jets so that she settled toward the surface feet down. "Dr. Frechet," she said, "you're not supposed to go off by yourself."

"What? Is it that no one knew where I was? How, then, did you find me?" He chuckled. "Beside, Uncle Waldo is with me. If anything were to happen, my 'invisible friend' Earthside would relay a warning."

Jacinta did not see any of the mobile units about. Of course, Waldo was quite capable of riding on a suit channel—sitting, Bird had once said, "like a bluebird on your shoulder."

"Uncle's a little slow out here," Jacinta pointed out. "With the speed-of-light lag, if anything happened to you—"

"Then Dr. Ku would receive an alarm from my marvelous body implant; or Captain Feathershaft would find my icon blinking madly on her screen—" He indicated the PANIC button on his chest-mounted command-and-display module, which everyone called "the accordion." "This place is not so vast that I could not be reached in seconds. I am quite as safe as one can be—considering where we are. But come. I want you to hear this."

The physicist was like a child who had found something new and was bubbling to show it to everyone. He wasn't going to come back with her until he had done his show-and-tell. Jacinta sighed and crouched beside him by the rock phone. "What are these?" she asked, pointing to a cluster of tiny pockmarks on the asteroid's surface. "I see them all over. Like someone attacked the Bean with an ice pick."

"An ice pick?" Frechet chuckled. "No, no, my little one. But perhaps the asteroid passed through a dense cloud of sand particles. Listen." He handed her the line for the rock phone and she plugged it into her accordion and heard . . .

A strange sound. It was a hiss that came and went. A little like a snare drum. A little like gravel spilling on a tin roof. Her ear refused to name it. "What is it?" she asked.

"There is activity underground," Frechet announced. "Something is moving."

Jacinta felt a tremor go through her. Something was active? Under their very feet? "Have you told Feathershaft?" she asked.

"Only this moment have I discovered it. When we debrief tonight I will have more information. Here, I download the graphic to your screen." Jacinta's visor telltale flashed <graphic received> and a three-dimensional sonogram appeared in a popper screen in the lower right corner. "I have recorded," Frechet explained, "at key locations, the shock waves of our explosions. Integrated, they present the model of the interior."

The drawing looked like a CAD wire-frame rendering, and Jacinta momentarily fancied the entire asteroid as a construction project. (And what a rigging job that would be for Flaco!) The Bean was augered out down its longitudinal centerline from the west end to about a third of its length, with the cavity lined with some denser material. That was the Big Engine. Within the lining were darker spots, nodules of some sort.

"The nodules," Frechet said when she asked, "are probably the injectors of fuel. Perhaps they generate magnetic fields to channel and focus the ionized gases. Otherwise, with just this one engine, how do they adjust attitude?"

He spoke with the same bland confidence as Total Meredith; but with a difference. Total's was a "no brag, just fact" sort of confidence, but Frechet just loved to spin theories. Oddly enough, no matter how confidently he explained them, he would just as cheerfully discard them when more data came to light. Jacinta imagined him as a scientific butterfly flitting from flower to flower. Perhaps that was not fair. Perhaps that was how science was done. But she was not interested in being fair to Alois Frechet. He was polite enough, though his blend of leering and patronizing did grate; but she could imagine him singing that old song, "Thank Heaven for Little Girls," and really, really meaning it.

"What are those dark, blocky objects forward of the Big Engine?" she asked him. "Um, at coordinate D-7."

"Who can say?" the Frenchman said in an uncharacteristic burst of caution; but then he could not keep from adding, "Machinery and controls, perhaps."

You could say "I don't have a clue." Jacinta thought. But that probably would not be as much fun. The sudden notion startled her. She had never thought of science as "fun." But, yes, she had his voice pegged now: delight.

There was a small void starside of Frechet's "machinery." "That space at C-7 must be the construction shack," she suggested to Frechet, just to prove that she, too, could spin certainty out of virtually no data. And now that she thought of it, the Visitors must have needed someplace where they could kick after a hard day's work.

Frechet responded with a bland "Ah!" Jacinta thought she may have offended him by usurping his prerogatives, so she asked about the larger void below the "construction shack."

"Certainly that is the 'mine,' " Frechet told her. "The Bean has been consuming its own substance as its fuel over the centuries. The sound you are hearing originates there."

Sounds from the mine. Maybe it *was* gravel . . . As Jacinta listened to the hissing rattle, an unaccountable sense of dread stole over in her. Thousands of antique, impact-style typewriters played by a thousand monkeys. A thousand crazed Brazilians shaking maracas. The sound still refused to come true. Then she unplugged the sensor from her suit, stood, and looked at the ground beneath her feet with genuine fear. "I don't think you should wait until tonight to tell the commander," she told Frechet.

She squinted at the sonar picture of the interior. Sounds from the mine. It was a Saturday, the calendar said. Maybe they were having a hoedown. "Too bad," Jacinta added, "we don't have equipment that can dig down there and find out what's happening."

Frechet highlighted a portion of the map on Jacinta's display. "Do you see that line?"

She pursed her lips. "That looks like a . . ."

". . . like a passageway," Feathershaft said.

"Jesus," said Chase Coughlin. Jacinta tore her gaze away from the ship's screen, where Frechet's diagram was now displayed, and glanced at the pilot. Yes. He'd felt the same frisson of strangeness as she had when Frechet first showed it to her. Vast engines where you dared not look . . . Even buried machines, inaccessible within tons of iron . . . These evoked awe, but not the shiver of expectation. But a passageway, a corridor, a doorway . . . That called up a different emotion. Someone would walk down that corridor. Someone would come face-to-face with the relics of the ancient Visitors.

Jacinta turned her attention back to the conference screens, where the *Cochran*s and *Sikorsky*s also studied the sonogram. "Where does it reach the surface?" Chase asked.

"It doesn't," said Zaranovsky. "I have examined that area." A blunt finger stabbed toward his own screen. "We built smelter just north of it."

Total Meredith shook her head. "I didn't see any opening, either."

"I'll go check," said Lonzo Sulbertson. "Be right back."

Feathershaft turned away from her screen to check that her copilot was joking. She did not look amused. A round-faced woman, she had—deliberately, in Jacinta's opinion—styled her hair and features to appear matronly. Jacinta had seen pictures from ten, fifteen years ago, and the mission commander had been decidedly hot. But command required a certain amount of parental authority; a certain "distance."

"You were not expecting one," Ku suggested through pursed lips, "and therefore your eyes did not see it. One shadow looks much like another—especially starside, where all is shadow."

"It may not be wise to poke into there," Feathershaft said. "Our primary mission is to install the rocket motors and direct the Bean off its collision course. We're already behind schedule, and"—dryly—"I'm sure no one wants to work overtime." To stay on the Bean past Departure Day meant staying there forever, since the Long Orbit home would then last longer than their supplies and none of the prearranged pod rendezvouses would synch. *But what,* Jacinta wondered, *if we aren't done by then?*

"Archaeology," Feathershaft concluded, "however fascinating, must take second place. Let Uncle Waldo handle it."

A chorus of objections erupted from most of the crew. Frechet looked appalled. He opened his mouth several times before words emerged. *"Madame!"* Bird tugged at his chin and muttered, "Don't seem right for someone who's not actually here to make the big discoveries."

Feathershaft calmly waited out the storm of objections. "Furthermore," she said when they had quieted, "that passageway may be booby-trapped, just as the engine area was. Yes, Dr. Frechet."

"That is most unlikely, *Madame* the Commander! The Probe of 2016 was destroyed because the Bean's automatic safeguards believed it a meteor that could damage the engine. No such logic applies to the passageway or the chamber it leads to. It must have been, as I have suggested, a temporary 'construction shack.' Why sabotage the way in?"

"To keep us out?" Zaranovsky suggested dryly. "Events of 2016 were *not* reflex actions of anti-meteor system, but deliberate. Bean identified origin of probe and altered course to strike Earth. There is active intelligence here, my friends—computer intelligence far more advanced than our own 'Artificial Stupids.' "

No one spoke for a moment.

"Mr. Coughlin," Feathershaft said. "You are preternaturally quiet."

Chase shrugged. "It's what Jacinta said earlier." He wagged his thumb over his shoulder in her direction. "Something's going down. We ought to know what that something is. I mean, what if we fire off our motors, and the Bean farts its Big Engine and makes a course correction, and all our work is wasted. We'd be right back where we started, only with a new impact date."

Jacinta could tell from the hangdog expressions that Chase had hit a nerve. Total Meredith and Yvgeny Zaranovsky nodded, as if they had already discussed the matter between themselves. "So you think we should go down there," said Feathershaft.

"I think we'd be hung back home if we didn't. Look, curiosity aside, the skinny Earthside is that this whole thing is an intelligence test. Well, it would be pretty dumb *not* to go look and find out what's shaking, wouldn't it? It'd also be pretty dumb to just shove our—" He glanced at Jacinta and flushed. "I mean, to go into the hole without checking things out first. I suggest we find the entrance and then send a mobile—*locally* controlled to avoid lightspeed lag. Total, you can handle that, right? That way, if there *is* a booby trap, we don't lose anybody."

Feathershaft nodded. "All right, that sounds reasonable. And I don't like the notion of something stirring underground any better than the rest of you. But we'll finish installing the rest of the sunside boosters, first. Then, if worse comes to worst, we can still turn this sumbitch off its path."

Jacinta had regarded Captain Feathershaft as a Wise Woman, somewhat like Mother Linda Fernandez-Jacoby at the silver apple's Torrance Refuge. She possessed the rare ability to sort through the advice given her and separate the wheat from the chaff. But there was a certain inner ribaldry that informed her posture and her language, and Jacinta suspected a wilder youth had grown into this shrewd, pragmatic adult. To some extent, Wise Woman was a mask she wore; but as long as the mask worked, Jacinta would not criticize.

The frequent one-on-one meetings with Zaranovsky bothered her more. If those meetings were more intimate than simple briefings, it was a chink in the mask that might prove fatal. Such behavior, to lonely men, could be heard as a signal. *Permission granted.* And the discipline and trust that bound them and assured their survival could disintegrate like a dandelion in the wind.

Perhaps she did the captain an injustice. As project manager, Feathershaft met individually with each of them; and the sessions with Zaranovsky might be no more risqué than those she held with Jacinta or the others. Yet, though it was impossible to strut in ziggy, there was something about Yvgeny's body language that seemed more than his own wishful thinking. All three senior pilots belonged to a generation that viewed such matters differently than she or Flaco did. When the fleet departed, Zaranovsky and Feathershaft would again be in separate ships; so perhaps the captain thought they need only be circumspect for the month and a half on the Bean. Yet, their very circumspection argued that, at some level, they recognized their behavior as wrong.

For her own protection, Jacinta assumed the persona of Kid Sister, using voices and body language that defined her as taboo. It meant being taken less seriously by some of the others, Frechet, in particular; but it might be a margin she would need later. Her two friends from the Academy, she felt safe with. To Lonzo, she really was Kid Sister; and regarding Total, Jacinta began to wonder if that sort of thing would constitute a betrayal of Yungduk at all. As for the others, if Zaranovky was "getting his" elsewhere, he was off the board; and Dr. Ku struck her as a man with no passions to arouse. Perhaps, having seen so many naked bodies in his practice, he had grown inured to the temptation. As for Flaco . . .

She was not immune herself to rogue feelings. Confined as they were in such close quarters, they could not avoid disturbing sights or contacts. She had come on Flaco one time while he was . . . But, no. That was not an issue. In Flaco, she had confidence. It was in his voice when he spoke of Serafina.

She realized she was deliberately narrowing the scope of her worries to Chase Coughlin. She was not naive enough to suppose that her onetime mentor had never glimpsed her in private moments. *Mitchell* was too small for that necessary fiction to survive analysis. And men did grow more lonely and arouse more easily than women. So take her own longings and multiply by five. Granted, Chase held his passions in a tight grip; but they might break loose, to both their regrets.

There was a door at the end of the tunnel.

All work had stopped while Total guided a waldo down the tunnel and Feathershaft knew better than to order them back to their tasks. The secret of command was never to give an order you knew would be disobeyed.

A door. The first undoubtedly alien artifact ever seen up close. And a door implies another side. Total and Waldo had taken pictures in every wavelength; they had tested its hardness and composition. Or tried to. Tools broke before shaving a sample and even the drilling laser failed to warm it. It was opaque to X rays. So the door itself was an exciting thing; not to open it was unthinkable.

Earthside viewership climbed near to a hundred percent when Waldo gripped the handle with a manipulator arm . . .

But the compressed air jets could not generate enough thrust to move the handle. All that happened was that the floater pulled itself toward the door. Total braced the other manipulators against the rock and pulled in on the teep controls, but she only succeeded in bending a strut. In the end, she gave up, and Jacinta could see how much that galled her.

And so it came down to a human in the end, after all.

It was redundant to ask for volunteers. The mission had been staffed with neither the reluctant nor the timid. So Feathershaft made a command decision. The three primary pilots and Dr. Ku were off the board. The others would draw lots. Chase remained stoic, as he always did under disappointment, but Jacinta could read his brows and his lips and the set of his jaw. Yet, she dared not use the Voice of True Sympathy, lest he misunderstand the nature of her care. *Thus does caution resemble coldness.*

The computer generated a set of random numbers and Jacinta won the draw.

"You shouldn't go," Chase said, once the conference call had been broken and the three *Mitchell*s faced one another on the flight deck.

He sounded both bitter and fearful, but Jacinta only said, "Uncle Waldo can't turn the handle. He doesn't have the torque."

Chase looked at the screen over her shoulder, the view relayed from inside the Visitors' tunnel, where the door stood unmarked and unmoved. "I didn't mean *no one* should go," Chase said.

"Just me?" She had heard in his inflection the tones of the Guardian. Perhaps she had played Kid Sister a little too well and Chase now felt the need to protect Sis from the Dark Unknown. "You don't think I can handle it?"

Of course, he did. He had seen how she had handled the malf on her training flight a few years back and how she had handled the wreck of the *Harry Stine*. "It's not that," he admitted. "It's just . . . I'd hate to see anything happen to you."

"Yeah," she said. "Me, too." With just enough Chase-like bravado in her own voice that he had to laugh.

"Okay," he said, throwing an arm around her shoulder and giving her a squeeze. A brotherly squeeze, right? "Just be careful. I'd hate to have to finish this flight with only Flaco to look at."

Flaco said, "I love you, too, amigo."

She turned to the rigger. "Flaco, round up the gear we decided on. Dr. Frechet thinks the mechanisms may be frozen after ten thousand years of cold and vacuum."

Flaco sighed. "Ain't nothin' built to last, these days . . ." Then he kicked aft toward the storage lockers.

"May need more than a pry bar," Chase said. "Or a block and tackle. Jesus, Flaco should be doing this. It's a rigger's job. That's what I meant before, about how you shouldn't do this. If the parts are vacuum-welded or something, you won't have the strength to force the handle."

It wasn't what he had meant, but perhaps he believed it was, and Jacinta let it ride. "If it *is*," she said, "The Cid himself couldn't budge it. Don't worry, Chase." But she knew *that* request was futile even as the words had left her tongue. "I better get suited up."

"Need help?"

Jacinta shook her head. "I'll call when I'm ready for check-out. I want . . . a little time alone."

In the suit locker, Jacinta began to tremble. Her hands shook so badly that she nearly jammed the zipper while opening her coverall. She looked at the hard suit clipped into its rack, and the helmet's blank visor stared back accusingly. Oh, a fine burglar she would prove! Break into a locked room when she couldn't even get out of her own clothes? She crossed her hands over her breast and called on her Inner Strength. *I control my own life. Let the world do what it will. I will choose how to respond. I can face danger or run from it. I can even accept the choices of others. But* I *will decide.*

A sound behind her. She turned to see Flaco emerge from the equipment locker with a bundle of tools tied up in a cinch. "I'm sorry," he said. "I didn't realize you were praying."

"I wasn't. Praying, I mean. It's a recitation the silver apples use."

Flaco shrugged. "If you say so."

Jacinta pulled down the lower torso and positioned the Snoopy cap. "Do you really think the door may be booby-trapped?" She wouldn't look at him.

"I could go, if you want."

Jacinta shook her head, gathered her resolution. "No, we decided. We have to know what's happening. If I refused, someone else would have to go instead. Then, if it *was* booby-trapped, I could never forgive myself."

"I don't think it is," said Flaco. "It wouldn't make sense."

It was useless to speculate on the motives of ancient aliens and what might have made sense to them. Ten thousand years of neglect could create dangers and deadfalls where none had ever been planned. "I better wriggle into the Iron Maiden," she said, putting a hand on the torso in the rack. "Go tell Chase."

When Flaco had gone, Jacinta turned and slipped off her coveralls. She had no trouble with the zipper.

Total Meredith was waiting at the tunnel's mouth with Bird Winfrey. When Jacinta alighted, featherlike, on the coarse surface, Total stepped forward and clipped a cable to Jacinta's utility belt. She laid a hand on Jacinta's arm. "Come back," she said over the two-way.

"It's in the action plan," Jacinta answered. "Step fifteen." Then, before she could think any more about it, she stepped into the tunnel.

The aliens must have been small, because even Jacinta had to bend slightly. She wondered how large a role chance had played in selecting the smallest crew member to squeeze down this narrow passageway. Had Feathershaft rigged the dice? The first few meters were strewn with rubble, presumably thrown in when the crater hiding the entrance had been formed. That chilled, that this tunnel was older than the crater. She moved a boulder aside. Her shoulder lights threw weird and ghastly shadows. Monstrous shapes loomed on the walls.

Uncle Waldo floated near the alien door. The module was soccer ball in size and floated just to the side of the chamber. The manipulators were folded up, which made it look, Jacinta thought, rather petulant. One was bent, where Total had tried to get leverage against the tunnel wall. "Hi, Total," she said.

A few moments later, the remote replied over channel twelve. "Jacinta Rosario, do you have any words for the audience here on Earth?"

"Yeah. Get a life." She switched over to channel one. "Captain? You didn't tell me I'd be broadcast." She had thought Total was still teeping the mobile from the relay at the tunnel mouth.

"DeepSpace insisted," Feathershaft replied. "If you get that door open . . . It could be important, what's inside."

"Then it should be scientists, not websters doing Waldo."

"The scientists are there. Waldo's got got major bandwidth. Don't worry about them getting in the way . . ." A pause. "Okay, Waldo's in see-only mode, as of now."

Jacinta eyed the device. She thought of how many different people were watching through the optics. *My name is Legion. I contain multitudes.* Suddenly, she wanted to laugh and turned away to study the door. One of the multitude, she was sure, was Yungduk. He would be watching her, and he was the only one who mattered. Impulsively, she blew a kiss at the mobile. The watchers would wonder at the gesture; perhaps ascribe some noble motive. But Yungduk would understand; and across seven hundred thousand miles she felt him return the kiss.

The door was circular, of a gray metal. Or perhaps a metallo-ceramic. Very hard. Waldo had been sent in with a Rockwell tester and the imprint had been microscopic. Drill bits tipped with fullerine-diamond might eventually bore through, perhaps even in her lifetime.

The truly alien aspect of the door was that it did not look very alien, at all. Perfectly ordinary hinges fastened it to the rock wall. The handle was a simple class two lever that appeared to move a set of ordinary pins. There were bolts or rivets. There were even what appeared to be weldments.

Not too surprising, Frechet had said. *One must extract materials, machine them, fasten them to one another. The properties of materials, the mechanical advantages of levers, are universal truths.* Whoever the Visitors had been—humanoid or giant spiders or something unimaginable—they had come to grips with the same physical universe and that, if nothing else, gave them something in common with humans.

There were some touches of the strange. The fastener heads were pentagonal, for one thing. Nor were there as many joints and welds as Flaco and Bird thought there ought to be. Most of the door consisted of a single large disk. How had it been fabricated and installed? Had the Visitors brought it with them; or had they fabbed it on-site from the asteroid itself? And the handle . . . No human hand would ever grip it comfortably.

When Jacinta laid her glove on the handle, a shiver went through her. She was the first living creature to take hold of it in ten thousand years; and the last hand to touch it might not even have been a hand.

Assume it has not been locked by intent. Frechet's voice during the briefing. Anxious and perhaps a little jealous. Speaking quickly, stuffing her mind with his ideas; so that something of himself would stand with her before the silver door. *They will have needed a work space, perhaps pressurized and with a breathable atmosphere—I speak of breathable by them—and when they left, they simply closed the door behind them. Whatever barriers there are to entrance are there by time and chance.*

So, first thing was: jiggle the doorknob.

Jacinta could hear the hush—in her earphones and, by imagination, among the Earthside audience.

The lever did not move.

Well, she thought, it would have been one hell of an anticlimax . . .

She pushed again on the handle, this time watching the rest of the visible mechanism in case something obvious was hung up. *This* moved *that* which pulled on *here* . . .

One of the fastener heads was glowing a dull blue.

"Dr. Frechet . . . ?" She put her finger next to the stud, not quite daring to touch it.

"Fascinating. Still functional after so long a time. . . ."

Functional . . . But what was the function? The Visitors must have had one hell of a quality system, even if it hadn't been ISO-registered. She looked closely at the other fastener heads and saw no sign whatever that they were indicators. Okay. Magic. In a way, it was reassuring to find something beyond the edge.

"There is activity on the sonar stations," Frechet announced. Over channel twenty, she heard a sound like the rush of the wind through the trees. The scratching of sandpaper. Jacinta looked again at the glowing bolt, which was now more green than blue. An indicator light. But what did it indicate?

She tried the handle again, but it still did not budge.

A motion caught the corner of her eye and, turning, she stifled what might have become a scream.

A torrent of questions erupted from her earphones. Frechet exclaiming. Total, over the waldo. Chase telling her to back away, back away. Instead, she moved closer.

It was a spider.

About as big as her hand, it scuttled rapidly across the rock face of the tunnel. The body was an oblate sphere with the same dull matte finish and gray color as the door. Five high-knee'ed legs spaced around its circumference scissored like knitting needles as it ran and Jacinta saw that the leg tips were points that actually sank into the rock. *So that's where all the tiny pockmarks came from.*

"Marvelous," Frechet remarked. "Marvelous."

"Only four of the legs are working," Jacinta pointed out. Indeed, the fifth leg was held tucked up. It was broken off, she saw, and slightly bent near the break.

"It is still marvelous," Frechet said.

The spider—the robot—paused near Jacinta. The high knees on the legs gave it a threatening aspect, as if it were crouched to spring—

"Jacinta," said Chase, "back away!"

—which it did. The knees flexed and a puff of vapor emerged from under the body and it sailed across the tunnel to the door. Halfway across, the legs reversed and it landed catlike on the door's face. The points scratched across the surface (without, she noticed, sinking in) and squatted over the fulcrum hinge on the door handle. *Something* emerged from the underbelly and entered the clearance between the bar and the housing. It looked to her like an oil, gleaming black and flowing sluggishly.

"Jacinta," said Frechet. "Can you obtain the sample of material? But certainly, those must be micromachines, perhaps even *nano*machines!"

"Frechet," said Chase, "are you nuts? Jacinta, don't be reckless."

"I think Chase is right," said Total. "Better come out of there and let Uncle Waldo watch."

Everyone had advice for her, but none of them were with her in the hole. Capatin Feathershaft had not spoken, which was significant. Jacinta could not ignore a direct order. Yet, she didn't think she *could* leave at this point. "I think," she ventured, "that when I jiggled the handle repeatedly, something in the door woke up and called the janitor to unstick it."

"Yes!" said Frechet, his voice almost cracking in excitement. "Yes, of course."

"There may be other mobiles," said Flaco. "Sometimes, I see motions among the rocks and shadows."

"If only we could secure one to study."

"No," said Feathershaft. "I won't allow one of those things on board our ships."

"But—"

"End of discussion."

The mobile moved to another location and repeated the process. Then it spurted away from the door and jetted to a niche on the wall, where it sat, apparently inactive. If there was ever a chance to nab it, that was now, but Feathershaft had forbidden it. Perhaps, later, when their primary mission was accomplished . . . *We're here to divert this Bean*, she reminded herself. Alien contraptions take second billing to the Big Splash. The immediate reason to look behind the gray door was not science, but the need to learn what might be going down on the other side.

"I think I'll try the handle again," she said.

"Go ahead," said Feathershaft. "But be careful."

Great advice, Jacinta thought. What did "care" mean, under the circumstances? She glanced at her tote. Pry bar. Block and tackle. Almost, she felt ashamed for the human race. Yet, humanity had semi-autonomous micromachines, Artificial Stupids, designer molecule plastics, magnetic levitation, and other things. DeepSpace had opted for simple, but reliable tools for certain tasks because the nearest repair shop was a long ways off, and because the real intelligence resided in the bioware, not the tools.

She gripped the handle once more and pushed. It was still binding. She could feel the resistance in the tight clearances between parts distorted by centuries of cold and vacuum. The handle moved; the latch retracted . . . And stuck again.

Jacinta glanced at the quiescent robot. "Thanks for the help," she said, "but do you want to give me a hand here?"

There was no reaction; Jacinta hadn't expected one. *The mothership has expended its micromachines,* she guessed. *And now it's chowing down on rock to make some more.* There was something artificial-looking about that niche . . .

The colored bolt had gone through yellow and was turning red.

What did that signify? To a human, some humans, red meant Stop! Danger! What did it mean to the Visitors? The color code was obviously running up the spectrum, so it might indicate a scale. Intensity? Volume? Readiness? Would it stop at red, or would it keep going, past the range of human vision?

She could stand here forever and ask questions that would take even longer to answer. She gripped the handle again, and this time she pulled, then pushed. The latch slipped in, then came out a little farther. She could see where it was binding, near the edge of the door. Pull. *Push!*

She felt it slip free.

And the door flew open with sudden violence, clipping her and tossing her against the rock wall of the cave, so that her head rocked inside her helmet and her vision went dark. Stars and snowflakes whirled about her and the wind lifted her up and threw her once more against the other wall.

The last thing she saw before darkness took her were the shattered remains of Uncle Waldo scattered in the white tornado and the alien spider sailing like a Frisbee. It had lost another leg.

18.

In the Belly of the Fish

Dead Man's Trip had been the bogie phrase all during training. Never spoken; never discussed; but always lurking in the shadows of the conversations. Everyone had known there would likely be casualties and everyone had hoped it would not be himself. But Jacinta was well liked by all—perhaps too well liked by some—and to have the hammer fall on her struck them all hard.

Chase watched *Mitchell*'s external viewscreen in horror as the tunnel down which his copilot had vanished erupted in a geyser of white. The plume spurted far into space, flashing off where the sun's rays caught it. A few feathery strands, curling back in response to the Bean's feeble gravity, coated the rocks around the mouth. The waldo view from inside the tunnel had gone dead. Cursing his helplessness, Chase kicked off toward the suit locker, only to be blocked by Flaco. Chase turned his curses onto the Dominican.

"Don't panic, '*mano*," Flaco said, holding him tight. "Total an' the Bird, they're *there*. They'll handle it." But Chase could hear Feathershaft's voice ordering the other two otters to get away from the freezing spray. So who was going to do jack to save Jacinta? Yet, when he struggled against Flaco's iron grip—and how could a man so thin have arms so strong?—the rigger only repeated, "Let Total and Bird handle things. Time you suit up, it won' *matter* no more."

Chase batted him away. He had not yet run out of curses; but Flaco only crossed himself and his lips moved and—who knew?—maybe blessings *were* more effective than curses. Chase turned again to the outside viewscreens—in time to see Total Meredith dart into the maelstrom. Bird waited as still as the rocks around him with Jacinta's lifeline gripped in his two hands. "Pull, you son of a bitch!" Chase hollered. He fumbled for Bird's comm channel. "Pull!" But if the NDT tech heard him, he gave no sign.

Time seemed to stretch like steel wire through a drawing die, pulling thinner and thinner, creeping up on its tensile point, ready to snap and whip like an iron lash. The torrent of snow coated Bird's suit with ice and slush, and still he did not move. "Do something!" Chase was near to tears.

And then . . . the Bird began pulling—steadily hand over hand, never jerking or tugging, until, incredibly, from the tunnel's mouth, Jacinta's ice-encrusted suit emerged with Total Meredith guiding it from behind. Squeezing down the frosty confines of a tunnel too narrow for her, Total had dislodged Jacinta's inert form and kept it from snagging against the rocks while she called instructions to the Bird. All the while the numbing sleet blew around them all, blinding them, battering them, encasing them in icy shells that sublimed into lingering clouds of vapor as they lifted Jacinta through the eternal sunlight to Cochran's waiting airlock. The vapor looked like comets' tails. Or perhaps the wings of angels.

There was no way they couldn't go back inside the Bean. It was only a question of who and when. Concussion, decompression, a wrenched shoulder . . . These were no trivial matter; but they'd been lucky. Lucky that Jacinta's suit had held, but for a slow leak in the shoulder. Lucky that Total had reacted so swiftly. Lucky that Bird had waited for Total's instructions and had not yanked and tugged blindly. Chase owed them both; and so Chase insisted on his prerogatives. Whoever else entered that alien chamber, now that the door had been loosed, *he* would go inside. If Sandy Feathershaft was inclined to argue the point, she held her peace. Perhaps she saw something in his face during the inter-ship teleconference that followed the accident. Perhaps she wrestled with her own previous misjudgment. In either case, she acquiesced. Chase would go.

"But the booby trap . . ." suggested Zaranovsky.

Frechet dismissed the caution. "Pfaugh! There was no booby trap, my friend." Alois Frechet was an Alsatian of the dolorous, long-faced type, so that, with his large nose and drooping cheeks, he reminded Chase of nothing so much as a bloodhound. "The 'snow' was oxygen, of course," he said. "Plus other gases. I analyzed a sample by its vapor spectrum; but I suspected it immediately. Certainly, it is the atmosphere of the control room. The asteroid's artificial intelligence sensed our dear Jacinta's attempts to enter and began the environmental preparations. Increasing the temperature sublimated the frozen air, which naturally created pressure inside the chamber. When the outer door finally unlatched, the atmosphere inside blew it open."

"Atmosphere. Yeah," said Jacinta. "It sorta felt like the sky fell on me."

The laughter of the others was nervous. Glad that it had not been more serious; all too aware that it could have been. Frechet frowned a little at Jacinta's joke, perhaps unfamiliar with the idiom. Chase turned and gave Jacinta, sitting in the spare seat under Ku's attentions, a brief, nervous smile.

She and Total, who had been tossed about in the outgassing, had been brought aboard *Cochran* and Ku had come across to treat them both. Jacinta's left eye was surrounded by darkened tissue where she had struck against the inside of her own helmet and her right arm was immobilized to relieve stress on the wrenched shoulder. A fine network of red lines on her cheeks gave a hint of what the slow leak would have wrought had Total been more attentive to her own safety than to Jacinta's. But Jacinta was conscious now and Ku had worked his magicks. Chase wondered if the doctor was secretly delighted to have had a patient at last.

Feathershaft said, "What sort of airlock opens without the inner door closed?" drawing Chase's attention back to the teleconference. "What about safeguards?" She sounded truculent, and seemed drawn and tired. Not only had she nearly lost a crew member, but she had to know deep down that had her order to get away been obeyed, Jacinta would have died. It was through that hole in her confidence that Chase had shoved his demand to climb, like Jonah, into the belly of the fish.

Frechet shrugged. "Undoubtedly, there were such safeguards once, but the telemetry failed long ago—a dead relay, perhaps; or a mechanical failure—and the Intelligence no longer *knew* the inner door was open. So impressed by those things still working, we forgot there were other things that might have failed."

Feathershaft seemed to sag. "All right," she said, looking at Chase. "We go back. Who else goes?"

The chamber was an absolute black, the sort of darkness that needed a shovel to remove. Chase's suit light captured a narrow circle of visibility. Incomprehensible shapes appeared within its circumference as he aimed it at various points, but it was like looking at a jigsaw puzzle one piece at a time. Chase pressed channel seven. "Pass me the worklight, Alois."

The physicist waited behind him in the corridor. He handed Chase a rod with a brilliant globe on its tip. A fibrop cable connected it to the power grid on the surface. It was so bright that for a moment, paradoxically, Chase could see nothing. "Well?" said Frechet with marked impatience. "Is it safe?"

"Just being here isn't safe," Chase growled. He knew the physicist had wanted to be first into the room. Chase had told him that he was too valuable to risk, which pleased the man's vanity; but the truth was that the mission could spare its physicist far more readily than it's second-most experienced pilot. Chase wasn't going through the doorway first to draw fire as point man for Alois Frechet.

Chase was not the reflective sort. He often prided himself on that, making virtue of circumstance. Just Do It had been the motto of his generation—slacker existentialism, Styx had once called it. *I don't waste a lot of time agonizing,* Chase sometimes said.

And yet, as if the mind could not help but contemplate itself on occasion, he could not avoid the odd moment of self-reflection. So he knew that he went through the alien airlock ahead of Frechet because Jacinta had been injured there. But he had no idea why that should be either a good thing or a bad thing and dismissed the whole notion with a mental shrug.

The smart thing, of course—as opposed to the good or bad—would have been to send Uncle Waldo through first. But in some odd way, Jacinta's accident had changed the dynamics among the crew. They hadn't said to hell with caution, but a consensus had emerged in silence that no machine would go where a human could. The bonebags would stick together; and the bonebags would blaze trail. If that meant accepting greater risks, well, they were stone for that. Like Chase had told Frechet, just being on 2004AS was a risk that millions of teeping herberts had not dared assume. What was one more risk on top of that?

First one work light; then another. Light grew in the chamber like a blossoming lily. Shape emerged from shadow. Frechet gasped and even Chase paused while arranging the equipment to stare about him.

Furry place mats hung on the walls. Tall stems, like leafless trees, rose from the nominal floor or projected from some of the walls. Long rows of buttons(?), switches(?), and knobs(?) were set on gooseneck panels at every which angle. There were no chairs (nor perches, nor pedestals), unless some of the floor-mounted devices had served some such purpose. There wasn't enough gravity to make chairs more than decorative anyway, and—as the placement of the equipment indicated—the Visitors had been content to work at a variety of orientations.

Frechet went through the room with weird confidence,

naming items and describing functions that Chase thought he could not possibly know. Those flat, furry panels . . . those were the equivalent of Gyricon screens, only using some MEMS-like technology. There was nothing that Chase recognized as a dial or gauge, but Frechet pointed to "bolt heads" and speculated on color changes and reading the magnitudes of light frequencies. When activated, this apparatus would function like a keyboard. Here were rockers that were probably much like continuous control knobs; and there, ranks of short stems that looked so much like switches that even Chase had to agree that they were binary controls.

Chase didn't touch any of them. He played his suit camera across the alleged "control boards" for the slavering audiences shipboard and Earthside. He and Frechet were here only to observe at first hand and report back. Touching something might . . .

Might what? That was the problem. There was no way of knowing what might happen. He opened the radio link to the mission commander. "Sandy, do you read me?"

No answer. Frechet had been right. But, hell, they were surrounded by rock several meters thick. Not exactly transparent, even to radio . . . He switched back to the fibrop line. "No go on the radio," he told Feathershaft. "Have to stick with the telephone."

"Proceed to the next level," Feathershaft answered. "Second man stays above until the first has checked things out."

"Roger that."

In the middle of the "floor" was a simple hole. According to Frechet's sonogram, the cavity below was the "happening place." The mine, he had called it. There were no guardrails around the hole, but with so little gravity you couldn't really fall through it. Chase grinned a little and slid to the center and floated above the void. Ever so slowly, he began to drift down. Taking Newton's elevator.

"Perhaps, I should go first this time," Frechet suggested.

For some reason, that irritated Chase. Step aside, boy, and

let the big-name scientist go ahead. "Better not, doc," he said smoothly. "Remember Jacinta." Frechet backed off. Reluctantly, Chase was sure. He gave the scientist that much credit. He hadn't come seven hundred thousand miles because he peed in his pants at risks. Quite the contrary. What was it that made some people discount danger? Frechet was no thrill-seeker, but he was perfectly willing to jump through a black hole into a cavern where some *intelligence,* busy at some unknown task, might not care to be interrupted.

Chase, on the other hand, had Jacinta to live up to. He had stood by twice now in his life while she had climbed into danger. And, yeah, Chase had skated the edge a time or two, but still . . .

The passageway was barely wide enough for him to negotiate.

"They must have been physically smaller than humans," Frechet said.

Chase didn't bother answering. He had learned after the first few comments that Frechet was speaking for an audience of Uncles watching with him through his suit's cameras, discussing their observations in a sort of interplanetary science internet chat room.

Impatient with his slow descent, Chase gave his suit a brief burst so that he dropped faster into the lower chamber. He played his suit light around the lower chamber as he fell, creating a vista of bright reflections and abrupt, shifting shadows. Toward the left, the rear of the asteroid, three large tanks made of the alien's dull gray metallo-ceramic were embedded in the rock face with only their circular tips showing. Chase's thermal scan told him that the middle tank was very hot indeed and he thought that, like Total's smelter, it teased oxygen and fuel out of the very rock. There were no gauges or readouts that he could see—but then why would there be in an autonomous system? Who'd be coming around to read the dials? The meter man?

Playing his light below him, he saw . . .

Spider City.

The floor of the cavity was crawling with the brothers and sisters and cousins of the little robot that had broken the vacuum welds for Jacinta. Chase braked his descent but could not stop himself from landing on top of them. Spindly legs snapped beneath his boots. Other spiders skittered away from under him like soap in a shower and he lost his balance. In any decent gravity field, he would have fallen. Here, he simply looked absurd, windmilling his arms and doing the buck-and-wing across the room with his boot toes barely brushing the floor.

Finding his footing at last, he turned to warn Frechet, but the physicist, hanging by his hands from the lip of the opening, lowered himself slowly, pulling one of the work lights after him. The little mechs scurried out from under, leaving him a bare spot in which to alight.

"They didn't do that for me," Chase said, aggrieved.

"They did," Frechet told him. "I saw. But you dropped too quickly for them."

"How was I supposed to know?"

Frechet never seemed to recognize rhetorical questions and had the annoying habit of responding literally. "But of course, you could not know. You did not have the benefit of watching someone else, as I did."

Somehow, that did not make Chase feel better. Neither did the way the spiders now ignored his presence. They scuttled back and forth between the rock face and the hot tank, going wide around him. When he moved into one's path, it simply sidestepped and pulled an end run, its peculiar legs pumping like crazy. Up, down, up, down, like some obsessed arachnoid Irish step dancer. It annoyed Chase that he had jumped not into danger, but into slapstick.

"Where do they get their power?" Frechet wondered, bending close over one of the busy spiders. "Certainly, they cannot carry batteries along with their micromachines! Perhaps they receive the beamed power, though I see no rectennae, either.

But perhaps their programming is external, as well. Yes. Are they true automata, or are they only remotes controlled by the Intelligence?"

Chase stopped listening. They could get their power from little windup keys on their bellies, for all he cared. These spiders were larger than the one Jacinta had found. Industrial strength, he thought. And there was a thin, glowing band of yellow-green around their equator. A mining laser? He also noticed that about a quarter were dead, or at least deactivated. Many had bent or broken legs. Others simply lay unmoving on the floor.

When Chase pointed it out, Frechet said, "Find a complete specimen to take with us. The captain cannot object to bringing aboard a nonfunctioning unit. Look for one where the carapace has come loose, so we can study its insides."

Chase grunted. Frechet always came on with that supercilious tone, like a polite, urbane version of Jimmy Poole. Chase didn't know if that was because the man was a scientist, a Frenchman, or both.

"They chew into the rock and grind it with their 'gizzards,' " Frechet announced. Chase, rummaging among the carpet of dead mechs, glanced up, realized Frechet was dudding with the teepers again, and returned to his spider hunt. "Then they carry it to the furnace for melting by perhaps the selective ionization." A pause, undoubtedly to listen to time-lagged learned discussion from Earthside domes. "We know from the spectra taken in '16 that the engine burns an iron propellant . . . a low specific impulse, but as you see around us, much fuel . . . *Mais oui.* Perhaps aluminum, as well. The rock contains feldspars; though the hydrogen to catalyze the— What was that, Dr. Jürgen? Ah. The residual 'slag,' I suspect, becomes the strange gray material we see about us . . . Directionally solidified, I am confident, which is why it is so hard. Surely, the Visitors knew how to use the microgravity to— No, I think Dr. Kubiyashi is right. This cavity is no bigger than it is because the Bean has seldom needed to fire its engines. A few course corrections following random perturbations, from meteor impacts or the like . . ."

This time, the pause was long enough that Chase looked up from his study of the broken mechs. Frechet was staring back and forth between the rock-eaters and the furnace. Then, abruptly, he snapped, "Coughlin! We must return to the ship. Immediately."

Chase and Frechet reported aboard *Cochran* personally. Flaco had come across from *Mitchell* to attend and Zaranovsky from *Sikorsky*. Teleconferencing was all very well, but there was a certain need to hear firsthand, from the living lips. For the straight skinny, there was nothing like looking another monkey in the mug. Jacinta, who could not move her shoulder to put a suit on, was stuck aboard *Mitchell*. Ku and Total had elected to stay with her.

They had all watched, of course. When Chase and Frechet had ventured through the door, most of the freaking world had gone with them, courtesy of shoulder cameras and telepresence goggles. Yet some things had gone unsaid on open channels and even Chase did not yet know what had spooked the Frenchman.

"Make it quick," Feathershaft said when they had gathered in the wardroom. Her voice flat and no-nonsense. "I don't want to ruin the schedule any more than it has been."

"There is something very ominous," Frechet said, "which I did not wish to discuss with all the Earth listening. The mining machines—let us call them stokers—they are busily stoking the furnace. Their scurrying makes the sound we have been hearing on the rock phones. The tip-tap of many feet—"

"Seems werry inefficient," said Zaranovsky.

Frechet shrugged off the interruption. "A paradigm trap, perhaps. What matters now is not their efficiency but that they are so busy. Why else does the Intelligence stoke its engines if not to ready itself for a course adjustment?"

Bird growled deep in his throat. "That was a possibility all along. We all knew it."

Feathershaft said, very quietly, "Do you say we should throw in the towel, Alois?"

Frechet's brow creased in a puzzled frown.

Jacinta said from her screen, "We can't go home without at least trying."

"We should blow it up," said Zaranovsky. "Those charges Sulbertson and I have planted at fracture points . . . If we shatter Bean this far out, pieces are slowly dispersing over time. When they reach Earth in three years, very few may hit."

"Great," said Chase. "A shotgun blast instead of a rifle bullet."

"Smaller pieces may burn up in atmosphere."

"Which is why it's our fallback plan," said Feathershaft, shutting down the argument. "Can we use the stress points in the underground chambers to maximize an explosion? Pack the control room and the 'coal bunker' instead of boring into impact fractures . . . Yvgeny, you're our demolitions expert. Do a survey. If Alois is right about the intentions of the Intelligence, we'll need the fallback plan."

"But, no," said Frechet, "I never said we should—what is it?—'throw in the towel.' No, we started hearing the sounds of the stokers very soon after we landed and began altering the asteroid, is it not? *But who does the Intelligence think alters asteroids?* Perhaps its own makers? So, it readies itself for our instructions."

That earned him silence. They looked at one another with varying degrees of wonder and skepticism. "That's a pretty wild guess, Alois," said Feathershaft. "But if you're right and we give it no instructions, then everything will stay on standby."

"Until we alter the course with *external* engines—engines the Intelligence cannot be aware of since they are not in its 'sensor net'—and whose effect it will certainly regard as an external perturbation."

Even Chase, who thought Frechet used the word "certainly" far more often than he was entitled, could think of few alternatives. Maybe the stokers were active because, small as they were, it had taken them five years to replenish the bunkers after the Burn of '16. In that case, once they had topped off the tanks, the Intelligence would return to idle. He wasn't sure he believed that; and he damn sure wouldn't bet the world on it. Never depend on the enemy doing what you hoped for; and wittingly or not, the asteroid's Intelligence was the enemy.

"The blowout when Jacinta forced the outer door," said Total Meredith. "It wasn't much, given the mass of the asteroid, but the outjetting must have nudged us off the original orbit. Why hasn't your 'Intelligence' adjusted for that?"

Frechet spread his hands. "If the intent is to strike Earth, the Intelligence may not care exactly where the blow falls. Such a small perturbation did no more than alter the point of impact. But . . . I have been wondering. How will the test be graded?"

Feathershaft frowned. "Test? Graded?" She looked at Frechet as if he had grown antennae.

"On Earth they are saying that this asteroid is a test of our intelligence. But is it a simple pass/fail test?"

"Pass/fail . . ." mused Ku, pursing his lips, and his eyes sharpened in interest.

"Obviously," the Frenchman went on, "to do nothing is the failure, and we are rapped on the knuckles—"

"More'n a rap, good buddy," said the Bird.

"But what else? Waiting for close approach and trying to deflect it is perhaps a D. To await the last minute is not the smartest behavior. To blow it up, as Captain Zaranovsky wishes, is a C, because though it reduces the threat, the center of mass will still follow the original trajectory and strike. Altering of the course, as we are doing, is a B."

"First time I ever got graded that high," said Bird, laughing.

Frechet paused—waiting, Chase was sure, for someone to

ask what an A was. Feathershaft, sounding irritated, finally did; and Frechet beamed in delight. He looked at them, one by one.

"Why, to gain control and fly it home."

After the meeting, they dispersed to their own ships or to their work on the Bean while Feathershaft conferred with DeepSpace over Alois's suggestion. Flaco and Bird returned to their rigging; Lonzo, to the power plant. Zaranovsky detached *Sikorsky* from its Salyut and dropped out of orbit to fetch a supply pod that was approaching "peri-Bean." Chase returned to *Mitchell.*

In the airlock he encountered Ku, who was returning to *Cochran.* When Chase hit the open-airlock button, nothing happened for a moment and he wondered if the mechanism had malfed. He was about to go around to the cargo lock when the door opened and he saw Ku coming out.

Ku saw him, too, and hailed him on the suit-to-suit. "Complete rest," he said sternly. "No work, understand? I come see." He eyed Chase. "*You* understand?"

"All the work schedules are whacked anyway," Chase told him. "We'll share out Jacinta's assignments. Yvgeny knows electrical and can pick up some of her tasks." Sandy would probably leave reassigning the tasks on him, as de facto number two for the fleet. Chase hated the administrative side of the mission. Yet ballistics imposed a departure window on them; and the work must be scheduled and scripted and assigned if it was to be done within that window. (And, given the inevitable foos, rescheduled and rescripted and reassigned.) Somehow, the byte juggling and drag-'n'-drop and PERT wrangling didn't mesh with the image of Chase Coughlin, gonzo space pilot.

Ku clipped his suit lanyard onto the mooring line that linked ship to ship. "Jacinta lucky girl," said before parting. "You know that?"

Chase snorted and entered the ship. Ku was playing inscrutable oriental again. The accent came and went on a whim.

Of course, he knew how lucky Jacinta had been. He had thought of little else since then.

It did not take long to slip out of his suit. He clamped the hard torso in its dressing rack next to Jacinta's smaller suit, fastened the lower torso below it, and attached the stay-together cord to the helmet, snoopy cap, and gauntlets. The air tanks he put into the recharger, reflecting for a moment on the strangeness that, thanks to Total Meredith's reducing plant, he was breathing a part of the asteroid itself—oxygen wrenched from the ilmenite that made up a portion of the Bean. Drinking it, too; since water condensing in the fluid bed had to be removed or the vapor pressure would build until it reversed the reaction.

When he had everything staged for redonning, Chase pulled his snoopy cap out, held it to his ear, and called Flaco on channel nine. "Hey, good buddy," he said. "How long you gonna be out there?"

"Bird and I got one last engine to install," the rigger replied. "On the south side. We figure to finish it up. Then tomorrow we can start fresh on the north side."

"Sounds like a plan. You watching your oxygen and all?"

"Commander's baby-sitting on *Cochran.* And I guess Dr. Ku is watching his board, too."

"Don't depend on them catching what you should watch for yourself."

"Hey! Who's gonna wire this bank up when we're done, with 'Cinta laid up an' all?"

"Zaranovsky. Jacinta can ride on his shoulder. Ku said she shouldn't do any physical work, but she can teep with Yvgeny. Take care. Out."

Chase ducked out from the helmet and pulled himself forward to the flight deck, but himself before he was more than head-and-shoulders through the interlock.

Total was kissing Jacinta.

It caught Chase off guard. He knew Total was lizardly—and wasn't that an almighty shame—but he had never thought Jacinta bent the same way. Yet there was some serious, closed-eye tongue action going on. Total ran her hand through Jacinta's close-cropped hair.

Chase licked his lip, brushed his cuff across his mouth. They must not have heard him come on board, since he had cycled in on Ku's dime. He ducked behind the lock hatch that, standing open, lay between him and the women. Then he retreated aft as quietly as he could.

On the utility deck once more, he dry-cycled the lock, then went to the suit rack, where he fiddled with the helmet and gauntlets until Total showed up, so it would look as if he had just unsuited. He helped Total don her own suit and ran the "buddy check" on her airtight seals.

"I've been wanting to thank you," he said, "for rescuing Jacinta."

Total paused before setting the helmet in place. "Didn't do it for you."

Chase flushed. "I meant . . . I felt so helpless up there on the flight deck, watching but unable to help, and I—"

Total laid a gauntlet on his arm. "If you'd've been there, you'd've done the same; and I would've been the one agonizing over the viewscreen."

Chase let out a breath and nodded. "Yeah. Yeah, any of us would have."

"Bird had the roughest job."

"How's that?"

"He had to stand there with her lifeline in his hands and wait for my word over the fibrop link when every instinct in his bones was screaming at him to haul, and haul hard."

Total cycled out the lock and Chase swam forward once more. The flight deck was empty, so he continued through the nose lock into the Salyut. "Honey? I'm home!" he cried in a mock-fifties voice. Jacinta was in the rec room screading a book, but she was scrolling the pages much too fast to be taking them in. She seemed agitated, and when she raised her head at Chase's voice, he could see flushed cheeks and wary eyes.

He asked her if anything was wrong, but she just shook her head and looked back to the monitor.

Chase tried again. "Those alien gizmos were freaking strange."

"I was watching over the video fiber."

"How's the shoulder?"

Jacinta slapped both hands on the monitor. "I'm stuck here!" she said. "I can't lift my arm to get into a hard suit; so I'm stuck aboard *Mitchell* for the rest of the mission."

"Sandy said she'd—"

"Yeah, the mission commander's going Beanside and get her hands dirty while I have to sit up here and watch the angel board."

"Lonzo slaved it over to *Mitchell*'s system?"

"Chase, I didn't come seven hundred thousand miles just to sit and watch others risk their lives!"

"You've done your share," he pointed out. "Maybe more than your share. Let Lonzo and Total take their turns."

Jacinta turned away from the book screen. "Total saved my life. That's the second time."

Chase raised an eyebrow. "Second time?"

"The first time was back at the Academy. I—nearly drowned in the buoyancy tank and Yungduk carried me up to the surface and Total gave me mouth-to-mouth."

Combining duty with pleasure, Chase thought. And Jacinta had married Yungduk. "You feel you owe Total something?"

She grabbed him on the forearm. "Wouldn't you?"

Chase covered her hand with his own. "Sure, but—"

Jacinta winced and, pulling her hand away, rubbed her right shoulder.

"Hurts?"

She nodded. "Wrenched it when the door whacked me."

A door harder than diamond . . . Chase didn't want to think

about the chance that it might have struck her helmet, shattered it; that everything that was Jacinta Rosario might have been sucked into vacuum. "Close call," he said uselessly.

Jacinta squirmed. "Problem with slings in ziggy is they don't stay slung. Dr. Ku tightened it up good, but it keeps riding up."

"Can I tighten it for you?"

Jacinta turned away—"It's a Velcro band in the back"—and she slipped her coverall off her shoulders.

The brace was wrapped around the right shoulder, leaving the left one bare. For some reason Chase could not fathom, the sight of that one shoulder and the gentle curve of her spine disappearing into the folds of the coverall filled him with a sudden, unbearable ache. "Hold onto something," he told her as he loosened the fasteners between her shoulder blades. "Tell me if I make it too tight." He snugged up the first fastener, but on the second she must have lost her grip because, when he tugged on it, he spun her round.

He'd had his own moccasins planted on a stay-put pad, but the unexpectedness of the movement caused him to pull loose, so that he spun the opposite direction from her.

Around once. Around twice. On the third round he grabbed ahold of her and checked both their motions. Jacinta was laughing and Chase laughed with her; then, as the laughter slowly faded he found her eyes, large and brown and round, staring into his.

Suddenly he was kissing her. He hadn't planned it. At least, he didn't think he had planned it. And after a moment of stiffness, Jacinta kissed him back, her lips softening and parting. They moved together. "Oh, God," she whispered and kissed him again, more urgently. His arms circled her waist, felt her supple curves and the promise in her tongue. He ran his fingers down the curve of her spine and she arched her back.

In ziggy, Newton's Third was remorseless. He pressed himself against her and she drifted away from him. To stop the motion, he placed one hand at the small of her back. His fingers found a band of elastic and slipped inside. "Please," Jacinta said, and Chase said, "I love you."

At that Jacinta gave a small cry in the back of her throat and pushed him away as hard as she could. Chase went tumbling toward the passageway into the ship, coming up hard against the nose lock. Jacinta, being the smaller, sailed father—forward into the main living quarters. Chase gathered himself and kicked off on the bulkhead and followed after her.

She had checked herself on a stanchion holding one of the zeolite trays in the "greenhouse." Her coverall was twisted around her waist and she was grabbing at it, trying to straighten it out. Chase started toward her, but she looked up at him with angry, wet eyes.

"We don't want to do that," she snapped in a voice that demanded obedience. And then, in the softer, little-girl voice she sometimes used, she said, "I depend on you, Chase."

"I didn't mean—" But he had. He had meant it fully. He couldn't look at her. The walls were friendlier. *You stupid asshole,* he told himself. *Why did you do that?* There was no answer on the bounceback. Something inside him didn't know, or wasn't telling. Or else the answer was too obvious for words. "You wanted to," he told her. Her lips had been hungry, eager. He could remember their velvet touch. "You wanted to as badly as I did. Otherwise, why'd you even pull that thing open and ask me to—"

"Yes," she said. "Yes, yes, yes. And that's exactly why we mustn't."

"Down in the tunnel . . . I was scared I'd lost you. Dammit, I love you."

When she shook her head a lock came loose from its band and floated above her face. "No, you don't. You love Karen. Me, you're just horny. Like me."

Chase shook his head. "It's more than that."

"Don't let it be! Oh, God, if it were only lust, we could

look back and say it didn't mean squat and it was just a slip and . . . But we both have people we love, people we owe our vows to."

"I don't love Karen any less—"

"Don't even think that way. Don't put me in a balance pan with her. That's not fair to her; or to me."

"—and I don't want to hurt her."

"Then don't. Don't make the rest of your life with her a lie!" She looked at her feet and tugged the coverall up to her waist one-handed, where she held it gathered in her fist. "Or mine with Yungduk," she added more softly. Then she tossed the stray lock out of her face and gave him a defiant look. "Come over here and finish what you started."

Chase jerked his head and his pulse thumped with a dizzying expectation. But, no. She meant he should finish adjusting her brace. Why? To prove they could overcome their desires? Or just to feel a few more gentle touches. He swallowed. "Maybe you should ask Total to help you."

"No," Jacinta said, perhaps a little too abruptly.

"Then maybe you ought to move into *Cochran* like Ku wanted. Trade billets with Lonzo. Or switch with Total in *Sikorsky*. I don't think you and me should be in the same—"

"What sort of message do you want to send the others?" she asked in a voice that Chase heard as flat and cold.

His hands felt bloated and awkward. He didn't know where to put them. He looked at his own anguish reflected in her eyes. "What do we do on the Long Orbit home?"

"Keep to ourselves, like we did outbound."

"That's a lot of months."

"One day at a time."

"Listen. I—"

"Forget it." It wasn't a dismissal, but an order.

Neither of them spoke again. He turned her around and she grabbed on to the zeolite rack with both hands and he first loosened, then fastened, the Velcro fasteners. Then he pulled the coverall up over her shoulders and she zipped it shut.

Afterward, they regarded each other warily—and perhaps a little hungrily. Flaco was still Beanside, Chase remembered. He and Jacinta would be alone for a while yet and there had been as much eagerness in her kiss as in his. He longed to feel her in his arms again.

But, no. To obsess on it would only make his fantasies real. Without another word, they parted—he, to the flight deck; she, remaining in the Salyut. Once alone in the captain's couch, Chase closed his eyes and sought relief, desperately calling on memories of Karen.

Four months on the Long Orbit. He could see the end of it as clearly as an oncoming train on the high-speed maglev line. One day at a time, Jacinta had said. And one day they would run out of days, long before *Mitchell* docked at Goddard City.

"The whole idea," said Uncle Waldo, "is phat stoopid. It is also the other kind of stupid."

Uncle Waldo in this case was no less than Jimmy Poole, who was teeping a mobile in the Bean's control room.

"Alleged control room," said Jimmy Poole.

Chase, who—as a former schoolmate—had been condemned to liaise with the remote control weenie, waved a suit arm around the equipment lining the walls. "It looks like a freaking control room, doesn't it?"

"How do I know? I'm no alien. Maybe it's a bathroom."

"And the equipment?" He touched one of the long, thin rods that stood out from the floor.

"Maybe they were really constipated."

Chase actually laughed. "You know, you could be right. They probably needed Porta-Johns as much as a construction shack. But Frechet thinks this is worth trying. Captain Feathershaft agreed, and the long arm of DeepSpace reached out and plucked you up."

"Right in the middle of prep-up for my next magsail flight."

Talking with Uncle was always a chore. The inevitable lag times gave the impression that the other was carefully considering his responses and thus the bouncebacks sounded more calculated than they were. Yet Jimmy was the sort to play mind games and his comment about the magsail may have been intended to remind Chase of what he had missed out on.

Or it might, given Jimmy's legendary self-centeredness, be no more than a complaining bleat over his own temporary inconvenience.

"Frechet thinks the Intelligence is in command-ready mode and all we have to do is find the commands."

"Oh, that's 'all.' Jesus, I don't believe you people. Frechet is what, a physicist? But you think, hey, science is science, and a world-class physicist must be a honking, mojo dude when it comes to the cheese. *Just find the commands?* You'll be lucky if you can turn it on."

Or unlucky. But Chase kept that thought to himself. "Look," he said. "We all got problems. If you can't handle it, say so."

The pause was longer this time. "I never said *I* couldn't handle it. I said *no one* could handle it."

"Everyone agrees it's a long shot; but everyone also agreed that if anyone could do it, you could."

"Sussing out an alien system? No clue to the architecture or the operating system? You don't even know if it's electronic or optical—or something we've never dreamed of. Plus you got a deadline."

"*We* do. Departure Day. But we can leave a few teep mobiles here and you can play as long as the Bean's in range. The real deadline is aphelion. *Our* programming, for *our* engines. The A/S we leave behind is supposed to light off when the Bean reaches its farthest point from the sun. That will raise the rest of its orbit higher above the sun, including the part where it would have intercepted the Earth. Problem is, if the Bean's engine corrects for our burn, this whole expedition's been a waste."

"So blow up the control panel."

"We would . . . *If* we knew that the Intelligence uses this equipment to control the engine. But Frechet figures this is only the tutor the Visitors used to train their A/I, not the A/I itself—which he thinks is a neural network dispersed through the living rock. Lieutenant Meredith found microscopic fibers in the rock fragments from our excavations." If that was true, the entire asteroid might qualify as some sort of living organism. Chase shivered at the thought.

"If it's distributed and massively parallel," Jimmy said, "you can't shut it down by cutting a few thousand pathways. Nothing short of total breakup of the asteroid would do that."

"That's why we need to try this."

The silence on the bounceback lasted a long time. "Jimmy?"

Slowly: "It would be the ultimate hack, wouldn't it?"

Chase gave the mobile a nod. "Win, lose, or draw."

"And you got to figure—those switches on the panel—they knew on/off logic, so down in the bone we're probably talking binary code."

"Works for me," said Chase, wondering what a binary code was.

"We'd still have to sniff the hardware . . ."

"That's why I'm here. Plus you can get a hardware expert to teep from Earth."

"I'll need a team."

"I figure you'll get whoever you ask for. Feathershaft says DeepSpace is very concerned about this problem."

"Yeah, and learn what they can about the Visitors. Either way." More silence. "I'll need Pedro the Jouster, SuperNerd, and Official Chen. All three can deep hack, down to the binary bone, and they're all more-or-less legit. The first two, I can round up myself. But to get Chen, DeepSpace has to play kissy-face with the Three Cities."

Chase thanked him and told him he'd made the right decision. Bottom line, Jimmy didn't have any choice and Jimmy probably knew it as well as anyone. But there was a difference between doing what you were told and doing your best.

It took three days to learn how to turn the equipment on.

You gotta figure the power switch sits in a catbird seat, said the teeper named SuperNerd. *Top left. Bottom right. Dead center. Something like that. It's probably* not *the fourth switch from the left in the third row down.*

Chase tried each switch, pressed each button that looked promising. Each time, he expected something to pop up or blow up; and each time, when nothing happened, he carefully reversed the switch or second-pressed the button.

His activities attracted attention. A few switches had refused to budge and, shortly, a small spider emerged from some hidey-hole and ejected micromachines into the slits and openings of the panel. The micromachines spread like a swarm of black nits, so many they looked almost like a fluid stream.

The hairy panels on the wall bristled, then flattened out, then flexed, somehow producing a deep indigo color. The hairs on the back of Chase's head did pretty much the same, except for the color.

Booting up, said Pedro the Jouster. *Good.*

Chase wasn't sure how good it was. It annoyed him that Frechet's guess about the panels had been right. He reported the results to Feathershaft, who, with Jacinta on light duty and Chase assigned to the control room project, had taken some of the fieldwork on herself. The captain expressed encouragement; but Chase could not help feeling that vast, slumbering powers had been awoken.

It took another two days to detect the microwave fields.

A network of microtransmitters and receivers, said Official

Chen. *Most intriguing. The pulses must flip the switches from yes to no and back.*

Bird Winfrey crawled underground with Chase and set up detection equipment under Earthside instruction. After that, it was straightforward to discover how each control perturbed the pattern. Official Chen wrote an A/S neural net to monitor the patterns and establish a "vocabulary," and squirted it to Bird's equipment via the microwave laser on Helios Light powersat, Total Meredith's Beanside receiver, and the fibrop phone line into the depths of the asteroid.

By the end of the week they had learned that some buttons were brain-dead.

There's so many buttons, said Pedro, *that they must be single function. If we knew what those ideograms meant . . .*

Official Chen hacked a second A/S. This one studied the small, complex inscriptions above each control and matched each against what happened when they tried it. Since mostly that was "nothing," the Visitor-Earth Translating Dictionary remained largely composed of blank pages.

The system may be fried, Jimmy Poole said. *That many buttons can't be dead on purpose.*

Some may only activate, SuperNerd cautioned him, *when the cheese is running.*

By the end of the same week, they had learned how to read the scales.

Blue means "off," said Jimmy, *and red means "on." No color means the control is dead. Forward is "off" and back is "on" for the switches and rockers. For the rockers, the lights above them run from blue for low to red for high on whatever scale the inscription means.*

They learned how to read "open" and "closed."

"What's that?" said Chase, who felt the vibrations through his boot soles after pressing the button. Turning, he saw the outer door, the one that had swatted Rosario, swinging closed. Jimmy and his crew became very excited, but Chase worried that he would be trapped, like Jonah in the belly of the fish. He pressed the same button again, but nothing happened. "Guys . . . ?" he said. But the fiber had been pinched off.

Chase stabbed buttons on the equipment Bird had installed and Chen's resident A/S flagged two dozen alien controls labeled with ideograms similar to the one that had closed the outer door. There were four in a cluster. The two right-hand buttons were dark and Chase guessed they were for the inner door, which had failed open, but which the Intelligence thought was closed. Chase realized that if the Intelligence ever learned better, they'd never be able to open the outer door of the airlock again. Quickly, he took a chance and stabbed the red button immediately below the first. The outer door swung open and the button turned blue.

This elemental symbol means door or perhaps airlock, Chen decided, once communication had been restored. *These others mean inner, outer, open, and closed.*

The "elemental symbols," Chase saw, were superimposed one atop another. With "open" inscribed over "outer," which in turn was inscribed over "door, or airlock." The net result was a pattern that looked to Chase like what he saw when a rock hit a windshield. "Those things are too complicated for anyone to read," he said.

Chen, who worked out of the Guangdong Republic, laughed, but said nothing.

In two weeks, with Departure Day rapidly approaching, Chen's microwave A/S switched from receiver to transmitter and beamed an instruction at the panel. The outer airlock door swung closed, and then open. That night, Earthside, Jimmy and SuperNerd got drunk together and Chase felt a little giddy himself. By then, they had identified a dozen functional controls, managed to display ideograms on the view-mats (whose many bristles were apparently MEMS-based, like the sign above the Sidewinder Bar outside Phoenix), and activated something very scary in the recesses of the asteroid.

Chase reversed that particular control quickly; but on Jimmy's insistence and Feathershaft's reluctant concurrence, repeated the experiment with Uncle Waldo down in the coal bunker and the whole Bean under microwave scan from *Sikorsky.*

It was the left-side tank, announced Uncle Waldo.

Something was activated at the head of the nozzle, Total Meredith told them.

Spectrum reading on emissions from nozzle, Jacinta declared from *Mitchell. Iron powder.*

Ah, said Chen. *So* that *symbol means "iron" plus "pump/injection/feed."*

Chen's A/S obliged by telling them where else on the board the elements of that ideogram appeared. One, an indicator light in the yellow-green range, was evidently iron storage. Half full, Chase noted glumly. Would the Intelligence wait for "full" before acting? But if *that* part of the ideogram meant "iron," then these others . . .

. . . those must be other pumps. Perhaps the oxygen . . .

The A/S designated the controls that were likely to mean oxygen feed pump and Chase took out some duct tape and marked off that whole side of the Visitors' control panel. "I'm not touching anything else over on that side until we know what'll happen when we do."

Jimmy griped, but Chase stood firm. The little twit back on Earth didn't understand—though Feathershaft, Zaranovsky, and the others did, and backed him up. He had injected fuel into an engine that could have swallowed the old Saturn booster main engines for breakfast. That was one step back from lighting the torch. The sweat soaked into his LCG and he did not even want to think about his suit diaper. He was uncomfortable, sticky and cold and hot all at the same time. Nevertheless, he did not return to *Mitchell* until he was certain that Flaco Mercado was already on board. He had contrived for the three weeks since his slip with Jacinta never to be alone with her again. Though sometimes, at night, perversely, Karen spoke to him in his dreams with Jacinta's voice.

On D-minus-Two, they screwed the pooch.

19.

The Battle of the Bean

The Bean was as busy as Manhattan on a Friday afternoon; and for much the same reason. The workers were getting ready for the long commute home. Time, tide, and launch windows waited for no one. Jacinta, confined to *Mitchell* because of her injury, watched the activity on the monitor screens with a mixture of relief, impatience, and frustration. Relief, because they were heading home at last; impatience, because she itched to help out; frustration, because they had not quite finished their mission.

The incident in the tunnel, the subsequent investigation, and the general reshuffling of work assignments had left several of the rocket motors uninstalled. Some assembled stacks ready for installation were lashed to the ground near the asteroid's nose, but nobody had volunteered to stay behind to finish the job. However, contingency planning had allowed for the possibility that not all the engines would be in place, and new burn software had been already uploaded from Earthside. Only, there would be that much less thrust available to nudge the asteroid off its anointed path.

Feathershaft, who normally monitored Beanside activity from the "mothership," helped Zaranovsky lay fibrop cable on screen one. Jacinta watched the two of them lope easily forward along the Bean's sunside, unreeling a spool as they went. *Yvgeny could have handled that himself,* Jacinta thought none too kindly and turned her attention to screen three.

That was the view of Beantown Power, at the asteroid's waist. She watched Total move methodically from equipment to equipment, shutting down the ilmenite reduction plant. Lonzo loaded a skid with filled oxygen cylinders and guided it on compressed gas jets toward *Mitchell.* He moved off screen three, then reappeared on screen five approaching the base of the mooring line, where the extra oxygen was being stacked.

Total had wrested plenty of O_2 from the Bean for the Long Orbit; but Jacinta was more concerned about hydrogen. At least two fuel pods had outgassed by the time Chase or Yvgeny snagged them. Using fuel to fetch fuel was okay, but not when the tank you finally captured was dry. The fleet was scheduled to rendezvous with additional pods en route home, but none of the pilots were happy with the margin.

Screen four showed the northside engine array near the asteroid's tail, where Flaco and Bird were securing the last rocket motor in an otherwise half-empty rack.

There was Dr. Frechet on screen seven, heading toward the entrance to the alien's chamber, on the dark side. "Chase," she said on the private ship-to-suit channel, "Doctor Frechet's on his way." Chase was in the underground chamber finishing some last tasks for Uncle Waldo. He would rejoin *Mitchell* as soon as he was done and start the departure checklist. The remote module would remain behind when the fleet left so teepers could investigate the alien equipment as long as the telepresence link could be maintained.

"Thanks." Chase's answer was short, impersonal. Jacinta wet her lips and rubbed her knuckles against her palm. Chase was trying to maintain distance; but it was a strain on both of them. He was not expert enough at voice and body to establish distance without sounding curt, or even hostile.

Dr. Ku called from *Cochran* and asked permission to board *Mitchell* to check the swelling in her shoulder. "It's almost gone now," she told him. It had been three weeks since the accident and she could move her arm through almost the whole range of movement, though raising it above head level still caused sharp pain. Rotator cuff. Ku had warned her the ache might be permanent. No one knew how bruised tissues healed in ziggy. Certainly, her black eye had been a very long time returning to normal and her face was puffier than usual for ziggy.

Honest, Mom. I didn't run into a door. The door ran into me.

Ku raised an admonishing finger. "Nevertheless . . ."

Jacinta sighed. "All right. Come on over." She signed off and activated the outer lock for Ku. To facilitate visits back and forth, each ship was tethered not only to the Bean, but to its neighbor. *Cochran,* in the middle above the north face, was linked to both of the other ships; *Mitchell* over the sunside, *Sikorsky* over darkside. Ku could clip onto the magnetic grapple that connected their two ships and scoot straight across.

A flash of light in the corner of her eye caught her attention and she looked up at the big monitor that carried the wide-scale view from the co-orbiting satellite. *What the hell was that?*

She switched frequencies and viewed the Bean in U/V, then I/R, then microwave. There was a hot spot in the throat of the Bean's nozzle and microwave activity like an uprooted ants' nest. She toggled Chase and hollered. "Chase! We got problems."

Chase knew something was wrong before Jacinta called him. Official Chen was preparing a new microwave pattern for input when the mat screens rippled and displayed a series of ideograms and other simpler pictures that must have been icons. One of the buttons in the panel began blinking deep blue. "What the hell is happening?" he said. "What'd we do?"

"Nothing," said Chen. "I have not activated the command."

"The Intelligence is active," Pedro said.

"No fooling . . ."

The screens froze; then ran through another series of ideograms.

"No. These are same symbols," Chen announced seven seconds later. "Repeating. Perhaps it is requesting input."

"It could be a warning," Jimmy Poole suggested. That was Chase's thought, exactly.

A bank of indicators flipped from blue to red. Some of them, Chase saw, were those they had tentatively identified as fuel and oxidizer feed pumps. "Guys . . . ?" he said.

"Don't touch the big blue button," said Pedro. "That will <execute pending command.>"

"Hit the big blue button," said Jimmy. "That's <abort pending command.>"

Thanks for the advice. Chase looked at the rippling mats of fur as their flexing hairs displayed the ideogram sequence over and over. Telling him something, or asking him something, or warning him about something. But what? But what?

Another indicator, near the feed pump controls, one that they had thought colorless and therefore dead, had turned blue and was rapidly brightening toward green.

"The power switch, quick!" said SuperNerd. "Shut the whole thing down!"

"Never mind the power switch," said Jimmy. "That powers *your panel,* not the A/I. Hit the abort! Hit the abort!"

Chase went with Jimmy. He wasn't sure why he trusted Jimmy more than the others; only that it felt right. *Trust the farce, Chase.* But having made a false start toward the power switch on SuperNerd's command, he now twisted in the microgravity toward the blinking blue light, with his fist already descending in an arc, when . . .

The main engine blew. Jacinta saw the flash, then a plume of orange light that faded rapidly into invisibility. She triggered the All Suits. "Return to the ships! Return to the ships! The

Bean is moving!" Then she looked up to the feed from the underground control room and saw . . .

Chase's fist missed the button because he was moving backward toward the open airlock. No, he was hanging in place while the Bean moved forward! He scrambled for purchase on the rocky floor, grabbed one of the floor-mounted mechanisms (and wondered for a wild moment if that was not exactly why it was there), and all of a sudden the control panel was on the ceiling, far above his head and impossibly out of reach.

Alois Frechet crossed the surface of the Bean in long, languid, ground-hugging bounds. As he hurried toward the tunnel entrance, he hummed to himself. He still felt the thrill of entering the Visitor control room for the first time, after that poor, unfortunate girl had pried the door open. Yes, he had seen immediately, very much a "construction shack." Everything had a temporary, field-rigged appearance. The airlock had been the simplest possible, with a handle where humans would have used a screw wheel. (By the blue! Similarly, they used rockers instead of knobs on their control panels. Perhaps twisting motions were difficult for them. What did that imply of the structure of their bodies . . . ?)

And now the computer experts were well toward solving the riddle of the equipment and even, as a lagniappe, progressing on the written language.

What excited him most of all was how close to human the Visitors' technology was. They had nanomachine automata. But humans had micromachines—although not yet true automata. And the odd screens. Humans used MEMS for many things, from the chameleon dresses of the Paris fashion houses to the microsurgery. Could the Visitors, due to some paradigm trap, have missed the cathode ray tube, the liquid crystal, the Gyricon screen? Difficult to imagine but . . .

There was a spine of rock ahead of him, splashed up by

an ancient collision. Frechet bounded with his suit jets to clear it.

But when his boots touched down, he skidded. Suddenly, and disorientingly, he found himself standing on the side of a sheer cliff. He staggered, found no footing, and twisted. He was falling! Falling? But how was this possible? The girl's voice hollered in his ears.

Twisting around his center of mass, Frechet struck the asteroid facedown and slid across the rocky surface, coming to rest at last in the angle formed by the ring wall of a small crater.

His helmet visor was very tough; but it cracked and splayed from the impact. Frechet thought, *How very odd! The fracture looks like a Visitor ideogram.* Vapor surrounded him. Oxygen leaking from his suit. *Through my cracked visor?* He held his hand up against the plastic to hold it in place and saw the long gash running up the arm of his suit.

The fabric was a tough composite, layered with Nomex and Kevlar. It could endure a great deal of punishment—but not sliding across sawtooth ridges and craters that had never known the softening kiss of wind or rain.

A strange peacefulness enveloped him as he reached into the leg pocket for the "duct tape." He wrapped the strip around and around the gashed suit arm, though of course the tear was far too large to be contained. Yet, no man would say that Alois Frechet had surrendered to Fate! The command and display module—his "accordion"—was smashed and a steady mist steamed from the high pressure oxygen connector valve. He pressed the PANIC button, but nothing lit up.

The suit was growing cold. He adjusted the temperature control, but it never got any warmer.

The earth often moved for Alexandra Feathershaft when she was with Gene Zaranovsky; but never before when they walked in their hard suits across the northern face of the Bean. The ground suddenly tilted under her, spilling her and her companion across the surface. The spool of fibrop wire went spinning and the Russian caromed off a small rill and bounded into space. Unable to maintain contact with the surface, Feathershaft tumbled after him. *Jack and Jill,* she thought wildly.

She was spinning. There was *Cochran*, the Bean, *Mitchell,* an infinity of stars, the distant green pearl that was Earth, the *Cochran* again. She hit the emergency stabilizer on her suit spews, and the embedded A/S clocked her on three axes, fired the gas jets, and brought her to a jarring stop way up in the middle of the sky.

Zaranovsky's strobes flashed at two o'clock high. His white suit was surrounded by the glow of gases. Leaking . . . She could see him trying to reach behind his own back. A hose torn loose? Dear God! "Gene!" she cried and jetted off after him.

"Flaco, old buddy," the Bird said. "From here the shit looks very deep indeed."

The two of them clung to the empty northside engine mounting brackets to keep themselves from falling off the wall that the world had suddenly become. The stars that had been "aft" were now "down," and as Bird had said, that was a very long way down. If they slipped off the rack, they would tumble "down" into the plasma from the Big Engine.

Nearly one-quarter gee, Flaco guessed from his own suddenly regained weight. *Oh, Serafina!* Desperately, he looked around to see if rescue was on its way; instead, he saw . . .

"Bird, let's blow this joint."

Winfrey looked where Flaco pointed. "Jesus H!"

The three ships were swinging toward the asteroid on the ends of their long tethers. And from where Flaco clung, *Cochran* looked a great deal like a fly swatter—with Bird and him as the flies.

Cling to the rack and get crushed by the *Cochran,* or drop off and be vaporized by the Bean's exhaust. "Use your jets, *'mano*," he told Bird. "Jump hard and fire jets full open and pray like you never prayed before."

Flaco flexed his knees and leaped, opening his jets full. He tumbled into the starry void and—abruptly—he was ziggy once more. To his right, strobes blinked on a red striped suit, so the Bird had gotten off, too. They were still moving forward with the asteroid, having picked up some velocity from it; but the Bean was still accelerating, pulling ahead—and if it pulled too far ahead, they would still find themselves engulfed in the plasma plume. Flaco looked about for a target, any target, and centered *Sikorsky* on his faceplate. "Aim for the *Sikorsky,* Bird!" And he told his suit's A/S to take him there.

The jets fired, angling him forward and starside. Though what did it matter? The ships were their ride home. As the Bean moved forward, *Sikorsky* would . . .

. . . swing around on its anchor cable and smash into the ground. Total Meredith saw that instantly, even before the shudder in the ground beneath her had settled into a steady vibration. She danced a little and grabbed hold of a feed line on the smelter and watched the other human figures around her topple and fall or spin into space. A small part of her mind took pride in being the only one to maintain her balance. Cat Foot Meredith! Yes!

But there was no time to waste. She let go of the feed line (and refused to think of herself as hanging over an infinite pit) and dropped into space. Centering *Sikorsky*'s airlock in her visor crosshairs, she said, "Target"—and the A/S took over, bringing her to a pretty halt, just by the lock controls. She slapped the cycle command with her left hand, and reached around with her right to disengage the ground tether and the magnetic grapple.

They were taut as violin strings. She pulled on the lever and it . . . Would. Not. Budge.

The outer lock door swung open and Total spewed inside and . . .

Jacinta felt the ship jerk. She tore her eyes off the horror on the screens and scanned her boards. All green. She looked again, more carefully, slowing her breath by willpower. Wait. Look for it.

Relative motion. Radar said the Bean was both pulling ahead and moving closer.

Lights flashed in the forward port. There, past the curving expanse of the Salyut module mounted to the ship's nose, were two sets of suit beacons. Whose? She ought to cast loose and retrieve them. From the inside, she could disconnect the magnetic grapple linking her to *Cochran,* but the "Bean-stalk" tether was a simple clip, manually attached to an external ring. She couldn't detach that one without putting on her suit; and she couldn't put on her suit without help.

The tether?

The tether!

Lonzo Sulbertson fell through space, tumbling toward the west end of the asteroid, where a fiery hell awaited. The cylinders of compressed oxygen he had been carting toward *Mitchell*'s staging point were scattered like chaff. It was as if the Bean had become a vast ocean liner, sinking tail-down into a vast, starry ocean. He knew that was an illusion, created by the acceleration reference frame, but that didn't stop his reptile brain from jibbering.

And there was *Mitchell*'s tether coming toward him like God's garrote.

Total fought the outrushing torrent of ship's air and struggled into *Sikorsky*'s flight deck, where she found the attitude controls more by instinct than anything else. Just one light slap on the toggles to burp the jets and she back-flipped the way she had come, shooting like a diver headfirst through the open man-lock; then, in the suit locker, springing off the supply room bulkhead, executing a perfect jackknife, so that the rush of air carried her out the airlock into space.

She snatched at the edge of the airlock and for one horrifying moment her hands slipped. But she was Cat Foot Meredith. She didn't slip. She *refused* to slip. The angry red light on the outside airlock control panel demanded attention. <Emergency Override. Outer Lock Open.> But she didn't have the time for normal 'locking. The push from the attitude jets had nudged *Sikorsky toward* the asteroid, and the ground was rushing toward her now, with her between the ship and the rock.

But, more importantly, she had relieved the tension on the tether.

Releasing it was a flick of the wrist; but she wasted no time admiring her victory. Back inside now. Never was she more glad of those long, grueling hours of physical exercise; the slow, painfully won mastery of her body that had made hands and feet and torso notes in a symphony. A deft movement of the hand as she passed through the airlock canceled the override and the outer door swung closed, stoppering the outfall of precious air. *I hope I didn't spill too much.* But air conservation would be moot, if *Sikorsky* collided with the Bean.

She entered the flight deck like a lance and she reached over the back of the pilot's seat, one hand stabbing for the magnetic grapple disconnect linking her to *Cochran* and the other for the Beanside attitude jets and . . .

There was only one thing she could do, Jacinta realized; but she couldn't do it for long. Maybe it would buy her time.

She demagnetized the grapple, which floated loose from *Cochran*'s hull and automatically reeled itself in. But as for the ground tether . . .

No time for the seat belt. Seconds might matter. Reaching across to Chase's panel, Jacinta toggled the flight controls over to the copilot's console; then eyeballing her rate of approach to the Bean, she lit the torch.

Lonzo had caught *Mitchell*'s grapple across the body and it jarred him badly, but he had the presence of mind to hold on for dear life. He felt like a tightrope walker who had fallen and now had arms and legs hugging the high wire.

He had to unloose *Mitchell* before it was too late.

As if hearing his thoughts, *Mitchell*'s grapple detached from *Cochran* and began to roll up into its scabbard. Lonzo held tight and let it pull him with it like a fish being reeled in.

Then *Mitchell*'s main engines lit and the ship bucked ahead, swinging Lonzo inboard. The ship's fuselage grew suddenly huge and hard in his eyes. He let go of the grapple before he was slapped against the side of the hull, and fired his suit jets. Jacinta must be trying to run ahead of the Bean to buy time; but she could not accelerate indefinitely. Once *Mitchell* ran out of fuel, the Bean would play crack the whip again.

Still, *Mitchell* could accelerate longer and faster than Lonzo's suit. If he wanted to close in, he'd have to sprint. Open his spews full and catch up. But if that wasn't good enough—if he missed or fell short—he'd drift through space with his jets dry, unable to turn or stop.

Flaco saw *Cochran* die.

The tail struck first, digging into the crater they had named Little Mo and raising a cloud of meteor dust and broken rock and metal. It paused for a moment, as if it were about to change its mind. Then the crater wall gave way and the ship continued its slide aft. Momentum carried it along, plowing a track through the ancient landscape, leaving parts of it scattered behind. The ship rebounded—a bird straining for flight—then hit again. The fuselage buckled at the waist; the metallo-ceramic composite tore, the aerogel substructure ruptured. Then the Salyut module broke free of the nose and, turning cartwheels on its own independent path, rolled off a splash of rock and jammed into a ridge on the nightside.

The hydrogen tank in *Cochran*'s midsection ruptured, spewing a strange and ghostly cryogenic geyser into the air. The onboard lights flared and went out. The ship moved again and slid a few more meters toward the rear before, its momentum spent as friction and its broken body impaled on the rocks, it came to rest.

Flaco and Bird were already well to the rear and sunward of the asteroid. They had tied themselves together with their belt tethers, not because they thought it would increase their chances of survival, but because neither one wished to die alone. *Serafina, ah, Serafina* . . . He would never see his wife and children again.

"Look at that, Chico," Bird said, in a sad tone that suggested a shaking of the head. "Now ain't that a dirty shame."

"Sure is, *'mano*. She was a fine-looking ship."

"Ship? I wasn't talking about the fucking ship. It came right down on top of the rocket engines we mounted on the north face. All that damn work we did, and for what?"

Lonzo's hands slid and snatched for purchase on the side of the *Mitchell*. He grabbed at the tether, missed, and grabbed again. Fingers closed around the line, and took hold. Jacinta's thrust had put slack in the line; but the cable's sheer length gave it considerable mass, and when he pulled on it, it resisted him. He was panting by the time he managed to release the buckle and let it float loose from the ship. *Don't panic,* he warned himself. *Think, then act. But don't take too long at either.*

"Jacinta, can you hear me? It's Lonzo! Stop the acceleration. I loosed the tether." There hadn't been any answer yet, and he didn't think he would get one now. He slid aft down the ship's aeroshell—like sliding down a hillside, only in this case, it was the hill sliding up past him. The airlock was already standing open for some reason. A nudge from his suit and he dropped straight toward the small round ledge it formed.

He took the landing with his legs, bending to absorb the impact; but as he rebounded, he fought for balance. Like a diver springing off the boards, he imagined for a moment executing a jackknife into a deep, black, sparkling pool. *Talk about your high dive into the deep end . . .*

But he managed to grab hold of the airlock rim and steady himself. Then, pausing only a moment to swallow his heart, he cycled through the inner lock into the suit locker, where he saw why Jacinta had not answered his calls.

She was dressed in her lowers and crouched under the hard torso. With her left hand she was trying to raise her right arm high enough so she could wriggle into her suit. There was blood streaming from her mouth and nose, drifting into globules in the microgravity of the cabin.

In blood and tears, she turned her face to him. "I couldn't do it," she said. "There was no time to buckle into the seat before I hit the burn and I fell through the gangway into the aft bulkhead. I thought I could suit up and run outside and unhook the ship and . . . But I couldn't bend my arm . . . I couldn't bend my arm . . ."

"It's okay, now, 'Cinta. We're unmoored. Now we gotta find out who's left."

He climbed up the ladder to the flight deck and hit the burn cutoff. Settling into the copilot's seat, his eyes automatically gathered in the ship's status. Fuel was badly depleted, he saw. Jacinta had used a lot to pace the asteroid as long as she had. But there was a good pod-full at the asteroid and—

He stopped. That pod must be quite a few klicks back along the orbit by now.

No, it might be ahead of them by now. The acceleration, first of the Bean, then of *Mitchell* itself, had raised the ship's orbit with respect to the sun, and that would slow them down, allowing the pods to catch up. Except the pods would be sunward now. He looked up as Jacinta took the pilot's seat beside him. "Okay, Jacinta, you're the navigator. Figure us an orbit to rendezvous with the pod farm."

Jacinta stared at him bleakly, then started setting the problem up on the ship's navigational A/S. The radio squawked at them.

"All suits," it said. "All suits. Lieutenant Meredith, aboard *Sikorsky*. Can anyone hear me?" Then, more desperately, *"Is anyone left out there?"*

Bai Deng Ku had been nearly suited up for his "house call" on patient Rosario when chaos struck. He looked forward to the examination. Rosario was fine-featured and smooth of skin, as proportioned as a work of art. It would be a delight someday to paint her.

When the acceleration began and the ship started its slow giddy swing, Ku rushed to the control room. He thought perhaps there would be something obvious that even an untrained person could do . . .

But the room had been as mysterious to him as that of the Visitors, and in the short time available, he could think of no better course than to fasten his helmet, strap himself firmly into his accustomed seat, and ride it out.

The impact had been bad. His head snapped back and he knew he would suffer whiplash because of it. He bounced and rolled within the harness and watched with bemused detachment as the outer skin peeled off, leaving him staring at the open landscape as it slid past, until his carriage came to a crunching, tearing halt.

How long he sat in a daze staring at the rubble and the gradually settling dust and debris he did not try to tally. It was shock, he knew. The problem with a medical education was that self-diagnosis left no room for illusion. Shortly, he disengaged the seat belt and climbed through the jagged opening onto the rocky plain.

The acceleration had ceased and the Bean was docile once

more. Ku looked around. There was no sign of the other two ships. Perhaps they had impacted below the horizon. Far to the east, the tower with the solar arrays still stood, held in place by its guy lines. He saw no other figure, nor any suit beacons. *I am alone,* he thought in desolation.

Perhaps there were survivors in the other ships. He chose the sunward side for no better reason than visibility. His suit jets kicked up small clouds of dust that seemed to sweep westward in a strange phantom wind. What a transient thing is man; yet here, his own footprints would persist for eons, to be found by future spacefarers. Perhaps by his own descendants. That would be fitting, that they would know and honor their ancestor. But perhaps by intelligent rodents, if Heaven saw fit to erase the slate and start anew.

He shaded his eyes against the sun and gazed upward. *The superior man recognizes the ordinances of Heaven,* he thought. That was if Heaven cared to set them. More often, silence was the response.

But this time, amid the confusion of stars, lights blinked. Harsh, actinic flashes. Strobes. One of the other ships, perhaps. Or others of the crew even more luckless than he. Or perhaps Heaven itself was speaking at last.

The superior man acts before he speaks; and afterward lets his actions speak.

Or, as the Americans liked to say, Just Do It.

Before he had even formed the thought, before he was aware of his own intentions, he had leaped into the sky and turned his face to the beacons. He directed his suit toward them and activated the jets. The distance was long, he judged; perhaps longer than suit jets could take him. Perhaps longer than any man in a suit had ever traversed.

If it was a ship, they would intercept him. If it was others like himself, they could die together. If it was nothing but his own deluded mind conjuring visions, he could—someday long past caring—fall into the sun.

One of these things would happen.

* * *

"In the name of the Father," said Yvgeny Zaranovsky, "and of the Son, and of the Spirit, Amen. Praised be His holy Name."

Feathershaft brushed her hand through his hair. "Hush, now, Gene. We're aboard *Mitchell*, now. We're safe."

Maybe. Rosario had used a lot of fuel saving the ship. It might be a problem returning to the pod farm. In a lower orbit, the pods would eventually lap the ship, so if *Mitchell* decelerated at the right moment, it would drop into co-orbit and rendezvous. The problem was that they did not have a fix on the pods; and if the maneuver failed they might be unable to rendezvous with the next set. Rosario was working on the problem and so was DeepSpace back on Earth.

Sulbertson spoke from the pilot's seat. "That was Total, again. *Sikorsky* just picked up Flaco and the Bird."

"Still no word from the *Cochran*?"

Sulbertson shook his head. "There won't be. Flaco and Bird saw it smash against the Bean."

Feathershaft nodded. She had expected it, but it still hurt. *Jackie Cochran* had been her ship for a long time. In test flight, in the high orbit and lunar trade, now on FarTrip II. Its loss left a hole in her heart. But she had known it in her heart when she had seen Lonzo Sulbertson aboard *Mitchell*. There was no one else rated to fly *Cochran*.

She weighed their situation. The remaining ships could support three each in comfort and four on short rations, and that meant eight, tops. For every individual they rescued, the odds of survival would drop. "Who's not accounted for?"

Rosario answered. "Ku and Frechet and . . ." Then, after a very long pause and in a smaller voice, "Coughlin."

And where were they now? Coughlin had been in the Visitors' control center; Frechet, going to join him; Ku, aboard *Cochran*. Were they still on the asteroid? Tossed into space? What did it matter? They had not been found, and now they never would be. Yvgeny, still delirious, still calling on his

Trinity, muttered ejaculations over and over. Count him as a casualty, too. She covered her face with her hands. What a ghastly failure her leadership had been!

"Ma'am?" said Rosario through her bloody split lip. "Your orders?"

Feathershaft checked her watch and was suddenly appalled. Fifteen minutes? Was that all it took to shatter everything so irrevocably? From beginning to end, a scant quarter of an hour? It seemed impossible that so much could have happened so quickly. Three dead, or as good as. One ship lost. The mission, a failure now that the Bean had shifted orbits. The wiring had not been finished and the revised programming for the strap-on boosters was now invalidated.

Unless the Bean's own long boost had shifted its orbit enough to miss the Earth.

But she didn't believe in that kind of luck.

Yet, it still might be possible to snatch mere disaster from the jaws of catastrophe and at least bring the survivors home. She took a deep breath and steeled herself. She would bring the fleet home or die. "All right. First order of business is to refuel *Mitchell,*" she said, "and Meredith needs to replenish her breathing oxygen. She's still in co-orbit with the pods and Mercado can help with the refueling. *Mitchell* will rendezvous with *Sikorsky* at the pod farm if our navigator A/S tells us it's feasible. Otherwise, we cut orbit for home and ration everything between now and the next pod rendezvous. Rosario, I need to know how much juice we have for our steering jets. Can we close when we rendezvous? I'll inventory the food and water." She glanced at Zaranovsky. "And medical supplies." She had considered briefly taking ship's command from Rosario, but had decided against it. Meredith would need a number two—and they would shift personnel at the next opportunity—but right now they had four pilots for two ships. Five, when Gene recovered. If Gene recovered. "Ask Meredith if—"

There was a clang on the hull and everyone but the Russian

jumped. A debris impact? Feathershaft read the alarm in the others' faces. But then the lock cycled and, shortly, Peterson Ku emerged onto the crowded flight deck. His helmet was already off and he gazed slowly from face to face with an eerily unnatural calm.

"Ah," he said in a matter-of-fact voice. "I had thought to find you turtle's eggs here. Could you not have waited?"

Chase Coughlin knew that no one would be coming for him. The vectors weren't right. There was not enough fuel. And, most important, four plus four equaled eight, and he was number nine. For that reason, he did not bother to join in the radio chatter between *Mitchell, Sikorsky,* and DeepSpace. He had not been unconscious long, and he'd heard enough on the ship-to-ship, and even from the weaker suit broadcasts, to piece together what had happened. The two remaining ships could take eight people home, if they were very careful and very lucky. They didn't need the ghostly voice of Chase Coughlin rubbing their noses in the Lifeboat Dilemma.

Besides, this would make the Long Orbit easier on Jacinta. There was a helluva thought. It was too goddam bad that he had never screwed her. He was glad he hadn't. He had kept her respect—and his own. Still, he could not help think about how sweet it would have been. Somehow, when you were dead, all the chances you never seized weighed more heavily in your mind. And Chase knew he was dead. Only the formalities remained.

Time to take stock. The air in his suit. Three-quarters. Total had some oxygen stockpiled at Beantown P&L, if it hadn't been shrugged off into space. And there might be something salvageable on the wreck of *Cochran.*

Which he wouldn't know until he looked. The Bean was near ziggy, now that the acceleration had stopped. That would make it easier to get around, provided the Intelligence didn't decide to cut loose again. But there was nothing to do about it if it did, so he decided not to worry.

He supposed in the long view of things that there was no point in what little life extension he could hope for; but the long view wasn't in it. He had heard what Feathershaft told DeepSpace about the Bean's orbital shift screwing up the programming for the rockets they'd worked so hard to mount. So, yeah. He would run out of air sooner rather than later. Not that he was some kind of hero or nothing, but he'd get the rockets reprogrammed first.

If Uncle Waldo wasn't broken.

He didn't know jack about programming, but he knew a guy who did.

Voices: Acts

. . . *the valiant attempt by the brave expeditionary force, has ended in failure to . . .*

Karen Coughlin took the photograph in her hands—smiles and lace and tuxedos and flowers and arms around her waist that she would never forget—and she brought it down hard on the dresser top, smashing the glass and cracking the wooden frame at the joints. "Damn you!" she said. "Damn you, damn you, damn you!" Then she sat down on the edge of her bed and covered her face with her hands.

Pomnim dyesyat' geroyev. Yvgeny Pavlovich Zaranovsky—iz Kharkova—spokoyniy chelovek . . .

It didn't seem right to use one of the original seven shot glasses, the ones he had set up in a row on the shelf in his office all those years ago; and so he had bought another package. It lay open now on his desk, the crumpled cellophane slowly uncrackling, the cardboard torn open on the end where impatience had warred with packaging. Forrest Calhoun held one of the glasses in his hand, filled with bourbon. The true quill, aged in an oak cask in a Kentucky holler.

His office at Glenn Spaceflight Academy was bedecked with his memorabilia. Ribbons, photographs, medals, trophies. He faced one of the photographs: his first class at Ames Field. Forrest and good ol' Ignacio Kilbride, surrounded by five shiny-faced kids. Flight school had been a lot more informal back then; a lot more one-on-one. He'd gotten to know the kids closer, the ones he'd trained back then. He lifted the bourbon to the photograph. "Here's to us, Chase. Who's like us?" He swallowed the drink in one toss, then considered the glass. "Devil a one," he said.

He took the emptied glass to the shelf and made a space, apart from the row of seven, and placed it mouth down, as two of the original seven were. Then he returned to his desk and sat with his hands balled and his chin resting upon them. After a time, he sighed and dumped the package onto the desk and took three more glasses to the shelf and set them next to the one he had emptied for Chase. Sulbertson, Meredith, Rosario. He placed them mouth up.

For now.

"À l'honneur du Dr. Alois Frechet qui a sacrifié ça vie pour sauver la planet . . ."

Ned DuBois had cried only three times in his whole life. Now it was four.

"Chune sie guy doe jook hoa Ku Bai Deng gae ling yung ging kay ton ying yon gae tie hone bo hung . . ."

Meat Tucker reviewed the ECNs for the *Lariat*'s upcoming test flight in his office in Goddard City. Three engineering changes to the preflight checklist. One design mod to the electrical system. He clicked the hyperlink and verified that the mod had been installed and tested by the Earthside design team, then he E-mailed the ECNs to his electrical and mechanical leads and clicked on the flight manifest.

The supplies—food, water, oxygen, spare parts—had come up by ram pod and were confirmed in co-orbit by Goddard Roads STC. He toggled over to the station's yard engine schedule, located the next open slot, pasted the move requisition and the pod's transponder signal, and marked it Planetary Defense/13th Deep Space Wing/High Priority. It wasn't really, but that was the only way you got things done these days. If you needed clean underwear, you stamped it Planetary Defense/High Priority.

King Boudreaux knocked on the doorjamb of the project office and wriggled inside when Meat waved. The rigger aimed his cliputer at the workstation, downloading his completed work orders on the I/R beam. "All done?" Meat asked him.

"No problemo." King hesitated, floating by the workstation, and—when Meat looked a question—said, "Wasn't that Coughlin dude a skillet of yours?"

Meat had been trying hard not to think about that. Marooned on the Bean; probably dead. Better off dead. "Sorta." They gotten drunk together a couple times, and they used to shoot the shit about bad old days in North Orange; but they'd never been especially close. Meat wondered if anyone had ever gotten very close to Chase; or only to the image of Chase. Flaco and Bird weren't off the sharp end yet, and Meat felt closer to those two than he did to his former classmate.

"Real sorry about what happened, dude," said King.

"He knew what he was getting into."

"He put his life between us and the Bean."

Meat wasn't sure if that was what had motivated Chase. More likely, it had been the chance to strut his mojo; but that didn't change anything. In the end, when you had it to do, "why" didn't matter, and all that was left were those who did and those who didn't. He remembered how Chase used to loanshark back in high school. He'd got in Meat's face one time over payments, and Meat had pulled a screwdriver on him. After that, they'd gotten along.

Meat made a note to send a letter to Karen. Tough cases, her with a kid and all.

"Yeah," he said to an empty room long after King had gone, "he was my skillet."

This just in from DeepSpace in Geneva. FarTrip II has reported a successful rendezvous with the fueling pods left behind after the unfortunate . . .

Ed Wilson swirled the gin sling around in its highball glass, watching the bright liquor build in waves. Below him, in the dusk at the base of the bluff, yachts and sloops dropped sail as they coasted into their marinas. The breeze carried the sound of tin drums from somewhere out along the beach. He could see a driftwood fire and dancing silhouettes in the cove where the headland bent east.

Annarosa stepped onto the patio behind him and draped her arms over his shoulder. "Time for bed," she said. He leaned back in his chair, resting his head on her breasts.

"In a minute," he promised.

Fingers massaged his neck, working into the tired muscles. Wilson sucked in his breath and let it out slowly. "Oh. That feels good." He placed his drink on the glass table and leaned forward so she could work her magic on his spine.

"Are you done working now?"

He thought about the ram schedules, maintenance due at Antisana, creditors calling. There had been a window for a two-year rendezvous. Too long for a manned flight; but not for warheads on long-range missiles. But now the Bean had altered course, and the launch window for the missiles had vanished.

Gentle hands lifted his shirt and tugged it over his head. "You're worried," she said.

"Yes."

"Is there anything you can do about it tonight?"

"No."

He pulled her around to sit on his lap while he untied her shirttails and reached up under the bright, wind-fluttered fabric. Her nails traced circles through the grizzled hair on his chest. He fumbled with the snap on her shorts, the urgency rising in him.

Later, gazing over her smooth, golden flank gleaming in the milky river of light from the moon-haunted sky, he located a tiny dot a few degrees west of Luna. He fell asleep beneath her warmth with that sight fixed in his mind. It was only in his imagination that it grew steadily larger.

"Allahu Akbar! Subhan'Allah. La howla wa la quwatta illa billah . . ."

Hobie was perpetually astonished at the number of babies in the nursery. Ranked in rows and columns, in every color of the rainbow. Some lay quietly; some waved their arms and jerked their legs in a simulation of perpetual motion. Some cried; some watched the strange kaleidoscope of light and shadow that was all their eyes could take in. Some had hair so scant as to seem bald; others were as shaggy as Zog the Caveman. Even so, Hobie wondered how the nurses kept from mixing them up. He had checked the bracelet on Ladawan's wrist against the one on the baby's leg five times before he had let the nurse take Olethia from the birthing room. Old quality control habits: identification and traceability.

A giant's hand came down on his shoulder, and having seen the reflection of Big Mike Hobart in the nursery window, he turned and embraced his dad. "You made it!"

"Shortage of wild horses back home," Big Mike answered.

"Mom went to see your wife. She'll be right up. Which one is it?"

"The most beautiful one, of course."

"IQ test, hunh? Why not just throw a rock at my head? That one there, right?"

And wasn't that objective evidence of his daughter's transcendent beauty? (Or perhaps of Big Mike's keen eyesight in reading the name cards hanging on each crib; though he didn't believe that.) "We're calling her Olethia."

"Good choice. Grandma would have been proud." Big Mike leaned close to the glass. He rapped on the window with a knuckle and waved. "Very alert, too. And you'll have to chase the boys away with a stick when she's older. How's Ladawan?"

They chatted about women and babies for a moment. Then Big Mike spoke with sudden gravity. "Damn bad luck about Coughlin. He helped pull my brother, Azim, from a very nasty pickle when we were with the blue helmets in Skopje back in '09."

Big Mike and Azim had been Marines, and that made them brothers, never mind that Azim Thomas was Hobie's age—had in fact gone to school with Hobie. That was a part of his father's soul that Hobie could never share, a reminder that he could not have all of the man. "Yeah," Hobie said. "Chase, 'he the Man.' "

Big Mike gave him a look to see if he was being sarcastic. "Boy," he said, "he done his best out there. You can't say more about a man than that."

"I'm doing my best, too," Hobie said. "These magnetic ships, they'll give us extra chances . . ." But even in his own mind it sounded not at all heroic. "The test flights have been looking real good."

Big Mike's arm fell across his shoulders and squeezed him. "I know you're trying, boy. We all are. We got to show these Visitors what we're made of."

Hobie saw Olethia playing semaphore with her arms and

legs. *I promise you, babe. I didn't bring you into this world just to die.*

Every now and then, when she had the dog watch in *Mitchell,* Jacinta put the Bean in the crosshairs of the outside telescope and played the image on the flight deck's screens. Sometimes she wondered, through an intolerable sense of loss, whether she had made all the right decisions.

20.

Casting Dies

The operation was a success, and Roberta did not know until she started breathing again how important that was to her and to the world. Mariesa's was a voice that gave hope and vision. Her weekly multimedia web-postings spoke the courage that people needed. Now, more than ever. With the failure of FarTrip II, there would be no rabbits pulled from hats; there would be nothing but pain and death and grim determination.

Yet there was more to it than that. Other reasons why she had come to the hospital. People weren't valuable because they were useful, but simply because they were.

When Roberta strode through the doors at St. Joachim's, the security guard saluted her. He might not recognize the patch on her jacket—a pair of tumbling dice showing six and seven—but he knew it meant she was one of the Defenders. "They will not pass," he said—though Roberta thought his voice sounded less certain than it might have only last week.

Roberta did not answer the salute. It was one of her last defenses against the *orderliness* of society, against the regimentation that the defense effort had wrought. McRobb had taken recently to wearing a uniform—and that scared her more than the asteroids.

They will not pass! A brave cry. Perhaps a necessary cry. The drunk tanks and the hospitals and the morgues were filling with those who failed to cry it. Yet, the Bean would surely pass through their defenses. The GEO and FarSide Laser Arrays, nearly half-done, might boil a part of it away, might create jets of superheated plasmas, might nudge the sucker a little more to the west; but no one now supposed that it would fail to strike *somewhere.* And already senators from Pennsylvania to Missouri were raising "a voice of caution against expensive and ill-thought-out plans," even as the seaboard states were pushing for it.

In other words—on someone else's head be it.

Roberta put on her smile before she entered the room.

The knifelike odors were those of hospital rooms for the past hundred years. Antiseptic, plastic tubing, metal, freshly washed linen; the smells of bodies and fluids. The IV drips, beds, and monitors would have startled few physicians of the twentieth century, although they might have wondered a bit at the absence of sensors. How did the monitors know the pulse rate, the blood pressure, the body temperature without connecting wires?

Mariesa van Huyten looked well, considering that the Roto-Rooter man had been through her brain. There was an unsightly bruise on her left temple and her simple bob had been spoiled by a bare patch shaved just above the ear. She glanced away from the threedy when Roberta entered the room. "I look awful, don't I?"

The Rich Lady did not seem especially disturbed; but then she never had been one for fancy looks. "How do you feel?"

Mariesa considered the question for a moment. "Clean," she said. "That's an odd word to describe it, isn't it? But that's how it feels. Clean, clear, more alert than I have felt in years. It's as if I have been reborn. I should be in the nursery, not here" She laughed.

"You took a terrible chance with that *thing* running around your brain." Roberta twirled her finger around her head.

"We all do. Every morning, we cast the die." She gestured with her free hand to the patch on Roberta's shoulder. "I can't say I was lucky. Dr. O' Neil's engineering and Dr. Held's surgical skills were anything but luck. But, yes, there was always the chance the dice would crap out."

Roberta fidgeted. "Well, I just dropped by to see how you were."

"Just dropped by Florida? They told me you were here all through the operation."

Roberta flushed. "Sure. Okay. But I had business down here anyway. For the Thirteenth."

"Yes. How is the project doing these days? You understand, I've been out of the loop recently."

That was the understatement of the year. Roberta pulled out a chair and sat down at the bedside. The TV had been muted, but Roberta recognized HLV-2, *Fat Albert*, on the news loop. With forty-eight engines, half burning hydrogen and half RF-1, it made the most spectacular—and photogenic—lifts in recent memory. HLV-1 had delivered three entire Shuttle-loads in one lift, only to sink after splashdown. But Mark Two had now made several successful deliveries and two more Heavy Lift Vehicles were a-building in the Recife Yards and another at Vladivostok. "Affairs continue, I see," Mariesa said with a nod toward the screen. "The world hardly misses me."

"It does. More than you think," Roberta told her. "Your weekly postings were . . . inspirational? Is that too strong a word?"

"An old lady with an obsession."

"An obsession that might save us." Roberta toyed with a loose pleat of the bedsheet and spoke with hesitation. "When do you think you'll feel up to making another? Another web-dress, I mean."

"Oh, surely people are not so eager as all that to hear me speak!"

"Maybe. Everyone's pretty discouraged right now, because of . . ." The words choked and it was a moment before she could continue. "A few uplifting words . . . 'Never say die . . .' That sort of thing."

Mariesa said, "Ah," and it sounded like all the breath going out of her. "Chase." Her hand found Roberta's and covered it.

Roberta pulled her hand away. "It's not just Chase. The French scientist died, and the Russian pilot may never recover from the anoxia. The survivors still might not make—"

"Chase always was a difficult boy."

Roberta balled her fists and pressed them into her lap. "He didn't used to be! He used to be pretty damned simple! A bully. A groper. And not exactly a bright bulb. But, you know; he tried. He wanted to become something better; and thanks to you and Dr. Karr and, and Mr. Fast and Ned DuBois, he did." She brushed the corners of her eyes with her sleeve. "It just seems like such a fucking waste. He'd just become a guy worth knowing."

"It's like losing a member of your own family . . ."

Roberta started to say, "The Lucky Thirteenth isn't exactly a family," but then she realized that Mariesa had spoken to herself. They sat together in silence. She remembered Chase whispering lust in her ear as she walked into school. He had grabbed her breasts at a party and wore her handprint on his face for a week afterward. How would history have changed, she wondered, if she had been the sort to spread her legs for him? Everyone's lives ricocheting off in different directions; not only Chase and herself—no Prague poet, no space pilot—but others, too. Chase had helped Jenny Ribbon run away. If he'd been porking Roberta that night (and Roberta was not so foolish as to think that, having once given in, they would not have seized every opportunity thereafter), so no "Mother Smythe," which meant no silver apples, which meant no Jacinta Rosario. And Roberta had gotten Jimmy Poole and Tani Pandya together, which would have meant no tempering of Jimmy's more juvenile impulses by Tani's calm wisdom.

We create the world, she thought, *with every day we live. We can never say our lives make no difference.*

Then the threedy news cycled to a fire or an accident—something, at any rate, involving photogenic flame—and the Rich Lady blinked and sighed. She reached out once more and patted Roberta's hand. "Soon," she said. "I will post a 'thrilling exhortation,' complete with videos and links and all the rest. You'll help me write it, of course."

Roberta left shortly after. Somehow, the joy over the operation's success had become diluted by the general melancholy over Chase and the expedition's failure. She hardly noticed where she was going, even as she thought, *Can't let da funk get you.*

A hand on her arm stopped her, startled her, caused her to suck in her breath and take a sudden, panicked step away. Then—

"Mr. Fast?" And why, after all these years, did she still call him 'mister'?" It wasn't as if she had shown much respect to any of her high school teachers. Yet, here she was, mid-thirties, and he, mid-sixties. Why did the gulf now seem so much narrower?

"How is she?" His voice was husky. It quavered. It never occurred to Roberta to ask him who "she" was. For both of them, ex-husband and ex-Alecto, there was only one "she."

"She came through fine. No complications."

Fast nodded. He was tall and broad-shouldered, though age had bent and withered him just a little. His smile had the remarkable property of lighting his face. Roberta remembered that from high school: that Mr. Fast had always smiled as if he meant it. "That's good," he said. "That's good. They wouldn't tell me anything, you know. I used to be her husband, dammit; but they wouldn't tell me anything. No complications, you said?"

"Good as new."

"That's great news." He pressed his palms together, rubbed them once, twice. "Well . . ." He turned to go. This time, it was Roberta who seized an arm.

"It's still visiting hours. Go in and see her."

He shook his head. "No, she wouldn't . . . I only came down to see if she . . ." He fumbled after words even as they ran from him; then, after a pause, "We didn't exactly part on good terms."

"You still love her," Roberta said with sudden astonishment.

"I don't know if I would call it . . ."

"What else can you call it, you fly down here from Jersey and hang around in the waiting room, just to find out how her operation went, when you could've stayed home and read it in tomorrow's papers?"

"Okay, I . . ." He ran his hand through thinning hair and looked off, over his shoulder, at the doorway. "Yeah, I guess I always have. The whole thing—the breakup—was my own stupid fault."

"She's not so rich anymore, you know. Not unless the Defense Bonds pay off someday. Most of her wealth went into the bonds."

He shook his head. "I never married her for the money. The money was always more of an impediment than anything else."

"Well, the bonds pay off more years down the road than she's likely to collect."

He suddenly grinned, and again that huge amusement broke through his face, as if the whole world were a joke and he had just now gotten the punch line. "Don't sell her short. She always had an eye for the dime. I wouldn't put it past her to hang tough long enough to see those bonds mature."

Roberta laughed, then sobered. "If *any* of us survive that long."

"I wouldn't worry about Impact. Mariesa would never permit it."

Roberta's tracey warbled the opening stanzas of "The Ode to Joy." Colonel Eatinger, she saw, glancing at her wrist. "I've got to take this call, Barry. You will go in and see her. I think it'll do some good." For one of them; perhaps for both. When Barry had passed from sight, she touched <answer> and Colonel Eatinger's face appeared on the wrist screen. He was grinning ear to ear.

"Better hop up here," he said. "We just got the Goddamnedest long-distance call in history."

Mariesa heard the door open and close once more and thought for a moment that Roberta had forgotten something and had returned; but it was Barry Fast who lowered himself into the chair beside her bed. Mariesa was so astonished that she could think of nothing to say.

Barry sat for a while with one hand cupped in the other until the silence had filled to almost bursting. Then he pricked it with a single, "Hi."

Mariesa's breath gusted out of her. "Barry," she said.

"I ran into your protégée outside." A nod of his head caused the pale curls on his forehead to dance. "She told me the operation went all right."

"Yes," she said. "The old gal's brain is scrubbed clean."

Barry nodded, squirmed in his seat, made to rise. "Well," he said, "I just thought I'd check . . ." But he paused as if paralyzed when Mariesa laid a hand on his forearm.

"Wait. Tell me . . . how have you been getting on."

"Oh—" He made a vague gesture. "Well enough."

"And that school of yours? The one in North Orange."

"Discovery School." He nodded and his eyes took on a livelier gleam. "Still going strong. The Dip almost killed us—we were this close to shutting down—but the mothers wouldn't let it happen. All the kids—our graduates, too—their mothers started showing up—and more and more, there are fathers, too. They cleaned the building. They cooked the meals. They did story time for the Ks and pre-Ks, and ran the day care. Carlos Sulbertson—his son was one of our first graduates—he brought boards and window plastic and half a dozen ex-bangers and they fixed everything that had broken except the furnace and the wiring." A brief smile creased his face. "You know how sometimes you wonder if anything you're doing matters a damn? Well, no one planned all that. It just happened. The word went around the 'hood and even the NO-men pitched in. I've never been told in plainer words by people with no ease with words that I made a difference to them. We've got our third charter, now—over in Eastport, this one."

This was a man, Mariesa remembered, who loved teaching. He came more alive when he spoke of it. "And the furnace?" she asked. "And the wiring?"

He shrugged with his hands. "An anonymous donation. A heating and electrical contractor pulled up to the school one day, and replaced everything, all bought and paid for."

"A donation."

"Anonymous."

They looked at each other quietly. "It must have cost a lot of money," Barry said after a while.

"I should think so," Mariesa answered. "But undoubtedly the donor considered it well spent."

Somewhere along the way, his hand, large and stubby-fingered, had covered hers. But that was just like him. He sneaked up on you, and before you knew it, he was in your life. "You're still plugging away," he said.

"Oh. One does what one can."

"I was worried."

The abrupt shift in tone caught her off guard. "Worried? About what?" A dozen possibilities flashed through her thoughts. Losing the school. The oncoming asteroid.

"I was afraid I would lose you."

"Lose me?" Gently, she extricated her hand from under his.

"Lose me? Barry, you lost me years and years ago."

He shook his head. "No. I lost a lot of things. Position, companionship, your love and my self-respect." His quirky smile flashed briefly. "Even Harriet's nagging. But I never lost *you*. The stroke, last year? I thought . . . I thought . . ." He stopped and took a breath and looked away out the window at the palm trees and sunlight. There were tears in his eyes, she saw.

"Tell me, Barry, what ever happened to . . . her?" There it was: the dread pronoun. She had known from the moment she saw him settle in the chair that she would speak that pronoun. In all the years since he had shown her Attwood's blackmail pictures, she had never spoken the woman's name.

"What?" He turned back from the window. "Shannon? Nothing. She moved to California. Her daughter was in school there and fell sick and Shannon went out to take care of her and decided she liked it there." He shrugged hugely, sadly. "That was the year after John died. Her husband. Maybe she was looking to make a new start. A clean break. I don't know. She needed someone for a while, and I was it. After a while, she didn't need someone anymore. Me . . ." He shook himself. "I wallow in the past too much."

And so the succubus was gone. Mariesa had not thought of the other woman in years and was surprised now to feel no hatred for her. Perhaps the Bean had made all such emotions trivial and irrelevant. "You wouldn't recognize Silverpond anymore," she said.

"I know. I've brought some classes out there." Teeth flashed. "Almost didn't recognize Roy." He grimaced. "Can't say I didn't feel a pang when you deeded the place to the Conservancy, but even though I lived there for five years, it was never really home to me. I never felt I belonged there."

"I don't belong there anymore, either," Mariesa said. "And I mortgaged and sold all my other residences for the defense effort."

"A poor, old homeless lady," said Barry with a grin and a

pat on her arm. "I've got a spare room. Maybe I'll take you in."

Mariesa laughed—but she shivered a little, too. His touch had conjured a host of memories from her body; and his words, though spoken in jest, had been spoken in earnest, too.

Jim Poole, Space Ranger! tacked his way up through the magnetosphere. This was the tedious part: climbing up from LEO in polar orbit, patiently kicking at perigee over magnetic north, where the field lines converged, until the ship was past the Van Allen headlands and caught the solar wind into open space. He needed three klicks delta to get over GEO Ridge and onto the flats around L-1 and there weren't no easy way to get 'em.

This would be a tough flight plan, but he was up to it. L-1 to L-4 to L-2 to L-5. One point shy of the Grand Tour, but close enough. He'd leave a Hobie parasol at each location, rigged with staysails to keep them from drifting off—especially at L-1, a potentially valuable staging yard for moonside shipments, but notoriously unstable. Programming the parasols had been a cute piece of hackery, what with the wind pulses caused by the "pinwheel" effect of the spinning sun. The sails had to be continually trimmed, lest the wind itself knock the parasol off the flats and into Luna Gulch or—worse—into Big Earth Canyon. But if Hobie could demonstrate that magsails could be used as skyhooks to keep satellites and pods stationary . . .

A challenge, yes; but Jim Poole (Space Ranger!) was up to it. His heart hammered at the thought and he wiped his suddenly moist palms on his jeans. Sailing the Big Empty was like approaching Tani—it made him scared and eager at the same time.

"We'll skip the intermediate phase," said the voice of Billie Whistle, "and go straight to the L-1 drop-off maneuver."

It was always a jar to shift his focus from the simulation to reality. A moment of disorientation. The stars beyond the viewport became mere lights; the Moon, only an image. The breath leaked out of him. It wasn't the same thing. It didn't have the same hold on his gut. He knew that real-timing the complete mission was neither practical nor useful. He couldn't spend days in the booth, and most of the flight was routine. Still, he hated to come out of the zone. "Wait one," he said, "while I reorient." The scene shifter replaced the view from LEO with the view from the approaches to L-1. The panel readouts reconfigured. Jimmy switched the A/S from *Harbor Pilot* to *Sailing Master.* Navigating in the wind was different from navigating in the magnetosphere. He glanced at the flight plan on the auxiliary screen and refreshed himself on the upcoming action items. "Okay, babe," he said when he was ready, "let's make it happen."

Afterward, when the exercise had concluded and he had donned his mirrorshades and kicked at the desk he sometimes used when he came to Building 29, he realized Billie Whistle was staring at him from her console across the room.

At first, he was not aware of it. He was thinking of a half-dozen things at once. Stevie's sixth birthday party; the school arrangements for first grade; Tani in the moonlight when he had pointed out to her the tiny speck of the Bean; flight plans for *Lariat*'s upcoming "Grand Tour"; reconfiguring the trim programming to compensate for the yaw discovered in last month's test: exploring the notion of "emergent programs" implicit in the Visitors' micro-automata. He had always imagined his brain as a massively parallel quantum processor, able to condense solutions simultaneously to multiple problems.

That was why he could stuff those last few minutes in the Bean's control room—before Uncle Waldo fried and the teep channel went black—into their own separate partition, where he could run the scenario over and over without bottlenecking other, more pending thoughts.

Gradually, he became aware of Billie Whistle's regard. He

looked up from his screen to see her two dark eyes boring into him.

"What?" in tones of annoyance.

Billie shook her head. "Nothing." She turned her powered chair away and went back to hacking cheese. Jimmy still hadn't gotten used to the prosthetic arm, so lifelike it sent chills up his spine. Adam van Huyten had bought it for her—for whatever reason only Adam and Billie knew. But why anyone would give up their interface for a simulated human limb escaped him. It seemed unnatural. Why limit yourself to arm's length when you could reach into cyberspace itself? At least she had kept the skull implants.

A few minutes later, Billie's sigh broke the silence. Jimmy swiveled his chair. "Something's bothering you."

Billie Whistle had a lean, predatory face, one that transmuted any expression into one of hunger. "It's been over a week and you haven't said word one about Chase Coughlin."

Jimmy blinked. "Was I supposed to?"

"You knew him from the time you were kids."

"Yeah, but that wasn't my idea."

Billie made a sound in her throat and Jimmy's computer shut down.

"Hey," he said, "don't do that!"

"Didn't what happened mean anything to you?"

"Mean anything? Mean anything?" Jimmy stood up and his chair rolled away from under him. "*I was there!* I watched the whole thing and I couldn't do a damn thing about it. Everything I tried was seven seconds behind the curve. Waldo had no leverage! I couldn't do anything!" He started to sit, missed his chair, and fumbled after it. He sat down again. "I couldn't do anything," he said more slowly.

Billie seemed taken aback. "I'm . . . sorry."

Chase had been too slow. He should have hit the abort right away. Jimmy had seen that right off, but Chase hadn't caught on until it was too late. Blue meant "off" or "stop" or "chill out" or however the aliens had conceptualized the notion. So what else could a flashing blue button have meant? Now, Chase had paid the price for his slow-wittedness.

Too bad, but at least he wouldn't be ragging on Jimmy anymore. No more sneers. No more put-downs. No more peeking at Jimmy in the locker-room shower stall while Jimmy de-stressed after gym . . .

And yet, there was a curious emptiness in his chest.

He still hadn't keyed another entry, he had not even turned around to face his terminal again, when Colonel Eatinger entered the office. Eatinger was not Jimmy's idea of a military man. Thin, gentle-voiced, scholarly, not a man of action—though the row of ribbons on his chest might contradict that if Jimmy knew how to read them. "Jimmy," Eatinger said. "Jimmy! Change of plans. The test flight's canceled."

He should have caught on earlier, warned Chase sooner. FarTrip II's failure was his fault and the hell of it was, no one knew that but himself. He shook himself. "Canceled? What do you mean?"

And Billie Whistle groaned. "Not now . . ."

Eatinger's face was a mixture of emotions that Jimmy could not read. "Coughlin's alive," he said. "He field-repaired the commlink on one of the waldos."

"Alive . . . ? But . . ." *But what good does that do?* was the first thought that popped in his head. Wasn't it better to die fast than slow?

Eatinger read his mind. "He figures he has water and air to last another week and a half, maybe a little longer if Meredith's reducing furnace is still working. He's been taking sightings, laying out the Bean's orbit. He wants to recalibrate the firing program for the remaining rocket motors, the ones that weren't destroyed in the chaos. Do you understand? *We've still got a shot at diverting the Bean!*"

"But why do we have to cancel the . . . ?"

"He wants *you* to do the reprogramming."

Jimmy hesitated. "Me? That's whitebread hack. Your grandmother could do it, if she had the cheese."

Eatinger shook his head. "He asked for you. He said, we only get one more shot at those rockets and he wants to be damn sure it gets done right. And that, he said, means Jimmy Poole does it."

Jimmy was silent a long while, staring down at hands balled in his lap. When he looked up, he looked at Billie. "Chase said that?"

"He said that," Eatinger answered. "Now do you see why we have to cancel the test flight? This is far more urgent."

"Colonel," said Jimmy, "can you walk and chew gum at the same time? 'Cause I sure as hell can fly the *Lariat* and noodle some kindergarten ballistic code at the same time. Ever hear of telecommuting?"

Eatinger might have had a comeback to that, but Jimmy never heard it. Instead, Jimmy had a sudden vision. An idea so *phat,* so *stoopid,* so phucking *there,* that for a moment it occupied his entire universe, crowding out everything else in his life. He gazed at the wall over Billie's head, seeing through the window overlooking the simulator, where silver moon gleamed in charcoal sky, as if the solar system had been captured and imprisoned within the walls of the sim room.

"We'll just have to rewrite the flight plan a little, is all."

21.

Voices, Crying in the Wilderness

The value of a thing, Chase had read one time, was determined by its scarcity and demand; and so for both reasons his days grew increasingly precious. There weren't that many left and he needed every one. The first of them he spent taking inventory in the wreck of the *Cochran* and its now-detached Salyut, and when it had been spent, he became acutely conscious that that was one day fewer left to him. And yet, he must not succumb to melancholy. Despair meant paralysis, and there was work to be done, which he set to with grim determination. If the Bean did strike the Earth, he did not want anyone to say that Chase Coughlin had not done all he could to prevent it. Not that he would personally care by then—unless his mother had been right all along about heavens and hells—but he wanted Karen and Little Chase to hold their heads up, high and proud. Little enough compensation for husband and father lost: but better coin than shame.

But to accomplish anything he had to ensure his own survival. Power, first. The Salyut's solar panels had become a million shards sparkling among the rocks or hovering in a shimmering trail that only gradually was settling toward the ground; and the power beam receptor on *Cochran*'s fuselage had wound up under the wreckage. The nuclear pile was intact, however; and promised to yield electricity for far longer than Chase was likely to have any personal need.

The ship itself was irreparably breached—the entire nose had been torn away—but the Salyut had survived and could sustain temperature and pressure. It was a straightforward matter to salvage cable and run it from the ship's pile to the Salyut's power inputs. *Let there be light,* he thought when he tested his handiwork. *Not to mention air and water regeneration.* And so it was.

That was morning and evening of the first day.

On the second day, he inspected the rockets that Flaco and Bird had installed, checking the integrity of each, verifying the command circuits, making notes on his wrist pad. It was a routine but absorbing task and for long stretches Chase would forget his situation. Then a chance glimpse of stars or wreckage or simply a pause for rest would bring it all back like a kick to the belly. He was never going home. Ever. And the last thing he would see in life would be not Karen's love or his son's smile, but endless emptiness and lonely desolation. When such thoughts stole upon him he concentrated more narrowly on the task at hand, blotting out everything else; but once, the sorrow came on so overwhelmingly that he let go his tools and floated on a tether clipped to engine South-Four and sobbed uncontrollably—not at all the chin-up, stiff-lipped behavior tradition demanded of its heroes.

Sleep was something he begrudged. Minutes were too valuable to be wasted. Yet on the other hand the objective was too important to trust to a groggy, bemused mind; and so he rationed out a few carefully measured hours, spent in troubled dreams in which Karen and his son stared at him in mute accusation. *You could have done something,* their eyes told him. *You could have come back somehow.* Their faces receded, fading into the dark, even as his fingers clutched for them, and he awoke feeling desperate and alone. The urgency of his work was not the only reason he avoided sleep.

He didn't even have their picture. That hurt most of all. The threedy of his family had gone with *Mitchell.* And he would never see them again.

Day and night became places, not times; separated, distilled to their essence, then confined each to its own hemisphere of the Bean. Without morning and evening to mark them, or a steady evolution of the heavens, he lost track of the days. The sky was iron glass: black, but at the same time transparent and possessed of infinite thickness, bursting with distant lights. Gradually, he came to accept these lights as huge balls of spinning plasma embedded in the crystalline heavens; and the great flow of white that ran like a ribbon across the sky as a starswarm so numerous and so distant that enumeration and distance alike lost all meaning, the individuality of particular suns as lost as a man's voice in the murmur of a vast crowd. It pressed down on him, hard, what an insignificant sliver he was in the vast, empty ocean of night.

With acceleration stopped, there was no longer a sense of motion on the Bean. There was no way to gauge his progress against the unchanging backdrop of stars. Perhaps the emerald crescent of the Earth crept slowly eastward against the sky; while gleaming Venus, west of the sun, moved toward her transit; and ruby Mars, perversely retrograde, slipped behind the solar disk. But it was a slow, almost stealthy motion, as if the planets moved only when he wasn't looking, giving no hint of the headlong velocities with which he and the Bean hurtled deeper into the void.

At times, his world seemed to have no edge to it. Iron ground blended into iron sky. Glittering fragments of PV cells scattered on the asteroid's ravaged surface simulated additional stars, until the mind accepted the ground as only as especially solid chunk of sky. At such times, Chase would stand in the SPP viewing bubble in Salyut's nose and imagine that he was still en route, had not yet reached the Bean, and that somehow the calamities that haunted his waking hours were but a bad dream.

Beantown Power and Light, its solar tower held in place by guy wires, had survived the acceleration without toppling, though a rain of loose rock and debris had damaged it and torn loose connectors and wires and shattered one of the solar mirrors. It took a solid day to trace the malfs and reestablish connections, but when he had finished, the grid of work lights that Jacinta had staged across the face of the Bean glowed once again, revealing a landscape of craters and ridges and spoiling the illusion of seamlessness with the sky. Afterward, just before sleep, Chase would sometimes turn the lights off again to re-create the vision of endless night—the illusion of flying en route. Thus did he separate the night from the day and reinvoke the passage of time.

Chase was not a very talkative man. He might have, in a moment of reflection, traced that to his father's command of "No back talk," enforced with offhanded cuffs. But he never wasted time in what-if or might-have-been and, in any event, he had long ago come to terms with his dad—once he had reached a size when "No back talk" could no longer be physically enforced and long-held words had gushed forth to the benefit of both and, perhaps, the salvation of one—for Danny Coughlin had never lifted his hand in anger since that day.

However it had happened, Chase had grown into the "tall and silent" sort, as he sometimes described himself. Save for the odd joke or banter, he spent most conversations just listening, which was no mean accomplishment. Many—like Jimmy Poole—had never mastered it. Still, words held back did accumulate and every now and then he had to unstopper the bottle and pour them out. This was more difficult to do alone, as he had an aversion to talking to himself, and so he resorted to Tanuja Pandya's recorder.

There was little chance that Tani would ever hear it. The world had deeper concerns. If he succeeded and the Bean missed, no one would ever bother chasing the asteroid just to fetch a micro-CD. And if he failed, µCD, *Cochran,* spiders, flex-mats, Big Engine, the Intelligence the asteroid itself and whatever was left by then of Chase Coughlin would ignite and explode in the Earth's boiling atmosphere.

It sounded phat stoopid. He almost wished he'd be around to see it.

All boosters confirmed as operational, except the northside cluster that Cochran *smashed up. Command and firing circuits tested and verified. Ditto on the explosives that Yvgeny and Lonzo buried. I've taken a series of bearings on Earth, Mars, and some of the fixed stars that should be enough to establish an orbit. I've got everything I need to finish the job except the firing plan. Still no contact Earthside. Be a hell of a note to get this rock all prepped then not know when to light the torch. I may just have to blow it up, and me on it.*

It's a weird thing, but I don't think I'm alone here.

Something moving out there . . . It's gotta be the Visitor spiders, right?

I just hope nobody knocks on my door tonight.

I figure there's enough food on Cochran *to last a lifetime. Of course, a lifetime's not so long anymore . . . <laughter, cut off short.> Jesus, that wasn't very funny. But this ship was supposed to feed a crew of four, and it carried extra rations besides, in case we missed a pod rendezvous or two. Today, I had Salisbury steak with mushroom gravy, green beans, and mashed potatoes. I'm no kind of gourmet, but it didn't taste especially good. Maybe I should send for takeout.*

Plenty of food, then. And the air gets scrubbed and recirculated (so I get to breathe the same molecules over and over. Wonder if they ever get worn out?). Ditto for the water—though I don't even want to think about that *recycle loop. Theoretically, I can last here for a long time. Robinson Crusoe, that's me, I got my hut, my food and water, my power . . . But where's Friday?*

Who am I kidding? Something will break down before too long. We don't build for the eons, like the Visitors. The air scrubbers will clog up, I'll use the last spare plug-in filter, and the CO_2, *will accumulate and choke me. The zeolite plants are already turning brown, so* something *isn't right. Or maybe the water will slowly poison out. Or there'll be a solar storm and I'll get sleeted by radiation without ever knowing it happened. Life sucks; but it beats the alternative.*

I found Alois today. He was sitting upright in the craterlet we named Agamemnon, just over on darkside. His suit was badly battered. Faceplate cracked. Right arm ripped almost the whole length. Thermo-regulator on his D&C module torn loose. Whatever oxygen didn't escape his suit settled out as frost on his cheeks and brow, so he was white as Frosty the Snowman, except where the blood had dried around his eyes and nose—which come to think of it did look like coals. He looked goddamn peaceful, froze up the way he was. God, I hope he asphyxiated before decompression burst him open.

About half his sleeve was wrapped up with the emergency

repair adhesive fabric. I liked that. I like someone who doesn't quit just because it's hopeless.

Never knew how lonely it was here until I stumbled on Alois. I can chatter all I want on this recorder, but I ain't getting bounceback, and I find . . . I miss it. What I wouldn't give to hear Karen's voice, or deal with Little Chase's endless unanswerable questions, or listen to Roberta read her poems or even whine about some new injustice she's discovered. Hell, I wouldn't mind playing the nines with Jimmy Poole at this point. He ain't maybe the best company in the world, but believe it or not, he's a couple cuts above none.

You know, Tani, when we were at Witherspoon together, I thought a lot about getting you between the sheets at the Bunny Wunny Motel down on Lenape Street.

Surprised?

You know where I mean . . . or maybe not. Hell, you probably didn't know the Bunny Wunny existed. Not your side of town at all. There weren't any pinned virgins back then—they'd've been laughed at, not paraded as role models—but I figured you "brains" didn't even know how to do it, so I used to dream about how I'd teach you. Not that I knew shit back then, either; but I thought I did.

The first time I got laid . . . I can't even remember her name. Dull brown hair and plain-looking, but lips that wouldn't quit. After that, I was looking for it every chance I got. Hardly ever got it, but I hit the jackpot often enough to keep me plugging the quarters in. I even slicked Greg Prescott once, when his girlfriend, Leilah, got drunk at a party. He'd been porking another cheerleader on the side and she found out and got her revenge behind some trees in her backyard. She sure had great pom-poms.

Jacinta . . . I think another couple months inside Mitchell *and I would have been inside her. It's not something I wanted, and it certainly wasn't something she wanted, but I could see it coming as sure as the astronomers could track the Bean. I could see her weakening. Abstinence is a whole lot easier* before *you've bitten the apple. Afterward . . . Well, if there's food lying on the table, sooner or later you get hungry enough to nibble.*

Not that it was all physical. I liked *Jacinta. I think you could say I loved her even if you kept sex out of it. In the end . . . I never met Morrisey except that one time, but he is one lucky dude. And the way Jacinta smiles when she talks about him . . . well, I just couldn't wipe that smile off her face, could I? So, I guess it's best for all of us—Jacinta, Morrisey, Karen, even me—that things turned out the way they did.*

But, Tani my big jones was always Styx.

I'll pause here while you pick your jaw up off the floor.

Yeah, she used to dress like death warmed over; but I always thought her and me were a pair. Outsiders. You and Jimmy and Jenny Ribbon and all the others, you were inside *the system. Even Meat Tucker. He was coasting, not taking anything too serious, but he was coasting on the inside. But Styx and me—and Azim Thomas, too, now that I think about it—we were on the outside, and glad of it. Hell, maybe even Azim really* wanted *in—like a kid pressing his nose up against the window of a candy store. But Styx and me, we didn't even want the candy.*

I put some moves on her once or twice, but she wasn't having it. Which is too damned bad, because now neither of us have those memories to look back on. I think the two of us could have been emperors of the world if we'd joined up. But we went our separate ways. She fled to Prague to be a famous poet; me, to flight school and then to the Moon with Ned DuBois. I ran into her once at a reunion, but it wasn't until she roped me into Project Lariat that we really saw all that much of each other again, and by then she was a widow and I was happily married.

But you know what? She was still hot. I can close my eyes and see us in the sack together, all wrapped around each other, me staring into those bottomless eyes of hers while we pushed and shoved. I always imagined it as sharp as broken glass. Love like a knife. The sort of thing you'd come away exhausted, and glad enough to do it all again. I think Roberta felt something, too, but that's probably the ol' ego talking.

But here's the strange thing. Here I am, marooned on a fucking asteroid, never a chance of getting back, free to fantasize to my heart's content—you, or Styx, Jacinta, Leilah, a parade of the "shameless nameless," threedy stars or screen morphs I haven't a hope of ever sacking—and what is it I keep thinking about?

Karen and me, the night we got married.

Go figure.

Waldo lives!

I didn't find many mobile teeping units when I did the survey three . . . five? A couple days ago. I figured most of them got tumbled free when the Bean took off and they're a bunch of klicks aft by now, floating in the void. Those I did find were smashed. Not as durable as the spiders, and they don't have those weird gripping feet that actually sink into the rock. (I wish I knew how that trick worked.) So Waldo got royally scragged.

Except one unit. Some dude at DeepSpace was trying to reactivate it and wasn't having too much luck. The main bus from the rectenna was loose, so the Earthside signal was only coming through intermittently, which is why I thought it was dead the one time I saw it. But it musta been him I seen moving around before. I don't know what the teeper was trying to accomplish. Maybe he wanted to study the Bean. Maybe a cow likes to study the knacker's hammer. Doesn't matter. I reconnected the wire and stood in front of his optics and waved and waited.

He must have crapped his pants back there in Geneva or wherever the hell he was teeping from. I plugged my jack into his socket and told him to patch me through to Jimmy Poole at Project Lariat. What I got on the bounceback was someone saying, "You're alive!" Well, hell, I knew that already, so I told him again how I wanted to talk to the Wizard of Baud. So, he passes me back to DeepSpace, which shunts me to Lariat, and Colonel Eatinger gets on-line, who hands me off to Styx while he goes dweeb-hunting.

I definitely gotta do something about phone service out here.

So. What do you say to a dead man? Chase heard that in Roberta's voice, in her every cadence. He heard it in the way she danced around the subject of his "situation." Oddly, Chase found himself resenting that; as if, having come himself to a measure of acceptance, he found her discomfiture vaguely offensive. Besides, he wasn't dead yet; only survival-challenged.

"I don't need your sympathy," he said, interrupting her hesitant remarks. "And I need cheerfulness even less." Chase had guided Waldo back inside Salyut. Wouldn't do to get into a heavy discussion outside and forget he was on bottled air. Roberta was code-dancing from a pee-phone crypt at some Florida airport and he was kicking in a ruined spacecraft on a receding asteroid. Reach out and touch someone.

"All I said," the reply came after the requisite lag, or perhaps a little longer, "was that I admired your determination."

"Yeah, stiff upper lips came with the standard issue kit. Admire it all you want, but I'd trade places with you in an instant." But bitterness wore harsher on his tongue than in her ears, and he regretted the words even as he spoke them. It wasn't anyone's *fault* that he'd been stuck here: and telling Styx he'd rather she was here instead of him was less than kind. "Ah, hell, Styxy. We got to do what we got to do. You find Jimmy yet?"

"Eatinger thinks he's in the simulator. There's a major test flight coming up."

"Yeah," said Chase. And that should have been *him* back

there safe and sound in the bosom of Project Lariat. But if life had gone that way, someone else would have been here, instead; or worse, one of the two surviving ships would have had more people on board than its systems could support. Or maybe nothing would have happened because everything would have gone different. It was useless to speculate. "How's the weenie doing?"

A longer pause in which the static of the sun and planets hissed. "Not bad," Roberta said at last. "It's like Jimmy said, 'Everyone's a nooboo for this kind of ship.' Thing is—maybe I shouldn't tell you this—but I think he's terrified of deep space. Oh, he rhapsodizes about the beauty and the vastness and all the rest of it, but I've seen pure fright in his eyes whenever he's about to go ziggy."

Chase couldn't put his finger on it, but her use of "ziggy" rubbed him wrong. Roberta hadn't earned the right to talk that way. Oddly, too, he resented her remark about Jimmy's fear of hard vacuum and radioactive sleet. What did she know about it? What did anyone know, except those who done it? It was a peculiar brotherhood that embraced both Jimmy Poole and Chase Coughlin, but there it was. Waldo watched him through lenses lacking all expression. Chase felt like a bug on a slide.

"Get Jimmy on the line," he said. "I'd like to get the reprogramming done before"—he hesitated only a moment—"before too long." He'd almost said *before my air or water or power give out,* but however much that thought might concern him, he refused to troll for pity. If others mistook that for bravery, that was their problem. The world had too many whiners already; it didn't need one more.

"Do you . . . want me to rig a connection with Karen? For later?"

Chase sucked in his breath. Styx always did have a talent for the jugular. He brushed at his face with his sleeve; studied the dying plants in the zeolite trays; watched the slow dance of a dangling hammock. He really ought to stow the thing properly. Batching it was all well and good, but what if some-one came calling? Almost, he laughed, but he could never have explained why to Roberta. Still, even a virtual visitor was a visitor. Chase pulled down one of the fold-out chairs out of line-of-sight of the messy housekeeping and clipped himself into it. "What would that accomplish?" he asked gruffly. The idea of talking to Karen terrified him. What could they say to each other? *Honey, don't wait dinner for me.*

"I thought . . ."

"Yeah, sure. Of course, I want to talk to her." *Just to hear her voice again. Just to say good-bye.* That was what Roberta had meant, but since when had she grown so damn delicate not to say so flat out? The bounceback was a long time com-ing. When it did, Chase heard a different note in her voice.

"The colonel has Jimmy. I'll switch you over. They . . . have a plan."

A plan, Chase thought. Jimmy was a top hacker—Mr. Cheeze Whiz, they said—but he could not possibly have worked up the new firing program in the time it took him to answer the phone. He didn't even know the number and placement of the motors. What sort of plan could he have?

Jimmy told him, and Chase's universe had to realign itself.

"Come out to the Bean in the *Lariat*? Are you whack? In case you haven't noticed, herbert, that's just shy of three-quarters of a million miles. And rising. It took us a couple months to get here in the first place and I"—it was a moment for ragged truth, and firm control of his voice—"I can't hold out that long. So let's just cut to the programming and can the comic book action plot."

"Chase," said Jimmy in the slow, patient tones that always set Chase's teeth on edge, "the *Lariat* can get a steady ac-celeration of one-thousandth of a gee, and—"

"A milli-gee? Whoa! Roadrunner, move over."

"Beep-beep, dude. That a milli-gee *constant boost.* You pay attention when you were training for this, or were you too busy pumping your handle? Go ahead, work the numbers."

Chase scowled. He'd been otherwise occupied; but now that he thought about it . . . He summoned the equations from the Salyut's deeby while Jimmy was still gum-flapping and found the equations of motion for falling bodies. Falling in Earth's gravity field was constant, one-gee boost. Elapsed time equals the square root of distance over half the acceleration. So, plug in point-oh-oh-one, instead, and . . . Hold it. Convert everything to a common base. How many centimeters in seven hundred thousand miles? Good thing there was a conversion filter for measurements. He finished the entries and the answer popped up on the spreadsheet. "Holy shit!" He checked again to see if he had entered the right figures.

"Right," said Jimmy. "I've got to match vectors, overshoot, then quench the loop and let the sun slow me to the right speed; but the way I figure, even with the tacking, I'll be there in eight days, more or less. Can you hang on until then?"

Chase, still stunned by the figures, said, "Eight days? Jesus. If I have to, I can hold my freaking breath that long."

"Good," said Jimmy. "Make sure the hardware's ready when I get there. I'll work your ballistic problem en route. Wait for me."

Chase gave Waldo the Look. "I wasn't figuring on goin' nowhere."

Afterward, when the connection had been broken, Chase returned to the suit locker. He'd been on his way to Total's smelter when he had encountered Waldo. He'd had some notion of coaxing a little more oxygen from the regolith. But for a moment, he couldn't even mount the suit in its rack, his hands shook so. His breath came short. His heart hammered and he found that his palms had gone damp with fear. He rubbed them against his trouser legs and wondered if maybe he ought to just kick for the next couple days. Short of a catastrophic failure, the recycler would supply air for well more than eight days, and every time he EVAded, he threw the dice against old No-Nose. A suit tear. A micrometeor hit. A solar storm. An accident—with the smelter spraying him with metallic plasma. He didn't *need* the extra oxygen, now; so why take chances?

If there was one thing that could hurt worse than despair and impending death, one thing that could slice through his belly like a knife, it was hope.

22.

Bread, Upon the Waters

Jimmy told Tani about his plan, and sat back in his chair at the dining table and waited with a broad and expectant grin on his face. It wasn't a long wait. Tani paused with a soup spoon half raised to her mouth, looked first skeptical, then astonished. The spoon clattered into the bowl spattering her beige blouse with red.

"Jimmy," she said, "you can't be serious!"

"It's the only way, Tani," he answered in serious tones. "*Lariat*'s the only ship humanity has that can reach the Bean fast enough."

"But why do *you* have to do it, Jimmy!" She pushed her bowl away and stood, walking rapidly to the living room. Jimmy, who thought it was perfectly obvious why he had to do it—no one else knew how to fly a magship—sat astonished at the table. Stassy had just brought the tureen out and now she looked around the table flustered. Jimmy motioned to her to serve Stevie, dabbed his lips with a napkin, and hurried after his wife. "Keep the soup warm," he told the cook, though she probably would have done so in any case. Rada, at the other end of the table, watched everything with cynical eyes and a knowing smirk and took Stevie in charge.

Jimmy found Tani by the big bay windows that opened on the back lawn and he came up behind her, placing his hands on her waist. "Tani, a man's gotta do what a man's gotta do."

She twisted away from him. "Don't give me that movie matinee crap! I want to know why you're taking the *Lariat* out to the Bean!"

"It's a dirty job, but someone's got to do it."

She turned and impaled him with a finger. "How many goddamn clichés are you going to throw up? Because I'm telling you, Steven James Poole, Senior. I'll knock every one of them down!"

Jimmy sighed. Maybe he should have known not to go for laughs. "All right," he said more seriously. "Who else is there?"

"No one . . ." this reluctantly. "But you could teep it. You could stay here on Earth—God damn it, you could stay in your goddamn Sanctum"—her arm stabbed out—"and run the whole show by telepresence! That's what you usually do!"

"Honey," he said, taking her by the shoulders. "You know better than that. Work the numbers. The Bean's over seven hundred thousand miles out and climbing. That's seven and a half seconds for telemetry to reach Earth and a return command to reach the Bean—not counting the time it takes the decision-maker to pull his thumb out and scratch his head."

And again he saw the Visitors' control room. The countdown to doom. Chase balking in confusion. Jimmy had ordered the waldo to strike the flashing button—knowing that the flashing button was four seconds in the past; knowing that waldo's response would be four seconds in the future, and that everything would be changed utterly before the floater could act. And with the memory came the feelings of impotence, of helplessness, of . . . rage *at the last transmission, from a waldo itself hurtling backward, of Chase tumbling and snatching frantically for a handhold, any handhold.*

"A lot can happen in eight seconds," he whispered.

"I know that, Jimmy. Don't you think I know that? Don't you think that's what worries me? What if the Bean's A/I doesn't *want* you to rescue Chase?"

He jerked his head up. Who the phuck *cared* what the freaking *Bean* wanted? But he answered Tani more gently. "Chase is a dead man unless I go get him."

"Better one dead man than two."

"But zero's better than one. If I don't go, he dies. I don't want that on my conscience."

"Since when do you have a conscience? It's the Visitors who killed him; or that Feathershaft woman for not being more careful; or Ned DuBois and the Selection Board for sending him out in the first place. It's not *you.* It's not *your* fault."

Jimmy was a long time answering. He turned away from her, to face the Karen Chong painting on the wall, a wickedly haunting one in which two parents in the background watched dotingly over a pair of children in the foreground—who watched in turn over a pair of doll parents minding their doll children. He focused on the painting, willing himself into it. *None of us matter by ourselves,* he thought, *we only matter as part of the Great Chain.*

Finally, a tentative touch on his elbow. "Jimmy?"

Did she even realize what she had said about him? Probably not. And yet, she was not the first, nor the only one to wonder whether S. James Poole had a conscience, or a sense of duty to anything outside his own skin.

"It's got to be done, Tani. They're stocking the ship right now. Food, water, compressed gas for the attitude jets . . . President Barnes practically shut down the orbital trade to expedite everything. Meat and his crew are running the preflight. The announcement's been all over the Web *and* the Lattice. How would it look if I backed out now?"

"That's it? Afraid of the flush of embarrassment?"

He turned and faced her once more. Tani was flawed—and didn't see her flaws—and, God knew, he had his own as well;

but no one demanded perfection in the Great Chain. Only that you tried your best before you passed the baton. "It's not that. Chase showed us all something we thought we had lost; and we owe it to him at least to try to rescue him. Don't you see that?"

She had no answer to that. Silently, they watched the clouds over the south bay darken into sullen rose. Her hand rubbed his back, slowly. "Oh, Jimmy, I suppose you *have* to go. I just don't know why you *want* to go."

The frustration in her voice wasn't fear, it wasn't possessiveness. It was genuine puzzlement. But Jimmy wasn't entirely sure himself why it felt so right. Take all the "have to" out of it. Postulate another ship available, or another pilot, or another whole option, and he would still have sought to go. Yet, how could he explain to another what he didn't understand himself? He took refuge in easy posing.

"Are you kidding?" he laughed. "It's Jimmy Poole to the rescue!" He swept his free arm through the air. Sometimes, it was easier to be accepted as the one they thought you were. Jimmy Poole, the Wizard of Baud, the cyber-hermit, the Ego. The persona had at least the comfort of familiarity. Not like the strange new imago he felt stirring like an alien larva in his breast. "It's like it was *meant* to happen," he told her, his words tumbling upon each other in their eagerness. "Think about it. Hobie asks me to write the flight software; then Chase gets drafted and no one else but me can fly the *Lariat*. Then Chase gets himself marooned and the *Lariat*'s the only way to reach him . . . No one else saw it. Not Eatinger, not Roberta, not Billie. No one saw the possibility but me." He realized he was bouncing on the balls of his feet—as if he could spring right through the window, up to the stars, and grab Chase by the short curlies on the rebound.

"No one thought the *Lariat* was ready for such a long cruise . . ."

What she had really meant to say, Jimmy thought, was that no one thought *Jimmy* was ready. But he was; he was. He'd been to LEO and GEO and even around the Moon on test flights. This would only be a little longer flight. That was all. Just a little longer. Okay, so maybe two weeks longer, out and back; but still, that was only quantity, not quality. "She's ready, *Lariat* is. I know my ship and I know what she can do. We've even loaded spare coils of hobartium, in case a sail needs replacing. We teleconferenced yesterday, before I flew out here. Me, Hobie, Eatinger, Otul, Zubrin, and the others and we worked out a flight plan; developed some contingencies. They're writing it up today. It'll work. I tell you, it'll work."

"When do you—"

"Tomorrow morning. I only came back to pack a few things and—"

"So soon?"

"The clock's running on Chase."

"You're doing it for him." She spoke slowly, as if tasting the words and unsure of their flavor.

Jimmy snorted. "I'm doing it for me. Chase harassed me all through high school. He never missed a chance to stick it to me. He thinks he's such a big freaking hero? How's he going to feel when it's *Jimmy Poole* that saves his ass?" He could picture the scene, he could. Himself standing in the airlock, arms and legs akimbo. Chase hanging there before him with his jaw slack.

Tani hesitated, then shook her head. "Revenge? That can't be it."

Well, no. Chase knew he was coming. So forget the slack jaw.

"No, it's not revenge," he said slowly. "Not exactly. It's just . . . I don't know. I was always the last one around the track when we ran laps. I was lost two seconds after they opened a car's hood. I couldn't cut a piece of wood square to save my life. Oh, sure, I always aced science, and almost always the other stuff, at least when they asked for facts instead of 'feelings.' But Chase didn't think any of that mattered. At least this time, he'll . . . This time, he'll have to . . ." He paused, confused at the turmoil in his own thoughts.

Tani stepped back and stared at him. "You want his respect."

Irritated. Jimmy chopped an arm through the air. "Not. You remember the guys who always tagged with him in school. Chase would say, 'Frog!' and they'd all go, 'Ribbit!' You think I want to be one of *them*? No. I'm doing this because it has to be done, and because I'm the only guy who can do it. That's all."

Tani's frown always created a little crease in her forehead right above her nose. Jimmy chucked a finger under her chin and lifted her face, catching the fading sunlight in her eyes. "It'll be all right. You'll see. Eatinger and the others, they wouldn't let me go if they didn't think it would work."

Tani's mouth twitched a brief smile and she bobbed her head. "Oh, God, I hope so." He kissed her and she returned the kiss. When they parted, she brushed her fingers across his cheek. "I better finish my soup or Stassy will be upset."

"We mustn't upset Stassy."

"Always keep the cook happy."

"Yeah."

Tani turned away, leaving Jimmy by the window with his own thoughts. He wondered if "the others" were letting him go in the hopes of a martyr to galvinize the public. By the doorway, Tani paused and looked back. "Jimmy?" she said, "What is it that Chase showed us that 'we thought we had lost'?"

Jimmy watched the red orb of the sun touch the crest of Butano Ridge. "Hope, dearest. Hope."

A minute or two later, when he followed Tani from the room, Jimmy noticed the μCD recorder on the end table by the sofa.

Jimmy pondered the instrument with a cold feeling in his belly. That couldn't be it, could it? She hadn't lured him out here just to pick his brain and learn his motivations so she could make her characters more real. And yet, her plea—*Why do* you *have to do it, Jimmy!*—could be read that way.

Oh, that was cold. That was chill.

He leaned closer to the input grille. Tani would probably not listen to this until after he had gone. He ought to leave her a little message. Maybe something scathing. Something to express the gall he felt.

I realized there were surprises buried inside familiar people . . .

Tani had recorded that herself on one of her first discs when she started her new project. She had been talking about Hobie, then; because Hobie had surprised her with his unexpected subtlety. But her own husband she could not fathom when he failed to conform to her template.

And yet, she herself could take most of the credit for Jimmy Poole, release 3.2.

So instead of the rebuke he had intended, he whispered into the grille, "Tani, I just wanted you to know something. I love you more than I love myself." And then, because he *was* Jimmy Poole and had an image to maintain, an image that Tani would find familiar and comforting, he added, "And you know how much love *that* is."

All during the outbound journey he snuggled within the confines of the Salyut living quarters as if it were a cocoon woven of steel and aerogel and glass within which struggled a caterpillar named Jimmy Poole. He sensed that at the other end of his journey, some new imago would emerge, but just what he didn't know.

Meanwhile, the cocoon was a comfort, shielding him from the immensities beyond, turning the void into viewscreen images. He could look at the endless starfield on the viewscreens and pretend he was watching a threedy show. Sometimes, he would summon the A/S and put labels on the stars. Deneb, Vega, and Altair . . . How many books had he read with adventures on the planets of distant suns? There was Polaris, inching toward the perfect pole position early in the next century. And there was Alderamin in the on-deck circle, waiting for its turn as the pole star when the calendar rolled over to 7500 CE.

If it ever did roll up that high.

A long time off. And yet, 3500 BCE was no more distant over his shoulder and the pyramids were still hanging in there. In paintings on the walls of ancient tombs nameless folk worked at everyday tasks: building, making, fighting, sowing, reaping. In one tomb painting that Jimmy had seen, the pharaoh's child slips food to a cat under the dining table. There was a strange sort of hope in that; that the things that made us truly human could survive the millennia.

When the depth of time outside his viewscreen grew too much, he could gogg a virtch-hat and actually watch a no-foolin' threedy—or cruise the virtch itself—and forget the endless down. He had serviced two clients on the way out, analyzed their problems, solved them, billed them, and transferred the funds to his badly depleted legitimate accounts. He had gotten so *into* it—he had hacked so deep into the zone—that when he surfaced once more, he half expected to find himself ensconced in his command chair in his Sanctum at home. Instead, he had found himself farther from Tani and Stevie than he had ever been in his life, farther from Earth, indeed, than all but nine other human beings; and more alone than anyone but Chase Coughlin, himself.

He even found Chase's ballistic problem more challenging than he had originally supposed, and the additional complication also helped insulate him from the awful reality outside the hull. Jimmy diverted his comm laser from Earthside to Beanside so Chase could send him Frechet's data on the asteroid's mass distribution, as well as the locations and bearings of Flaco's engines. Problem was: only three banks were functional, *Cochran* having smashed the incomplete fourth, and the vector sum of their thrusts did not actually pass through center of mass. One possibility—and it intrigued him more and more as the days wore on—was to use the Bean's own engine to compensate. Now that he knew which controls on the Visitors' panel injected the fuel and the oxydizer and could make a reasonable guess about the firing stud, it might be possible to jury-rig something that would impose the requisite microwave pattern on the "tutor" and light the Big Engine at the appropriate time.

Sadly, he rejected the option. Too many unknowns. What was the Big Engine's thrust? Was the panel in the alien chamber in fact the tutor to the Bean's Intelligence, and could it override the Intelligence itself? Jimmy thought he could make some reasonable suppositions, and the hometown crowd could estimate thrust from the measured change in the Bean's orbit following the recent debacle; but he wasn't sure he wanted to wager his planet on a few suppositions, reasonable or not.

And yet . . . And yet . . . Gradually, a notion grew on him. A coup so immense that he hung suspended in ziggy for two hours like a dead man in Raritan Bay, so deep inside his own skull that he missed a check-in point on his mission plan and had to spend fifteen minutes calming Tani. Yes, everything was copacetic and he had forgotten to log in only because he'd been deeply involved with a programming problem. Tani laughed, a little nervously, and said, "I think I'd almost rather lose you to another woman than to a logic diagram."

Another woman? Jimmy puzzled over that for much of the remainder of the day. Did Tani think other women found him attractive? It was an astonishing thought, and flattering in its way. It had never occurred to him before. Women were said to find wealth attractive—a spin-off of the hard wired protect-the-nest instinct—but in that case, Jimmy ought to have had groupies lined up ten abreast at his door.

Maybe he had, and he was just too much of a dweeb to notice them. He laughed at the thought. Jimmy Poole, superstud. Just like Chase Coughlin—except that Chase, so far as anyone knew, was straight-edge. Jimmy, remembering the sharp-edged, narrow-eyed, tight-skirted girls that had trailed

Chase like waste gases trailed a spacecraft, could only wonder. Chase could have had any of them; and probably had. Now he kept it zipped—from choice.

The gentle, but persistent acceleration gave the ship an up-down orientation, enough so that he began to think of the sails as "above" him and not "forward." Dropped objects tumbled aft toward the "floor." He had to monkey swing a few times to get to a cabinet or a control, and he made damn sure he was tied into his hammock when sleep shut him down for the night. A milli-gee wasn't much, but he'd hit the "aft" bulkhead at just over two miles per hour if he ever fell out of bed. About the speed of a brisk walk—but try walking into a wall sometime.

He made copious notes on facility layout. Standard Salyuts were designed for ziggy, and although some modifications had been made for *Lariat,* with platforms and ladders to accommodate constant boost, it was clear that the design team had not fully appreciated the difference between ziggy and a low-gee, uniformly accelerated environment. They had thought of "loggy" as "almost ziggy," but that was like calling a woman with a freshly fertilized ovum "almost a virgin." The two system states were very close, but they lay on opposite sides of a fractal boundary. There was a greater difference between "something" and "nothing" than there was between "something" and "something more."

The outbound trip was uneventful, the one excitement being a sudden gust in the solar wind. On the average, the charged particles surged past Earth orbit at a million miles an hour, with a steady pulse from the pinwheeling induced by the sun's rotation. But averages masked extreme values. Every now and then—Jimmy always thought of it as a burning log dropping into the glowing coals—the sun would belch and send out a shower of sparks. When that happened, Alaskans and Canadians and the like would ooh at their night sky and millions of threedy viewers would subject their receivers to a ritual slapping to expel the Static Demon, while far above them the otters at the lunar mines and the GEO construction sites would duck for their storm shelters.

Jimmy did not need a storm shelter, since his whole ship was encased in a magnetic bubble and the solar sleet skidded around him, raising phantom colors in the thin mist of waste gases that his ship exuded. Well, okay, the ionizing radiation was still a problem, but his water tanks were enough to block that. It was just a gust, not a blizzard; not the sort of storm that could shred a man's cells like an assault rifle on full auto, but it provided a few minutes diversion as the magsail ran before the wind, pulling the craft above the projected flight path, while Jimmy and his A/S tacked the primary loop against the new vector. The added speed was all very well, but finesse was called for, too. It wasn't enough to *reach* the Bean, he had to match its orbit.

Let's see you do that *by teeping,* he thought with seemly satisfaction when the wind finally died down.

The cause of pain was possibility. When there had been no possibility of rescue, Chase could accept his situation, even come to terms with it. Now a seductive "maybe" had wriggled like a worm into his gut and he found himself shying from risk. With no other ending in sight but death, he had taken whatever chances were needed to get the work done. Perhaps, he had even half hoped for an accident. After all, at best he could only drag things out. *Now* there were two possible endings: death or life. *Now* what he did could make a difference.

"Don't do anything foolish," Karen told him, once a link had been established and Chase had found the courage to speak to her. Fine advice for an environment where "foolish" equaled "dead," but even breathing carried risk. Even if he did *nothing* to prepare the asteroid for its diversion, even if he sat on his freaking *butt* and waited for Jimmy Poole—Jimmy Poole, for God's sake!—to come and pull his nuts from the cracker, there were a hundred things that could go wrong. He had added up the probabilities once, accessing component and subassembly failure rates in the *Cochran*'s system reliability deeby, and discovered that the odds said he was already dead. After that, he ignored the math.

"They're calling you a hero," Karen said, with something like accusation in her voice.

"It's not like I stayed behind on purpose," he answered. "But as long as I had to hang around here, I figured I might as well make myself useful." Yeah, right: aw shucks. Did that make him a hero? His actions had been forced on him by circumstance. Heroes faced a choice. Jimmy Poole, now. Jimmy Poole was a hero, because he didn't *have* to come. The only choices Chase made these days was getting out of bed in the morning.

Which, all things considered, might be heroism enough.

"They say you've repaired all the damage . . ." Karen said.

"I did what I could. Mostly to keep busy, you know. I didn't want to sit on my thumb all day, waiting to—well, waiting." But everything was as ready as it was possible for one man alone to make it. It needed only the software to bring it all to life, and Jimmy Poole was handling that. In fact, the software would arrive by transmission before Jimmy himself. After that . . .

It might not work out. The Bean's Intelligence might foil whatever they did. But, by damn, he owed it to the planet that sent him at least to try.

"When you get back," Karen told him, "I want you to stay home. I don't want you to go out again."

Chase hesitated before pressing the TALK button. Flying was his life. It was the one time when he was totally free. And yet, Karen was his life, too; and bondage to her a different sort of freedom. She had never tried to hold him back, all those years together, though he knew what sort of fears she felt when he went aloft. It wasn't as if Earthside jobs were anyways less dangerous. Electrical linemen, police detectives . . . Hell, a desk could kill you as sure as any solar flare. Layering on the fat and the anxieties until you coughed and croaked and your face fell into your keyboard. It just took longer and didn't make headlines. He pressed TALK.

"Once Jimmy gets me home, you won't be able to get rid of me." He didn't know if it was true. He didn't know how badly his heart would ache for the open void; but he knew that, at this one moment, he *wanted* it to be true; and if the only price was wistful nights gazing at heavens he could no longer reach, he could pay that price, and smile.

"We'll have a party," Karen said eight seconds later, "when you get back."

That was bad luck—tempting the gods—so he made a joke of it. "I got the invite list all made out. You. Me. Now, where'd be a good place to hold it?"

Karen told him on the bounceback. Either she didn't know the radio link was open, or she didn't care.

"Coming at you, dude," said Jimmy Poole.

Chase, suited up and standing near the western end of the nightside, studied the quadrant of the sky where his radar had detected the oncoming ship. He could see nothing against the backdrop of stars. *Lariat* was not a large ship, he remembered. Basically a Salyut with a parasol on its prow. A fraction the size of a Plank-based DSV. A test-of-concept vehicle, it had never been intended to haul freight. He'd probably not see it until it was alongside. Yet there was something about signal acquisition in the visible light bands that meant something to him. It had drawn crowds dockside for centuries, to search for sails on the far horizon.

"Can't see you, yet," Jimmy Poole said. "Wave a handkerchief, or something."

"Hurry it up, man," Chase told him, "so we can finish the debug and blow this joint."

"It's not a debug," Jimmy answered. "My cheese is bugless. Money-back guarantee. We're fine-tuning, is all. 'Sides,

I got a phat stoopid notion on the way out that I want to run past you."

Chase waited to hear the phat stoopid notion. Jimmy could no more help bubbling over with his own cleverness than a boiling pot. But the dweeb stayed mum, and that began to worry Chase.

A faint spot of iridescence seemed to come and go against the stars. That sometimes happened when he stared into the endless night. Cosmic rays could use your eyeballs as a bubble chamber. "The sparkles," they were called. Old Story Musgrave had noticed that way back when he fixed the Hubble. A man's irises grew to the size of Jupiter's moons and he saw things that no human eyes could see. Now, Chase could make out pale sheets of green and white, hardly perceptible, dancing and rippling in the night. There was a circle, then a lozenge then a circle again. "I can't hurry any faster than the wind'll take me," Jimmy went on. "Gotta tack, now; spill some vee so we match when I ease alongside you."

"Is that you making the colors?"

"Yeah. Phat, isn't it? The magfield is so intense that the solar wind creates an aurora in the mist that seeps out of the ship."

Chase saw the ship now, coasting silently toward him. The circle was the parasol support structure. When the guy lines "reefed" the sail, it turned edge-on, so that it looked like a lozenge or ellipse. On those occasions, he caught a glimpse of the Salyut module behind it.

Jimmy eased over to the sunside of the Bean. The parasol had a wide diameter, so Jimmy had to moor farther off than the Planks had. Otherwise, the loop would foul against the asteroid. Jimmy kept up a running commentary on his maneuvers that began to get on Chase's main nerve. Why did Jimmy always have to let you know how smart he was? And all that sailing crap he kept throwing in . . . Reefing. Docking. Throwing up a staysail. Chase had no idea if it was right or not, but it began to bug him, too. It wasn't until he heard

Jimmy address Hobie that Chase realized that the commentary was for the Earthside research team. This might be a rescue, but the project still wanted feedback on how the ship handled. Still, Chase suspected that Jimmy would be doing his monologue, regardless. It was in his nature.

When *Lariat* finally entered co-orbit, Chase breathed a silent prayer of thanks. He didn't know if any gods were on the receiving end of that particular transmission, but it didn't matter. The relief spilled out of him. He waited for Jimmy to open the lock and bring the mooring line down.

And waited.

He switched his radio to the ship channel. "Problem, good buddy?"

Jimmy's voice came back gaspy, as if he were short of breath. "Suiting up," he said. "Take a while."

Chase waited some more, while he counted through the suiting procedure in his mind. He reached the end—fasten helmet neck seals and check internal pressure—and gave Jimmy a long ten-count. Still no dweeb in the airlock. Chase considered the distance between the Bean and the *Lariat*. That was a pretty damn long free jump, now that he thought about it. Not near as far as what Peterson Ku had leaped, but not the sort of EVAsion you took lightly, either; even for an old hand like Chase Coughlin. He thought about what Roberta had told him and some of the things he'd heard on the grapevine.

"Hey, Jimmy," he said. "This ol' Bean is not the happening place. How 'bout if I come up to the ship, instead? You can noodle the software and then, later, we'll come down together to finish the Beanside shit."

Jimmy's answer was fast and the relief in his voice, palpable. "Sure. If that's what you want. Must be pretty boring down there."

Chase nodded to himself. Yeah, give the weenie a check mark by his name, if he was that scared of EVAding, but had flown out here regardless. The ship-to-suit radio chatter wasn't high power enough to be heard Earthside—not unless Jimmy had his Earthside link open—but Chase wasn't about to mention the matter for ears that hadn't even come. He checked the levels on his suit jets, then activated his faceplate display and centered *Lariat*'s Salyut in the crosshairs. "Target," he told the A/S that controlled his spews. "Go there." And they lifted him from the surface of the world that had been his home for so long.

The airlock opened before he reached it and Jimmy Poole, duded up finally in his hard suit, stood framed in the circle of light. One hand waved; the other gripped a handle. The toes of his boots were tucked into two other handles. Chase bit his tongue. Two people in suits cycling through a standard lock was not the roomiest maneuver, but he gave Jimmy credit for getting that far. His suit's brain calculated distance and a spurt from his forward jets brought him to a stop by the airlock. He could see Jimmy's face through the helmet: grinning so hard his face almost split in half. Part ego, part happy, and part pure terror.

"Need a ride?" Jimmy asked.

"What kept you?" Chase answered.

23.

When Hope Shall Sing Her Triumph

In all the years he had known Chase Coughlin, Jimmy had felt a great many emotions. Hatred, for the most part; for the bully who used to beat him and take his lunch money. Contempt for the smallness of the other's mind. Disdain for his strutting arrogance, for a man who acted as if ignorance were a virtue. Later, a grudging admiration for him as a copilot on the Skopje Rescue, on DuBois's Moon Jaunt, and even during the magship project, where he showed a thoughtless instinct for finding the envelope of the simulations. Finally, respect, knowing him as a trouser snake from way back, for the man's fidelity to Karen. But never before had he felt gratitude.

And that was backward! Jimmy was the rescuer, not the rescuee! Yet, as Jimmy waited paralyzed in the airlock, unable to cross the yawning gulf that separated him from the Bean, Chase had jetted up to the ship instead. It was not that he no longer had to leap the chasm alone that evoked his gratitude. By itself, that merited only relief. No, it was that Chase *must* have known the reason for Jimmy's hesitation and had said nothing—not to DeepSpace, not to Jimmy; not then, not ever.

There was a message there that he had never anticipated. Chase respected him. It was a thought so startling that even after they had stripped to their LCGs and donned the buckskin-colored coveralls of Project Lariat and kicked in the common room of *Lariat*'s Salyut, Jimmy could find no words. It was Chase who first broke the silence.

"So, how was the trip?" he asked, just as kick as hell.

Jimmy had never expected Chase to blubber all over him at being rescued, though this was carrying sangfroid to an art form. It wasn't in the man to gush. If Jimmy talked too much—and Tani had assured him, lovingly, that he did—then Chase talked too little. But because of that, each word he uttered was freighted with more meaning, like a bit bundle that had been compressed for transmission. Jimmy saw how Chase's eyes danced around the vessel, taking in its details. *How was the trip* . . . He wasn't asking after Jimmy's flight; he wanted to know, as a pilot, how the ship had handled, how it felt when it came alive under the yoke. He wanted to know what this *new thing* was like.

"It was . . ." What? A piece of cake? Routine? The A/Ss did all the work? ". . . scary and wonderful at the same time. Sometimes I wondered what I was doing there." He let the words lie, but if Chase had any thoughts along those lines, he said nothing. But then what sort of herbert bad-mouths his ride home?

"So," Chase asked after a silence. "Why'd you come?"

"Pick you up, dude." Jimmy tried to make light of it. For some reason, the question made him uncomfortable.

Chase pursed his lips, glanced down at his hands. He seemed strangely hesitant. "No. Why'd *you* come?" And the emphasis was there this time, enough for Jimmy to hear the real question.

He shrugged. "Never seen an asteroid up close."

Chase studied him for a long moment; then, with the ghost of a smile, shook his head. "Okay, I'll give you the VIP Beanside tour later. But . . ." He stuck his hand out. "Thanks for coming, anyway. I don't care if there wasn't anybody else, and you had no choice. What you did was phat stoopid, know what I'm saying? You were stone, and I want to shake your hand."

Jimmy looked at the hand, looked at Chase. He looked for the high school bully in the narrow set of the eyes, in the curl of the lips—and couldn't find him. Instead, he saw a man in his mid-thirties who was already losing his hair and who seemed flushed and tired. So much for showing up his old nemesis. That Chase was long dead, and in a way he could not fathom, Jimmy was suddenly very glad. "Yeah." He grabbed Chase's hand. "I had to come. You still owe me that drink. Hey, on the way back, you want to conn the *Lariat*?"

Chase's eyes blazed. "You sure?"

Jimmy could be kick, too. "All that simulator time you spent," he said with a wave of the hand. "Be a shame to waste it all."

Otter. Jimmy Poole had never satisfied himself on the origin of that particular slang. Legend had it that the LEO construction crews had coined the term to compare their maneuvers in ziggy to the playful antics of the Earthside mammal. Others claimed it came from the odd way people and objects moved on orbit, with those who had mastered the environment being declared the "odder." Whatever the truth of it and whatever an otter really was, Jimmy Poole knew he was not it.

Oh, sure, he could conn a magnetic sail, but you could teach a *machine* to do that. He had handled this strange new ship because he had written the programming and he had helped Hobie build it. But he had never really been anything more than a glorified passenger. It was only when he came to the lip of the airlock that first time and found himself unable to move that he realized that he was well and truly a bunny; that perhaps he would never be anything more than a bunny.

But how many bunnies got to step onto another world? Chase tethered their suits together, slaved Jimmy's jets to his own A/S, and escorted him to the Bean. Jimmy found the company comforting, though his gut still crumpled into a prune.

Once *on* the Bean itself, his jitters calmed somewhat. The gravity was almost imperceptible, but it wasn't ziggy that tortured him. He *loved* ziggy. It was that awful, endless emptiness below his feet. So even though there wasn't all that much "down" about the Bean, what there was of it—plus its comforting solidity—stroked his hindbrain and sang lullabies to his sense of falling.

It was almost like getting land legs back after a long bout in LEO. The Bean did not want to stay put. Legally, it was below him, but sometimes it seemed to float beside him, or even hover over his head. It was a hell of a universe.

Jimmy discovered, too, how much more difficult it was to work on the Bean. His first try at untorquing a nut on an engine rack put him into a spin and he might have struck his helmet against the frozen iron if Chase hadn't checked his tumble. Still, for his firing program to work, he and Chase had to alter the alignment of some of the motors. Chase did as Jimmy directed him and asked no questions.

Not even when they reversed one motor apiece on the starside and sunside racks and two on the south face.

Of course Jimmy just had to see the alien control room. It was *the* hot tourist spot in this part of town. After they had finished most of the realignments, they took a break, replenished their oxygen tanks, and Chase led him down the tunnel into the chamber.

It was just as he remembered from his visit as Uncle Waldo. The odd stems projecting from the floor and walls; the MEMS-like viewscreens; the control boards. Nothing had changed; and why should it? The only difference was that he was *here;* but that made all the difference in the world. Jimmy moved slowly about the room, touching things, handling them physically, for no other purpose than to savor their reality. It wasn't just an image on a pair of wraparound goggle screens. How different from the Core where he and his allies had confronted Earp four years ago. Nothing then had been real, except the risks.

As he studied the control board, with the scrawled notes and markings that Chase had added during their study, he struggled with a variety of emotions. Pride for what he and his colleagues had accomplished (or had almost accomplished). Comradeship with the Fingers and the bonebags who had helped. Frustration at the manner in which they had been thwarted; and more than a little anger at the vanished aliens who had so *inhumanly* threatened his wife and son.

Indicator lights glowing in a rainbow of colors showed that the tutor board was still active. Jimmy snorted contempt. What, no sleep command? He checked the indicators for the engine feeds and found them comfortingly dark. At least the Bean wasn't prepping for a burn. He leaned close over a stud that was bright yellow. Apparently solid material, like five-sided bolt heads. How did they manage that color change? And why pentagonal? Wouldn't hex-bolts be more efficient and easier to make? You could cut a hex shape with three parallel cuts, but five was a prime number. What kind of weenies were these aliens, anyway? He wanted to unscrew one of the bolts for study (assuming they did unscrew), but he sensed that this would not be an optimal strategy.

Strange ideograms stood out in bas-relief on the mat-screens. Every now and then, a ripple passed across the screen and the ideogram changed. A million tiny football fans in the stadium bleacher's holding up their colored cards on cue. Jimmy wondered suddenly if it worked in reverse. If he traced an ideogram on the screen, would the Intelligence "read" it? An obviously more advanced technology, but at the same time one that seemed "clunkier" than what humans used. Almost like an old Windows interface. Or was that only familiarity clashing with strangeness?

Down in the "bunker," he and Chase watched the spiders scurry back and forth between the "mine" and the reducing kettle. The "spiders in the basement" were still busy, though the level of activity seemed much lower than what he remembered from the earlier broadcast. More evidence that the Bean was thankfully now quiescent. More evidence, too, of the Visitors' odd design choices.

Jimmy shook his head as he played his light around the chamber. "Seems pretty inefficient. Like a horde of coolies loading a ship in Shanghai, when a crane and conveyor would do the job."

Chase managed to display indifference in a hard suit. "Doc Frechet told me it was probably a paradigm trap."

Jimmy grunted. "They couldn't even trap two nickels. No, I'll bet they opted for flexibility. A whole bunch of independent robots with self-adaptive emergent algorithms could react to unexpected changes in the operating conditions."

Chase snickered. "You can argue it out with Doc on the way home."

Jimmy said nothing to that and swallowed a thickening in his throat. Hauling a corpse home on board *Lariat* spooked him; but Frechet's wife and his mistress had both asked that he be brought back to Earth for burial. In his whole life, Jimmy had never seen a dead body. Closed coffins at grandparents' funerals were as close as he'd come. That was why Frechet's suited cadaver was the one tourist attraction on the Bean that he had not gone to see. *Lariat* didn't have storage bins. So where did you put the stiff?

In the suit rack, of course. But Jimmy refused to let Chase stow the deadhead on board until they were ready for departure.

"Why didn't the Visitors leave pictures of themselves?" he wondered aloud as he and Chase returned to the upper chamber.

"They weren't trying to *communicate,*" Chase said. "They didn't leave sticky notes, either. Oho!" Chase reached into a niche in the rock wall of the chamber and pulled out the shattered sphere of a teeping module. He held it up to his visor. "Alas, poor Waldo," he said; then, turning, "I knew him, Jimmy: the dude was a lot of laughs."

Jimmy snorted. That must have been the unit he and the Fingers had been using. In a way, it *was* his skull Chase was sporting with. A segment of fibrop wafted from a damaged port. He shivered. It was like looking at your own corpse. "They were trying to whack us," Chase went on. "The Visitors were. Why should they care if we knew what they looked like?" Chase tossed the skull back into the corner. It bounced off the rock and spun a little in the air before slowly settling to rest.

Finally, with a longing look at the alien computer, Jimmy said, "Let's go. We got two more motors to reangle."

"Ah, crap," said Chase. "I'm dog. Let's just set the timer and blow the joint. We're coasting farther from Earth every day."

It was the first time Jimmy had heard Chase give in to the impatience that must be gnawing at him. "It's a quick trip home," he told him. "We just tuck and dive and then deploy sails to skate across. Don't forget, altitude doesn't correlate with velocity for sailing ships."

"I didn't forget that," Chase answered. "But you don't have unlimited supplies, either. And . . . well . . . I don't have the strength left. I'm tired, Jimmy. I'm used up."

"We only have two more realignments left."

"I don't know why you're being so finicky." Chase snapped and waved an arm at the alien control panel. "Doesn't *matter* how fussy you are. The Bean gives one good fart and it's all a waste."

Jimmy could not read his friend's face through the visor. "If it's a waste of time, then why did you wear yourself out repairing and rigging the equipment, even before you knew anyone could reprogram it?"

"Hell, Jimmy, it was something to do. Just to keep from going crazy. And . . . I had to let the Bean know we didn't just give up. So yeah, let's get your programming all set up and give it our best shot; but there's no point in fine-tuning it."

Jimmy asked, "Can DeepSpace monitor our voices down here?"

"Sure," said Chase. "Radio waves go right through solid rock."

Jimmy ignored the sarcasm and considered his options. He ought to tell Chase. The man certainly knew that reversing the four rockets meant Jimmy planned a retrograde burn somewhere along the way. He might even suspect why Jimmy had insisted on keeping the one functional Waldo aboard Salyut. He didn't want anyone Earthside seeing what he was doing. So Chase had to know that Jimmy was Up To Something, but he hadn't asked—which might mean disinterest rather than approval. Approval might depend on how he thought of the Bean's Intelligence: as malevolent or merely inquisitive.

"All the way out here," he said at last, "I kept thinking about something your Dr. Frechet said, when you asked me to recruit the hack team. How he said the smartest thing of all is to fly this sucker home."

Jimmy heard suspicion in the answering hesitation. "Yeah . . ." Drawn out; half a question. "Except we don't know how to do that; and even if we did, you and me can't ride herd for a three-year trip."

"We don't have to. We set it up and our A/S lights the torch."

"And the Bean does a course adjustment and we're not here to stop it."

Jimmy shook his head; then realized the gesture could not be seen. "No. I figured it out on the way. The Visitors are testing the Earth, everyone says. That doesn't mean they rigged the test. The Intelligence won't try to thwart *every* move we make. In fact, there's one orbit I guarantee it won't try to correct." He grinned and waited for Chase to see it; but he got no joy on the bounceback. Instead, an impatient cough. Jimmy sighed. "Look, if your Frechet was right, then the one orbit the Intelligence won't correct is the orbit that demonstrates our mastery."

"Okay, smart boy. I'll bite. What's that?"

"An Earth-capture orbit, dude. Chase, you and me are gonna give the world a whole new moon."

Okay, so it was a mad dog notion, and even Chase was impressed: though he worried as they passed through the tunnel back to the surface. No, Jimmy told him, he hadn't cleared the plan with DeepSpace. "Because they'd freak out, that's why."

"Because you want to thread the needle between the Earth and Moon? Can't see why that would worry them."

Jimmy snorted. Subtle sarcasm was not Chase's métier. "Don't worry, dude. We got an ace palmed. Remember I told you I brought an extra sail?"

"In case you needed to replace yours . . ."

"Climb the mast and rig a new sail en route? No way. I'd

need a whole crew for that. No, it was Hobie's idea. Remember that day you all came to my place to get me to finance the project?"

A pause. "Yeah," Chase said. "Yeah, and Hobie talked about rigging sails to the asteroid and flying it home. But . . ."

"But the sails we've developed so far won't get enough drag off the wind to navigate a body this massive. What they *will* do is give the Bean's vector a constant starward acceleration that no ballistic computation can account for."

"Like a continuous radial burn. The burn point becomes the perihelion of a new ellipse. So . . . No, wait. It keeps on going. So the perihelion keeps sliding along each new ellipse . . ."

"If we rig the sail to the Bean we can make up for some of the thrust that was lost when the northside rack was smashed. Hobie and Zubrin and Otul worked out the parameters during the outbound trip. All we gotta do is lasso the asteroid."

He could hear the grin in Chase's voice. "That's all, hey?"

They emerged from the tunnel and headed toward dayside, where *Lariat* was moored. As the magsail rose above their stunted horizon, Chase sucked in his breath. "Lookit that," he said, pointing. "Man, that is one pretty sight."

Jimmy followed the outthrust arm, and saw their doom.

The staysail he had left active so that the *Lariat's* A/S could maintain its anchorage was shimmering like the ghost of a rainbow. Sheets of pale green and yellow and red chased across the disk and around the rim. Jimmy checked his radio and found the channels hissed with static. He closed his eyes and sucked in his breath. A solar storm, a strong one. He looked again at the pinwheel colors. A *very* strong storm. The charged particles interact with the field and . . . Yes, the ship was moving steadily toward the Bean. A lee shore. How long for the A/S to detect, analyze, and correct? How soon before the main sail support ring impacted and twisted and snapped? Too long. Too soon.

Suddenly, Chase saw it, too. "Oh, shit! Jimmy, it's drifting into the Bean! We gotta stop it before . . ." More static, cresting like a wave upon a beach, drowned his words.

"Radiation," he told Chase, lifting his suit arm where he could see the dosimeter already clouding up. It must be one hell of a burst to make the sail light up like that. A lot of hard rads. And here they were standing out where it was *always* the noonday sun. He grabbed Chase by the arm and pulled. "Darkside! Put the Bean between us and the sun!"

"What good'll that do," Chase shouted, pointing to the ship, "if we don't have a bus?"

"As much good as a bus with a dead crew." He shoved Chase, hard, and the otter stumbled into the shadows of the darkside, but the effort pushed Jimmy completely off the surface of the Bean onto the dayside, and before he quite knew it, he had turned on his jets and was speeding toward the drifting ship. There were attitude jets on the Salyut, he remembered. High pressure gases. He didn't need to wait for the slow reaction of the magsail. He kept his eyes fixed firmly on the airlock and refused to look at the depths that engulfed him. "Ship," he radioed. "Bo'sun. Command. Airlock. Open."

He had to repeat the order three times before the housekeeping A/S named *Bo'sun* understood the signal beneath the noise. But the airlock door did swing open on his approach.

The static stopped when he passed within the sail's magnetosphere. Objectively, he could no more feel the enveloping shadow than he could have felt the body-piercing gamma rain he had just passed through. And yet he did, in his bones.

He lost precious seconds cycling through the lock; more, as he bounded forward to the controls. He fired the steering jets along the entire axis of the ship, including those at the masthead, and the ship shuddered and jerked, the impulse knocking him loose from his handhold and bouncing him against the forward viewscreen.

Afterward, he did not look at the dosimeter strapped to the

left arm of his hard suit. Not for two days did he look at it. By then, he didn't have to.

It was just bad luck, was all. But when luck went bad, it went so far down the toilet you didn't even need to flush.

"Can it be fixed?" Chase asked.

The aerogel support for the main sail had nudged hard against the ragged surface of the asteroid. The ring structure itself was undamaged, but a great many guys, control wires, and micromotors had been torn loose. Jimmy, who was writing furiously on the Gyricon screen of his cliputer, paused and ran a hand across the raw skin of his forehead. The blisters felt soft and tender, ready to burst. He thought for a long time how to answer.

The storm had died and, after a long, close survey of the damage to the ship, they were once more aboard *Lariat*. Chase drank orange juice from a closed cup, his face as neutral as tension could make it. Jimmy bent again over his stylus.

"We could fix the ship," he said at last, "or we could finish rigging the Bean."

"Screw the Bean, then."

Jimmy would not look at him. "Chase, it'll be a nine-day trip back. I'll be dead before we get there."

"You don't know that!" Chase snapped.

Jimmy looked at him, surprised that *his* death could make Chase angry. "This isn't just a bad sunburn." When he rubbed a hand over his cheek, he winced. The blisters smarted. That they had shown up so quickly was not good, either. Morbidly, he had looked up the symptoms of radiation sickness in the ship's deeby. Reddened skin; loss of hair. In high doses, nausea, blisters, destruction of the mucous lining. The description would have made him lose his appetite, except that he had no appetite to lose.

"Look," Chase insisted, "those photographic film strips—sure, they're cheap and light, which makes them perfect for space flight—but they can *way* overestimate the dosage. Way overestimate." He grimaced and looked away. Jimmy wondered if Chase knew how flushed his own face was. He'd picked up a bad dose, too, even though Jimmy had pushed him nightside, putting the asteroid's thickness between him and the sun. And there had been that minor squall during the outbound flight; and possibly others during the time Chase had been incommunicado. The sun grew brighter just before a storm, and the luminosity gave advance notice of the slower sleet of charged particles coming along behind; but during the time when no one knew Chase was even alive, there had been no storm warnings sent to the Bean, nor had Chase had any way to hear them. Jimmy had noted Chase's flushed complexion and thinning hair on arrival; but he hadn't realized then what it meant. Chase had been building up his own fatal dose, just a bit more slowly than Jimmy.

If we hadn't been in the underground center, we would've heard the warning . . .

If Chase had restored the fibrop link down there, we would've heard the warning . . .

If we had just packed it in and left as soon as I got here . . .

That was the "If" that hurt. He'd been so full of his grandiose plan to sucker the Bean's Intelligence, and he really had no proof beyond his own self-confidence that it would work. He could have just loaded the original program, debugged it, and hoped for the best when the boosters fired at aphelion. No one would ever have known that he hadn't done his best. No one but himself. "I really screwed up, didn't I?" It may have been the first time in his life that Jimmy Poole had uttered those words.

Chase blinked, then shrugged. "Could happen to anyone."

His anger flared over Chase's studied nonchalance. "Well, don't get so hysterical . . ."

Chase shook his head. "I ain't making it back, either."

He knew, then. Jimmy sucked in his breath. He stared at

the cliputer, rolled the stylus between his thumb and finger. "Doesn't seem to bother you."

"I've had longer to get used to the idea." He shook his head. "I knew when the fleet left without me that I was a dead man. Just didn't know exactly how it would happen. You coming out here, I started to hope; and that should have warned me right off. I wish you'd never come. I goddam wish you had never come."

Jimmy wrote another line of code, noticed an error, and excised it. He looked up at Chase. "This isn't the way it was supposed to turn out."

"Never is."

"All the way out here. I thought it would be so stupy to rescue you. I thought, Dude! Show off a new kind of ship, save the hero, get my name in the books . . ." He ran out of words, grimaced, and shot Chase a challenging look.

"That why you came?" asked the pilot.

"I guess."

"Not friendship?"

Jimmy snorted. "You and me were never friends."

That shut Chase up. He retreated behind his eyes. After a while, he said hesitantly, "I always admired your brains."

"Yeah? You had a funny way of showing it."

"You had to know my dad. I knew I could never beat you in smarts, so . . ." He spread his hands in mute apology.

"Okay," Jimmy said, and he put down the stylus. "You know what always griped me? I couldn't get a horny man to follow me into a whorehouse; while you, the guys would line up to follow you into hell. Why?"

"Morbid curiosity?" Chase suggested.

Jimmy shook his head ruefully. "You don't get it. *I followed you out here.*"

"Not the smartest thing you ever did." Chase paused thoughtfully. "Well, I guess you 'n' me are friends now. Best friends in the whole world, at least in this one. We'll be friends for the whole rest of our lives."

Sometimes, it hurt so bad, you had to laugh.

"I would have liked to see Karen again," Chase said after their laughter had subsided into a self-conscious silence.

Jimmy didn't want to think about it. He glanced at the waldo that was their only link. They'd be getting antsy, Earthside. Only what do we tell them? Oops? *Oh, God, Tani!* "You know what they'd find when they open the ship," he said. "Wouldn't be right to do that to her."

"Yeah." He rubbed a fist with the other hand. "I'd be looking pretty bad by then. Let her remember me handsome and virile. But, still . . ."

The pain that pinched his face was not physical, Jimmy knew, because he felt that same ache, himself. He wondered what Tani would remember about him. Grief? Contempt for a herbie stunt? Maybe she would only be relieved that he was out of her life at last. He checked the ballistic computations on the ship's computer and rewrote the code that he had botched. He felt mildly nauseous. That was due to ziggy. He told himself firmly that it was due to ziggy.

"Why?" asked Chase. Jimmy looked him a question and Chase pointed to the cliputer with his juice cup. "Why bother now?"

"Because," Jimmy said simply, "it's all that's left."

The Salyut was dark, save for the pearly glow of the distant Earth and Moon that washed through the viewport bubble at the far end of the vessel. Jimmy pushed himself out of his hammock, careful not to disturb Chase, sleeping beside him, and he floated dreamlike to the bubble. *This* is *all a dream,* a part of his mind insisted. *In the morning you'll wake up, and everything will be like it was.*

Causes and effects; options and choices. Searching backward, Jimmy wondered how he had started down the road that led to this night. One thing led to another, but no one thing led to it all. It was a seemless whole, receding ever backward. From Jimmy's own bravado to Roberta's begging to Adam van Huyten's obsession and OMC's secretiveness. Chase the roots of it far enough and you'd have to blame the Big Bang for everything.

The air system hissed quietly in the background. Outside, a river of stars poured across the endless night, giving no answer. Fitting, indeed, that night be endless and he, restless. Endless night lay before him, and beyond it, rest eternal.

Roberta had had a hand in it. Shaming him into Project Lariat with her scolding over the stock market. Or Hobie who, pursuing his own single-minded dream, had made the whole scenario possible. Adam van Huyten, tearing down the pillars of the temple. Old Mariesa van Huyten, fleeing from her demons, sending out the probes. There were plenty of other players running their own agendas. Even the Visitors, rigging their deadfall traps millennia in the past. From the right perspective, the whole thing had a sort of inevitability, like the third act of a Greek play, and choice and will were not even on the table.

But that perspective was *too* far off, as godlike as the stars that filled the night. By explaining everything, Fate explained nothing. In the end, he had come because he had discovered it was not in him not to come. It had been a surprising discovery, to Jimmy himself no less than to Tani or Roberta or Chase; and, in a way, that discovery was almost worth the price of finding it.

He could have kept his mouth shut when that vision of glory and subtle revenge had blazed in his mind. If anyone else had thought of using the *Lariat,* he could have begged off, said the ship wasn't ready, said the programming wasn't ready, said the freaking *pilot* wasn't ready. No one would have doubted him. No one would have known, except himself . . . and Tani.

He would have lived; but what kind of life would it have been, knowing for all the years to come that he might have made a difference. What sort of character would that have made for Tani's book?

And so, even Tani had had a hand in it, because in the end, he had been posing for her expectations.

They finished the job, of course. As Chase put it, they had nothing better to do.

DeepSpace was not happy with an Earth-capture orbit. "Too risky," the mission director told them, as if anyone Earthbound understood what risk meant. But both Jimmy and Chase were certified planetary heroes now, so there wasn't much DeepSpace could say and (as Chase pointed out afterward to Jimmy) not a whole lot they could do about it.

And so they rigged the sail and Chase disabled the ignition circuits and Jimmy installed the software and ran a diagnostic dry fire. The results were satisfactory, as he knew they would be. Barring a hardware malf, everything would work.

And after that, there was nothing but the waiting. Waiting for the rockets to fire. Waiting to die. Jimmy's hopes for the future came down now to one thing only: that the second not happen until after the first.

"They're calling you heroes," Tani said in one of her almost-daily calls. It cost plenty troy to occupy bandwidth on the Helios microwave laser. From Earth polar orbit to the rectennae on *Lariat*. Talk about your long-distance charges. But DeepSpace had donated the transmission time. How could they not?

"I ain't no freaking hero," Jimmy said, stealing one of Chase's best trademark lines. It wasn't the first time she had told him that; so it couldn't be that she thought he didn't know. She was only speaking to herself. It was a way of convincing herself that it all had meaning. She'd had time enough to grow numb to the idea that Jimmy wasn't coming back. Long enough for the anguish and remorse to settle into the consciousness like a chronic cough. But behind the far-too-calm words Jimmy could still hear the pain. "You can have your heroes," he told her.

"No, God damn it, Jimmy!" Angry now. "You damn well better have saved the world, because anything less than that is just too damn little."

For the prices paid, she meant. Jimmy was thankful for the eight-second lag. It gave him time to think between responses, to gather his composure. If only it didn't feel so much like exchanging monologues. How he wished he could see her, sit with her, explain himself to her. He longed for the intimacy. He longed for the touch of her hand.

Silently, he flexed his own hands. The bright skin pulled parchment-thin against his knuckles and he winced at the pain. No. Some sights are better hidden. "Tani, if there was any way I could go back and do it over, I'd be off in a nanosecond flat. There were so many points where things might have gone different . . . I'd rather have your arms around me than the adulation of any crowd. We don't even know yet that it'll work. We won't know that until—later." By a common, unspoken consent, they avoided any mention of death; any direct confrontation with the stinking, foul-breathed reality. They consigned it instead to the hiatuses, buried it in the ellipses and the hesitations.

"Hey," he said suddenly, "I've been thinking about those schools we looked at for Stevie. I think the public charter—Mountaincrest—looked pretty good. So did the Karr Academy. What do you think?"

Tani's reply this time lagged by more than the canonical eight seconds. "Stevie won't go to any of them," she said flatly. "I'll be selling the house, leaving California."

Her announcement pierced him like a knife to the belly. It was as if she had announced a sudden divorce. "How could you?" he stammered. "That's our house."

"That's exactly why," came the bounceback. "What good is 'our' house if there isn't a 'we' in it? I got a letter from Barry Fast. You remember him from Witherspoon? He's offered Stevie a spot in one of his schools and he . . . I remember he was a good teacher. He'll have a good set of colleagues."

"Sure he will, Tani. It's a good choice. Make a fresh start, away from memories. Only, Tani? Don't get too far away from those memories." It was as close as he dared come. Her memories would be all that was left of Jimmy Poole. The real Jimmy Poole. The one that played with Stevie on the rug, and made bad jokes at dinner, and tried as hard as he knew how to make his family happy.

"I won't forget you," Tani promised. "Ever." Jimmy bit his lip and looked away from the speaker grille and the smashed viewscreen. Chase, in the far end of the Salyut, scread a book-disk and pretended not to listen. "I just wish that I could see you."

"An unexplained malfunction in the optics," Jimmy told her. Chase, who had performed the malfunction with a hammer, glanced up and smiled crookedly. The blisters had broken and the hair was coming out in clumps. Jimmy had certain standards of appearance he wanted to keep up. He didn't want Tani to see him like this.

"Tani, I've got an announcement to make. Is DeepSpace recording this?" They ought to be. Famous last words from the heroic duo. Scholars would study them, probing for subtext. Debunkers would, in another generation, use them to expose the clay feet.

He realized that he was thinking in terms of there being a next generation; or at least one concerned with more matters than shear survival.

"Hobie's magship worked better than anyone hoped. It cut months off the transit time. If we had packed it in when I got here instead of finishing the job"—and, oh, God, how he wished he had!—"we'd be home already. Constant acceleration is the key to the solar system. Tani, and you others who'll be hearing this later: Roberta, Hobie, Meat. Adam. Ms. van Huyten. Colonel Eatinger and Solomon Dark. Listen up. I've got a little money I've squirreled away over the years.

I'm giving it all to you. Except what Tani needs, and I've set that up in a separate trust. Use it! Build the ships! Scores of them! A fleet of magsails—and hunt down every freaking one of these asteroids and castrate them. Put our people on the Moon and Mars. Bring in the steel and minerals from the Belt. You've heard people waving their hands in the air and crying, 'It's the end of the world!' Well, wave your hands in the air, because it's only the beginning of one."

When he logged off, he didn't look at Chase for a moment. When he did, the pilot was still screading. "Nice speech," Chase said without looking up.

"Well. I rehearsed it a little."

"Yeah. Heard you last night." Chase sighed and closed his book. "Wish I coulda flown me one of those sails. Think they'll build 'em?"

"Try to stop them."

"How you gonna make sure they get the money? I mean, I figure it's all hidden away in secret accounts and shit, on account of—"

"On account of it wasn't all got legal. Yeah, I'll take that chance if anyone wants to come out here and arrest me. I've had a logic beaver out cruising the virtch disguised as an Association patrol 'bot for the last few years. I patched a whistle into my voice transmission just now. Once 'Jimmy's Last Testament' hits the Net, the whistle will activate the beaver and the beaver will open up the trust funds I set up." He hesitated. Hard to know how people would react to charity. "Set one up for Karen, too. Hope you don't mind."

Chase didn't say anything for a moment. He ran a hand across his jaw. "She'll do okay. She's got a good practice. But, thanks. When did you set that up, and how'd you do it from here?"

Jimmy pushed out of his seat and floated to the pantry. There were some bland soups there. Flavored broths. Sometimes he could keep them down. He wasn't hungry. He'd never feel hunger again. But that didn't mean his body could go without fueling. "Didn't do it from here," he said over his shoulder. "Set it up before I left."

There was a long, loud silence from Chase and when Jimmy turned with the dehydrate packet in his hand, the pilot was staring at him.

"Before you left."

There was no question mark to that, but Jimmy answered him anyway. "I ran the system reliabilities. There was a ten to twenty percent chance of failure. So I figured, you know, just in case."

"Ten to twenty percent. And you came anyway?"

"I was betting on the ninety. The odds were with me."

"You lost."

Jimmy shrugged. "If you don't play, you can't win."

There were pills that Ku had kept in his medical locker aboard *Cochran*'s Salyut. Taken in moderation, they relieved pain and brought on sleep. Taken in sufficient quantity, they ended all pain and brought endless sleep. By common consent, he and Chase moved into the derelict. *Lariat* would be left behind when the boosters ignited, and Chase thought it was important for the two of them to stay with the Bean. Jimmy was too tired to argue with him by then. He had not eaten in four days, except one small meal that his digestive tract immediately rejected. That was another reason they abandoned *Lariat*.

"What about Frechet?" Jimmy asked Chase. He resented the other man's greater endurance and mobility. Chase was still able to don a suit and jet across the surface of the Bean.

"I put him down in the Visitor center," Chase told him. "If you plotted the right trajectory and the Intelligence doesn't interfere, he'll ride home with us. It's only right."

Jimmy didn't rise to the provocation. Of course, he had plotted the right trajectory. At least, Chase hadn't dragged the Frenchman on board the Salyut module with them. Jimmy almost laughed. Who was he to object now to bunking with a corpse? He turned to Chase, who was hanging his suit carefully in the rack. Did Chase expect to don it again? The pilot's skin was bright red and peeling now. When he smiled, the skin at the corners of his mouth cracked. He had always shaved the hair on the sides of his head, now the hair on the top was going, too. He hadn't gotten the blisters like Jimmy had, but then he had built his dose up more slowly. In the end he would be just as dead.

"I'm scared."

Chase turned to look at him, and grunted. "Yeah. Me, too." He guided himself from handhold to handhold and settled into a sling beside Jimmy. "I guess the historians'll have to come up with some noble last words for us to say."

"Yeah, like: 'Can we try this over again?' "

Chase laughed. "Yeah, like that." He scratched his head and another tuft of hair came out with it. "When did you say those engines would go off?"

Jimmy pointed to the digital clock on the Salyut's main computer. Chase had run all the controls through the module once it became clear that Jimmy would no longer leave its confines. "That's the countdown," he said. "Eight days, the south bank goes. Then." It was hard to catch his breath. "Then, Earthside and starside. In tandem. A few. Hours. Later."

Chase shook his head. "Sounds like quite a sight. I wish I could be around to see it."

"Me, too," Jimmy agreed. "That would be so phat."

Jimmy had not even roused while Chase stuffed him into his hard suit so he was unable to lend a hand. It was a long, slow awkward process and Chase was grateful that Jimmy had lost so much weight, both personal pounds and courtesy of the Bean's gravity field. Even so, Chase had to stop and rest a few times before he got the dude all packed and sealed. Then, because he *was* so tired, he went back and double-checked the seals—and found one ring that had only been double-seated. Unlikely that Jimmy would accidently twist the ring, but Chase locked in the third twist because a three-motion seal was phat impossible to unlock by accident and because, by God, you did the job right or not at all.

Climbing into his own suit was hell on wheels because he had no one to help him, and for a time Chase wasn't sure he could finish. But he gritted his teeth and pressed on. It seemed to take a long time, and he even wondered if he was running a fever again and was imagining the whole thing. His breath hissed between his teeth. If he was going to imagine something, why couldn't he imagine being healthy and home?

The Snoopy cap felt funny with no hair to buffer it. Bare fabric against bare skin. He wondered what its real name was. Snoopy cap. It must have had a name before the cartoon dog went off to fight the Red Baron.

Richthofen? Baron von Richthofen?

He realized that he was drifting and shook himself. *Focus!* He glanced at the clock and saw that only twenty minutes remained. Yet, he went through the checklist systematically, item by item. No one would ever say Chase Coughlin got sloppy toward the end! An i-dotter and a t-crosser. Yeah. You got a problem with that?

When he was ready, he toggled the radio link to DeepSpace. "Shuttin' down," he said. He signed off without waiting for the bounceback. What could they say? Good luck? As for Karen, he had said his good-byes many times over during the last week. One more wouldn't do either of them any good.

"Jimmy?" he called over the suit-to-suit. There was no response. He'd have to wrestle the weenie through the lock like a sack of potatoes.

The hell with that. Chase entered the airlock's manual override. Four times, because the A/S required tell-me-three-times and the first time he hit a wrong key.

The inner door opened; then the outer. Chase was prepared and braced himself against the sudden surge of air racing for the door. Loose objects swirled past him. Styluses. Cliputers.

Nuts. A tube of gelatin. A screwdriver caromed off his suit, causing him to flinch. Then, gathering his companion in his arms, he leaped through the portal onto the Bean.

He landed badly. Off balance because of the deadweight he carried, he staggered for a while searching for an elusive balance. Until he realized he was standing upright on the rocky surface and it was his own mind that was spinning. He clamped down hard with his teeth. He hadn't eaten now in two days, but that didn't mean the stomach couldn't come up with something vile.

He fumbled Jimmy upright. "C'mon, buddy," he muttered. "Let's get hopping." And he slaved the other's suit jets to his own suit's brain and leaped for the centerline mooring ring. He kept it low and controlled—the Superman maneuver—because this would be a heck of a time to spew off the surface into the Big Empty.

When he reached the mooring ring, he checked the clock again. Five minutes? The time sure flies when you're having fun.

The ring was an eye bolt driven deep into the rock. *Cochran*'s tether was still clipped on and Chase left it that way so the wreck wouldn't slide off the back end of the asteroid and maybe trigger the Big Engine the way the probe had in '16. Instead, he took his own suit tether and ran it through, doubling back to clip on itself. Then he did the same for Jimmy.

"Jimmy?" he called. Then, more sharply, "Jimmy!" He shook the suit, upped the volume. "Jimmy!"

"What? What is it? Where . . . ?"

"It's showtime, good buddy. Three minutes." Jimmy groaned. Chase planted his feet and gripped his tether. "You gotta hold on, Jimmy. The acceleration'll make the Bean seem like it's tilting nose up." And, oh, how well he knew *that*. "That's right . . . Brace your feet. Now grab hold. Great. Think like you're rappelling down a cliffside and you've stopped to rest."

"Rest," said Jimmy. "I'm tired."

"You can't quit on me yet, Jim. The rockets should let go pretty—"

The jerk that ran through the rock beneath him was nothing compared to the fierce buffeting he had gotten from the Bean's own engine, but it was definitely a kick. He could feel it building—or was that his imagination?—as it overcame the asteroid's inertia.

There was no other sense of motion. Nothing was close enough for parallax. The stars, too pitilessly distant. But he knew they were moving, thrusting steadily ahead, rising a little and then a little more from the previous orbit. Raising all the other points on the orbit. Raising them, at the other end from the bull's-eye of the Earth to some empty zone between the Earth and the Moon.

That was the theory. Jimmy said his burn program would do that and Chase trusted Jimmy on that score. Whether the Bean would counter the move remained to be seen. So far, nothing; but the Intelligence was capable of biding its time and waiting for an optimum correction point. In the meantime . . .

He hung on to his tether like a drover with a runaway team. "Yee-hah!" he shouted. "Jimmy, I'm flying a phreaking planet!"

"Not. Planet. Just. Asteroid."

"So it's a little planet. First steps are always baby steps. But, Kool Beans! *We can do it!* Jimmy, we can fly mountains! This time. Next time. And the time after that."

"New. Kinda ship." Jimmy agreed. "You're prime pilot."

A grin split Chase's face. Split, literally, because he could taste the blood well up in his mouth. This was it. This was the ultimate. Just as well the game was over, because after this there would be nothing worth flying. His feet slipped a little and he repositioned himself.

"Jimmy," he shouted. "You're navigator! Lay me a course."

And Jimmy lifted a shaky arm and pointed to the bright

green crescent, now in their forward quarter on its lower, faster orbit. "Home," he said. "Let's take this sucker home."

Beneath Chase's feet, the planet rumbled and shook. It vibrated his boot soles, and the rings on his arms and legs, and the waist bearing and the neck bearing. It filled his suit with a noise that grew and went on and on and on.

Epilogue:

21 October, 2023, Silverpond Observatory

The sun was only an hour away, rolling west in a tide of light, and the clouds to the east had grown an anxious pink. In the south, a pale, washed-out half-moon lingered in heavens that were now more gray than black. It was a bad sky to watch against.

And yet, Mariesa van Huyten could not imagine doing anything else on this morning. Her telescope's A/S knew *where* to look. No orbit in history had been watched and tracked more closely than this one. If her eye refused to pick out one particular pinprick against the brightening fabric of the sky, it was not for lack of looking.

"Have you found it yet?" Roberta asked. She squatted with her son, Carson, who was playing with a variety of improbable plastic creatures on the floor of the observatory. Roberta wore a red-checked "lumberjack" coat. She had never liked goofball when it was fresh, let alone the retro-goof that fadmeisters were trying to resuscitate; but warm was warm. The dome opened on a fall morning, and the chill breeze brought a dry, leafy smell with it.

Mariesa studied the picture on the Gyricon screen. The A/S had given it a "false night" coloring, but even the cleverest programming could not compensate for lack of input. Mariesa scrolled a menu and applied a template of the Fixed Sky against the CCD data. The knuckles of her hand hurt when she bent them. Partly, that was the morning chill; partly, too, joints rusty with age. Really, she ought to use the Voice Command interface; but she rebelled against talking to a piece of hardware. People were unresponsive enough, thank you.

"There it is," she announced at last. The A/S had subtracted the Fixed Sky and displayed what was left: Things That Moved. And there was the Bean, a tiny mote west of the Moon. Algebra had succeeded where the senses had failed.

Barry Fast stepped up beside her and traced her finger across the screen. "This?" Mariesa nodded. "Hardly seems big enough for all the fuss."

"It's not the size that matters," Mariesa said absently while she noted the coordinates and ran them through her simulator. More powerful observatories than hers were watching the Bean's approach; had been watching it for months. Silverpond was better equipped than most amateur observatories, but it was not the big leagues. Still, this was something she had to do.

Roberta said, "I'll turn on the feed from JPL."

"I can do it!" Carson cried and ran for the channel wand. "What's the number!"

Mariesa looked up from her work. "Enter channel one-three-seven, dear."

"He always wants to do things himself," Roberta said.

"We all prize our independence, children most of all." She smiled at a suddenly conjured memory. "Harriet never did learn that, no matter how old I grew."

"It's amazing what kids pick up. He'll turn six in February."

"Yes, thank God."

Roberta gave her a startled look, then relaxed. "JPL confirmed the miss months ago."

"And I"—Mariesa made one final adjustment, then ran the sim—"am confirming it now." She studied the projected orbit, then settled back in her chair and swung to face Roberta. "It will go into orbit," she announced.

"Did it need your permission?" Barry laughed hugely.

Mariesa sighed and her hands lay limp on the keyboard. There had been a time when her permission had been needed for a great many things, and was therefore sought by a great many others. She had once been a star, as fixed in the firmament as any of the objects in the Known Space database. She had watched it decline slowly for many years with a mixture of sadness, frustration, and relief. Now, others carried on—or pursued their own agendas, taking the world on paths she had never imagined, even in her deepest fears and hopes. Chris used to consult her from time to time. But Chris was retired and Adam ran VHI, and her phone never rang. "I feel so useless."

Barry laid a hand on her shoulder. "Never that."

Trust Barry to razor in on the truth. If the affairs Mariesa dealt in were not so grand as they once were, they were certainly as important. Carson Albright. Chase Coughlin, Jr. Stevie Poole. Olethia Hobart. Will Sutherland, the young boy from Skunktown who had so loved the trees and flowers. There were worlds to be saved there, as well; though she did not expect to see this new cohort's final bloom. She could surely nurture the seeds. Perhaps with Barry and his schools. Belinda Karr, were she still alive, would have understood, and approved.

The wall screen flickered and showed someone's face, enormous and distracted. The unself-consciously disheveled look of those with work to do, and neither knew nor cared if they were on-screen. The image wiped and another view took its place. This one of the outside of Goddard City. A voice said, "Clear. Check the audio, wouldja, Pete?"

Barry folded his arms. "They need a professional director."

Mariesa gathered herself. There was no use wooling over what could not be helped. "Oh, that's the raw feed, straight from JPL," she said. "The networks and webmeisters filter and arrange it more aesthetically."

"Maybe we should log onto a live webcast, then."

"No, I've always preferred my news unfiltered and 'unarranged.' "

"Look!" said Carson, clapping his hands. "Spaceships!"

A child's life, Mariesa reflected, was all exclamation

points. Everything was new and wonderful. Adults lost that. Sometimes.

The ships were lined up starward of Goddard City. Four vessels, bright and gleaming, the stockpiled inventory of long-defunct North American Pressure Vessels, with their mastheads reaching out like the stems of some living plant. Mariesa remembered the men and women who had labored so desperately to build them while the capitalization slowly ran dry. She wondered how many were watching now, and whether they took any silent pride in the fruits of their labors. *We could never have built three fleets this quickly without them.* And without Jimmy's fortune.

The ships had not run up their sails yet. The mission was still in preparation and rehearsal.

"It's not over," Roberta said as she studied the ships. "I wish it was over."

Mariesa left her chair by the telescope and she and Barry joined Roberta by the threedy screen. Mariesa lifted Carson in her arms. The boy was almost too heavy for that sort of thing; or she was too old. "That's FarTrip IV," she told him.

"Which one? That one?" A stubby finger poked at a vessel.

"No, FarTrip is the name of the whole fleet. The ships . . ." They all looked pretty much alike, so she supposed it didn't matter which name she gave to which. "The ships' names are *Leonidas, Horatius, Alexandr Nevsky,* and *Divine Wind.*"

"Who was Divine Wind?" Carson's face, upturned, reminded Mariesa of a much younger Roberta. He had the same deep eyes as his mother. When he frowned, as he did now, he conjured up his father's somber ghost.

"Not 'who,' but 'what.' The Japanese don't name ships after people. The Divine Wind was a typhoon that wrecked an attacking fleet and saved Japan from conquest. As for the others . . ." And she told him about Leonidas and the Three Hundred, about Horatius at the bridge, about Nevsky on the ice. She wasn't sure how much the boy understood, but he was young, yet; and someday he would. Throughout history, there had always been those who had placed themselves between their homes and desolation.

"Somehow," said Barry, "I thought when Chase and Jimmy captured the Bean, that the other asteroids would . . ."

"Stop?" Mariesa shook her head. "I don't think ballistics allows that."

"No, but . . . Why isn't the test over?"

" 'Repetition is the mother of learning.' " A Russian proverb that Mike Krasnarov had taught her once; many years ago, when everyone was young. "You don't test a student with only one problem."

Roberta clenched and unclenched her hands. "One of them *will* get through, won't it?"

"Possibly. Or we might capture them all, as we did this one. Now that we know what to do, thanks to Jimmy and Chase. Or we think we do. Maybe the Bean was just 'level one' in some awful sort of game. We'll know soon enough. Captain Eustis and FarTrip III will rendezvous with Left Hook on Friday, and Captain Nieves"—Mariesa nodded toward the screen and FarTrip IV—"will leave for Rabbit Punch in December."

A voice from JPL said, "Insertion burn coming in five. Mark, try the view from SPS-2. They should have the best panorama." The image on the screen shifted, then shifted again as technicians tried different feeds. Roberta made an exasperated sound. In the foreground: a maze of struts and panels. A word crawl under the image read: HIGH NAIROBI SOLAR POWERSAT, followed by a string of coordinates. Azimuth, bearing, inclination. A clock in the corner rolled toward zero. Did anyone, Mariesa wondered, really need thousandths of a second? Or was it only a gimmick to heighten the anticipation.

There was a quick cut to the Bean itself, showing that the crew of the *Lodestar* had left the surface of the asteroid, and the magsail ship had cast loose, letting the solar wind push it starward. *Lodestar*'s command pilot said, "Initiate retrograde burn," and the viewpoint switched back to SPS-2.

"Look!" shouted Carson when the scroll reached zero. Flames had blossomed around the image of the Bean captured on the SPS's hubblescope. The engines that Chase and Jimmy had turned around to slow the Bean into capture orbit—plus those the "salvage crew" on *Lodestar* had added in June.

She thought of those long, lonely days on the asteroid—first Chase, alone; then with Jimmy helping—and of the awful time after the flare had written their death sentences and they had made the decision to stay and finish the job. She had no words for that, no way to express either her grief or her pride. They were the first of her "children" that she had lost. But they had done it; they had held the pass.

Abruptly, she stood and walked to the door of the observatory dome that led to the encircling catwalk. On that same catwalk, she had once stood with Ned DuBois's arm around her; she had cuddled with Belinda Karr and made love to Barry Fast; she had named the infinite stars for a young poet named Roberta; and she had stared skyward in trembling fear.

This time, knowing where to look, she could make out the asteroid with her naked eye. The roaring engines ensnaring it in Earth's gravity well had created a first magnitude star in the cerulean sky. The crisp morning wind raised a tear in her eye and she wiped it away. The burn would last for five more minutes; and when it was done, Earth would have a new moon. A mine? A habitat? A xenocultural study center? A shrine? No one was quite sure what to do with Jimmy's Gift, and already conflicting proposals were flying. Old treaties were being dusted off and studied.

They don't need to mine that one, Mariesa thought. *There is plenty more ore where that came from.*

Shortly, Barry joined her, and laid his arm across her shoulders. Roberta brought Carson out and pointed out the bright spark in the heavens and told him what it meant. Whether the boy was impressed was difficult to tell: his countenance was so often full of awe. Roberta kept a firm grip on him with her left hand; with her right, she held her cap in place against the breeze. "Windy," she said.

"It always is, out here."

"*Lodestar* has departed from the Bean, JPL said. Captain Rosario is bringing them back."

Mariesa didn't ask who she meant by "them." Jimmy and Chase were coming home. And the Frenchman, Alois Frechet. Too many forgot him; yet it had been he who first suggested they fly the asteroid home.

"Will you be at Sky Harbor when they come down from orbit?"

Mariesa shook her head without speaking. The plan was to bring the bodies down from LEO on the *Henri Farman* with great pomp and ceremony. There would be bands playing triumphal marches and speeches by important people; and they would give folded UN flags to Tani and Karen and Dominique Frechet and tell them what heroes their husbands had been; and the widows would endure it all with whatever stoicism two years' mourning could provide. Mariesa didn't think she could bear it. "Whatever honor was needed," she said, "Jacinta Rosario and her crew have already given."

Roberta nodded and fell silent for a time. There were painful memories for Roberta, too, Mariesa knew. Roberta had known Jimmy and Chase most of her life; but not until it had been almost too late had she known them as friends. And the ships for FarTrip V were named *Coughlin,* and *Poole,* and *Frechet,* and *Zaranovsky.*

Soon enough, the spark in the sky winked out. Mariesa sighed and retreated inside with the others, where she began closing everything down. Twenty years ago, even ten, she would have marked this occasion with a party—albeit a solemn one. She had invited more than twenty to her lodge at Jackson Lake to watch Forrest Calhoun set foot on the Rock, back in '10. Now, a few companions seemed sufficient.

The slit in the observatory dome closed with a satisfying clang, like a book clapped shut. Mariesa looked up at the dome. "I can't help feeling that something has come to an end."

Roberta took little Carson by the hand. "I can't help feeling that something has just begun."